To Elinor

To Elinor

a romance in two voices

Jane Beaton Bartow

with excerpts from
original WWII letters written by
Darrow Beaton

iUniverse, Inc.
Bloomington

TO ELINOR
A ROMANCE IN TWO VOICES

Certain characters in this work are historical figures, and certain events portrayed did take place. However, this is a work of fiction. All of the other characters, names, and events as well as all places, incidents, organizations, and dialogue in this novel are either the products of the author's imagination or are used fictitiously.

iUniverse books may be ordered through booksellers or by contacting:

iUniverse
1663 Liberty Drive
Bloomington, IN 47403
www.iuniverse.com
1-800-Authors (1-800-288-4677)

ISBN: 978-1-4759-8231-2 (sc)
ISBN: 978-1-4759-8232-9 (hc)
ISBN: 978-1-4759-8233-6 (e)

Library of Congress Control Number: 2013905175

Printed in the United States of America.

iUniverse rev. date: 5/17/2013

Elinor

Darrow

For Amanda.
Women's options have changed since your grandmother's time.
You have more choices and the opportunity to design your future.

And for Lydia and Elliott.
Love still exists even when the entire world
seems full of hate and war.

Table of Contents

Introduction

THIS IS HOW IT began, my birth as an unintentional novelist.

My sister flew into Minneapolis. We had already divided up most of the things our parents had left us—jewelry, household items, boxes of odds and ends we had found in their garage. We were down to the last boxes, the photos—pieces of our history—and we knew they'd be difficult to sort.

We traipsed into my basement and located the three file boxes Dad had taped up and sent via Fed Ex when he knew he hadn't long to live. I wiped the lid of the top one and then slit the tape that Dad had wrapped around the gray box. A puff of old dust rose into the air. A nip of mold. The smell of age, of years in one garage or another. I sneezed.

We dumped the contents onto my sewing table and sorted photos from the early 1900s. Cars from the early part of the century. People we had never seen before. Shots of family and friends that only our mother would recognize. Too late for identification now.

We untaped and lifted the lid of the second box. Photos from our youth. We luxuriated in the black and whites, some photos so small we could barely see the subjects. We laughed. We told stories. After a while we went upstairs for a cup of coffee. We blew our noses.

Now we each had a pile of memories.

My sister couldn't go on. She slumped in her chair. She said her eyes hurt. Memories are hard on her. Migraines slow her down. And, after all, the afternoon was pretty well spent.

One more? That last big box?

She closed her eyes. She nodded twice. We plodded to the basement again to finish the job. My sister plopped into a chair. I got her a refill of coffee and then cracked the lid of the last box. The label read "photos," but sheaves of onionskin filled the container. Hundreds of pages, mostly typed. And envelopes. With old stamps in their corners.

We looked into the chaos. I gasped.

My sister shook her head. "Not interested," she sighed. Too many words jittering around in that crate. "It makes me dizzy."

I resealed that box and settled it into the closet again.

But in a few months, when school was out for the summer, the box drew me. I shuffled to the storage closet one lazy summer afternoon, found it, and lifted the lid.

I sat a moment, staring at that crate of paper. There were more than a thousand sheets, I later discovered. Most of the letters were single-spaced and typed in capitals. I had only a few weeks until the start of a busy new school year. I thought about tucking the box away again to work on it one day in the future—maybe after retirement, a time when days would stretch out, empty, before me.

Nevertheless, I reached into the box. Corners of aged envelope flaps and loosened stamps cracked off in my hands. The papers crinkled. Bits of parchment dust drifted into the air.

I lifted an envelope. A dull green propeller-driven airplane flew in a stationary bombing raid on the corner stamp. I slipped the sheet of onionskin from the envelope. It unfolded in my hands. My father's handwriting. 1941. To Elinor.

During the war, my father bought stamps in the States before each of his journeys, then mailed letters with those stamps in the corners from faraway ports. After a long flight through the war in a plane—like the propeller-driven one on the stamp—this stamp had arrived at my mother's home in Fargo. And it actually looked none the worse for wear. Or time. It had, after all, languished in that dark box for more than sixty years.

I couldn't stop reading. Here was a young, hopeful guy. A brave man heading to war, riding on thousands of barrels of aviation fuel, camping out with his radio and a pack of Luckies above tanks and armaments which had been secured on the decks. A cocky fellow, even with torpedoes sandwiched next to the fuel, deep in the bowels of the ship. Something he never mentioned to his daughters.

One by one I opened the envelopes and read. These were disjointed chunks of history, and I needed to piece the scenes together. The project became a jigsaw of reading, a love story that children are seldom privy to, and it took almost a year to decipher.

Many of the letters had no date. At least no year. "January 7." I found pairs of "January 1" and other dates. But which years were the letters from?

Other letters had "Letter Four" or "Letter Twenty-eight" written as a heading. Whenever Dad started a new voyage, I discovered, he numbered the letters. They didn't arrive on the home front in sequence, and he thought it would be a way to preserve the order of his days. It was also a way of figuring out which letters hadn't made the trip. But because he started with "Letter One" on each trip, there were duplicates with the same numbers in that big stack. What to do with two copies of "Letter Five"? Or three of them?

Some envelopes were stuffed with onionskin, several missives taking up residence in one space. One had nearly 20 pages squeezed inside it and double stamps in the outside corner. Those were the only papers that looked like they had been damp at one time, maybe on the ship as they, along with the men, rode out one of turbulent tempests Dad wrote home about. Other envelopes clearly had the wrong letters tucked back inside them. And some envelopes were empty, just along for the ride.

Most had been censored and had the stickers to prove it. More than a few had holes where the censor had used a razor blade to excise a line or a few paragraphs. I tried to fill in the blanks, but that was impossible. A couple of letters were mailed with just a note in the corner where the stamp would've gone. "Sailor's Mail" jotted there was enough to get the message back to the home front in an emergency.

There were V-mails and Mackay communications—modern inventions—letters written on form paper. The sheets were microfilmed and shipped home at less cost than planes full of onionskin. When they arrived in the States, those V-mails were enlarged and delivered in their nearly original size.

Some letters were dated in one month but postmarked from a port several months later, which is, from my reading, just how our men had to mail them. Dad would pile his letters together, and when the ship landed at a port (a port where he could leave the ship, a port with mailing facilities) he would quickly get the envelopes into the mail there. Once in a while, when the ship came into port for only a few hours, and no one disembarked, he would pass the letters to a native in a bum boat who, Dad hoped, would deliver them to a Sparks in a ship that had docked for a spell. Any fellow radio operator would try to get those envelopes into the mail.

And once in a while, Dad's ship was in and out of a port so fast that he didn't even have time for that. The letters kept piling up.

Each letter was mailed with a prayer. A few rest today in Davy Jones' locker, along with the daring pilots of a few of the mail planes that dodged enemy fire among the Pacific islands.

I started by sorting those letters that included date and year. I began to see the outline of a story. The letters with only Letter Number Somethingorother I organized into separate stacks. Same with the ones with a date, minus the year.

I forgot about my life—the house and the approaching school year. I read all the letters and found I could fit many of the unidentified ones into developing plotlines.

The letters began in 1941, in December, just after my father met my mother. The letters continued until the end of the war, which, for my father, was November 1945, the month he came home again.

This book, then, is the story of Darrow "the Beat" Beaton falling in love with Elinor Landgrebe. From Gallups Island Radio School and then from the oceans of the world, I've included excerpts from the many pages of Dad's letters.

In the background of their rollercoaster romance lie Elinor's fledgling dreams and the reality of the effect of the war on women's lives on the home front. Lives where old friends risked everything, even death.

Lives with no possibility of making plans for a future. Love lives put on hold.

As men headed to war, they often gave their girls rings. Even though she had no intention of marrying, Elinor kept the rings, wrote to the men who were devoted to her, and planned to give the diamonds back at the conclusion of the fighting. She followed the rules in Emily Post's books. No "Dear John" letters from her would deflate a fellow in battle. A bishop's daughter had to maintain some standards.

Elinor had no intention of being just another housewife, under the thumb of any male. The generation of Rosie the Riveter saw opportunities open before them. Some tried out independence, imagining what women's roles might be and forging new opportunities.

And a few, like Elinor, reached for the stars.

This novel is my attempt to reconstruct my mother's story. Though mostly true—based upon the events mentioned in my father's letters, my research of the war, and family history—my story is fiction. The excerpts from the letters are authentic, however.

Prologue

Late October 1944, 7:45 a.m.

ELINOR FOLDED THE LETTER in her hand, replaced it in its envelope and set it on the desk, along with the others.

Was that the train whistle? She checked her Christmas watch. Sure enough. The morning *North Coast Limited* would be pulling into the depot just five blocks away. A faint light crept under the blackout drapes in her father's den. She squinted around the brightening room. The night had slipped away!

Her daybed, which rested along the wall opposite the desk where she sat, remained a narrow couch. The sofa pillows lay piled at one end, her purse on the other. Elinor hadn't even thought to turn down the sheets or to take the chenille bedspread off its shelf in the closet. She hadn't thought about sleep. But Ching, the family's Siamese cat, now stretched his length, dozed comfortably with the daybed to himself.

The threads The Fates had woven had untangled, and now it was up to Elinor to take control. To stitch her destiny.

Her coffee cup, empty again, sat on the right hand side of her father's large desk, close to the copper ashtray he kept there while he smoked his pipe and mulled over the synod work or a sermon. The acrid odor of yesterday's ashes brought her back to the issue at hand.

Her father. How would he respond? Elinor fumbled on the desk for her hanky.

Strewn in front of her on her father's desk lay hundreds of pages of letters, some hand-written but most typed, single spaced, on onionskin paper. The envelopes in which the letters had arrived were decorated mostly with pink or green six- or eight-cent stamps, each with an airplane, fat with mail, hovering in the corners. No more stamps with the Zeppelin or biplanes from another era. These stamps looked official, modern, like the mail service.

And most of the letters had arrived. Well, a few probably rested in Davy Jones' locker, sunk along with the ships that had carried them. That was to be expected in wartime, when letters had to crisscross the world, over all that water, through all kinds of weaponry and weather.

But here, piled on the desk, rested the hundreds that had arrived, a testament to the efficiency of the U.S. military mail system. From all over the world, planes and ships carried letters to her, letters stuffed with words. But not one phrase, not even a hint, about where her "old friends" were or what they faced. War secrets.

Her father's new Royal typewriter stood solidly on its metal stand beside the desk, dust cover in place, ready to be rolled closer when needed for writing. He had inserted a fresh dual-colored ribbon just yesterday so he could type in black for the sermons and in red for Biblical quotations. The phone squatted, its black Bakelite belly on the shelf her father had built into the wall. Its frayed cord had been stuffed into the alcove to prevent any more damage from Ching's claws to the thick brown fabric that wrapped the wires.

Someone stirred upstairs. One of her sisters, she thought, either Mickey or Irene, tiptoeing to the small family bathroom. Soon her mother and father would wake and, joining her sisters, arrive downstairs, ending her privacy.

Elinor roused herself, stood and carried her empty coffee cup to the kitchen sink. The cold brew she had sipped throughout the night had, at least, kept her focused.

Ching's blue eyes blinked. He scrutinized her, then stretched and yawned.

"Had I known how this would turn out," Elinor thought, "would I have taken that train to the coast? The Fates have certainly been in charge of my life since I met Darrow."

But, first things first. She rushed back to the desk.

She stretched a thick rubber band and wrapped it around the packet of letters she had been reading. Then she stuffed those back into their cardboard box, along with the ones she'd read earlier in the evening. She forced the lid on.

Ching stood then and, with a last glance toward Elinor, jumped delicately off the sofa bed and padded away into the awakening house. Elinor heard him lap at yesterday's water in his bowl in the kitchen.

She moved the daybed to stash her collection behind it. She reorganized the pillows and her purse after she pushed the bed back against the wall. Concealing her letters was a practiced art, a war secret of her own.

She entered the family coat closet, the space she used when she was at home, when she returned on weekends from her teaching assignment. She squeezed her outfits between the family's winter coats and boots.

She felt around in the cool dark. Her stationery box, her pink jewelry box and the vial of Christmas Night perfume Darrow had brought her from Egypt lay hidden on a back shelf behind the blue Singer vacuum.

Elinor located her stationery and exited the closet, straightening her back and then her hair. She set the box on her father's desk and removed two pieces of lavender paper and a matching envelope. She spread the first stationery sheet on the pull-out shelf over the top left-hand drawer of the desk. She smoothed it. In the center desk drawer, she found her father's Parker fountain pen. She unstopped the ink bottle.

Now! No more lollygagging. Time to let him know, she thought. "Those people" were not coming. No chance of a visit at all. She blew her nose once more, then straightened in the chair.

She gripped the pen in her right hand and faced the empty sheet. How to begin?

Darrow prowled the Pacific on his tanker now, delivering aviation fuel, ammo, and tanks. He must wonder what was happening back home.

Elinor tried to picture the port where he would receive her news. But, other than photos in her father's *National Geographic* collection, she had no idea what a South Pacific isle looked like. Not a war-torn isle, a bombed out beachfront.

Instead, she imagined his ship. Easy, since she had toured it in Seattle in June. A lifetime ago.

Elinor scratched her head and then pushed her hair back from her forehead. She pressed the white button on the fluorescent desk lamp. It blinked three times before waking completely. Her tongue rested on her bottom lip as she filled the fountain pen in the ink bottle.

"Arrive safely," she whispered. "Across seasons. Above the stifling heat of the South Pacific and between typhoons. Through torpedoes, mines, bombs. Past those damned Japanese planes. Directly to Darrow."

What Had She Been Thinking?

The night before at 11 p.m.

ELINOR WAITED UNTIL THE family had snuggled into their beds upstairs. Her mother and father's voices, their nightly murmurs to each other, had slowed and then come to an end. At a quarter to eleven she had heard the last creak from Irene's old cot in the bedroom overhead.

The coal furnace struggled to send steam through its pipes to the upstairs rooms. Elinor heard the shivering in the walls as the plaster cooled. She listened to the clicks in the foundation and the gentle hissing in the radiators as the house adjusted to the cool night air. When all the family's activity had ceased, 1135 Third Street North thrummed and sighed, its heart still beating.

When she was sure she wouldn't be discovered, Elinor had slid her narrow daybed away from the wall. She had located her stash, the box of letters from Darrow. She hefted it onto the daybed and pulled off the lid. Letters, bundled together with thick rubber bands, filled the container.

Elinor unwrapped the tan rubber band on the first pack and stretched it over her wrist. Letters spilled over the desktop.

She took out the earliest notes Darrow had penned to her. She remembered those days, back in the winter of 1941.

The New Guy

December 21, 1941

UNTIL SHE MET DARROW, Elinor's life had streamed along, a compliant eddy, a more or less gentle issue, rippling consciously within its banks. No unexpected twists or turns.

But that evening back in December of 1941, her spirit approximated a flooding river rising riotously, plunging recklessly in new directions, unseemly for a bishop's daughter—especially a 25 year-old maiden daughter schooled in the precepts of her faith and the manners of polite society.

Without checking the time on the Elgin watch her parents had given her when she graduated from college—the most reliable brand on the market, her father declared—Elinor bounded upstairs to the small bedroom where her two sisters slept. Without so much as a knock on the door, she hopped into bed with Mickey.

Mickey shot upright, eyes open wide, her mouth unhinged. She tried to scream but couldn't find her voice. Elinor giggled. Finding her sister beside her, Mickey unclasped her hands from her chest and slugged Elinor in the arm.

Elinor put a finger to her lips. Then, by way of hand and head signals, Elinor led Mickey out of bed and down the stairs to the living room, where they settled on the old horsehair sofa. The room was dark. At first, the girls sat there, still, listening for any sounds from upstairs.

Nothing. Irene must still be asleep.

The streetlight on the corner of the avenue barely crawled in around the edges of the shade pulled over the window, perfect blackout mode. In time, as their eyes adjusted to the dimness, the sisters could see each others' faces in the shadows.

Elinor inched closer to Mickey's ear. "Well, what did you think?" she whispered. She bounced once on the horsehair sofa.

"About what?" Mick yawned.

"HIM!" Elinor still whispered, but squinched her eyes at her sister.

Mickey shook her head. "Who?"

Ching jumped up beside her out of the darkness and settled on the sofa, stretched out his full length. Mickey scratched behind his ears, and he purred softly. With her free hand, Mickey pulled a crocheted afghan over her shoulders.

The house felt cold, but their mother would be up soon to tiptoe into the dark basement where she would stoke coal into the firebox on the old furnace. "The octopus," they called it because of all the arms radiating from its boiler.

Their father had caught the overnight train to Montana. Some parish there needed his help. And their brother, Yupps, lived at the seminary these days. The women of the family were alone this evening.

Elinor jabbed her younger sister. "Mickey, you stood there when we were introduced. Remember? Outside the church. Wake up!"

"You mean . . . Darrow? Why?"

"He and Bruns were exiting the church after a wedding of a friend. He walked home with us, Mick."

"Well, with you. I walked ahead of you two. With Betty."

"We had so much fun tonight walking home. He kissed me in the snow." Elinor's voice was more audible now.

"Kissed you?" Mickey tried to control the volume, and her voice raised nearly an octave. "You barely know the fellow. But, wait! I thought you had a date tonight with Johnny."

"Shhh! You'll wake Irene. My date with Johnny was later. When he arrived, I walked Darrow to the door. I introduced him to Johnny." Elinor bounced up and down on the sofa. "Darrow was polite, though he smiled through clenched teeth when I bid him goodnight. There's something about him that . . ."

"You got me out of bed for this?" Mickey's voice was louder now.

"Just wanted to know what you thought."

"In the middle of the night?"

Ching jumped off the sofa when Mickey stood up. Mickey yawned and stretched. She was a tiny woman, even with her arms above her head. She fiddled with the bobby pins in her hair as she questioned Elinor.

"You've lost me, Bunny. You were going out with Johnny Holsen, even though you're engaged to Walter? And when Johnny arrived to pick you up, you were with Darrow Beaton?"

Elinor nodded. "But I didn't wear Walter's ring." She grinned and held her hand up to prove her finger had no ring.

"Here's what I think, Bunny. Go to bed. Get some sleep. We can talk more in the morning." Mickey stepped toward the stairway.

"I want company tonight, Mickey. I really need to talk. I'm too wide awake to sleep." Elinor knew just how to manipulate her siblings. "Walter wants to elope this weekend to Brookings. But Johnny is talking about marriage, too, before he's drafted."

"Bunny!"

"I have a feeling that The Fates have something else in store for me."

"Can I go back to bed now? I think The Fates have some sleep in mind for me tonight." Mickey yawned again.

"Darrow asked me if I am rationed. In short supply. Isn't that cute?" Elinor smiled. "I told him I have a few 'old friends' that I see. I didn't mention the engagement ring."

"But, Bunny . . ."

"Wait, Mick. Here's the thing. Tonight I felt something when I was with Darrow." Elinor shrugged. "He's different from the others. Makes me feel bubbly all over."

"'The Beat?' Isn't that what he calls himself?" Mickey smirked. "Who has a name like 'The Beat'? Elinor! Darrow's a playboy."

Elinor hung her head.

"TOO cool." Mickey laughed. "I hear he has a gang. They roam around the area playing basketball. But mostly drinking." Mickey wagged her finger toward her big sister. "Think about your family, Bunny. Mother and Dad love Walter. What will it look like if you drop him after all these years? Two?"

"Three," Elinor mumbled. She looked at her painted toenails. Red. No one saw them now in the wintertime, but she was compelled to always look her best. They matched her fingernails, also red, with the exception of the half moons and very tips, the latest style. She carried matching red lipstick in her purse.

"So you drop Walt. You plan to marry Johnny?" Mickey's hands rested on her hips, just like Grandma used to do when she scolded the girls.

Elinor couldn't help herself. Laughter tickled at her lips for an instant. Then, adopting a look of sincerity, she met her little sister's eyes. "I don't know, Mickey. Must a girl marry? Aren't there bigger things to accomplish in life than marriage and a family? Or teaching?" Elinor shrugged.

"You're restless, kid. The whole country feels agitated. Pearl surprised us. And now the Japs are in on it." Mickey yawned. "This war is getting to everyone. Let's make a pot of coffee to settle you down."

They crept into the kitchen, feeling for the light switch. As soon as the ceiling light flickered to life, Elinor grabbed the coffee pot and began separating the parts. She washed out the soppy grounds from the last batch of coffee and handed the perforated basket of the pot to her sister. Then she filled the bottom of the percolator with water. Meanwhile, Mickey found the coffee canister and measured the grounds carefully. Together, they assembled the pot, plugged it in, and then leaned over it, waiting for the first whiffs of their favorite aroma.

"What are you doing up at this hour?" Irene appeared from around the corner.

There stood their prying oldest sister. The tease. But now, just for a few minutes, Elinor and Mickey wanted to be left alone.

Elinor turned around to face Irene. Mickey just looked over her shoulder.

Elinor tried a diversion. "We got thirsty for some coffee. Want a cup when it's brewed?"

"I thought I heard you talking about boyfriends," Irene hinted.

"Just getting caught up on our dates," Mickey replied. "What did you do tonight, Irene?"

"I worked."

"Who brought you home?" Getting her off-track wasn't too hard.

"Sammy."

"Oh, Sammy," Mickey and Elinor sang in unison. "Didja kiss the guy this time?"

Irene blushed. "You always tease me about my boyfriends. Leave me alone." She turned away. "I'm going back to bed," she whined. She disappeared into the living room. The girls listened for her footsteps as their oldest sister climbed back to the upstairs bedroom.

Elinor heard the springs on the old cot as Irene plopped back into bed.

Elinor and Mickey, assured they were alone again, poured themselves cups of dark coffee and stood to look out the window. The clock on the wall read 3:30. Soft snow still fell. For hours it had swirled outside, fluffy flakes, collected now into communities on tree branches, roads, and yards. The girls regarded the white piling up in the backyard and alley while their coffee steamed.

"Another Christmas," Mickey sighed. "A few more turns of the world and we'll be in 1942. We're getting older, Bunny."

Ching curled his body into the kitchen. He walked over and inspected his empty water bowl. He brushed past Mickey's leg. She reached down and aimlessly patted his head.

Elinor opened the refrigerator and took out the fresh bottle of cream, left by the milkman just a couple of days ago. "And the world is changing so quickly. With every turn there's something tragic in the news." She poured a dab of cream into her coffee cup.

Mickey lifted Ching's water bowl to the sink. "That's for sure. It changes nearly every minute these days, Bunny." Mickey turned the spigot and filled the bowl with fresh water. When she set it down, Ching lapped twice and padded back into the dark house.

"Ed's in the Navy already, and Johnny expects to be drafted into the Army as soon as school is out. He'll be gone in June, I suppose." Elinor blew on the liquid in her cup to cool it and took a tentative sip.

"Bob and his National Guard group are already in training. California." Mickey tried her coffee, too.

"Our lives will be different." Elinor ran her finger around the rim of her cup. "Not much to do without the guys around. Except worry and pray."

"Bunny, what do you think will happen to all the women waiting for their men, the guys who won't come home?" Mickey set her cup on the countertop.

Elinor patted her little sister's hand. "Don't say that, Mickey! We have to hope that they'll all be back."

"Okay, but say this war lasts a few years. A decade, maybe. No one is predicting how long it's going to last."

Elinor interrupted. "Well, what if the fellows all come back? Let's just say that no one is injured. Let's say The Fates have been good to the guys we know."

"We'll be too old anyway, won't we? To be married, I mean." Mickey released one spitcurl from her bobby pins. "Or to have children, kid." She opened the bobby pin, using her teeth, and then repinned the swirl of hair more tightly.

"The experts say that we have to have children when we're young— before we're thirty—or we're guaranteed problems with the kids. Physical or mental things that could go wrong." Elinor sipped her coffee. "That is, if you plan on having kids."

The Bavarian cuckoo in the living room popped out of her nest and cheeped four times. Then she disappeared behind the doors of the clock, to nap for another hour.

Mickey sighed again. "So, while the men are at war, giving up their lives, we're on the home front giving up ours."

Gertrude (Mickey)

Mickey

A Bigger World Out There

January 1942

It was a cold January Saturday when Beat's first letters arrived. Elinor had returned to Fargo to spend the weekend at home. During the week she taught and roomed in Gwinner, a small farming town nearby. But on most weekends, to save the cost of two days' room and board, she rejoined her family.

As usual, Irene, the family mailbox and telephone sentinel, pounced first, even as the mailman tossed the morning's messages through the mail slot in the porch door. She gathered the scattered envelopes and carried the assortment to the kitchen table where the girls gathered to open their letters. Coffee steamed in their cups as they sorted the mail.

"A letter from Ed," Elinor said. "Here, Mickey. For you. One from Bob."

"Thanks, kid," Mickey said. She used the letter opener from her father's desk to carefully slit the envelope and release the papers inside. She straightened the notepaper and began to read.

Elinor slit open the envelope from Darrow.

"Something from 'The Beat'?" Mickey smirked.

Irene found an envelope addressed to all three of the Landgrebe girls, ripped it open and pulled out a homemade invitation with a black construction paper cover.

"An announcement!" she proclaimed, standing.

Mickey looked up from her letter.

"The Thorstensens are having a Blackout Party at 8:00 on Thursday," Irene continued.

"Clever idea, putting Pearl Harbor and all the war news into a fun format," Mickey said. "Walking over there in the dark would be an adventure." She returned to Bob's letter.

"But what would you wear to a party completely in the dark?" Elinor grinned. "Who will see you? You could wear anything. Or nothing. Why, I might go nude!"

Even their mother had to smile at that. But, of course, she would. Trudie loved a good joke and a shot glass of Four Roses once in a while. For her health. The Landgrebes had open minds about some things other preachers expounded against. And they were proud of their independent children.

Late that morning, after Reverend Landgrebe and Trudie had driven off to Minot to tend to a congregation there, the Western Union courier rang the doorbell. His breath steamed in the frigid air. Elinor popped the door open a crack and snatched the envelope. From Walter, of course. Elinor laughed when she read it. Walt never gave up. Now he wanted to take a weekend jaunt to Brookings, South Dakota, to finally marry.

"He wants me to meet him at the bus stop when I come into town next weekend," Elinor explained to Irene over a cup of coffee in the kitchen. "I've put him off for so many years. And I am getting older. Maybe we should just finally tie the knot."

Walter managed the Fargo Paint and Glass Company and had more money than the other guys Elinor was dating. He was tight, though, reluctant to spend his hard-earned money. Nevertheless, he promised to take good care of Elinor. Her parents loved him. And she had accepted his diamond, though she seldom slipped it on. Perhaps that was enough for a gal in wartime.

"Why not, Elinor?" Irene asked as she slipped into her heavy winter coat.

"Well, I've always wanted a more romantic ceremony. And they say you should be in love to get married, you know." Elinor sipped her coffee. "But as long as I have Walt's ring, no one can call me an 'old maid.' I'm an engaged woman."

Irene stopped and turned toward her sister. "How does it feel to be engaged, Bunny? To have a ring and everything?"

"To tell the truth, it's nothing special. Not knock-you-off-your-feet special anyway."

"Mother and Dad have always wanted us to have church weddings with all the trimmings," Irene sighed. Her eyes took on a dreamy look. "So beautiful. You know. The gown. The flowers. The cake. And all those presents!" Irene wrapped a scarf around her neck and snapped on her galoshes.

"Never mind there's a war on, kid. Do you see many guys around here to marry?" Elinor looked out the kitchen window to emphasize the point.

Irene sighed. "Not these days."

"A wedding isn't really in my future," Elinor said. She poured herself a refill of coffee. "Though who can know what The Fates have in store? I do think there's a plan for every life, and no matter what we do, no matter how we struggle against it, that plan comes to fruition. Maybe I'm fated to remain single."

Irene laughed. "We'll all have to get married one day, Bunny," she explained. "It's the way of the world."

"Maybe not. Gals don't have to stay at home and live with their parents when they are single. It's not like the old days, like Aunt Dorothy having to live with Grandma or a brother for protection." Elinor sipped her coffee. "Girls can make their own living. They're running around this country these days, living on the coasts doing war work. They can do more interesting things. Modern women don't seem to need all that old-fashioned protection. Even in wartime."

Irene checked the clock. "I've got to dash! I'll be late for work!" She interrupted her sister's reverie, slipped into her gloves, and grabbed her purse. She hustled out of the kitchen.

"Wait!" Elinor called to her. "Do you have your uniform hat this time?" She stood to help her sister.

"Don't worry," Irene shouted back from the front door. "I remembered."

Elinor set her cup into the kitchen sink while Irene scooted out the front door to her work at the downtown café over a busy lunch hour. She'd have to run part of the way to be on time.

Elinor picked the telegram up and stared at it. "I'll stall Walter again," she muttered.

There was a bigger world out there somewhere. Even for a gal.

Irene

Irene

Hi, Sweetie

Early 1942

The Young Men's Christian Association of Fargo
Wed. nite

Hi, Sweetie,
Hear you're going to get married Friday—"Don't do it. Life's too short," quote from Miss Elinor Landgrebe, 1941. Maybe this is a New Year and all, but how about holding out for a couple more months?

Monday

Hi, Elinor,
Guess who!! And pardon the pencil and general untidiness of this letter. I just wanted to write and say that I'm sorry for that 3 A.M. call last Saturday. You see, teacher, it's this way. After work I headed for Dilworth. There's a bartender there that serves me after midnite. The fellows and I really had a good stag party and soon women became the subject and phone calls became the order of the evening. I'll say,

though, it wasn't the Beat that talked to your mother.

How's Tarzan? Suppose you're married by now. I see Walt every once in a while. He's O.K. Drop me a line, maybe, yes?

Your friend,
Beat

Where's Walter?

March 1942

THE COFFEE STEAMED. GEORG and Trudie stared into their cups.

Reverend Landgrebe sighed. "Mmmm. That coffee smells good tonight."

The clock on the wall of the kitchen marked a few minutes past eleven. It had been their bedtime ritual for years to have a last cup of coffee and a snack, a chunk of sausage or some cheese, while they reviewed the day. They secluded themselves at the dining room table, bent over their cups to inhale the aroma of the freshly brewed coffee. They raised their heads. Their eyes met.

"*Vas denkst du?* What are you thinking about, *Tay-Air-Oo?*"

Trudie laughed. He loved spelling her name in German. He called her "T-R-U" for short when he wanted to cheer her. It was always "*Tay-Air-Oo-Day-Ee-Ay*" when he needed her.

"Georg, I don't know." Trudie shook her head. "Maybe it was that phone call . . ."

"I remember. A bit past 3?" He set his cup on the table and looked at his wife.

"I rushed downstairs to answer it so it wouldn't wake everyone up. I didn't think you even heard the phone, Georg."

He touched her hand. "Vaguely. I checked the clock when you climbed back into bed. Not an emergency, then?"

"Whoever wanted Elinor was pretty soused. He didn't say who he was." She hesitated before going on. "Most of the fellows who drop in here to visit the girls are good men, but have you noticed . . ."

Trudie got up. She poured each of them a bit more coffee, then sat down again. Her blue eyes looked into her husband's. She noted how red-rimmed his eyes looked. Nevertheless, she needed to talk this over.

"Georg, Bunny seems cool to Walter when he comes to town. Have you noticed?"

"Hmmm."

"She seldom wears his ring."

"What's going on?" Georg sliced a second piece of summer sausage.

"She's not so eager to see some of the others who drop in to see her, either. Yet she seems to perk right up when Darrow arrives late at night."

He blinked at her. "Darrow, hmm."

Trudie lowered her eyes. "He arrives after Elinor's other dates have left. So late."

Georg placed his large hand on Trudie's delicate one.

"She's nearly twenty-six. But how does it look? I think he's staying most of the night. What must the neighbors think! I think he's a wild one, Georg. Irish." There! She had said it. Trudie took a sip of her coffee.

"I'm sure Elinor will sever any connection with him after that call." Rev. Landgrebe finished his favorite sausage and gulped the last of his coffee. "She's a free spirit, Trudie, but one day she'll have to settle down."

Trudie slid off the chair. Her housedress caught on the seat cushion. She gave it a yank, then walked into the kitchen and turned to the sink. She set her dishes there, ready for washing in the morning. Turning to gather her husband's cup and plate, she asked, "Ready to go up to bed then?"

Georg moved slowly. It was difficult for him to extricate his lanky frame from the table. Trudie could see how tired he was from that last trip to settle things in a congregation in Montana.

Together they moved into the living room to wind the cuckoo clock, their final chore before bedtime. As Georg pulled on the chains, they heard the porch door open.

Trudie motioned to her husband. "Pssssst! Someone's at the door now." Seeing Elinor on the porch, Trudie returned to the kitchen to make certain she'd turned off the stove. She unplugged the coffee pot. It could wait for cleaning until morning. She removed her apron and hung it on the hook by the door to the cellar.

Georg followed her to the kitchen.

The front door opened and then closed with a muted click. Elinor brought Darrow into the kitchen to grab a last cup of now lukewarm coffee. The four of them greeted each other warily. Elinor took Darrow's hand as they retreated, cups in their other hands, to the living room.

Trudie sighed. She raised her eyebrows at Georg, then turned out the kitchen lights and the Landgrebes padded upstairs.

After they closed the door to their bedroom, Trudie whispered, "Let's invite Walt for dinner next weekend. Maybe we can revive that relationship."

➤   ◄

from the 1942 journal of the Rev. Georg Landgrebe

Friday, March 13
Elinor came home from Gwinner. Ma had prepared a delicious chicken dinner. Walter was guest.

Jimmy Doolittle

April 18, 1942

ELINOR HEARD A KNOCK on the front door. The doorbell rang several times. She flipped the porch light on, saw who it was, and threw open the door to let him in. "You're early," she laughed. "We have time to see the late show downtown."

She breathed in the musty aroma of damp soil. The old snow banks, now gritty and gray, had started to shrink. It would be planting season soon. Her parents had already started this year's victory garden seeds. The tomatoes and nasturtiums and broccoli plants and peppers would pop into the world any day now in bedding pots arranged in every south-facing windowsill of the house. One could smell the change of the seasons, the fresh optimism of the country, in the air.

"Have you heard the news?" Beat was grinning, his worn leather jacket unbuttoned and the smell of bourbon on his breath.

Elinor laughed. "I've heard a thing or two about it," she answered. "Come on in." Of course she had heard the news. Her family had gathered much of the day around the Scott radio to garner as many details as possible.

He stepped into the house, fresh air and cigarette smoke mingling in a cloud around him.

"How do you think they managed to do it?" Elinor asked. She couldn't wait to walk to the theatre on this mild spring evening.

As Beat helped her into her coat, he whispered, "Jimmy Doolittle. What an adventure!"

Americans felt vulnerable after the bombing of Pearl Harbor in December. Of course, the U.S. declared war immediately and secured the coasts. Submarine nets. Blackouts, air raid drills, rationing to help the troops. No one laughed at threats against the mid-section of the country. It was said that the Germans could fly from Norway, which they had now occupied for two years, over the pole, and their bombers would end up over the fields and towns of the Midwest. There was no way to completely secure the country, to guarantee the citizens' safety.

But Jimmy Doolittle. Now that was something. Today, Saturday, April 18, 1942 would go down in the history books. Now the Japanese would feel vulnerable, too.

Sixteen bombers with four bombs in each had launched from the *USS Hornet*, secretly floating somewhere in the western Pacific. The planes, formerly land-based, had been outfitted and modified in Minneapolis—so close to home. They took off in enemy territory, in the waters just 600 miles east of Japan. And six hours later they climbed over their intended targets, flying single file to avoid detection. Tokyo, Yokohama, Nagoya, Kobe. Such funny names.

"Well, those Japs had it coming," he said. "Can you believe it? Flying planes off a ship's deck? Oh, honey, I'd like to be on one of those things, sailing. Or flying."

Beat leaned in to give her a kiss.

She angled toward him, smiling. Bourbon. He must've been celebrating a bit on his way to her house. She snuggled deeper into her coat, then snapped her rubbers over her pumps.

Elinor was ready to see a movie, but Beat needed to talk. "It must've been scary for the men in those planes," she offered as she guided him closer to the door.

"The Navy and the Air Force worked together on the plan."

"Think you'll join up?" she asked.

Darrow hesitated. "I know some fellows who are joining the services. Their numbers are coming up, and they don't want to be fodder for the Army."

The draft numbers were chosen in October of 1940—before Pearl. Each man was assigned a number and, for this first peacetime lottery, those were put into cobalt blue capsules for the drawing. Even FDR had been present at the beginning. He had addressed the nation, then, saying, "You who will enter this peacetime army will be the inheritors of a proud history and an honorable tradition . . . Ever since that first muster, our democratic army has existed for one purpose only: the defense of our freedom. It is for that one purpose and that one purpose only that you will be asked to answer the call to training."

Of course, every male knew his number and could predict the approach of his draft date. Some of the men wanted to avoid the draft, so they rushed to join other services before their numbers came up. Others sensed the inevitable. Many joined the Army right away and a few waited for the Army's invitation.

Mickey's boyfriend, Bob Dodd, had joined the National Guard. At first the boys were simply playing at war, like grown-up kids, a gang of buddies. Now he was about to ship into the Pacific, into the war.

"Geez, to feel some action. That'd be great," Beat said. "But with two years of college left . . ."

"Even movie stars are enlisting, Beat," Elinor encouraged. "Jimmy Stewart, Jackie Coogan, Douglas Fairbanks, Jr." She waved a good-bye to her parents who had entered the living room to settle into their chairs.

"Clark Gable, Joe Louis, and even FDR's son James." Beat continued the list as he held the door for her.

Elinor sighed. "Those Navy uniforms . . ."

Beat laughed and put his arm around her waist. They dashed out of the house, nearly skipping, to see *How Green Was My Valley*. In a few days surely there'd be an updated newsreel about Jimmy Doolittle's daring raid.

I Like You in the Damnedest Way

May 1942

YMCA
Monday evening, May 4

Dear Hon,

Everything's O.K. here now. In fact even better than ever because soon your ol' school will be out and we're going to have lots of fun.

I've definitely quit drinking for the duration. 'Tis a bad habit. Just one or two with you once in a while. We've got something to drink to—that ideal arrangement. May it always hold. I think we ought to have a couple of "Cokes" Thursday nite. I've got some things to explain and straighten out.

                                        Bye now and love,
                                                    Beat

From Reverend Landgrebe's Journal

May 7, Thursday
Elinor comes home in evening

May 8
Elinor and Johnny drive down to Gwinner, back in evening,
a distance of 180 miles.

Monday evening, May 11

Hi, Cleopatra,

From 2-3, me. From 3-7, Johnny. From 7-?, who? Musta
been someone, hon. How about signing me up for all
three shifts this weekend? And a few more, too.
   Write, huh?

                                        Love,
                                        Beat

Thursday, May 14

Dear Elinor,

It's really cold today. It might be something I
said or did. Have I done something that has caused
us to split—that is, that you're mad at the Beat?
And the best remedy seems to be a good drunk.

But I'd never let a woman cause me to feel bad and then drink. Not that it wouldn't be fun.

I like you in the damnedest way. I can't figure it out. Maybe I'm too stubborn to admit more, but we certainly do have something between us that means something to me. Oh, m'God, I just read that over and it sounds like I'm on my knees in front of you. That'll never do.

I like you a lot. It's probably too bad you know that.

Love,
Beat

Wishes on the Table

May 1942

"WHAT ARE YOU THINKING?" Darrow asked late one night.

He and Elinor sat in the Aquarium at a small table in the corner. Beat settled his cigarette into the ashtray and looked into her eyes.

Elinor stared past him. She watched the tropical fish in the tank behind the bar. The largest specimen swam to the end of the aquarium, bumped into the glass, turned and did the same on the opposite end. Elinor wondered if the fish had any idea how trapped it was.

The end of another school year was upon her, and Elinor needed to start planning her future. She wanted to quit teaching. But what to do?

Johnny would be leaving soon. Army. He wanted Elinor to wear his ring. And then wait for him.

And there was Walter, in and out of town, depending upon his business. His brother was lost somewhere in Italy, but Walter had opted to stay out of the service due to his bad back. Elinor had returned his engagement ring again, but Walter hounded her to take it back. Her parents felt he was perfect for her.

And now another twist complicated her life. She and Beat had devised the Ideal Arrangement. That's what they called it. She would date whomever she wanted on weekends when she came home. But after she had sent her date on, usually before midnight, Darrow would appear after walking—or, most often, running—to her home from his job at Interstate Seed where he worked after his daytime classes at the college.

When her parents were out of town, visiting distant parishes, Elinor had more freedom to hang out even later with Beat. They both enjoyed late nights in the bars and restaurants of Fargo.

After midnight, they could welcome the new day together. The two of them had developed a routine. First, they would stop at the Comstock, the Powers, or the Aquarium. He would order a Tom Collins for her and a bourbon and water for himself. He was, after all, nearly legal drinking age. He'd be twenty-one on the seventeenth of May, their shared birthday.

They would talk to the bartender and anyone they knew and then listen to the music until the place closed. Once they saw Peggy Lee at the Powers, before she became so famous. Beat knew the guy she was dating back then.

After the Comstock, they would stop at the Metropole or Gene's for a snack. They sat closer together and whispered to each other as the night wore on. Joking, flirting, breaking their sticks.

It struck her now as the silliest thing. She had thought it up one night while drinking with Beat at the Metropole. She'd had one or two. And she thoughtlessly broke one of the cocktail sticks that had arrived in her drinks.

"What are you thinking?" Beat asked.

"Just wondering. About this war. About the future." She leaned toward him.

"Breaking sticks?" He grinned, his eyes squinting behind his glasses.

"Mmm. Kind of like . . . like wishbones, I guess. You break them and think about what you wish for." She laughed. "Not so many chicken wishbones available these days with all this rationing."

"So you use the sticks instead . . ." He fingered a stick from the pile on the table. "What are you wishing for?"

"Silly! You can't tell or the wish won't come true."

They had laughed at that, but Beat began breaking his sticks, too. And Elinor wondered about his wishes. When their bar hopping evenings came to a close, the two of them regularly left a pile of wishes on the table.

So their friendship developed. Convenient, cozy. They snuggled in their favorite corners of their usual haunts. They wondered about the future, what would happen to the world after the war. They discussed religion and movies and music. Some nights they would sit together in the living room to talk, drink coffee, and spoon.

How late he stayed depended upon whether her folks were upstairs in their bedroom or out on the road in some parish of the large Lutheran district over which her father presided.

And once in a while Elinor would awake fully clothed in her daybed. She had a time remembering how she had gotten home. Pie-eyed, she supposed. But it had been so much fun, that delightful oblivion.

She knew she was playing with fire, and she promised herself that she'd have a long talk with Beat. Their relationship surely wasn't appropriate for a Bishop's daughter. She couldn't go on like this!

Elinor blinked as Beat's voice repeated the question. "What are you thinking?"

"Nothing," she whispered. She took another sip of her drink.

I've Ruined Things, Probably

May 1942

YMCA
Monday, May 18

Hi, sweets,

I'm really more than somewhat worried, hon. I've been blaming myself all day for it. When I keep thinking how I act sometimes—especially last nite—Right now I'm just hoping and praying that everything is O.K.

Say, would you please thank your mother for supper last nite? When I tried to, there were preachers on each hand and it just didn't happen.

Really is swell to have birthdays. How many more rings did you get?

I've reserved my right and left auricles for you (that's part a my heart y'know).

Bye now,
Beat

P.S. You can have the rest of that heart, too.

YMCA
Thursday, May 21
10:15–11:20 P.M.

Hi, Hon,

Or am I supposed to be calling you that any more? Your sister Irene says (tonight in the Fargo Café) that the folks are mad at me—very mad.

I realize that last Sunday was far from the ideal date from either yours or your folks' viewpoint. But, darn it, hon, I had to bluff, be rough, hurt myself and others to get out of that mess. It won't happen again, but that's an awfully poor and useless thing to say now.

Really it kinda hurts in me someplace when I look at your picture and think that I've ruined things probably.

Love,
Beat

May 27, Wednesday

Dear Elinor,

Thanks for the letter. 'Twas a pleasant surprise. And it certainly sounds as if you are busy down there.

I'll call you Friday at 7:00, 8:00, 9:00 and 10:00, etc. until I find you at home. You'll have to give me a few hours.

Love & such,
Beat

Something Big

June 1942

ELINOR SIGHED. THE CUCKOO wobbled out of its nest and chirped three times. Elinor watched the wooden bird settle back into the clockworks, and then she stepped into the kitchen to deposit the cups in the sink. Darrow had just left.

She arranged her bedding on the day bed. When she was finished, she flipped off the last lights and threw back the covers. She sat on the edge of the bed. If only Mickey were around! She needed to talk.

The evening had warmed up. Perhaps that's why she felt so restless. Elinor stood. She turned the den lights back on and went into the kitchen to see about any cold coffee left in the pot. Coffee grounds remained in the percolator's basket, no liquid, not a drop, in the silver carafe.

She left the kitchen and walked through the small dining area, to the living room, then to the front hallway, and finally back to her father's den on the main floor. It was cramped when the Landgrebes' grown children arrived home. Two bedrooms on the second floor for the six of them. And there were always visitors—relatives or pastors from the district—who needed a rooming house. That meant that the adult children camped out around the house, depending upon how many people were in residence.

Of course, this home was better than all those parsonages they'd lived in. This was, at last, their own.

Elinor coolly assessed how the family was living. "An unabridged dictionary and a shelf of books. A collection of *National Geographic* magazines. Lots of musty old furniture." Elinor wrinkled her nose. She hated that horsehair sofa from the turn of the century. "Mom doesn't even have silver or a decent china pattern," she thought. Could you count the Scott radio or the unabridged dictionary as "riches"? Or the snazzy Royal typewriter that had replaced the old German one—the typewriter with the umlauted vowels?

Elinor shook her head and sighed.

Her parents had lived through some difficult times at the turn of the century. They had made it nearly intact through the influenza epidemic of 1918. Her father had to attend to many of the dying, among them her newborn sister. Their small-town doctor recommended that Georg have a sip of bourbon before each visit and a smoke afterwards. And, following Doc Lorentzen's advice, Georg had lived through that epidemic.

The First World War followed. Americans, naturally, were skeptical about Americanized Germans. Georg preached in his parents' native tongue despite the mood of the country.

Prohibition followed. There was wine then only during the communion service once a month. The mammoth bottles arrived in a locked crate which Georg picked up at the train station in Bismarck. He kept the key to the wooden box in his desk drawer in his church office.

And the Depression which followed prevented her parents from amassing anything much. Her father hadn't been paid for years of preaching, instead receiving a chicken or some pork pieces once in a while and some eggs when the parishioners could spare them. Now this tiny two-bedroom home held all they had accumulated over a lifetime.

A country preacher's life hadn't been designed to be lucrative. All the hard times meant that her parents had even less to show for their years together.

Elinor admired her parents for the ways they maintained their standards and dignity. But she was determined not to marry a clergyman, despite her parents' hopes. In college she had avoided any man headed to seminary. She was just so tired of being poor.

She sat on the piano bench in the living room. It was too late to make music without waking the family. She touched the music cabinet her grandfather had crafted. She rubbed her fingers over all the carvings on the music shelves—the golden inset pattern of a treble clef, then the angel harp—and she wondered about him, a preacher who loved woodworking. They'd never met. Did he play piano? Was this the way he tried to beautify the basic living of his profession?

She retreated into her father's study and settled in for a short night.

And, as fate would have it, in the next morning's mail came a postcard from Mickey. Several weeks before, her sister had left home to work in Chicago with her best friend Betty, and the two girls had found jobs. Things happened there. Mickey had boyfriends already.

Elinor shook her head. Was everyone else busy with life? Why should she be stuck in Fargo?

1135 Third Street North

Beat, Too?

July 1942

ELINOR GRABBED THE MAIL and poured herself another cup of coffee in the kitchen. She carried her cup to the front porch where she stood, sipping and contemplating the small town activity. Someone mowed. She followed the milkman's path down one side of the block and up the other.

Elinor pushed her hair back from her forehead. She opened the envelope and read the letter, then reread the first paragraph. She smiled.

"Darling, you maybe feel the same way as I
do. So darn lonesome for you. I love you
so much and you can save this letter for
evidence if you ever want to sue me. And
I want to marry you, too. So there."

Darrow certainly had a good sense of humor.

She noted the hotel stationery he had used and ran her finger over the return address. The Nicollet, in Minneapolis. The Cities! She imagined the crowds downtown, the shopping, the bars, the energy.

So, he'd been to the Merchant Marine office. He wrote,

"They don't want me!! That is, as a common
seaman. They can probably use me at their
Boston Radio School. That would give me a

real education in six months and then to
sea as an officer. The only hitch is that
my eyes aren't up to standard, but my
education is way above. So they will waive
the eye test if I can see pretty well in
the morning. You can bet I'll be in bed
early tonight."

Elinor laughed. No big night on the town for Beat. She folded the letter and returned it to its envelope. Then she opened it again to take another peek at that P.S. "I'm nervous all over."

The boys were leaving for all kinds of adventures in the war zones. As they left her, they called out so gaily, "Have you heard there's a war on?" She certainly knew.

And when they were gone, they wrote. Phil, Clarence, Dale and Bob Flynn were already in training or overseas. They were scattered into the various corners of the known universe. Johnny was in training in California. Bob Dodd, Mickey's boyfriend, was in the Pacific. Now Darrow. The men would see the world, though no one on the home front would have much of an idea of which parts they'd see. She thought about the wartime newsreels she'd seen. It wouldn't be long before a few of her "old friends" might be starring in them.

Elinor sighed. School was out. The rest of the summer stretched out before her, boring months. She enjoyed dates when her "old friends" arrived back in town on their leaves before shipping overseas. But their visits were rare now, and their minds were on the war.

There were still movies being made, but no one but Walt, 4F, to accompany her to the theatres. According to the draft board code of regulations a man classified as 4F was "not acceptable for military service." Elinor began to feel that he wasn't acceptable for dating service either. It was shameful to be seen with someone in civilian clothing. She preferred dating men in uniform. Navy uniforms were her first choice, though there weren't many Navy men around on the prairies of Dakota.

The war meant more work now, and everyone on the home front

was expected to pitch in, too. Some served as blackout wardens who checked for any light coming out of buildings during an air raid drill. Some worked for the metal drives, collecting tin and iron for use in the war. Elinor supervised ration coupon distributions.

She heard a few children at play and then the low moan of the Great Northern whistle as the train approached the station a few blocks away. She looked up into the sunshine.

"I can't stay here," she thought. She remembered Mickey's postcard.

Mickey's apartment could be a safe haven for a couple of weeks, a vacation. Chicago! Elinor ran her fingers through her hair. She pushed it behind her ears again. She would look for a job, perhaps cook for her sister. Certainly there must be something an English teacher, a German speaker, could do in such a place. And there'd be shops to browse, new people to meet.

Elinor stepped back into the house. Ching met her at the door and followed her into her father's study. Relieved that her parents were out of town, Elinor sat at her father's typewriter. She set her cup on the desk and removed the dust cover from the typewriter.

Before beginning, she stood up and reached Post's *Etiquette* book off the bottom shelf above the desk. She turned to the index. "Resignation, letters of, 586. She located the page. She had to be certain that her letter was appropriate and written according to the latest etiquette.

"Oh, damn," slipped from her lips. She looked around to see whether anyone had heard her, then laughed. "Mom and Dad are out of town. Irene's at work. There's no one here but Ching." She leaned over to scratch him behind his ears, then returned to her research.

Emily Post had written the manners for resigning. From a club. Something every woman should know.

"What about women who work?" Elinor snorted. "She's one of us. There should be some direction in how to give up a job."

She found a piece of plain onionskin, no imprint of the synod on it, in her father's desk. She rolled the stationery into the platen of the typewriter and began. "To Whom It May Concern." She wanted to jump out of the big chair and begin packing but, instead, focused her energy on the words that spilled onto the page.

It was easy. She resigned. No more teaching. She would search for something else, something that would provide the finer things of life.

She tucked the letter into an envelope and walked to the table by the front door. She would catch the mailman when he arrived for the morning or afternoon delivery. For a moment, she wondered what her parents would think about this resignation. But, Chicago! And she'd be safe there with Mickey. There were sure to be adventures in her future. This might just be what The Fates had in mind.

Elinor returned to the living room and settled on the piano bench. She played softly at first, her fingers moving lightly over the keys, one song after another, joyous, dancing melodies. She could breathe again.

The next week, she packed her small valise, kissed her parents, turned her daybed over to Ching, and appeared in Chicago.

Perhaps, with a bit of luck, she'd be discovered, like the Andrews sisters from Minneapolis. And Peggy Lee from Jamestown, North Dakota, for Pete's sake. The possibilities! Perhaps she, too, could become Something Big.

Apprentice Seaman

July 1942

Andrews Hotel, Minneapolis
"Strictly fireproof, near everything, popular prices"
July 29

Well, Darling,

I'm all set now. It's 3:15, and we've been sworn in and all is ready for the departure. Lots of papers, etc. to sign. Also about three officers gave us serious talks about dangers and that stuff, not mincing words, so that we knew what we were signing up for. The pay is going to be darn good, and if the fellows at the school are half as nice as these fellows here, it will be fun. Right now I'm a very enthusiastic guy about this deal. We had coffee and doughnuts and cigarettes at the Red Cross place and got acquainted.

We leave here tomorrow morning at eight and arrive in Chicago at 2:40—the *Zephyr*, I believe. We have two hours there and then sleepers to Albany—on a crack streamliner. We arrive in

Boston at 2:40 Friday afternoon. And that's what I call really making time.

Well, I'm apprentice seaman Beaton now, so I guess I'd better pinch myself again.

I'm yours, darling,
Beat

Gallups Island

July 1942

His train to Gallups Island waited on the outbound track at Chicago Union Station. Beat bounded up the corrugated metal steps of the *Empire Builder*. Squeezing his body and pack down the aisle, he settled his mind on the moment, finding a seat. He located one at the back of the car and stowed his duffel.

He ran his hand over the soft seat before he settled on the upholstery. Beat was used to rougher riding on the railroads, from his days hoboing in cattle cars. A comfortable ride would be a dream come true.

Elinor had actually met him for his layover, their last two hours together before the war would come between them.

He saw her scanning his train car, straining to see him, and he leaned to the window for a last wave. "I love you," he mouthed.

She grinned.

When the Merchant Marine had accepted him into its ranks, they had given him one week before shipping out to the East Coast for training. Beat had taken the train to visit Elinor in Chicago. They spent his last days in the Midwest together, bumming around the Windy City, staying up most of every night, and sleeping late the next morning.

Perhaps her parents would never know about this adventure. It was another war secret. Mickey knew, of course, but was circumspect. Besides, she was busy working and barely noted Elinor's absence. She was probably grateful to not have to share her twin bed with her sister for a few days.

But the time had come. He had to leave Elinor in Chicago and return to Minneapolis to join the group of radio officer candidates for the trip to their Boston school.

Now the trip from the Cities had taken him back through Chicago for this bittersweet two-hour layover. A second good-bye.

Elinor turned to go. He turned to his seatmates.

In the next seat lolled an Army recruit, probably fresh out of high school. Two sailors—Navy boys—faced them. As the train began to rumble down the tracks, they chatted about the war and their final destinations. Although Beat had just said goodbye to his girl, he talked about his radio training and his dreams of action with the bravado of servicemen on the way to war.

The conversation lagged as the train, rattling with a familiar rhythm, rocked along its steely path. He leaned back in his seat. Beat closed his eyes and remembered how he had traveled by boxcar in his youth, those high school summer days when he desperately wanted to see the oceans. He and Bob Bruns had found their way to San Francisco and the Golden Gate Exposition. Then to New York City and the World's Fair. Riding the rails had been their way of sightseeing.

Beat stretched his legs. He remembered 1939. Both fairs in one year. Both oceans, too.

The two of them had traveled to the World's Fair in the Big City. The fair was all about the "Dawn of a New Day" and promised to give the millions of visitors a real look at "tomorrow." Roosevelt's opening speech was televised in New York City on NBC, and over a thousand people watched him on a couple of hundred TV sets scattered around the city. Einstein made a televised speech about cosmic rays. There were futuristic cars on display, TVs and even a voice synthesizer. Imagine air conditioning! Or color photos. He shook his head. The world of the future had looked so bright then, just three years ago. Before the war.

He got up and walked through the cars to the Tip Top Tap car, just behind the engine, where he could find a drink. The train rattled on while he sat on the red cushioned chair, a cigarette in the ashtray and a drink in his hand.

He changed trains again in Albany for the last leg of this journey. Not even two days from Fargo to Boston. Unbelievable!

When he exited the last of the trains, he strolled the streets of the port city. He entered a bar full of servicemen and ordered a bourbon. He met a couple of sailors on liberty who had no war experience to share. However, they expected to ship out soon.

After a few drinks, Beat headed to the wharf to catch the water taxi to Gallups Island, a tiny island just six miles into the Atlantic, off Boston Harbor. While he waited for the launch to pick him up at the assigned pier, the India Wharf, he followed the movements of the glittering ocean, the rising and swelling of the water, then the retreat as the foam washed up on the shore. The glare of the sun on the seas hypnotized him. He breathed the salt air and took out a cigarette. He lit it, took a drag, and continued to stare, nearly motionless. He scratched his neck in the heat of the late summer afternoon and wished for a cap.

He sat on his duffel then and studied the ships going in and out through the nets. Submarine nets had been stretched out across the bay, installed at all of America's ports to keep the German U-boats away from the harbors. He spotted oilers, destroyers, cargo ships, and troop transports, ships now outfitted to hold men and supplies and ammo. He looked at the decks to see what had been lashed aboveboard, and he speculated about what might be stowed in the hold. He guessed where each was heading and recalled what he knew about the war in those parts of the world.

"One day," he thought, "I'll be on one of those."

Others gathered with him to catch the water taxi to the Island. Some knew what lay ahead—guys returning from liberty, teasing each other, swearing, or sitting stupidly in some stage of hangover. The rest were raw recruits, the boots.

Beat supposed they were all, like himself, a bit nervous about what lay ahead.

When the taxi moored, he grabbed his pack and stepped aboard.

Gallups Island from Boston Harbor

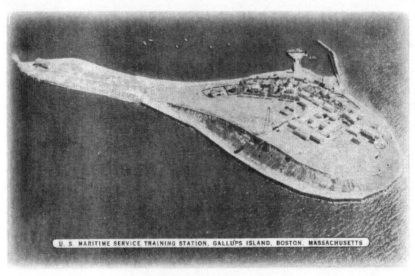

U. S. MARITIME SERVICE TRAINING STATION, GALLUPS ISLAND, BOSTON, MASSACHUSETTS

Aerial view of Gallups Island

We're Cooped Up Here

August 1942

Saturday, August 1
Gallups Island
Boston, Mass.

Dearest Elinor,

I love you, and boy, I know it more each night. This school is about the roughest and toughest deal I've ever seen—and I love it! But if I'm one of the lucky fellows, I'll be O.K. in 6 months to really rake in the sugar.

The fellows are cooped up here—no women on the island—and they talk and act rough. The fellows treat me swell because I've used a little bluff so far and not acted timid like the others mostly do.

I just looked out the window and the swellest blue sea is coming up on the rocks. It's beautiful, this ol' Atlantic. This harbor is full of war. Convoys, battleships, cruisers, destroyers, and big patrol planes and mine sweepers.

I love you, darling. Most of the fellows I'm with have girls so you can depend on us.

Yours,
Beat

Is Walt home yet?

August 2, Sunday

Good morning, Darling,
I'm sitting on a cliff looking east into the Atlantic. We're about 75 or 80 feet above the water with our legs dangling over. A swell sea breeze is blowing and the sun is shining. From here we can see the submarine nets across the harbor throat. We're outside them, and we watch the ships come and go through the only opening. All these ships have seen a lot of the world.

These sea gulls down below us make the only noise on the island, except the swearing and fighting, shouting, etc. that accompanies every meal. You've got to yell for everything you want passed.

One out of three pass the course. The course has been lengthened to seven and a half months. Some of us have been moved up a class to R-19 so my address is R-19 instead of R-20. This is a very good break—means sooner leave.

We had some real lifeboating in the Atlantic today. The water was rough, and we all got wet and cold, but it was really fun. This afternoon we were given drills on *how to abandon ship*.

All about fires, winds, swimming, etc. They demonstrated some of those rubber suits, and they work fine. Also all ships have $5,000.00 insurance on their men. So it's a good deal, if and when I get through.

Last night we had a thrilling sight among thrilling sights that are common here. A convoy was sighted way out at sea and then it "hove to." This was about 6:00. It was still out there at dusk, and when dark came a fellow read its blinker that "an undersea craft or more was in the vicinity, according to listening devices." Big searchlights, planes, destroyers, corvettes, and we all watched that water like hawks. Then all blacked out, and we couldn't see anything. The ships could be seen only as shadows passing through a small opening in the submarine nets. They all made it. It really was a tense situation.

Yours,
Beat

Elinor, you'd better tear this up or something after you read it.

⇒   ⇐

Wednesday, August 12

Dearest Darling,

Say, honey, you don't—you can't—realize how a letter from you sets off the smiles and happy feelings. As soon as I read your letter this noon, I just sat and looked into space, to be rudely awakened by the fellows laughing at me. They called me "lovesick." Maybe I am, but it certainly is a nice way to be sick.

Darling, no matter how much you say, "Don't think too much about" you, it's there day and night. I'm yours all the way. That soldier was right when he said he'd go "over the hill" for you. I would, too, if I needed to. I mean to keep you loving me and waiting for the few months that we have left.

I know that wherever you are that Walt is there. And others, too. Some day you'll be all mine, Elinor. I'm waiting and working for that day. Tell Swede to leave you alone. He's a wolf, hon. I know.

About telling fellows to look after you, I don't remember telling anybody that. Tell those guys you love me. That'd make me feel so much better. Say hi to the folks and your sister Irene. Maybe Walt, too, if it's wise.

I pray for you, darling,
Yours,
Beat

❧   ❧

We just had our fingerprints taken down at the office. All we need now is our "blues." That's our uniform for dress. "Is" is right, too, because they're singular, they say. Sounds funny to a guy like me, though. But then a lot of these accents and things that end up here are funny.

When I get out of here, I'll be able to eat almost anything. Not that they don't cook well, but they have so many things that I never ate before—this Eastern type spaghetti and meatballs and fried potatoes for breakfast. So you won't have to learn how to cook, darlin'. We'll eat at restaurants anyway.

Last nite there was a movie on syphilis from the Army. Now I know that I won't take any chances—and I surely am glad I haven't got it. They say you can get those things from cigarettes, kisses, glasses, etc. I'm not taking any chances around here, believe me.

⇛   ⇚

This course is an IF course for about five months. IF you pass the tests each week, you stay in school. Otherwise, it's goodbye to If Isle. So this can't be planned on either, unless you can say that hard work is a cinch to get you through the course.

⇛   ⇚

August 13, Thursday

Hello, Sweets,

You've never seen real fog in North Dakota. Let me tell you about the fog here—so thick I can cut it with a knife. All the bell buoys around the island are ringing out their warnings, and the foghorns are blowing, too. Now I know why they issued us raincoats.

In one week we've had two years of algebra, a

half year of Ohm's Law, and a half year of trig. In code we're already a week and a half ahead of any other class that ever went through. They tell us that today after pushing us all week. But I like it so far.

I have two cents until payday a week away. Guess I won't be doing much smoking or running around.

I saw the short. It was a special rerun of that Army picture on the perils of venereal diseases so I went to see it. Quite gruesome. We got some literature from headquarters on the same stuff today. They say this town is infested with it. But I needn't worry! There's a very good article on sex for men—saying it is a very unnecessary part of a single man's life. And the chances that a fellow takes inflicting those horrors on a wife and children . . . Well, I've got to write something, and this is what happens around here.

In a weak moment today I was laughing to myself, smiling, about your luck. Every time it seems that one of the fellows comes to town, the others just leave. How do you manage it? You seldom have complications, but now from your letters you seem to be having quite a time keeping them all happy. What a life, eh, sweets? I miss you, darling. Maybe you shouldn't be so beautiful. Then I might not have to think about those other fellows.

I'm always yours,

G'nite, Elinor,
Beat

Fate

Midsummer 1942

ELINOR FIDDLED WITH HER toast. Chicago hadn't panned out for her. It had been tight in Mickey's crowded apartment. There were no jobs that earned more than a teacher's salary.

She had returned home. But her "old friends" had left. Maybe there was only so much excitement in the world. When a world war came along, as they seemed to be doing with regularity these days, most of the energy migrated toward the action there. And there was a near zero level of adventure on the home front.

American ads promoted service as a way to see the world, and after the Great War and the Depression, seeing the world didn't sound so bad. In addition, having regular meals was a draw for men like Beat who had never had enough to eat during the Depression. The men were leaving their provincial towns to explore a wider universe.

But a gal didn't have many prerogatives.

Elinor nibbled at one corner of her dry toast, then set it down. "Dad, I've had an offer. Teaching. In Pelican Rapids," she said.

"A bigger town, Bunny, and you're a good teacher," her father replied. "Good news! Pelican is in lake country, where we vacation every year. Good Norwegian souls there."

Reverend Landgrebe was the head of the congregations in the Dakota District of the American Lutheran Church. He was in charge of making sure that everything functioned in the parishes of the Dakotas and Montana. He knew less about the Norwegian Lutherans across the border in Minnesota, a different synod, a separate universe, from the German Lutherans.

"But I quit teaching last May, Dad. I've left the classroom behind."

"Come now, Elinor," her father coaxed. "Pelican Rapids isn't far from home." He knew his daughter loved being home. Still young at heart, having trouble separating. Maybe it was because she had advanced two grades in elementary school and was the youngest in her class at graduation. Or maybe it was the car accident that killed her younger brother, Georgie. She had stayed home from college the year after Georgie's death to grieve with her family. "It's close. You can come home every weekend, just like when you taught in Gwinner."

Elinor knew her options. She could rot as an old maid in the family. She could marry Walter and move deeper into Dakota. She could wait for Johnny to come home from the war, then marry him, and become a schoolteacher's wife. A gal's basic choice seemed to be marriage.

Nevertheless, in the furthest corner of her dreams, Elinor held out hope. She had heard the stories. Movie stars were discovered every day in Hollywood. A girl'd just hang around in a drugstore, drinking an icy Coca-Cola. She'd chat with a friend or count her change, cross her legs, and some agent would come over to talk. The next step was the movies. Stardom!

No one would ever be discovered in Pelican Rapids, no matter how many Coca-Colas she consumed in those downtown cafés. She had to get out into the world where agents were on the lookout. But she didn't know how. A gal couldn't just leave her father and go alone to the coast. Not a bishop's daughter. Not in 1942.

After breakfast Elinor reluctantly signed the contract, smiling ruefully at their closing. "Love"? Did these people not even know proper business letter procedures? She slipped the paper into the envelope, added a three-cent stamp, and walked her future to the mailbox on the corner of Broadway and Twelfth Avenue.

At supper, her father suggested, "Perhaps we should drive next week to Pelican, Bunny. We can find you a nice rooming house there."

Elinor nodded. She wondered whether her parents were tired of sharing the small place with Irene and her.

On Monday morning the Landgrebes filled their striped steel thermos with coffee and they stuffed their tin lunch box with doughnuts from Leeby's. They packed their snack and themselves and Elinor into the Pontiac. They rolled the windows down halfway. Then they swooped out of the alley and headed across the river, through Moorhead, and down U.S. Highway 10, which began in the prairie but drove right into lake country.

They passed farm fields green with wheat, oats, and knee-high corn. "Looks like a good year for the crops," Georg smiled. But prairie weather could be so volatile. "Trudie, remember those dust storms in western Dakota? And our crops that died for lack of rain."

"The winds that ripped crops out of the ground before twisting into the distance," Trudie added. "It's a good year, though," she smiled across the large front seat toward her husband.

"If the weather holds," he added with a sigh.

They turned onto State Highway 34, and in a few miles, they passed lakes which shimmered in the hot July sun. Most boats were docked at this time of day, rocking in the water, oarlocks creaking, as waves and seaweed slapped their sides. The air smelled moist, heavy in places with the fusty odor of beached fish.

As they drove into the city limits of Pelican Rapids, Elinor rolled her window down completely. The Pontiac crawled down the main street. Two banks, Knutson Furniture, Westland Motor. They slowed past the creamery, then the West Ottertail Service Company building. Elinor grinned when she discovered the Park movie theater and The Cow, the local ice cream parlor. Georg was the first to spot the Norwegian Lutheran Church, with its lofty clock tower. They discovered two cafés—the Pelican and the Uptown, both clean and busy.

There were no bars at all. Pelican Rapids was a dry town. Georg smiled. And Elinor began to plot ways to get back to Fargo on the weekends. There might be train connections, she hoped, as they drove over some tracks.

The town was busy, nearly lively, in the summer, as city people gathered into small resorts like Dunn's, or the Oak Lodge, or cabins tucked between lakes. The summer people tracked into town for groceries, sand between their toes and sunburn on their cheeks.

The family drove up and down Broadway a few times, to get a feel for the town. They located the high school at the end of the main street.

"Let's look at the closest rooming house," Trudie suggested, after they had traversed most of the streets, threading north and south, then east and west. Elinor opened her purse to locate the rental list she had received from the school offices.

They drove the five blocks to the Nettestad residence, a fashionable brick, two-story home close to the Frazee Mill. It was a beautiful palace with an arrangement of porches to catch a breeze no matter what the direction of the wind, a welcoming front door, and sturdy chimneys.

As the three walked up the stairs to the front porch, they noted the gardens, everything in bloom and healthy.

Mrs. Nettestad met them at the door. Georg removed his hat and explained their mission.

Mrs. Nettestad cheerfully showed them the room to let. It was on the second floor and overlooked the large back yard. The room contained a single bed, a dresser, a small desk, a dressing table with a silvery mirror and a second-hand chair in the corner. The bathroom, shared with the family, was just two doors down the hallway. Breakfast could be arranged as part of the rental, and suppers could be had downtown at either of the two cafés. The Pelican and the Uptown would bill a teacher monthly.

Mrs. Nettestad gave the Landgrebes a tour of the large home. "This place was built for the owner of the Frazee Mill at the turn of the century," she explained. "My husband is in training now. The Army. We haven't had roomers before, but because of the current situation . . ." She smiled. "We thought a teacher here would be a good example for the children. Do you smoke?" She addressed her question to Elinor.

"Oh, no," Elinor replied.

"Of course you'd understand. No men allowed upstairs."

"Of course."

"And breakfast comes with the room."

"I like this, Dad." Elinor smiled. It had taken money to pay for the woodwork and the leaded glass windows on the main floor. The fireplaces were elegant—solid brick with carved wooden mantels. The large spaces downstairs were clearly meant for entertaining numbers of people. "It's a beautiful home. Kind of expensive, but I will afford it."

Elinor counted out the down payment in cash.

While her parents settled on a picnic bench in the park for their coffee and doughnuts, she stopped at the postal station just off Broadway to arrange for her mail and her own post office box number. She would have to write to all her "old friends" to let them know.

And before school started Elinor counted her savings and made a long distance call to Mickey. "One last adventure?"

It wasn't too late. The Fates might still rescue her from the classroom.

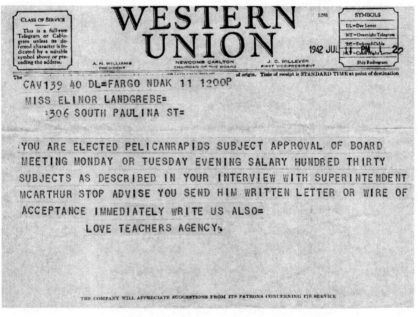

Telegram from teachers agency

A Hermit's Paradise

August 1942

August 17, Monday nite 4:50

Dearest Elinor,

If my writing is any different, it's because I've got a very sore right arm. Our whole ninety-four had typhoid shots and another Wasserman. Four fellows fainted. My arm feels just stiff and dead-like. Over half the class left the last code class early, and we found them lying on their bunks here. As I look around me in the barracks, I can see eleven of the ninety-some men out of bed. Some have been very sick and are in a dead sleep now. Here I sit on my upper bunk eating chocolates that I got from home today. Some of us are just lucky, I guess. We've got two more shots coming.

My blues are in the tailor shop and I'm planning on a weekend in Boston after payday Thursday. They have a lot of swell serviceman's clubs. If you don't care, I might even go to some sailor picnics with girls. The other guys plan to do that Sunday, so I probably would end up with them. The girls are supposed to be from Wellesley and other good schools around here and the picnics are on the up and up with nothing but a lot of fun and swimming. As long as I'm trying to be broad-minded, maybe you should be too. Just like you, hon, I can have loads of fun with the opposite sex and not do anything off-color either. Maybe a little of that kind of entertainment will help me get along in school better.

> I'll always love you, my darling,
> Beat

❧   ☙

Hi, darling,

I've lived on this hermit's paradise for four weekends and haven't had a real thought of wanting to get ashore. Really it doesn't excite me a bit, but it is something to look forward to . . . we're going to have a few Tom Collinses. No girls, I promise you again. I'll break all my sticks, and I'll probably be staring off into space and dreaming that I'm at Gene's with you.

> Forever yours, Elinor,
> Beat

Sunday morning

Dearest Elinor,

Oh, it's hot here. These woolen uniforms and all make it really uncomfortable. Last nite I had one of the poorest evenings of my life. Every time I had a drink, I broke the sticks and would then hold them for the longest time. The fellows that I was with must have gotten pretty tired of my talking about you.

We bunked up at the Seamen's Club. There I made some good friends, some that had seen a lot of action. In one of the bars we met and talked with some English Merchant Marine men who had been on the North Atlantic for quite a few years.

I'm at the Buddies Club here. They have given us—five sailors and five soldiers—an invitation to a dinner at 1:00 in Cambridge.

Last nite I couldn't get my mind off what you were doing in Fargo. I almost called you at 9:00 (7:00 there).

Yours,
Beat

THE BUDDIES' CLUB, ON HISTORIC BOSTON COMMON, IS
A RECREATION CENTER FOR MEN OF THE ARMED FORCES.

Buddies Club post card

He's Irish

August 1942

ELINOR AND HER MOTHER sat at the dining room table, sipping homemade lemonade from frosty glasses, thanks to two aluminum ice cube trays in the freezer compartment of the refrigerator. That Kelvinator had come with the house, along with a stove and the wringer washer in the basement. Manufacturing new appliances wasn't at the top of the list for production these days, so the four Landgrebe girls muttered a prayer of thanks every time they emptied those frosty trays or turned on the oven. Prayers were distracting, though, when using that wringer on the washing machine. A laundress had to remain alert because of the possibility of losing part of a hand to inattention.

Trudie wiped her face with a white linen handkerchief to dry the moisture collecting on her forehead. She put her hanky into the pocket of her housedress, then tried fanning herself with her hand.

"Your father says they might start rationing sugar," Trudie ventured. "He heard it the other day on the radio. With the Philippines out of action now, the sugar supply is short."

"And our soldiers will need it, I guess. We'd better appreciate it while we can get it." Elinor and her mother, laughing, lifted their glasses in a toast. "Our soldiers need all the aluminum, the nylon, tin, and even our gum."

"Don't forget cigarettes and film, Bunny."

Being a patriot meant sacrificing for the military.

The curtains on the dining room windows, along with all the

window coverings in the house, had been closed at daybreak to keep out the heat of the sun, but the sweltering air seeped in, despite those preventive measures. The family owned one fan, which whirled uselessly in the living room, moving the sultry air around.

"You know," Trudie ventured, "your cousin Arlene is planning to marry." She leaned in toward her daughter.

Arlene lived in Illinois, and Elinor had met her just once. "A wedding! I suppose you'll go?"

"I'm not sure your father can get away. Anyway, the man she's marrying?" Trudie looked around, then whispered, "He's Eye-talian."

Elinor swallowed a gulp of her lemonade wrong. She coughed a little.

"Some people think it's a problem when people start mixing," Trudie offered. "Mixing cultures, I mean."

"Why?" Elinor pushed her hair back behind her ears.

"Well, tradition. Wouldn't it be better for the children to come from one group? One country?"

"So the traditions of that country could be passed down," Elinor said. "Like not mixing a Catholic and a Lutheran because it would confuse the children?"

"Yes, because the parents would have the same holidays and customs. And religious beliefs." Trudie smiled at her daughter and leaned back into her chair. "No arguing about which church to go to or how to raise the children."

Elinor sighed.

She was definitely German. Her grandparents on both sides of the family had come to the United States from *Deutschland* in the late 1800s to serve as Lutheran missionaries to the settlers in Iowa. Her father, in his turn, had been the first Lutheran missionary to Elgin, in western North Dakota. He preached in German to German-Russian immigrants who had fled the Russian uprisings in the early part of the century.

Elinor had minored in German, an easy batch of credits for a bilingual girl. She was accredited to teach English, German, or history, and for the coming school year the Pelican Rapids Schools had offered her one class of German, along with the various levels of English. There wouldn't be many high school students taking German these days, with Hitler striding around the Fatherland, stirring things up. It was surprising that those innocent German people, good souls she was sure, marched with him.

Because of the anti-German sentiment in the country, Elinor decided to advertise her French side. She imagined that someone in her long European lineage must have married a French woman. "Just call me Frenchy," she asked her beaux. And it made her happy when they did.

Funny what a lineage could do in times of war, aligning oneself on the correct side of the action.

Her mother got up from the table to refill water over the leftover ice in their glasses.

"I just hope Arlene will be happy," she said as she returned to the table. "Eye-talians are very different from Germans, you know. Even their food."

"I've heard." Elinor picked up her glass of water. "I don't think I know any Italians, Mother. There are so many Norwegians and Swedes around here."

"Pretty much everyone we deal with is German. And Lutheran. Makes it easier for us to understand each other. I hope you find a nice German boy to marry, Bunny." Trudie reached out to pat Elinor's hand. "A Lutheran German."

Elinor released herself and finished off her drink. "Well, I suppose that makes Walter a more favorable match?" Elinor glowered. "Because we all eat sausages?"

"And speak the same language, Bunny. And celebrate in the same ways when holidays come along."

"Does it really matter—a man's background? These days we're all fighting together." Elinor ran her finger around the rim of her glass.

"Not the Eye-talians. They are against us. And Arlene is marrying one of them."

"Mother, the Germans are against us, too. Would you really want me to marry the enemy?"

"Well, it's Hitler. The Germans are good people, Bunny."

"I've dated a number of Germans. Clarence, Walter, Phil, Dale. Good people. And I'm not in love with any of them."

"Oh, Bunny." Trudie stood, mopping her brow again. "You just need time to decide on marriage. Maybe one day you'll find the perfect husband."

"Well, the perfect one doesn't live around here any more. The men are gone—the German men and the English men and the Norwegians, too. Do you want me to marry a 4F German?"

"Walter is a good man," her mother soothed. She replaced her handkerchief in her pocket. "Poor dear. He has such a bad back."

They heard the clink of the mail slot at the same time. Elinor rushed to gather in the mail. Sure enough, an envelope from Gallups Island lay on the porch floor. She picked it up, along with the rest of the mail for her parents, and returned to the dining room table.

She set her parents' mail on the table in front of her mother. "A letter from Beat," she explained, as she studied the envelope she still held in her hand.

"He's Irish," her mother reminded her. "And we are not."

"Yes, Mother."

Elinor put her letter into her skirt pocket. Then she took her mother's empty glass and her own and carried them into the kitchen where she set them into the sink.

"You know what they say about the Irish," her mother added, following Elinor into the kitchen.

"I've heard," Elinor replied. "They drink. They're lazy. Poor. Can't make anything of themselves."

She touched the envelope riding in her pocket.

She turned to her mother. "But they fight with the Allies."

Jews, Irish and Germans

August 1942

Hi, sweets,

I feel like an Irish philosopher tonite, the humorist kind. All I've had for the past day is trouble. First, you didn't write. You probably are still mad at me. I know everything will be all right when I stop to think it out. After all, I haven't done anything wrong.

We got our tests back—a so-called tough test on radio theory. I had a perfect paper, but didn't get 100%. I got 104%. You see, they had 26 questions at 4 points each. It was a cinch if one studied. I did, so . . .

This afternoon we were informed for certain that we were to get our second typhoid shot. They gave us that and on top of that, they threw another vaccination on my left arm. Both arms are in tough shape. I can't even lift them above my head. Most of the fellows are asleep.

Then, on top of this they told me I'd have to move. I'd just gotten some Scotch tape and had your pictures put up inside my locker door. Then BANG!! Now I'm below an Irishman from the

Bronx by the name of Sullivan. All around me are the Jews and Irish and Germans from New York, Brooklyn, and Joisey. Boy, what a mob. They all have fun and we're great friends.

There is a lot of war activity here, but today was something special. A lot of extra planes went to sea, and we heard a siren sound on the island. All the Navy ships hustled out on the double. Maybe something big, but you'd hear about it as soon as I would.

I was surprised to hear that I had to stand fire watch from 4 to 6 A.M. I lost a few hours sleep guarding over $200,000 worth of equipment.

Muster just was blown by the bugler over the loudspeaker.

Nite now, m'love,
Beat

❧   ❧

Last night on watch I saw the start of the longest convoy I've ever seen. All day they've been going out—way over 100 huge ships. We saw them loading when we were on Liberty boats. Maybe I shouldn't write this, but they had British flags on them and were escorted by American warships. They were loaded above-deck with huge invasion boats—below with I don't know what. Lots of huge tanks, too.

❧   ❧

August 26, Wednesday

You hurt me quite a lot when you said, "I think it might be wise to call our little affair off altogether." You're the only one that can possibly do that. Then, if you do, you'll still not be breaking my half of this "little affair." I'm going to marry you just as soon as it's possible, if not before.

Now that I've explained how I feel to you, I can put my mind on theory. We're in resistances, pressure, amperes, etc. Honestly, there are such simple explanations for electric lights, etc. if one just takes time to study them.

➤ ◀

Morse Code (I love you)

I do, too.

ARMY AND NAVY RECREATION CENTERS
Boston, Massachusetts
SPONSORED BY BOSTON SOLDIERS AND SAILORS
COMMITTEE

Saturday night

Dearest Elinor,

I'm here again. There's a gang at the piano playing Army and Navy songs and singing loud. This morning we took three rolls of film out at Harvard. We were in church at the famous chapel there for services.

The Navy is taking over the Merchant Marine so we're in a muddle here. Write some time, huh?

Yours,
Beat

Monday evening

Dearest hon,

Say, what were the old ladies kidding you about—I mean being the first bride in the new church and all? Do they think you're going to marry a preacher yet? I hope they won't be disappointed. But if I have to, I'll go to seminary. I would, too, to marry you. Someday you'll be my bride in that cozy little church. I just hope I can work hard enough to really feel that I deserve you.

Remember Minneapolis and Chicago? We had

such good times together. Just like married people. I'm staying attached to you, and the fellows here know it now. They admire me for it. Some of the fellows sneak and look at your pictures and then they tell me they realize why I'm in love.

We took some pictures yesterday and I should have them here by the end of the week. I've got one that shows the thirteen buttons on these Navy pants. It's murder to button and unbutton. The rest of the pictures will have Harvard's ivy covered buildings as a background. It's a beautiful college.

We had our biggest and last typhoid shot today, but it didn't really bother. Just have a huge lump on my arm. I watched them put it in and pump the stuff in and pull it out, just to see that I could. Other guys look at the wall. Nobody fainted this time, but a lot of them have reactions tonite.

Poor little ol' you!! School starting two weeks from today. All those young farmers should have their crops in by then. Please set aside time in Pelican to write me, hon.

Yours,
Beat

Sigma Chi pin

Tuesday night,
September 1

Dearest Darling,

Here's our pin, darling, and you take care of
it. It will have to be the link between us
for a few months and then we'll probably have
something better—not better in love, but in a
legal sort of way.

The pin is for you, forever, darling. Every
pearl stands for a million things I plan to
do for you and with you. I've lived under the
sign of that cross forever, too, really being
true and good. That's the way we both want each
other. I hope the pin is nice enough for you to
wear. I should probably have asked you about it,
but, gee, it was fun to buy it for you.

I'll pin it on you by long distance. When
we see each other again, I'll pin it on in an
appropriate manner. You can bet on that, hon.

Forever yours,
Beat

Well, two more days of school, and we have one sixth of our school completed. Five months more and we'll be out of here. Maybe about six months.

Tonite if I'd been near a railroad, I'd have been on my way home. Chins up for a while and everything will be all right.

✧   ✧

September 5, Saturday night

Hi Darlin',

Just happened to get a room at the Union Jack Club and I've been here for about three hours just talking with British merchantmen. They have some heroic tales to tell. They've all lost buddies in this war. They talk comically, but it's easy to understand after one listens a while. I'm hearing them tell of the girls and wives they left over there. I told them I know how they felt. At least you're within reach of me—a week's reach if I should quit this school. But I won't.

All I can think of on this Saturday night is that you might be tiring of all this. You haven't written for a while. Your last letter wasn't too long. I can see where you might be in doubt about all this, hon. I don't really know how I ever deserved a date with you, let alone all the time I've had with you.

So far today I've had some six or seven whiskey Cokes with my classmates, Johnny McCall and the fellow from Germany. This fellow from Germany has been telling me a lot about Hitler first hand. He lived in the Saar at the time of the plebiscite.

We saw a ship come by the island and later saw it on the way in. It had a huge torpedo hole forward. It was at the water line, but the ship had struggled in. Quite a sight. We also saw the *Aquitania* and other huge passenger ships leave with soldiers on them. Don't say anything about this, hmmm?

Forever yours,
Beat

᠉   ᠊

I think I mentioned the ship that came in with a huge torpedo hole forward. We met a fellow from that ship Sunday at the Seaman's Club. Three fellows were killed in the engine room. That's what you call "action." Someday I'll have some stories to tell.

᠉   ᠊

Tuesday afternoon in the galley

Darling,

How can I possibly tell you how much I love you? All I know is that for eight days I didn't hear from you and today they came up from the P.O. in a little package. All this time I worried about you. Maybe you might be tired of writing. Maybe you were sick. Today your letters make me feel like a million. You might put yourself in my place. If you hadn't received a letter for quite a while, it's tough.

That domestic life that you're leading lately ought to keep you in shape for our life together. We'll have a maid in every room—old, homely ones—and you just tell them what to do. All you have to do is make the coffee. That's the kind of life I want, and we'll really have it soon.

The pin means a lot to me—to us. So you like it, hmmm? I'm so glad. You wear it for us and think of me when you touch it. Remember that soon it will be properly hung on the prettiest and most wonderful girl in the whole world. You'll find a lot of Sigs in the world. Most of us try to be good fraternity brothers.

So, darling, let's settle down to a few more months of long distance love.

Love,
Beat

⟫   ⟪

I'm proud that I'm in service. You probably know how I wanted to get into this thing. I love my old America, all I've seen, anyway.

⟫   ⟪

Saturday, September 12

My darlin',

This is a really great Saturday night. On my bunk six fellows are playing poker. For the last hour and a half, I've been talking with fellows, and in between I read some of the real old letters you wrote me from January and February. We really had fun then. My mind wandered back to those times when I had to call at midnight or so to see you. Even then I loved you but didn't let myself tell you because of all the other fellows and all. Those weeks used to drag by. Then I'd go through some nervous hours on weekends calling for you, always trying to see you. We did all right considering all—as we used to call it, "the ideal arrangement." At the time it might have been O.K., but deep in me I wanted you to be mine alone, to see shows with me, walk with me, laugh and play together. Those things all came so true.

You ought to hear me lead the place in the "Sweetheart of Sigma Chi." Every night I take a shower and sing that. Most fellows, fraternity or not, know it. You'll know someday, if you don't now, just how much I really love you.

What's Walt doing now? Just wondered where he ended up. What are the other fellows doing? Have you heard from Dale since you wrote him?

Forever yours, sweets,
Beat

Monday evening, Sept. 14

My darling—

Some Negro fellows have come to the school. Nothing unusual to you or me, but it's causing a Civil War on the Island. All the Southern boys are arguing with us. They mostly really hate the Negroes. It's an unchangeable idea. They are talking now of going to the O.D.'s office and demanding that the Negroes go or they will dis-enroll. When three Negroes were put at a table in the galley, four Southern fellows got up and walked away. Let's hope it works out.

Now that you're away from Fargo, I hope you won't be too lonesome. Remember how lots of us fellows have to live. We're away from home for some time, and, besides that, we don't see regular people very often. Automobiles, buildings, stoplights, people rushing around, and all the other things seem so far away while on the Island. One of my favorite likes is to go into a cafeteria and order just the things I want to eat. That may sound foolish, but here we eat what is given us. The variety is not too great. One finds that out after being here a few weeks.

I can hardly wait to have some of your coffee in that new breakfast nook your father and your brother Yupps built.

Xmas isn't so far away now, and you and I will be together again. I just want you with me every place I go so I can reach out and find your hand and hold it. You make me dream such nice, sensible dreams. And you're doing so well in keeping up my morale by writing.

Hi to all the folks in Sleepy Hollow. I love you, *mein schatz*!

Yours forever,
Beat

Right now the barracks are quiet. There is a program on the radio devoted entirely to the Merchant Marine. We're finally getting a hand from the people of the country. They realize just how much this service counts now. Even a letter from Roosevelt has been read, quite a flattering one, too, all about bravery, etc. Hope I make the grade and can rate the praise they're now giving us.

IMPORTANT: Our superintendent has just been introduced. He's now speaking. His speech is about the importance of the radiomen—how dependable the men must be, the distances to be covered, the material to be carried. We're really up for a big and important job. He just said we're specialists and officers of the highest ranking. Boy, it's interesting!

Thursday evening

My dearest Elinor,

So now you're the popular new teacher again. You'll be even more popular before you leave, darling. Everybody likes a pretty girl like you. You're beautiful and full of pep. No wonder the red-headed boy and twenty-four others joined the German class. I would've, too.

Darling, I'm sorry I didn't get a letter to you for your first day there, but I wasn't quite certain you'd be there and I wasn't sure of where to send it. So Dale beat me to the punch, darn it! What's he doing lately?

Our big boat ran aground today in the fog. What a bunch of Navy men will do. They brought it off at high tide so they will get the fellows to shore tomorrow all right. We have had three big blackouts here in Boston with sirens and all-clear signals and all. Quite a thrill at first, but routine now.

Yours, darling,
Beat

Saturday, September 19

Dearest Elinor,

We've had a few blackouts lately. They seem to come about 10:15 at night, just as we are getting to sleep. The sirens wail from all the islands near us and here. They sound off for about fifteen minutes. Then comes a period of quiet and then a couple of long blasts on a steam whistle about 100 yards away. After that, we go to sleep again.

   The last few days we've had fog that one could cut with a knife. In the morning at 4:45, when we go to work, it's eerie. Usually the fog rises about two or three in the afternoon. Honestly, we never have seen a real fog in North Dakota. The air here is as salty as heck. The bell buoys ring out, and it is just like the sea pictures we've seen in movies.

   Save a little room in your dreams for me.

                                              Beat

Monday, September 21

My darling,

I think I'll quit sending you so many letters if it's going to make the other teachers jealous. Try to keep them friendly, hon. Friends will count for a lot out there—women, I mean.

   Tell me more about that Casanova guy. If he doesn't weigh over 110 pounds and isn't over 5 feet tall, I'll send my gang after him. I'm glad you're not going out with anyone. You really are being so good and true to me, darling, and I love you for it.

So Phil has written you a very pretty proposal. Maybe someday I will think up a pretty one. Did I ever propose to you? The first time it was brought up, I remember you brought it up and we told the gang that we were going to be married. Remember? We just were kidding about it then. Look at us now.

I really would like to propose to you by letter some time, but, in our case, a proposal would probably be called "excess baggage."

So, I'm asking you, my darling, to be mine for the little time we have to wait. I promise to work hard for our future happiness and be ever so faithful. I'll never let you get away.

If only the thousands of miles could be melted down to about 40 and I had a car and a ration card, a clean uniform and a liberty card! Tonite we can't possibly get together except in our dreams. That's a cinch, gal!

All my love, sweets,
Beat

≫　≪

So you're making some clothes. And that fur coat—I'm taking out a long-term contract on the job of being the number one and only moth to cuddle in it. The coat sounds so darn soft and pretty. Hope you get it.

≫　≪

High Fashion

September 1942

ELINOR GLANCED AROUND HER small room. Another Wednesday evening. She set the letters she'd picked up at the post office after school on the pile of Correspondence-to-Be-Answered. The stack leaned precariously again. Her eyes took in her antique dresser, her dressing table, and the wooden chair in the corner with her clothing for tomorrow's school day already carefully laid out. On the corner bookshelf she noted the pile of essays that had to be read soon.

But not tonight. She wasn't in the mood.

Walt's letter lay open on her bed. An invitation to Minneapolis for an adventure. He promised that they'd have separate rooms. While he did his work, she could shop, and they'd go to the orchestra concert on Saturday night. But how would it look . . .

She picked up her Sears catalog. Even in wartime a girl had to dress right. She paged through the current fashions again.

In the front section, girls posed in simple dresses of rayon or viscose, man-made fabrics. There wasn't much available in wool; servicemen needed wool to keep warm on the battlefield. She got cold, too, in this frozen Norwegian town. But she could sew with wool from dresses she no longer wore or the out-dated clothes that Aunt Dorothy sent the family. Not everyone had an aunt who was a banker's wife.

Clothes these days were styled from leftovers. Factories were turning out parachutes instead of fashionable fabrics. Mending and remaking clothes . . . that was patriotic. And some of the latest styles were made from several fabrics, mix and match, to encourage using up fabrics on the home front.

The latest styles showed suit dresses with a jacket-like top and slim skirt. Or softly pleated skirts, some slightly A-line. Skirts gored in the front. There wasn't as much fabric in the styles these days. But the new styles made it easier to convert older dresses with all their pleats and balloon sleeves into the slimmer new fashions.

Fashions in plain colors—black, wine, cadet blue, soldier blue or forest green. Designers used serious colors during wartime. At least the girls in the States could use trims, buttons, and gathers or soft pleats—all prohibited in England.

When she found a design she liked, Elinor noted the page and wrote it in the front cover of the thick catalog. She planned to stitch copies with her mother during Christmas break.

There it was, the page she had turned down. The dyed coney coat. "Full draped tuxedo, dressy looking, converts to closed collarless style. Gay, small-waisted flaring silhouette does wonders for the figure." Who would ever guess it was fashioned from rabbit, dyed to look like mink? Anyone would shine like a movie star in something like that. And a hat, of course.

Just $82.50. $82.50! What was she thinking? What teacher had that much money lying around? She surely didn't. Maybe she could buy it on time, paying some of her salary each month to the Fur Coat Fund.

She paged further into the catalog and looked at the shoes. She couldn't imagine wearing those "sturdy welt oxford" ones with the big soles and nearly flat heels. She preferred pumps. Suede or patent leather, the toeless model. Pretty, but $3.98! If a girl added a hat, an outfit could cost nearly $20.00!

Elinor flipped the pages quickly when she came to the beginning of the undergarment section. She wondered what kind of girl would pose for those shots. In their underwear! Turning the pages more slowly, she studied their faces. Such pathetic lives. What could've brought them to this? And what must their parents think? Posing half-nude for a photographer in some studio. In New York, she supposed. Life was different on the coasts. Here in Dead Stick Landing, her HQ, a girl wouldn't think of it. Couldn't think of it. Everyone would talk.

She exited the lingerie. On to hats. A girl could dream. Of style, of a coney coat, jewelry of 24 karat gold, and diamonds.

Elinor leaned back in her bed. She closed her eyes and imagined that she was on stage. Like Peggy Lee. She began to hum "There Are Such Things."

Singing, sure. Peggy Lee was good. Anyone could sing. But Elinor could play piano, too. You never heard about Peggy Lee on the piano. A gal who could sing and play piano had a chance to live the life of a star and have all the coney coats she wanted. Maybe even a real mink.

Perhaps one day she'd be discovered. First she'd have to escape Pelican Rapids somehow. She'd have to nudge The Fates a bit.

My Darling Bunny

September 1942

Thursday, September 24, 1942

My darling,

How are ya? Bunny. Isn't "Bunny" the nickname you liked so well, hon? In the last couple of days, I just decided that I would get up the nerve to timidly enter "Bunny" into one of these letters. How do you like it? As for me, I think it's pretty and very appropriate. You're cuddly, soft, and very pretty.

Last nite I had liberty! And it wasn't a weekend. We had a two-hour basketball game, and then steaks, and we all went to The Cave for a few drinks. The Cave is the best place in Boston. $2.00 minimum and pretty classy. After spending my two bucks, I went to the Buddies' Club to write you and guess what. They had a stage show and Horace Heidt there and it was packed. Bill Robinson, the Negro dancer, was there and he's good!

While at the Buddies' Club, there came a real blackout. Two unidentified planes were heard fifty miles out. The town was really scared, but the planes turned out to be U. S. Army planes off course. Really these cities have perfect blackouts—not a particle of light—just like camping out in the woods in Minnesota, pitch black and quiet.

That bus ride between Pelican and Fargo must be kinda rough and tiresome. Maybe you should spend more time with the natives in Sleepy Hollow.

So you have to get up at 7:30. We get up at 6:00, but we are asleep at 10:15 or so. Get a lot of sleep, darling. If you lose any, you can make it up when we're married. You look so darn cute getting up in the morning, just so sleepy looking.

Hon, that Minneapolis meeting is something that sounds perfect to me. Let's stay a couple of days—just the two of us together with nothing to do but be happy. We'll see each other all the time possible.

I'm kinda afraid to write things in these letters. Remember our experience with Irene snooping!

Wish we were in Chicago again, you in those pink pajamas.

Always yours,
Beat

September 25, Friday

Dearest Elinor,

I've been pounding my brains out for three straight hours—really nerve wracking, this stuff. Really, a person can say what they want, but some things ARE hard to learn. This week we've covered a tremendous amount of material. We have to know coefficients of resistivity in positive, negative, and zero for 15 metals. Then for those fifteen metals we have to know all the resistance in ohms per 1000 feet. With those we can find temperature changes, resistance changes, etc. according to length, temperature and ohms. What a complicatedness it is when they word a problem as they do! Hope I pass this.

Just three months from today is Christmas and on Christmas Eve we'll just sit at home and talk and you'll play the piano. Then Mickey and Yupps and Irene and the folks and you and I will all have coffee. That's the perfect evening to me.

Be mine. I'm yours.
Beat

⇥   ⇤

Remember Chicago? That's the test. You said to see if I loved you in the morning. You should have known better, sweets. Whenever I see you, you look like the person I love and want to love me.

Monday, September 28

Dearest Elinor,

Only twenty of us passed that "power" test. I just made it. Then tonite I practiced code an hour and started my work on batteries. This is very important, too, as you could guess, as all our radio power comes from batteries while at sea.

Tonite I have a fire watch from ten to twelve in barracks two. Then I'll roll in until six in the morning. Our job is to check the barracks every half hour for fires, etc. The rest of the time we sit in the "head." That's what sea-going men call the crew's washroom. So if I say that when I get home, you'll know why. There are lots of terms that I use naturally now.

I like when you write that you love me. It makes this fight to stay on top and in school so much easier. And what a fight it is. The Navy served notice today that they aren't fooling with us. They're going to kick the guys out right and left.

How's the big financial deal going? I mean the fur coat. That fur coat will be something to see you in when we're in Minneapolis. You'll come off the train, into my arms, and, darling, I can hardly wait.

Yours,
Beat

Thursday, October 1

My darling Bunny,

I've got the ambition and really want to get ahead. You're the reason that I work so hard. This week we've been so damn busy. Batteries are a big subject to cover in one week. I have been in study hall every night. We read books on local action, sulphation, low capacity, voltage, loss of sulphation and a million subjects like those. We learn the causes and ways to rid cells of sulphation, the chemistry of a battery, charging and discharging. We'll always use this week's work. In fact, it's about the only work we have on a ship, besides sending and receiving. Tonite I'll go down to the battery lab for an extra class.

The barracks is a racket, everybody shouting and yelling, a few pillow fights. You wouldn't believe it, but it's one of the few minutes we've been able to relax all day. They keep us moving. Taps is coming soon, darling, so I've got to close for now.

Love,
Beat

ARMY AND NAVY RECREATION CENTERS
Boston, Massachusetts
SPONSORED BY BOSTON SOLDIERS AND SAILORS
COMMITTEE

Sunday morning

My Bunny,

I'm back in my element again. The place is quite crowded, but it isn't at all noisy. My appetite has been appeased—a steak, no less—and I feel great.

Just before coming in here, I was standing in front of a cemetery at Old South Church. Built in 1729! Paul Revere, Samuel Adams, John Hancock, and Benjamin Franklin are buried there. Doesn't that make a person think? Those "guys" gave all they had to start a great country. And there was a tombstone of someone buried in 1625! Must have been a Pilgrim. History is interesting and this city has it. Oh I should keep these thoughts to myself. They maybe sound like kid hero stuff. Anyway, they did their part. I'll do mine.

Forever,
Beat

For the last couple of days, I've been lonesome as all heck for you. I even got the funny idea of wanting to get married at Christmas. Maybe you won't realize just how much I want that. At the same time or a few hours later, I tell myself to be fair to you and me. When I've made a trip and have a good job and am pretty well oriented it will be such a nicer wedding. How about a June wedding, Bunny? You're everything that's worth working for, and I love you so.

Monday, Oct. 5

A huge convoy left today and the perfect ship was in it—a huge tanker with a superstructure with a big roomy radio shack. I watched that ship all the way out and wished I were on it— through this school, married to you, and doing something important.

A neighbor of mine was sent to the Marine Hospital in Boston with—maybe you'll guess it—a good case of gonorrhea. He's a New Yorker that's been keeping up with the sailors' reputation. In fact, hon, I've had a lot of arguments with him and predicted this for him. I'm not in any danger of catching it, as it's not "catchy" and I haven't even talked to him for quite a few days.

Tuesday, October 6

Did you notice in Hank Hurley's column in the *Fargo Forum* those service pictures? They brought back a lot of memories. All those fellows are old friends and now they're on New Caledonia. What a war!

So you are alive. I was wondering, hon. Got your letter today, and it made me feel some better. I waited all week for that letter you promised to write last weekend. Then I felt inside me that something had happened to change your plans. And, believe it or not, but I knew there was an "old friend" in it somewhere. Bet it was good to see Clarence again and I don't blame you for going in to Fargo to see him. You see all the "old friends" and the folks now, 'cuz when Beat comes home, you're going to have one date from the time I arrive until I leave. O.K.?

Thursday evening

Dearest Elinor,

Last nite a bunch of us had an *Esquire* marriage chart to pick out or rank our girlfriends. When I got through counting up, you were "one in a million." And I ranked the thing honestly, too. Honest. I did.

When I'm in The Cave with the fellows, I often think to myself how I'd like to be walking through the door with you. To see all the fellows stare. They think I'm a quiet guy who doesn't like girls. Someday soon you and I will be in Boston and New York and we'll do all the things we've ever wanted to do together. Remember Chicago? Well, we'll do it a lot better than that, only I don't believe that I could be any happier than I was there.

For quite a few days I worked to get my locker looking neat. Most of the fellows just let it go. Today comes locker inspection. What a farce! The old braid takes one glance into the lockers and walks on by with a pompous grunt. So, the guys razz me and call me the Industrious Farmer (jerk). Guess I'm the only fellow that does his own washing. Seems I feel better when I see nice white wash on the line all dry. Then I have accomplished something and it helps to save a couple bucks a month, too. Those bucks might buy a few Toms at Christmas. That's what keeps me broke—sending home over half my pay. Got to wait until payday to buy some stationery, even.

Beat

Unanswered Mail

October 1942

ELINOR SAT AT HER desk, fiddling with her hair. She twirled a few strands around her index finger, then sighed. "Stuck in Pelican again," she breathed. She stared at the pile of essays she'd promised to have back in the hands of her students on Monday. There were too many papers to read, the style of writing simply too basic. There was not a natural writer in the group.

She stretched.

She wrinkled her nose at the stale bacon smell which had hung in the air since the family's breakfast. She could never abide a heavy start to the day. She just grabbed a cup of coffee most mornings, and maybe a bite of toast, as she dashed out the door for school.

"I should have gone home this weekend," she thought. "But there's nothing to do there these days. Nobody around. Just Irene, and she just shadows me."

She put the papers in a new order, leaving the toughest reads for the end.

She read an essay, marked it with her red pencil, and set it aside. She stood again and paced the length of her limited space a few times. Ten steps. Stop. Ten steps back. Then a second essay. Red pencil. Pace.

"If I can get those essays half done by suppertime," she thought, "I'll get to that game." Against Barnesville, she remembered. Leonard had said he'd be there, and she needed some companionship. Maybe he could tell her how he handled all those themes from his Shakespeare class. She went back to work.

After a few more essays, Elinor thought, "Fresh air might just do the trick." She felt a little light-headed from all the reading.

She removed the bobby pins that she had inserted in her hair and found her brush. She ran the boar bristles through her fine dark hair a few times. Then, slipping on her black sweater, she left her bedroom, walked out the front door and into the world.

It was unusual for her to be in Pelican on the weekend. She was paying room and board by the day, and this weekend would add two more days to the month.

But she needed to get her schoolwork caught up. She planned to stroll the couple of blocks to the post office to check her box. She suspected that most of the letters mailed to her sat on the dining room table in Fargo, in wait for her next trip home.

Elinor savored the autumn air. Smoke from the backyard incinerators around Pelican reminded her of autumns past, autumns when she was in high school or walking on campus at college. She kicked at the leaves on the sidewalk. She loved the sweet decay of summer before a person had to face winter. She loved the sharp bite of a mum's fragrance in a homecoming corsage on her shoulder.

People worked in their gardens, harvesting or closing them for the winter, as she sauntered past on the narrow sidewalks. Elinor waved.

In no time, she neared the compact downtown. She smiled and nodded as she greeted people on the street. A few of the high school students dashed about, meeting up with friends to gossip over a Coca-Cola at the Pelican Café. Cars, mostly Fords, were parked diagonally at the curbs on both sides of Broadway. Black vehicles lumbered up or down the main drag looking for a place to settle. Saturday was the biggest shopping day of the week, and this weekend held homecoming besides. The town felt full, energetic and busy. It was just what the doctor had ordered—some fresh air and movement to get her going again.

She stretched her legs as she picked up the pace in the gaggle of shoppers. She held her hand, visor-like, to her forehead and looked up.

The sun glittered in a nearly too-blue sky. Feeling the warmth of the day on her face, she realized that she missed weather when she was cooped up in that stale school building day after day.

She arrived at the town post office, located her box, and put her key into the lock. She pulled the door open. Reaching in to pick up her mail, she wondered which of the men she corresponded with had written. She loved the attention of her "old friends," but the task of writing back pressured her.

An English teacher couldn't write a sloppily constructed letter. Each took time to compose. Emily Post had published, in 1922, a book of manners. And the new book with a war supplement was due to be on the bookshelves soon. Elinor knew most of the letter writing rules by heart.

First, a correspondent had to consider the choice of appropriate stationery. Certain kinds of papers for different ages. Gay designs for young girls, but plain paper for mature women. Oblong envelopes for business, but square for personal use.

Dates must be written out in full. No abbreviations, though rebels thought those were in fashion. Post felt it less confusing to write out January 9, 1941 instead of 1-9-41.

The form of address announced your relationship to the addressee. What messages might a casual address or closing give a fellow! Dear Beat or Love, Elinor? She had to be careful.

After reading so many badly written essays, Elinor felt she couldn't put quality sentences to paper at all. And she rued the day she had chosen English as her major. Now she had taken on the responsibility of teaching these big children how to write without, as Post said, "prolixity, pedantry, or affectation."

Then one must consider the message. Well-bred people shouldn't write badly. "Pretentiousness is an infallible sign of insincerity and lack of taste." For simplicity of expression, Post suggested as a model— the Bible! Elinor closed her eyes and shook her head. The Bible and "simplicity" in the same sentence! Had the doyen of manners ever read the Old Testament?

So, when Elinor found a letter from Phil or Johnny or Bob or

Darrow in her mailbox, she added it to the pile of letters that needed an answer. The stack grew higher as the school semester progressed. And the next letters from her beaux begged her for mail. The guys asked why she wasn't writing. She knew she should. Making the boys happy while in the war zones, well, it was her duty! "Have you heard there's a war on!" she would mutter before facing the job at hand.

She stood at the post office and sorted through the stack—a letter from her father, a short note from Mickey, and three envelopes from Beat. She tucked her mail into her purse and walked toward Broadway for a quick lunch at the Pelican Café.

The place hummed just at noon. The homecoming display in the window paraded the school colors, everything edged in black and orange. Go Vikings! Three farmers sprawled in one corner, in overalls and work boots, coffee cups in front of them on the table, getting caught up on the news. A few women had set their bags down and flopped into tables in the small space. There were high school girls giggling in the furthest booth from the door. The jukebox spread "Jingle, Jangle, Jingle" through the place, and the noise of conversation drew Elinor in.

She checked to see whether any other teachers were at the restaurant for lunch. Finding no one, she slid into a booth. A waitress arrived with a glass of water. Elinor ordered a tuna sandwich and a cup of coffee. The waitress spun off to place the order at the back window, and Elinor relaxed into the wooden seat. She needed some time in the real world, and this part of the world would have to suffice.

She retrieved the letters from her purse. The delicate envelope from Mickey would be dessert. Elinor opened the letter from her father, then the ones from Beat. She scanned the news from Gallups. She sighed. Beat wrote so often. She managed a letter or two to him each month, but he always wanted more.

Her sandwich and coffee arrived just as she opened the flap on Mickey's letter.

The light inside the restaurant dimmed a bit as a cloud covered the sun. Elinor squinted at the tablet stationery. She gulped her coffee and reread the two handwritten pages. Then she stuffed them into the envelope and back in her purse. She looked around the restaurant to see if anyone had been watching her, then took a deep breath to collect herself.

"Darn," she thought. "What next? I've got to get home next weekend to find out what's going on." Her sandwich sat, mostly uneaten, on its plate as Elinor exited the restaurant. She walked intently through the village.

She heard them first, their wild, lonely honks filling the sky. As she looked up, as a skein of geese veered across the treetops. "Not a vee yet," Elinor thought. It would be a while before those geese would be migrating. Time. That's what she needed.

She plodded up to her room and threw her purse on her bed. "Irene!" she muttered. "What has she gotten into now? This'll be big news in any congregation that gets wind of it."

She stared at the essays strewn around from the morning's work. "Oh, darn it!"

As Elinor plopped onto her bed, her vision began to sparkle. It wouldn't be long before the geometric designs would arrive. She found her purse beside her, removed a few Anacin tablets from their tin, and fumbled her way to the bathroom for a drink of water. She moaned as she swallowed her pills. Another migraine.

Remember Me in
Your Dreams

October 1942

Sunday afternoon

Hi, ya, sweets,

How come you don't like to write me once in a
while? All week, hon, and no letter. If you're
kinda "fed up" with all this, you probably
don't think too much about me, or something
like that, tell me, Elinor. I can take it, and
I would like to know it now. You know me well
enough to know that I like to keep things clear
and above-board, so there won't be any little
"white lies" or anything. What I'm trying to do
is to let you know, hon, that I don't want any
of that kidding that you might have given some
of the other guys. You always have been honest
with me, and I've been honest with you.

Hope you don't mind my getting honest or just
a little downhearted. One thing I realize is
that you don't have to depend on a "gob" like
myself to be happy. You've always had all the

men you wanted. You're the first gal I ever met that I wanted to marry, to make happy. When we were together, we were both happy. That's what I'll always want—us together.

This isn't a letter to find fault or anything, just maybe a suggestion to help you over a so-called "difficult situation." How's about it? I want you to know what I'm thinking. So to a quiet and relaxing weekend—

Yours forever,
Beat

ARMY AND NAVY RECREATION CENTERS
Boston, Massachusetts
SPONSORED BY
BOSTON SOLDIERS AND SAILORS COMMITTEE

Sunday morn.

My darling,

I caught the 8:30 boat in for a real ride on a big sea. A couple of fellows got seasick. When I lick my lips, even now, I can taste that good ol' salt. We all knew the *Queen Mary* was in, so I wanted to see it while in drydock. It's monstrous when sitting in the water. I saw it in New York a couple of years ago, and when it is up keel and all it's something you can't imagine. The battleship *Massachusetts* came in last night by surprise and it looked tiny alongside the *Queen*. And that wagon is no baby!

The town is full of limeys. They're a bunch of swell fellows when they're not drunk. One of them is playing the piano about ten feet from me now—all lonesome home songs, and the English boys are singing or just standing around with a stare on their faces. Dreaming of home, I know.

For a couple of minutes now I've been sitting here listening to a soldier play "Moonlight Cocktail." He's good and that music is quite a memory restorer. Now it's "Sleepy Lagoon." And now "Sunrise Serenade."

Remember me in your dreams,
Beat

Wednesday

My darling,

And I mean that more than I did! This morning
your letter came, and I feel good all over. First
we'll go into statistics. You mentioned that
I was letting down in my writing. My, my—only
twenty letters in the last month. In fact, 23.
And you squawk! Five in the same time. You see,
hon, I like to write to you, but as you said, it
leaves a lot of doubts in a guy's mind when mail
call after mail call passes and no letters. I
must admit that there were a lot of excuses for
you not writing but they weren't the ones I had
figured out. We've always told each other that we
wouldn't lead the other one on if something came
up—as it could very easily for you. So for about
ten days, no letter. What was I to figure except
maybe you've found something new and different.
    You have your doubts about me—that feminine
intuition again. Please, darling, trust me.
There's not a reason in the world to do otherwise.
No matter how much you get me mad at times,
I'll never let my temper and doubts lead me
to anything that wouldn't be right. "Right"
includes not drinking heavily, as well as girls.
This school is too tough to have a foggy mind.
Remember this and be mine forever.
    If you happen to see Walt say hello for me.
He's a nice fellow as far as I know. You can
make the fellow happy, but be mine, hmmm?

Yours, always,
Beat

Thursday

My sweet,

Tonite we'll have to study, and I mean study—but hard. This week and the next three or four get us past the "hump" of this course. Then we start applying all the things we've learned. That's what we're all awaiting—to do some actual experimenting, watching ammeters, voltmeters, oscillographs, and other machines proves that the problems and theories we've been working with were, after all, really right.

Our class is getting smaller right along. They say we have the best class in code that ever came here! In theory we're known as the worst teacher-baiting class there is. Two teachers won't even try to teach us any more. We have a few fellows that know electricity, and they constantly ball up the chiefs. These Brooklynites continually get in the laughs and barbing remarks and make teaching a tough job. One of the chiefs quit because a bunch of them always laughed at his schematic drawings on the board. They would sit and smile at him after he'd put a masterpiece on the board. He even threatened them, but they just came back with, "How can we help how we look? We were born this way."

Another thing that gets the chiefs sore is the way the fellows answer at muster. Of course, they can't help what kind of a voice they were born with, but Mother Nature surely pulled a lot of dirty tricks on this class if that is true. You probably have your troubles, too, in some of your classes, but they couldn't possibly be as bad as these. All of them are quick-witted and can make up a lie or a wisecrack in a millionth of a second.

Right now I'm waiting for the chow call bugle to go eat some more of this Navy food. Since they took over, we've had beans about six or seven times a week. The food has been getting a little worse since we first got here, but that's because of the additional six or seven hundred students.

Our Navy pilot ran the boat into the dock today but luckily there wasn't a lot of damage—only hurt feelings as all the guys aboard wised off about the efficient Navy personnel.

There goes the mob. The bugle just blew.

Love,
Beat

ARMY AND NAVY RECREATION CENTERS
Boston, Massachusetts
SPONSORED BY
BOSTON SOLDIERS AND SAILORS COMMITTEE

Sunday morning

My darling,

Last night I missed you so much. "I'm Dreaming of a White Christmas" seems to be quite popular now, and every time it's played, I dream of you and me at Christmas. That leads to other thoughts, just thinking of you so far away in a town full of wolves on a Saturday night.

Maybe a few things that happened last night would interest you, hon. We had a big gabfest. Then I showered and was sleeping. The guys woke me up. One of them, a ranchman from Texas, wanted to know how to spell "Jesus." He was writing a letter. I kidded him and he smiled in his quiet way and admitted, "I'm not up on such stuff, I guess." There was no reason to laugh as he is a very serious and clean-cut guy—just big and kinda backward on everything except ranching and electricity.

We tossed the firewatch in the shower because he woke us up at eleven. He called the O.D. These Saturday nights on the Island aren't as restful as they used to be.

A sailor next to me just asked how to spell "shipped." We got to talking and he told me his last trip he'd shipped to Russia. Quite "fighting water" he says, alive all the time. One thing for certain I'll be hard to scare after all the things they teach and show us at the Island. Damon Runyon says we have the toughest branch of service of all, and a few other newspaper columns have given us some good "hero stuff," too. Naturally, we don't mind.

Have you read this far? If you've been waiting for a meal at the Pelican Café, it probably wasn't such a bad way to pass time.

All my love, forever, darling,
Beat

Mayo Clinic

Late October 1942

"GEORG, WE OUGHT TO try something." Trudie bustled about gathering a small midnight snack. The two of them had walked downtown to see a movie, a rare treat for such a busy couple. "I think these migraines have gotten worse for Bunny. Since her fall."

Georg relaxed in the new breakfast nook. He sipped the hot coffee Trudie had just poured for him. "Well, we could try Mayo. They have a good reputation." He stirred his coffee to cool it a bit.

"They couldn't help Irene though, Georg." Trudie set the leftover chicken neck, her husband's favorite piece, on a plate in front of him. She sighed and plopped down on the bench across from his.

Georg held the neck to his mouth and began nibbling around its edges, taking small bites to stretch out the culinary experience.

"Mayo can't cure nervous conditions, Georg," Trudie continued. "I guess no one can. So we deal with Irene one day at a time. But Bunny might have a chance at some cure. The girls and I get these headaches, we all do, but no one suffers as badly as Elinor."

"*Tay-Air-Oo,*" he began. He patted her hand. "I think we should give it a try."

"Will you look at your calendar?"

A few weeks later, Elinor traveled with her parents to the clinic in Rochester. The doctors there ran her through different tests. They examined her head and approved the patching that the Fargo physicians had done. "Skull bones are mended nicely," they told her. She didn't want to be reminded about the weeks she had spent in the hospital in a darkened room after falling on the icy steps at college. Or that she had to change her major from music to English because she had missed so much school.

They checked her intelligence, and she passed those tests easily. Hearing. Nothing missing in that realm. Blood tests. No problems noted.

Eyes. "Perhaps some glasses would help with the focus," they suggested. "Poor vision can cause headaches. Migraine is a multi-factorial disease," they added. "The continuing headaches could be caused by stress or by food allergies. Or even something wrong in the female organs."

Elinor certainly was cursed with migraines accompanied by painful periods. She could predict some of her headaches by her menstrual cycle. But others arrived like unwanted visitors, sneaking up on her, barging in.

She would crave anything chocolate. Whether she gave in and ate some chocolate or not, she ended up with sudden a smack in the head. The aura of beautiful shapes and colors would've been interesting to view—like modern art—but she felt so nauseated that she couldn't abide the movements of the purple, pink, hot yellow zigzags behind her eyes. Her brain throbbed. It felt like it was coming apart at the seams, at the fractures pasted back together after her icy fall. For two or three days she vomited and hid in the dark. On the last day of each headache she would collapse in bed, exhausted.

Migraines became her private war, a monthly half dozen days—a disaster for her classroom and for her love life. Elinor found it useless to make plans. Her life was unpredictable.

The doctors warned her. When migraines brought a woman to her bed for so many days just at that time of the month, pelvic inflammatory disease could be the cause. Endometriosis, they named it. She would most probably not be able to bear children.

Elinor could only nod. She thought of Irene's problem. This news actually freed her to have more fun. She didn't want children at any rate. One couldn't argue with fate.

On the ride home, her parents rode quietly in the front seat, circumspect. They waited for Elinor to share the diagnosis. Trudie sat upright and scouted for dangers on the road. Georg leaned back in the driver's seat, his foot on the gas. Once in a while he hummed a hymn. Trudie nudged him then and nodded toward the back seat.

The car rolled silently along the roads back to Fargo.

After nearly a hundred miles, Elinor cleared her throat. Then she spoke up. "I need new glasses. I guess that's it."

She went back to Pelican with her new glasses. "I just hate to wear them," she confided to her new friend, Ginny, one evening in the Uptown Café. "They make a girl look old. Old maid-ish, I guess. And they don't help me one bit. Really."

Before long she put the glasses into their case and tucked them into a drawer in her dresser. Could anyone imagine Peggy Lee in lenses?

Blue

November 1942

Hope your eyes don't bother you too much, darlin'. In our class something like ten or fifteen of the fellows have bought glasses in the last couple of weeks. Eyestrain had bothered them all, and the doc told them to get glasses. You'll appreciate them a lot. I know.

⁂

Thursday evening 5:00
October 29

My darling Bunny,

Just about an hour ago, I was shocked. On the front page of this paper was an article about the death of Bernard Starhenberg. We used to do a lot of things together, and we both took the same courses. I remember him so well, and the day he left with the rest of the gang. I'm going to put his picture up on my locker door, just to have something to really work for, to get even for him. It will make my ever so small problems seem easy to forget. We really don't realize just what this war is until we get close to it, and I know I'm about four months away. By that time there will be other fellows to remember. Really we're all awaiting the day.

Seems to be just like a football game. You train for so long, but you don't realize what's going to happen until you get in it. Then things come naturally and easily. In a football game it was always easy to play all out. This should be even easier to fight for. We only hope that by that time, we have an even break and can do some fighting. Return a few of those slugs in the back.

The fellow that they shipped out to the Marine Hospital for a disease is back. He hadn't had it after all. The doc said it was only overstrain! Maybe he should have some of that "breakfast of champions." The hospital is full of seamen from the Merchant Marine with all kinds of troubles. He has some interesting stories to tell.

You'll be in Minneapolis this weekend. Really it would be—well, I wish that I could be there. You'll have lots of fun, I know. Tell me all about it, hmmm? As for me, I've got $1.85 so it will be another weekend on the Island probably. And another weekend closer to seeing you again. Less than two months! That isn't very long, is it?

Here it is November already. Next it will be the first of December and then home to you. I'm going to love that. But what are you going to do with coffee rationing setting in?

My love forever, honey,
Beat

Tues. eve, Nov. 3

Dearest,

I'm broke so I'll mail this tomorrow or with Thursday's letter. We get paid then. The next few checks will have to go home so I won't spend it! Our vacation ought to be some fun. The fellows say so, too. "For all the fun I'm missing," they say. But really, I'm having loads of fun in my own way.

Today we had an interesting lecture on, of all things, mines, torpedoes, and bombs. An old bo'sun's mate gave us a lot of tips. Many of the fellows have taken out a book that's standard reading here. The name, *How to Abandon Ship*. Lots of fellows lose their lives because they don't know little things and because they get panicky. We learn how fast a ship will sink according to where it's hit. What side to lower away from. How far to get away so the suction won't pull the lifeboat under. How to ration food and water and navigate. A million things. Probably it's the most interesting subject we have!

Guess the themes and things kept you pretty busy last week, hmmm? And for all I know, you probably were in Minneapolis, hmmm? Maybe you didn't go. Say, I'm really wondering.

Beat

Thursday evening, November 5

My darling,

Do you want a really "blue" letter to read? Continue in this one then. 'Cuz I'm feeling as low as I ever have . . .

Today has seemed like twenty years ever since morning muster. An announcement—Station Order— was read to the effect that no long leaves will be granted for any of the holidays. That's put the damper on everything that I've worked and saved and planned for. Seems the war can't get along without us, and we go to school every day but the actual holidays.

And your last Wednesday letter is a week overdue. You can't kid me, hon. This is quite a burden to you. You're among people you know, people who like you. Damn it. I should be drunk tonite. I'm in a thinking mood.

Since I've gone, you've been busy and all, thinking of me once in a while. After a while, things began to seem a lot farther away to you. As I went through the letters the other night, the length of time between them and length of the letters showed that. There it is, and I know it. Sometimes I've wondered just what it would feel like to have you write and tell me everything is off.

This course would have to take up all my interests. I'd finish and go to sea. The trips are long and keep a fellow "interested." That way I could finish out the war. You probably will doubt this very much, but I don't believe that there will ever be another woman in my life. Sounds like

True Story, doesn't it? For anything in the world I'd trade for a night and day with you now.

With all this money to spend, I'm going to go in Saturday night and get good and drunk. But I know now that the first stick that I break will turn the evening into another one of those dreaming evenings. Then on Sunday I sit down and write you letters and hope you'll like them and that they can partly make it seem as it once was when we were together. Lately, I've kinda given up on the idea of letters taking my place, even though I enjoy writing when I have time. So, sweets, I'm in the position of a Walt, Johnny, Phil, and the rest. Just wondering, but due for a lot of things.

You'll wear my pin, won't you? And be good. Never drink if you are with men. NEVER. I promise to be the most faithful guy you ever had or have. Now that that's off my heart, darlin', I feel a lot better.

Yours forever and ever,
Beat

⤜ ⤛

Remember Peggy Lee at the Powers Coffee Shop? Last week's *Look* magazine had a full-page picture of her, telling of her popularity with Benny Goodman's Orchestra, her recordings, and hometown history. And I remember the day she sat at the Aquarium with Johnny Quam. They broke up when she went to WCCO in the Cities. Quite a surprise to see her so popular, though, isn't it?

Why Don't You Do Right?

November 1942

"Just look at what happened to Peggy Lee," Elinor exclaimed. She and Mickey sat at the dining room table, reading the women's pages of the newspaper together.

Their mother was in the kitchen pouring coffee for Georg who sat in his chair in the living room, his corner table strewn with his smoking equipment. He reached for his pipe and settled it between his lips, teeth holding the stem while he popped open the can of Revelation and tamped some tobacco into the pipe's bowl. A few flakes escaped and dropped into his lap. Several landed on the floor. He struck a wooden match and puffed the pipe to life. The lamp threw a beam on the front page of the *Fargo Forum*, Sunday edition, which Georg now picked up from his lap, dispersing a few more stray flakes of tobacco to the floor.

The girls gathered at home as often as they could on lazy Sunday afternoons. Since the death of his namesake, his oldest son, holding the family close had heartened their father. Today Irene was absent, staying with her grandmother and aunt in Illinois for a stretch.

The family hadn't changed clothes since arriving home after services. The girls both wore hand-knit sweaters which they had added to their costumes, necessary in the cool of the house.

As they hunted for the crossword puzzle, Mickey and Elinor happened upon an article about the hometown girl.

"She's from Jamestown, a North Dakota girl. I remember her hanging around in town singing at WDAY, in one bar and on to the next. Beat knew her boyfriend." Elinor buttoned her cardigan and reached for her cup of hot coffee. She wrapped her fingers around the cup and shivered just a bit as the coffee warmed her hands.

Mickey turned the newspaper article toward herself to get a good look at the black and white photo. Places in the room which didn't have lamps were shadowy and dark, like Dakota Novembers. She focused the article under the light.

"She has a smoky voice, Bunny. That's what jazz players like."

"Singing in Benny Goodman's Orchestra already," Elinor sighed. "Just 22 years old. I wonder how she did it." Elinor studied classical piano.

"Well, she probably slept with a lot of guys to get where she is. The article here says that after she left the Cities she headed to Chicago. Now the Benny Goodman Orchestra." Mickey laughed. "She moves fast, Bunny."

"New York City, Mick."

"She's on to bigger things than North Dakota now." Mickey studied Peggy Lee's outfit.

"Have you heard 'Why Don't You Do Right?' She wrote that herself," Elinor said, rising from her chair.

"It's not on the Hit Parade yet, though." Mickey stood, too. "Let's get to the crossword."

Elinor stood and walked to the kitchen to refill her coffee cup while Mickey dashed to the den.

"I hope I can find a pencil with a good eraser this time," Mickey called to her sister as she dug through her father's desk drawers. She scoured around among the papers on the desktop. She couldn't disturb those too much. Then her eyes lit upon a pencil tucked away in the phone alcove her father had built into the wall.

Elinor sat at the piano. Steam rose from her abandoned coffee cup on the dining room table. She experimented with a few chords, then led into "Why Don't You Do Right."

Want To Be Happy?

November 1942

Wed. noon, November 11

My own,

We just had a big chicken dinner. Armistice Day. We had five minutes of silence this morning, and more than one of us was praying for the fellows of the last war and friends in this one. Makes a guy feel so much better to get things out of his system, and now all of us feel that we are really doing "our part." Really, it won't be long, and we'll be in things and see what's going on, have a gold service bar and a few stars on it and a classy uniform to wear on shore. Will be a dream come true.

Want to be happy? 'Tis a long story and some doubt attached to it, but here it is. Seems they are giving R-15 a week's leave about November 21. From then on in they plan to give all the platoons—in order—a week's leave. That means we would get ours at Christmas!! Dec. 19 to Dec. 27 or so. Your letter today, this news, and my promotion and raise. I'm sitting on top of the world! We'll have only a few days together, but they'll be every minute together. And we'll cuddle in that fur coat—probably wear it out!

You have been busy, haven't you, sweets? I can't realize, I guess, just how busy a person can be. But on the "outside" there seems to be less time for writing than here. A bit of news of what you're doing and thinking is ever so important to me.

Say, guess what? This is the truth and quite cute, too. We had locker inspection today and Seabag, the old bo'sun's mate, came through and looked over the lockers. At mine all he did was cast a glance inside and then look at your pictures. He smiled and walked on. All this time I had to stand at attention, while behind him Koester and McCall smiled. But when he went on by, we all had a good laugh out of it. So tomorrow if I'm called to report mast, I'll know the reason why: he wants an introduction.

Forever and ever,
Beat

Decisions

November 1942

THE OLD BUS GROUND to a halt. The driver turned in his seat. "Fargo," he called back to the passengers.

Elinor stood. She sighed. Just two months into the school year. Maybe it was the shortening days that had darkened her mood. Homecoming excitement was over and the academic grind was in full swing. She needed this break in Fargo, a weekend vacation in her parents' home with no essays to read. Half of Saturday, most of Sunday, and then she'd be catching the Greyhound back to Pelican. Monday morning would find her sitting at her desk at Pelican High.

She grabbed her valise from the overhead rack and then pulled her purse strap back up over her shoulder as she walked to the door. She thanked the driver with a smile, then exited the bus and began the walk toward Third Street. The morning air, crystalline, clean and brisk, encouraged her to hustle. The sky, of course, drooped gray, the color of Dakota in November. Elinor quickened her steps.

She hadn't packed much—just a nightie, some clean underwear, and basic make-up. She planned a girls' weekend. Her parents were in some congregation in Billings for Sunday services. Mickey was the only one at home, so Elinor doubted that they'd have the energy or commitment to get out of bed on Sunday morning. She didn't want to dig a church outfit out of the closet in her father's study. Whatever she found in there needed to be pressed before she could be seen in it.

Elinor noted the white patches of snow on the lawns as she walked through the residential area. She could see her breath, frosty in the air. She tightened her scarf and made a mental note to remember to pack up her galoshes when she left for Pelican again. It could be an icy walk to school from her rooming house if there were significant snow on the ground—or ice—both of which were sure to happen any day now.

"Elen-O-rah!" Mickey ran toward Elinor as she shouted. Her wool scarf flew behind her and she held on to her hat as she hurried down the block.

Elinor laughed to hear her name shouted as her grandmother used to call her. She picked up the pace. They met on the sidewalk at the cheesemonger's front yard, just a few houses from home. The refrigerator in Fargo always held a brown ceramic crock of the Wisconsin Old Tavern cheese he distributed.

First, a big hug. Then the sisters strolled together toward home, Mickey carrying her older sister's valise.

"I thought that bus would never come," Mickey exclaimed, a bit breathless, fog forming around her lips. "I have so much to tell you."

Elinor teased. "How about some letters? Pelican does have a post office, you know."

"Sorry I haven't written in a while. I know I should've. But I knew I'd see you one of these weekends. And we could talk . . ."

"In person. Well," Elinor began, "I have some things to talk over with you, too." They reached the house and ran up the front steps, laughing as they squeezed side-by-side through the narrow porch door.

Elinor rubbed her hands together to warm them. "Let's brew a pot of coffee," she suggested as they entered the house. "I need to warm up." She wondered where she had stored her woolen gloves last spring. She'd need those in Pelican, too.

She threw her small satchel and her coat on the daybed in her father's study. Mickey moved ahead to the kitchen and began running water into the bottom chamber of the Coffeemaster, the old pot they'd used for so many cups of brew. With no one home to ration them, the girls added three generous scoops of Victory coffee to the basket in the pot. They waited for the percolating to begin.

They settled into the breakfast nook their father and brother had designed and built together over Yupps's summer break from seminary. The walls of the small alcove were newly lined with redwood, and a slender shelf for the growing salt and pepper shaker collection ran the three-sided perimeter of the area. Mickey sat on a built-in cushioned bench on one side of the narrow table, and Elinor sat across from her, their knees touching.

"Here's the lowdown," Mickey began. "Bob is in Guadalcanal. The headlines from there sound horrible, Bunny. The first land battle in the Pacific campaign. He's been there since mid-October."

Elinor interrupted. "I just hate to listen to the news these days. It sounds so desperate. But, as Papa always says, 'This too shall pass.'"

"I wonder when this will be over," Mickey said. Then she smiled. "But I did hear something sweet."

"Oh?"

"Yeah. Betty knows the girlfriend of one of the fellows in Bob's unit. And she said that the girlfriend told her that Bob drives around in an old Jeep with 'Mickey' painted on the side."

"Oh, Mick. He's a gem. You're lucky you've found The One. At least I think you have. Right?" Elinor smiled. Her peppy little sister was so lucky with men.

Settling on a guy was hard in wartime. What if you allowed yourself to fall in love and your man didn't return? What if he became an invalid? Or fell in love with some infirmary nurse? Or was somehow drastically changed by the war? Commitment seemed impossible. Who dared take such big chances?

"Well. Melvin and I still go out once in a while. And remember Chicago? Arthur? I loved sailing with him on Lake Michigan."

"How could you do it! We never did learn to swim. What if something had . . ."

"Oh, Elinor. You worry too much. A girl's gotta have some fun," Mickey laughed as she scratched a match across the front of a Fargo Café matchbook. The tip flickered to life. She lit one of her precious Luckies.

The pot percolated, gurgling on the kitchen counter.

"So what's on your mind, Bunny?"

Elinor had been planning this conversation in the bus on the way to Fargo. Still, she didn't know where to begin.

The warm aroma of coffee drew her attention, and she listened for any last percolating. She looked over at the pot to see no coffee bubbling up in the crystal knob of the lid. It was finished. She got out of her seat, reached into the cupboard for cups and poured. She carried the coffee to the nook, handing one cup to her sister. The other she held under her nose, drinking in the warm perfume of a really dark cup of coffee again before taking the first sip.

"Well," she began slowly as she sat back down. "Walter and I are engaged, as you know."

Mickey nodded. "I guess so."

"Off and on again, but it's handy to be engaged sometimes," Elinor continued.

"I understand that, Bunny. But you were with Darrow in Chicago." Mickey took a long drag of her Lucky Strike.

Elinor stared at the tablecloth on the small table. "Walter's invited me to go with him to Minneapolis next time he goes. I think in a week or so. He'll be there for business. We'd spend a long weekend together. I know it doesn't look good."

Mickey released the smoke slowly from her lips. "That's for sure, kiddo." She shook her head. "You're toying with old Walter again, I think."

Elinor looked up, directly at this little sister who understood how the world worked. "But I would so love to shop. Browse in the windows of Dayton's, Quinlan's even. Wouldn't you love to pop into one store or another to see what the latest fashions are? And Walter says he'll take me to hear the orchestra for some classical music." Elinor moved Mickey's ashtray to the side. She was having trouble seeing her sister with all the smoke between them. "Besides, getting out of Pelican . . . Well, I need an adventure!"

"What would you ever tell Mother and Dad?" Mickey released smoke from one corner of her mouth.

Elinor took a large gulp of her coffee. "Would they have to know? Walter could pick me up in Pelican and I'd return there. I don't think he'd mention it to them." She stood up and walked to the refrigerator. "Do you?"

"Well, he might. You know he wants to put some pressure on you to finally marry him. You've been going together—'off and on', as you say— a long, long time." Mickey flicked the ash end off her cigarette into the glass ashtray that had a permanent home in the nook. "And that reminds me. Johnny. Where does he fit into your scheme?"

Elinor returned to the table with a knife and a block of sharp cheddar.

"Well, he's a good guy and fun to be around. Walter left to go here and there to attend to the paint business and then to his father's business. I got lonely. Johnny and I saw each other every day in school in Gwinner. We had fun until he enlisted."

"What'll you do about his ring?"

Elinor sliced the cheese and popped a small chunk into her mouth. She covered her mouth and began to explain. "I'll give it back after the war. You know the rule. Emily Post—actually everyone—says we can't disappoint a guy away at war. You can't break up once they leave for the service. They can't stay clear-headed. Might be distracted in some desperate situation. And that's my real problem." Elinor passed the cheese and the knife to her sister.

"What, Elinor?" Mickey set the cheese and knife on the table. She continued to enjoy her Lucky Strike. Smokers supported the war effort with these smokes. The American Tobacco Company was no longer using bronze or chromium in its packaging. They advertised that the U.S. could build 400 light tanks with the metals they no longer used. Imagine! So no more green on the package. Luckies now came in a white pack, "the smart new uniform for fine tobacco."

"Well, there's Darrow. Beat. He writes all the time. He takes it for granted that we are going together." Elinor shook her head.

Mickey exhaled. "You saw a lot of him in Chicago in July. Looked to me like you were getting along."

"There's something about Beat. But . . . Well, seriously, I've tried writing just a couple of times a month, but he persists."

"And?" Mickey exhaled.

"His letters are interesting, Mick. But, well, now he is talking about his upcoming leave from Gallups. December. Meeting in Minneapolis for a rendezvous. I shouldn't have encouraged him last summer, but . . ."

"He was the only guy around for a while there. But, Bunny, you've got to drop him. Think of Irene." Mickey set her cigarette into the ashtray. "You know how Mother and Dad feel."

"Yeah . . . They love Walter." Elinor downed the last of her coffee. "Darrow can be so much fun. But you're right." She set down her cup. "He isn't the one for me. But I can't seem to tell him. He doesn't listen when I try."

"Elinor, you have your troubles!" Mickey teased. "Two fellows want you to go to the Cities with them. Bob, Clarence, Phil, Darrow, Johnny, Walter all want to marry you. Tom, Dick and Harry. Kid, just pick one and let the others get on with their lives."

"You know I have trouble making decisions, Mickey."

"Yeah." Mickey took a last drag of her cigarette.

"I don't think I'd make a good wife. I have these darned migraines. I'm slammed into bed, vomiting, for days. My life is unpredictable, to say the least. And no one can fix me. What guy could live with that? How could I possibly run a household?"

"Do you think it got worse after you slipped on the ice at college? Kid, you were in the hospital a long time, in the complete dark, while they tried to paste your skull back together."

"It's not just the headaches, Mickey. I don't want to run a household. I don't choose to do housework. Or take care of snotty-nosed children. Or be at any man's beck and call. I want to do something else. I just don't know what."

Elinor stood up to put the knife in the kitchen sink. She wrapped the cheese back up in its waxed paper, then walked to the short refrigerator and placed it back on the shelf.

Mick stamped out her cigarette in the glass ashtray before freeing herself from the breakfast nook. She dropped the butt into a mess of ashes, then picked up her cup of coffee. "Well, kid, you have to decide. One day you'll have to decide."

"Let's sit in the living room. It's more comfortable. I want you to help me resolve this. Seriously." Elinor poured herself a refill of coffee and waited. "I have to tell you about the Mayo report. I need to tell someone."

Crossing Off the Days

November 1942

Sunday afternoon

My sweet,

December 19 we'll be leaving this city at 2:30 P.M. We'll be in Chicago at eight the next morning. Then we'll catch the *Hiawatha* to Minneapolis. We'll be there at about 8 in the evening on Sunday. Now, maybe, I hope, please—if things could be arranged, you could catch an afternoon train to Minneapolis and I'd meet you at ten when your train pulled in. If it can't be arranged, I'll catch a Northern Pacific or Great Northern train out of Chicago and be home early Monday morning.

Dreaming tonite, hon, of a Sunday eve five weeks from tonite. We'll maybe be together in Minneapolis. Right now it seems quite far away, but the time will go as we'll both be busy. We'll be together from that time on until Christmas night at about twelve. The way things stand now, that'll be the train I'll have to catch.

Keep crossing those days off the calendar. It really isn't so long 'til Beat will be home.

Yours, hon,
Beat

※　※

TUESDAY, NOV. 16
[TYPED IN ALL CAPS, AS THE "MILL," THE RADIO OFFICERS' TYPEWRITERS, DID]

HIYA, SWEETS,

THE GENERATOR IS BROKEN DOWN, SO WE CAN'T TAKE CODE THIS PERIOD. THEY TELL US TO PRACTICE CODE SENDING OR TYPING—HERE I AM. WE HAD A PERIOD OF ROWING LAST PERIOD THAT TURNED OUT TO BE ANYTHING BUT. SEEMS THAT ALL THE BOATS ARE BEING REPAIRED.

TODAY A FELLOW FROM R-12 CAME BACK. WE LIVED IN THE SAME BARRACKS AS THEY DID AT FIRST AND LATER HE WAS MY DETAIL BOSS. HE'S ON A SHIP IN BOSTON HARBOR AND HE TOLD US ALL ABOUT IT. HIS SHIP IS BEING LOADED WITH BAUXITE. THEY CALL ALL CARGO THAT NOW. THE CARGO IS LISTED AS HEAVY MACHINERY—WHICH MEANS ANYTHING FROM TANKS TO MUNITIONS. AND HE WON'T KNOW UNTIL HE IS OUT AT SEA WHERE HE IS GOING.

HE SAYS THAT THE RADIO SHACK IS THE PLACE HE HAS TO GO EVERY TIME THAT THERE IS AN AIR RAID OR EMERGENCY—AND THAT IT IS PROBABLY THE SAFEST PLACE ON THE SHIP AS IT IS STEEL AND CONCRETE REINFORCED!!!

HE IS SECOND RANKING OFFICER ON THE SHIP AS I WILL BE SOMEDAY AND LISTENS ONLY TO THE

CAPTAIN. WHEN WE GRADUATE, WE GO TO NEW YORK AND IMMEDIATELY ASSUME THE RANK OF CHIEF RADIO OPERATOR.

THE FOOD IS GOOD AND HE SITS AT ONE HEAD OF THE TABLE OPPOSITE THE CAPTAIN. THEY HAVE A MENU AND WHITE LINEN. HIS CABIN IS LARGE AND ROOMY AND PRIVATE.

THE SHIP HAS THREE ELECTRICIANS THAT KEEP THE POWER IN GOOD SHAPE—THAT IS A MAJOR WORRY OF RADIO MEN. NO SHIP LEAVES PORT UNTIL THE RADIO MAN IS SATISFIED WITH THE CHIEF ENGINEER AND THE SUPPLY OF POWER.

AFTER EVERY TRIP A FELLOW GETS AN AUTOMATIC 21 DAY LEAVE. AND THEN SIGNS UP AT THE END OF THE LIST FOR A JOB.

WELL, HONEY, THIS STORY OF THE REAL WORK AHEAD HAS ME STEAMED UP QUITE A BIT—DARN IT, I CAN HARDLY WAIT. CAN'T YOU KINDA FEEL IT, TOO? AND IT WON'T BE SO LONG, EITHER. I KINDA LOOK FORWARD TO SEEING WHAT REAL ACTION IS—AND I KNOW THAT I'LL LIVE ALL RIGHT—IN FACT, THAT IS ONE THING THAT NONE OF US EVEN DREAM ABOUT UNTIL WE HAPPEN TO RUN INTO IT LIKE THIS—AND THEN IT IS ONLY A PASSING THOUGHT. AND WHEN I READ THIS OVER A SMILE COMES TO MY FACE—SOUNDS LIKE THAT CORNY HERO STUFF, DOESN'T IT!!!!

ABOUT 32 DAYS TO GO. LET'S HOPE AND PRAY THAT NOTHING GOES WRONG—AND THAT YOU CAN ARRANGE THE MEETING IN MINNEAPOLIS. O.K?

YOUR LOVIN' SAILOR,
BEAT

We Use the Same Equipment We'll Find Aboard Ship

*Trainees at Gallups Island learned to handle a ship's
radio, nicknamed "the Coke machine"*

Nov. 17-18

My hon,

We had a beautiful moon last night. It came in a long trail across the dark ocean, and I thought to myself that it was shining out in Pelican, too. This morning the moon had moved around and as we walked to chow it lit our way. You know, it is awfully dark when we go to chow now.

Today was the first time any of our class went "code happy." That's a malady that hits everybody sooner or later to some degree. This fellow got it to a really great degree in the middle of code class. He got up in his chair, tore off his ear phones, tore out his paper, was going to toss the typewriter through the wall when a couple of fellows jumped him. He went to sickbay for a few days' rest. That happens quite often in the older classes so the instructor wasn't at all surprised. But we were!

Only four weeks from this Sunday, and we might be hugging each other. Sounds so close now. But not half as close as I'm going to stay to you for a few days. Everything points to our vacation now. We won't have our uniforms by then, but if the 'boots' have them, I'll try to borrow one.

Every once in a while, studying pops into my mind, and I've dismissed it, but this can't go on all night. This is a tough subject—tubes. So that's what I'll be doing for the next couple of hours.

Yours forever,
Beat

Friday eve (11/20)

My honey,

The days are really floating by now. The constant thought is of going home. I want to be with you and see you and feel that you're near me. Today in class I remembered that dress—the white one with the red cape, kinda. You know the one. And the blue polka dot one. This month had better go fast.

We got paid today and I have exactly $5.63 left. Bought some war stamps, $4.00 worth of postage stamps, paid $9.00 in debts. Johnny owes me $4.00. The rest was spent at the canteen. We really need the money when payday rolls around. Everybody is broke. This weekend I'm staying on the Island to rest and save some money. We get $33.00 on the fifth of December and another $33.00 when we leave, so I'm all set for the trip home. And I've got money at home, too. Pretty poor system for a two-year accounting course graduate!

Did I ever tell you about our fresh air fiend? We all used to get quite cold here until we put him in the showers a few times. Last night he opened the windows after taps. It was a nice crisp room this morning. He called a few guys "babies" for saying it was cold. Guess what! This afternoon he was put up in sick bay with pneumonia. And all of us are awaiting his return to call him "baby." Quite interesting—a New Yorker that talks about fresh air.

The radio is playing Christmas carols, the first any of us have heard, and we all are

enjoying them and singing. One of my favorite
memories is the one of you playing the piano.
And I like to close my eyes and sit in the big
easy chair and listen to you play.

This weekend I'll have a lot of time to write
you. Lots of time to think about Christmas and
our time together.

Now what did you do? You never tell me what
ya do from Saturday 'til Sunday in that soldier-
infested town!

Be mine,
Beat

Dreams

Thanksgiving 1942

"Come, everyone," Trudie called. "Let's have a little something before you all leave again."

Elinor sighed. The weekend was almost over. It had been a quiet one, lonesome in a way. No one had mentioned Irene's absence. The Thanksgiving feast wasn't the same without everyone in their respective chairs.

Trudie set a plate of blood sausage, Limburger cheese, leftover turkey, and some bread on the dining room table, along with some oleo and the leftover homemade chokecherry jam.

Elinor roused. She grabbed a bite for herself and then sat back down on the sofa. Trudie made up a plate for her husband and one for herself and then joined Georg and Elinor in the living room. Elinor and her father sat together as they finished the *Forum*. Trudie sipped her coffee.

Between bites, Georg smoked his pipe, the aroma of Sunday afternoons. He sat in his easy chair in the living room. The corner table by his chair was littered with his coffee cup, his tin of Revelation tobacco, his copper ashtray from the Black Hills, and the lamp which lit that corner of the room.

Elinor perched on the outdated horsehair sofa next to her father's chair, close enough to exchange newspaper sections, close enough to gather in the edges of the lamp's light. She itched to sit cross-legged, but in her Sunday dress—the slim one she and her mother had just finished—it was necessary to sit properly. Ching dozed nearby.

Georg handed his daughter the front pages, news of the action in the war. But, as she read, Elinor's thoughts drifted. Being in the service. She had stopped at the recruitment centers downtown earlier in the weekend to see what she might do. Now, as she read the news, she tried to imagine what role she might play if she joined. Not nursing. What else was there? Perhaps German translation. Or secretary. What did women do exactly?

Elinor stood to set her section of the paper on her father's lap. Then she headed into her weekend space. Her mother had packed a lunch for Yupps. He had his suitcase packed for his trip back to the seminary. Mickey was out with friends. With everyone occupied, Elinor entered the family coat closet.

She, too, should start packing. She had a bus to catch. She'd be in Pelican by bedtime. But first.

She took her dainty pink jewelry box from behind the box of winter boots and sat on her daybed. She settled the jewelry box in her lap and waited for a moment. At last she snapped the lid open and looked at her collection—her most valued earthly goods. She fingered her fake pearl earrings. Then the brooches she loved. The birthstone ring her parents had given her for confirmation rested there. It still fit.

She dug out the small box holding the engagement ring that Johnny had foisted upon her. It lay safely in the velvet-lined case of its own. She slipped the band on her finger and shook her head. She hadn't been able to turn her former teaching partner down when he was heading into war. She'd give it back when the fighting was over, when Johnny returned to the classroom. Elinor removed the ring and placed it gently into the velvet pleats of its box.

And there was Walter's ring, a miniscule diamond with no case of its own. She kept it in a slit in the lining of her jewelry box. Could she wear that ring all her days? She'd return it again when Walter came home from Washington. Walter was so cheap. Why did her parents love him so much? And why on earth did she spend so much energy pleasing them and putting up with Walter? She wondered whether other girls had so much direction from the home front.

On the narrow shelf in her pink jewelry chest lay the Sigma Chi pin Darrow had given her. She'd worn it on some of the snaps she sent to him at Gallups. But it mostly stayed in this box. She wasn't exactly sure how to pin it on correctly.

She remembered reading in Emily Post's *Etiquette* that "a man's fraternity usually means everything to him, and if he gives a girl its official pin, he must think a great deal of her."

Elinor stroked the pin. She remembered her adventures with Beat— the days they spent together in Chicago. And the nights. Her parents wouldn't believe the things they'd done! Beat was an adventurer, and they always had so much fun together. Too much fun. She was once such an innocent. Now she found herself testing her parents, even questioning her life.

She returned the box to the closet and then rejoined her father in the living room.

"Could I see Hank Hurley's column, Dad?" Elinor asked. "I want to see which of the boys he's written about." Darrow had been one of the subjects lately. She had to keep up.

Her father riffled through the Sunday paper. He handed her the sports section with Hurley's column which featured the war exploits of Fargo's former high school and college sports stars. Elinor opened the section and located the column. She and her father continued reading, side-by-side.

Like most people on the home front, they read the paper to keep up with news of the war. The *Fargo Forum & Daily Tribune* arrived at their doorstep in the mornings. At suppertime, the paperboy delivered the *Fargo Forum & Daily Republican*. On Sunday the paper, a volume of reading, came once.

Elinor set her section of the paper down. "Dad, what do you make of the fifth columnists? How could anyone appear to be on the side of the U.S. but, in fact, support the enemy?"

Georg turned the page in his newspaper before setting it on the corner table. "Spies for the enemy. It's hard to believe of any American."

He reached for his pipe. "You are too young to remember the last war, Bunny. Speaking German was *verboten*. Or writing to relatives in the homeland." He hung his head a moment. "A minister in Minnesota was tarred and feathered when he prayed in German with a dying parishioner." Georg looked directly at his daughter.

"Gosh, Dad! It must've been awful."

"Mmm-hmm." He drew on his pipe, then tamped the tobacco a bit.

"Now some Japanese are forced into internment camps in California just in case they might be traitors or spies?" she asked.

"The same old thing." Her father grunted, then puffed on his pipe once more to keep it lit. He picked up the paper and went back to reading.

"Funny," Elinor mused, "how countries are lining up in this war. Like friendships, cliques, in a way."

"Mmmm," Georg commented from behind the paper, an agreement. The newspaper rustled as her father lowered it to look over the top.

"Do you remember, Bunny, when Stalin signed a pact with the Nazis?" Georg settled the newspaper on his lap. He arranged his pipe in the copper ashtray. He continued, "And then the Germans launched that surprise attack against the Soviets last June, in '41. Attacking the people aligned with them. So Stalin turned right around and joined with the Allies. Who wouldn't? With friends like that . . ."

Elinor mused, "So they changed teams."

Georg added, "But those Soviets, now on our side, can't really be trusted no matter how much they're needed. The Russians are dangerous. Mark my words." He picked up his newspaper and continued reading.

Elinor pictured the world. Nearly a year after Pearl Harbor, the sides were settling in: basically England, the US, Russia, and China against Germany, Italy, and Japan. She tried to imagine how three dwarf-sized countries could cause such havoc in the entire world.

"Why, the world has divided into fraternities!" Elinor blinked at the crazy thought.

The Axis countries could take some advice from Emily Post. When attending fraternity House Party Week, she advised, "Don't take up more than exactly your share of the closet space and drawer space."

Elinor had read that just the other day in her newest edition of *Etiquette*. She had picked up the latest, a 1942 copy, with a new wartime supplement at the back—Chapter 54. These days the Axis countries were advancing all around the world, grabbing land.

Elinor wondered whether there was an Axis Emily Post. And if she were shaking her head in dismay.

"Here, Dad, look at this," Elinor pointed to the newspaper section in her hands. "There is now a Women's Coast Guard. The services are opening up to more women in their ranks."

Georg picked up his pipe again and continued smoking. He turned a page in the front section of the paper.

Elinor spoke louder. "Dad, I'm thinking of doing my duty and joining something. The Coast Guard, maybe, or one of the services."

She stood up and moved into her mother's soft chair, next to her father. She leaned toward him. "There are the WACs and the WAVEs, too. I'd have a chance to see the world. And to help out. Maybe use my German."

Georg set his pipe back into its copper ashtray. The paper he slapped on to his lap. "I don't like the idea of women in war, Bunny. It's too dangerous."

"But, Papa, the women don't go to battle. They support the troops."

"You can do just as much good here," her father replied, eyes looking heavenward.

Elinor leaned toward her father. She held her hands in her lap, folded, because they threatened to shake. "Women don't go to the front lines, Dad. The soldiers would protect me."

Her father sat speechless. He stared at his daughter.

"I'd be in no danger. And the job sounds interesting." She noticed that her knuckles had turned white. "I want to find out how to sign up," Elinor declared.

"You don't need a uniform to do your part." Georg picked up his pipe and the paper. A wisp of smoke rose into the air from behind the *Forum*.

"I could see more of this big world, though. And meet people. And have an adventure." Elinor spoke to the newspaper. "I would have a life, Dad."

Georg lowered his paper and raised his eyes again to his daughter. "You have a good life here. You know, you're doing a lot of good teaching, Bunny."

Elinor leaned back in the chair. She sighed. At any rate, she'd have to wait until June to join up. She was under contract. And a gal could break a two-year teaching commitment at the end of the first year only if she were getting married or going into the service.

She closed her eyes. Papers to grade. The Glee Club. The plays. Lessons in subjunctive mood and subordinate clauses to high school students who couldn't care less. She had to do something. Her life spun in circles, around and around, uselessly.

Thanksgiving on the Island

November 1942

November 26

My hon,

Thanksgiving Day and we had a huge dinner. Right now I feel like sleeping. Everybody has a liberty from last night until tomorrow morning, but I'm spending the day in study.

Bet you're having a big dinner and a good time with the folks. A guy would get homesick if it weren't for the thought of other fellows in much worse situations. What a fatalist they make of you around here. They show a guy that you take what comes, and if it's bad, you just shrug it off 'cuz there's not a thing one can do about it.

You don't seem very excited about meeting in Minneapolis, so we'll probably skip that, hmmm. That means that I'll be there about 6 A.M. on Monday. We'll get together in the afternoon if nothing else comes up, and it will surely be great, darling.

I'm going to jump at detector amplifiers now, hon. We've got a lot of big diagrams to learn to draw and operate.

Yours, forever,
Beat

Coney Coat

Friday evening

My dearest,

Hi, beautiful! The pictures are perfect, hon, and so good to have 'em on my door. Guess I've spent most of the day standing there looking at them. A new picture of you just keeps me interested for a long, long while. The fur coat is pretty. I can hardly wait until we cuddle up in it.

   Since getting your letter, I've changed my plans for the weekend. I'm going to a dance party or something like that out at Wellesley

College. Lots of the fellows have been going and say that it's a swell way to spend a Saturday night. And I'm going in on a shoestring, with a gang of fellows. It will be one of those "platonic" evenings, I am certain. I want to know what it's like to talk to a girl and be near one. We'll just consider it as one of the "old friends" or something, hmmm?

Glad that you and Walter had a nice time. He's a guy I'd like to know some day—yeah, as friends. Suppose he'll be home during the holidays. Wish I could come and go as I pleased.

Three weeks from tomorrow I'll be on my way home. So get rid of all the "old friends" for a few days and give a guy a break, please? We'll be together soon and talk all of these things over—and you in my arms. Heaven on earth!

Yours,
Beat

Thanks again for the snaps, hon.

Nov. 29
(Sunday)

Good morning, my sweet,

Right after writing to you yesterday, I put the
"bite" on the fellow who runs this place, a
personal friend, thank you. He gave me a couple
of tickets to the Army show, "This Is the Army,"
with the instructions not to tell anyone.

To say the show is terrific is putting it
mildly. Irving Berlin, himself, sang. Ezra Stone
is one of the leading men. They have choruses of
"girls" and it's a riot. There is a Navy number
that was a build-up for the sailors. The whole
company is on the stage in the finale, and all
these old dowagers—rich people and all in their
boxes—gave them eight curtain calls. It was the
last night in Boston, so it was a big night for
all and a sell-out, as were all the nights for
the two-week run.

We went to an exclusive club then—The Fox and
Hounds. Ed knows the piano player very well and
we spent a half hour there talking to him—and
all the beautiful gals you ever want to see.
They just thought these sailors were "so nice"
and so we danced a couple of times with a couple
of officer's gals or wives or something. This
fellow said we were probably the first gobs ever
to be in there, and they treated us swell. We
hated to leave, but we heard there was a fire
at the Cocoanut Grove, so we left with a couple
of the orchestra.

We went to the fire and helped pull a few
bodies out. And we did guard duty for a while.

The uniforms let us in and we worked along with soldiers, Coast Guardsmen, policemen, Marines, and air raid wardens. The last we heard this morning at 4 o'clock there were 476 known dead. We saw hundreds piled in garages, etc. around the place. Something that I don't want to remember for a while—you can imagine—lots of servicemen couldn't take it for long—the sight—

All my love,
Beat

Sunday evening

My sweets,

We just came in here, checked our coats and Ed has started dancing. And he had a couple of very cute WACs, but I ducked him and them. They were playing "I Don't Want to Walk Without You," and I just had to come over and let you know I'm thinking of you.

We went to dinner in classy Dedham. The people are swell, well-educated, Yale, etc. They invited a couple of girls over, and their daughter is pretty swell. They wanted two college men between 20 and 22, so we fit right in. We had a grand time, a regular New England day and evening. We ate and ate, sang songs, talked our sections of the country over, and really got to be friends after a while. We've a standing invitation to come over any time we wish. Hope to go again as the people are so friendly and homelike.

Why don't you come down to Minneapolis? Only three weeks from now we'd be together an extra night, and it would mean so much to me, hon. I guess it's quite impossible—damn it! But all this cockeyed dreaming won't do any good, so to hell with it! Pardon my language, but it's exactly what I feel.

That house this afternoon—the party, I mean— just put me in such a good mood. You see, the people we visited have a daughter, very attractive and a junior at Radcliffe. She could have any guy she wanted, but she makes no passes at anyone, just is very pleasant and a real "buddy." Seems there's a man, a draftee who worked his way up to a looey. He's in Egypt now and hasn't seen her for over ten months. If a guy could only let him know just how swell she is, it'd make him very happy, I know. A fellow, no matter where he is or how much he loves the girl, gets a bit suspicious at times. 99% of the time he is just the most trusting guy in the world. But I'm one of the guys that always seem to pick that 1/100 of the time to write you.

Yours forever and ever,
Beat

I don't have any real enjoyment from fooling around with the girls here. Is that love, my darling? Or is it just plain craziness, as the fellows from New York say? Until a few of their other statements come true, I'll be a guy that's in love. O.K.? Such statements being:

1. She'll always run out on you. They always do.

2. There's no such thing as a virgin today.

3. They'll always write and tell you they don't go out, but they do and tell the new guy, "My boyfriend is in the service, but you're so much nicer." Then when you come home, she tells the new guy, "He's coming home for only a few days, and I really should see him—old friends and all." He's a generous guy and will give the serviceman a break. So the gal tells the serviceman, "It's you I love. Joe Blow and I are just good friends. He likes to take me around, and he's nice."

Well, the few of us that do believe in love take this with a smile. And, sweets, it sometimes takes a lot of willpower not to soak up just a little of that—not because they say it, but I've found the same thing to be true while running around.

December 1

Hi, hon,

We slept in the big jail Sunday night. They
have a place for servicemen who are broke. And
we were (and are)!!! Many of the guys had their
uniforms still dirty and stinky, and I mean
stinky. We compared stories and in the paper
was listed as dead our assistant platoon leader.
He was one of the first ones to arrive at the fire
and is credited with saving many lives. Later we
found that he was overcome by poisonous fumes,
and he is now in the hospital recovering. We're
going to throw a party for him when he comes
back. We'll pin a big paper medal on him.

Hurley wrote today, and he's going to be
drafted just before I come home—December 19,
he figures. He's worried about his mother as he
is the only one to support her. Funny how fate
works. When your number is up, it's up.

Two fellows were kicked out this week. Kinda
hard to see a fellow go, after being with him
for so long, and they worked hard, too. The
stuff just didn't come to them.

I get paid Friday and hope to get my ticket
Saturday. Not so long now, my sweet, until we'll
be talking and laughing together.

Yours,
Beat

December 4, Friday noon

Good afternoon, sweets,

'Tis a great day, after a meal of codfish. Can it be true? Even that hasn't put the damper on me today.

And, hon, 'tis only two weeks from tomorrow that I'll be starting home. So I'm taking care of myself and keeping up my record. Just think, sweets, five months without a kiss. I'm practically a virgin again. And that's on the level, too. Honest.

I'm happy that you considered the WAVEs. They really are a swell outfit, I think. You wouldn't go in without a commission, and you'd be quite busy. But when would we ever be able to see one another!

Last weekend I had some glorious ideas of going in and going to a party, just to show myself that if you could go out with Walt, I could go out with the sailors. But, honestly, it just doesn't appeal to me, and I figure that as long as I've come this far, what the hell. I might as well be able to look you squarely in the eyes and not have even the slightest doubt in my mind that I've been faithful to you. Not a tiny little kiss. Doggone, I've really been TOO good.

As you won't be coming to Minneapolis, I probably will come straight through. But there is a possibility that we might stop off someplace. You know how I celebrate and these fellows from out that way are all planning to have a vacation—a regular Midwestern time. I hope to be home Monday and want to be home Monday and will do my best to be home Monday. And that ought to satisfy everybody. Right? You're going to be all mine for Monday, Tuesday, Wednesday, Thursday, and Friday!! The rest of your vacation you can spend on the folks and Yupps and Mickey. Just forget the "old friends."

Got the candy yesterday, hon. It's swell. All the guys have been eating with me when we study. Thanks a million. Got my teeth examined yesterday. No trench mouth. Today I took a Wasserman—purely voluntary and everyone should do it three or four times a year. And I had an X-ray for TB and am perfect. So look me over, darling.

Yours forever,
Beat

Bay State Club
ON BOSTON COMMON
Sponsored by U.S.O.
Greater Boston Soldiers and Sailors Committee
Dec. ?

My gal,
Guess I'm just a little cockeyed. So that's maybe why I'm writing you.

I'm just a little bit worried. Tonight I was all set to call you. 'Twas about 6:00 there. Then I decided to wait a while. Now I just haven't the nerve to call you. For quite a while your letters haven't been too regular, and although they seemed full of all that I wanted to feel was true, you tripped yourself up every once in a while with little "white lies." So all the while I have doubts in my mind—and last week no letter.

The craziest feeling came over me when I was going to make the call to you. Seems I had the feeling that you wouldn't be there, and that the best way to avoid any trouble was to forget it.

Hope all of this isn't foolish, sweets, but I feel a little low tonite, have all week. You'll write me a letter soon, and all the doubts will be gone again. But in between, darling, what the hell do you do on weekends, anyway? Couldn't you squeeze in just a few minutes to drop me a line? Does it always have to be the routine of Monday night? And then sometimes forgetting to mail it for a couple of days? You used to laugh to me when you'd say you hadn't written Walter or Johnny for a while, and—truthfully—I didn't like it. Anyway, I'm sure to find out whether a guy is a sucker to go for the "one girl" while a long way from her.

All I hope is that my coming home isn't going to complicate things for you in any way. Just tip me off quick, like you used to. That's one thing about me. I'm generous and broadminded—you said so yourself. Meet me at that train Monday morn and tell me that I'm all wrong. We'll start all over again as we did when we first met and have loads of fun. How's about it, sweets?

Be seein' you,
Beat

Bay State Club
December 6

My bunny,

Honey, I hope my hair grows out a lot longer because it's worse than anything you ever saw. And right now it's been growing for two weeks. Guess I haven't given much of a thought to trying to look like a Romeo while here. Our platoon barber took me at my word when he "cut it short." They've been calling me "Head" out at the Island because of the short hair.

But we've got pet names for everyone—Lips, Nose, Sheepherder, Tex, Depot, etc. The fellow we call Depot went to New York. He's from Minnesota, too. When he came back, he mentioned Grand Central Station as the "depot." The New Yorkers really jumped him on that one, and the name has stuck.

Yours, forever and ever,

Beat

But He's Interesting
and Funny . . .

1:00 A.M.

THE STUDY REMAINED WRAPPED in shadows except for the glowing pattern of light from her father's fluorescent desk lamp. The cuckoo had chirped the hours, one after another, and there were still hundreds of letters to browse through. Elinor stood up and stretched. Ching's ears twitched, but he refused to be awakened.

At least Darrow's letters were interesting and worth saving. She remembered how she had discarded so many of the others' letters and wondered that, even early on, she had kept Beat's letters in their envelopes. She enjoyed reading them over and over.

Elinor reread the letter from December 6. She smiled, reading about those GI nicknames. No one still called Beat "Head," now that his hair was growing out. He probably liked being the "Grain Man."

She loved her nicknames. The high school kids in Pelican had named her Glamour Queen. Some of the guys she dated called her Bunny. A few called her Frenchy, but that was just in the first years of the war, the years when she downplayed her German heritage.

Elinor tiptoed into the kitchen, turned on the tap, and filled a glass. She gulped the water and then returned to the study. She settled back into the desk chair, averting its squeaks, and listening for movement from upstairs. Ching got up, then settled himself by a sofa pillow and curled into a tight ball.

Where did Elinor come from? And spelled that way? *Sense and Sensibility.* Austen. Was that what her parents had hoped for? A good girl with sense? Manners? Someone who went along with the codes of behavior, the expectations for a Bishop's daughter?

Eleanor Roosevelt, First Lady, had an aristocratic spelling.

"I know it's against the law in this family to admire a Democrat," Elinor thought, "but Eleanor Roosevelt . . ."

Roosevelt, they said, had been shy as a younger woman. But she'd certainly learned to speak up for issues she believed in.

Elinor had to admire Eleanor's style. Well, not in clothes. Hard to imagine Mrs. Roosevelt as a debutante at the Waldorf just 25 years ago. Eleanor's passion was what made her life significant. Just about twenty years after women's suffrage, Eleanor stood for the 48-hour work week and minimum wage for poor women who needed to work.

Eleanor Roosevelt defended the African Americans. Marian Anderson had wanted to sing at Constitution Hall, but the DAR refused to allow an integrated audience. 1939. Before this war. Eleanor stepped in and Marian was singing—on Easter—to an audience of 75,000 at the Lincoln Memorial. The Landgrebes and millions of others had gathered around radios to listen.

Mrs. Roosevelt did the same thing for the African American Tuskeegee Airmen by flying for over an hour in a plane with one of their student pilots. That alone gave their movement more prestige and some extra financial support.

Eleanor amounted to something, despite her lack of beauty. When the WWI vets, the Bonus Army, marched into Washington in 1932 to demand the bonuses they had been promised and had certainly earned, Hoover chased them away with tear gas. When they marched again the next year, FDR, the new President, settled the vets down by sending food, his greetings, and his wife.

Eleanor held press conferences with only women in attendance. She wrote articles for national magazines. She wrote a syndicated column called "My Day," too. Because her husband had been paralyzed, she took a larger role in the politics of the times.

Mrs. Roosevelt was Something Big.

And although her father didn't know, Elinor admired the First Lady and her courage. She loved to think of Eleanor saying, "A woman is like a tea bag. You can't tell how strong she is until you put her in hot water."

Elinor was certainly in hot water after that last appointment with Doctor Klein. She wondered how strong she really was. She opened another envelope.

Christmas Plans

December 1942

ELINOR'S VALISE, CLOTHES PACKED neatly, lay open on her bed at the Nettestad's. She had finished. Her outfits for the weekend of Christmas shopping in Fargo lay assembled and folded. She had packed her red woolen sweater, tight, as was the fashion; her new black and red plaid skirt, knee-length; and the white blouse with the sweetheart neckline. She wished she had nylons, but they were hard to get. The boys needed nylon for parachutes. At least she had the coney coat!

In her hands she held a letter from Beat. He wanted her to meet him in the Cities for an overnight date on his first night back home. There was simply no way she could get away to meet him in Minneapolis. What would her parents think of such an arrangement? What excuse could she ever come up with that made sense?

It might've been a big mistake to invite him to Christmas Eve dinner on the last night he'd be in Fargo. But it was proper for citizens to include servicemen in their meals. A duty to country. Emily Post said so.

Elinor knew she had to end this friendship before Beat went off to war. Her parents didn't approve. And she couldn't keep up with all this letter writing. Beat expected so much.

She'd have to have a long talk with him. She'd break things off once and for all.

The floor creaked in the same spots as she made her way from one side of her rented room to the other over and over again.

Elinor parked Beat's latest letter on her bed, then picked up her hairbrush and sat at the dressing table. She stared into the mirror and began her routine, as was her habit, 100 strokes every night.

Cardamom. The sweet aroma of Christmas cookies in the oven in the kitchen below curled into her room. Mrs. Nettestad was baking again. There'd be enough *krumkaka* and *fattigman* for the Army! Elinor put down her brush, picked up the novel she was reading and set it on the table with her purse, ready for tomorrow's early morning bus ride.

As she arranged her hairbrush in her suitcase, she wondered whether her mother had already made the *springerle*. Those German anise cookies needed aging time to soften. The family often had to enjoy them in January because they hadn't been started soon enough in December. *Springerle* had become a family joke, like the cranberries they forgot at Thanksgiving. After the pumpkin and mince pies had been served, someone was bound to remember the bowl of red jewels cooling on the sun porch. "*Ach*!" Trudie would laugh. "Again!"

Before getting into bed, Elinor settled Beat's latest letter into her purse. She could answer it this weekend from home. She was due to write a long letter. She closed the suitcase and snapped its brassy latches, set it on the floor by the door, and then turned out the light.

❧   ❧

Darrow strolled the streets of Boston much of late Friday afternoon. He and Johnny McCall had decided at the last moment to catch the water taxi into town for a weekend of lonesome drinking.

And Beat needed to shop. His goal was the perfect gift. He looked in the windows of the stores and wondered what a guy could do without more money to splurge on his girl. He had to show Elinor that he would be a more devoted suitor than the others who had already proposed to her. He hated to think of them hanging around "his" girl.

His girl? He had to admit. She'd never really committed to him.

"Beat," Johnny laughed. "You sure she's still going with you? You haven't had a letter from her in a while. She's probably got someone else."

Beat laughed. He wanted to wrestle Johnny to the ground, like he would in the barracks. But this was Boston. He'd play along.

"She's special, Mac," Beat grinned. "C'mon. Give me an idea. What could I get?"

Johnny laughed again. "Spend your money on bourbon, Beat."

"Hey, I've got an invitation from Elinor to spend Christmas evening with the family."

Wasn't that promising?

The two fellows had purchased train tickets already. Darrow's was in the secret section of his wallet, which he stowed in his back pocket. The expense of the train ride, the money he owed his buddies, and his trips to Boston had left him with next to nothing. $5.63. Hardly enough for a special gift for the girl of his dreams. And he didn't want to appear cheap, like Walter.

Beat patted his back pocket often, just to make sure his wallet and the train ticket to Fargo were still with him. He paced the now shadowy street, already crowded with other servicemen and their dates. The winter dark arrived early these days, always a surprise.

He and Mac ducked into a nearby bar. Beat ordered a sandwich and a couple of cool ones. Of course, he'd write to Elinor. Mac ordered, too, but he was on the lookout for a girl to dance with. The music set his feet a-jangle.

The band, warming up, was already loud enough to cover the subdued noise of conversations and whispered *tête-à-têtes*. The volume in the place would increase as the night grew long, as more sailors and servicemen packed the joint.

Beat found a quiet corner. He began a new letter. Actually, it was a promise. For the next weeks, he planned to stay on the Island and study, saving his upcoming living allowance for a few drinks and some special times in Fargo.

He thought about calling Elinor. He had enough money left to give that a whirl. He dumped the change from his pocket. He gulped the last of his drink. He stood.

On second thought, he wondered whether she'd be home. Saturday night. She probably had plans. He didn't want to look like a fool. Again.

He sat. He ordered another drink. At last, with the bourbon relaxing him, his mind cleared. He devised a plan. Easy money—pennies from heaven. Heaven only knew he needed some dough.

He wondered whether prayer really helped. He ordered another drink.

⇒ ⇐

Elinor boarded the early bus to Fargo on Saturday morning. She stared out the window, lost in thought. She gazed as the sunrise crept over the fields, blotchy now with frost around the stubble of last summer's crops.

Last summer. Chicago. She remembered the long, lazy days hiking around the city with Beat. The baseball games. The bars at night. She couldn't remember laughing so much in her entire life as she had that week.

She remembered his kiss. She felt warm and loosened the top buttons of her coney coat. Then she dug into her purse, found Beat's letter, and leaned into the light to read it again.

Well, she had already invited him to the family Christmas celebration. Too late to change. She'd have to remember to talk with her mother about that. She would assure her *Mütterchen* that she'd use the occasion to end the relationship.

⇒ ⇐

Late Sunday afternoon, Beat returned to Gallups Island, liquor on his breath and nothing for his girl.

The Boston shops showed expensive gadgets, things she'd love, things he couldn't afford. He had roamed through the jewelry shops with empty pockets. Even costume jewelry was out of his range. Flowers? Chocolates? Not enough to impress her.

He gathered his spare change and pooled what was left of his paycheck. Then, shoulders back, teeth clenched, he joined the fellows at Ed's bed, where a high stakes poker game was in progress.

He smiled at the gang and sat at the edge of the game, on someone's bunk. He reached into his shirt pocket for his cigarettes and a matchbook from the Fox and Hound, a swell place. It showed he had some class.

"C'mon, Beat," the fellows urged. "We'll show you how to play."

"Nah," he replied. "Not my game."

He lit up and contemplated his classmates until the betting reached fever pitch. He stood then. He fingered the gold World's Fair coin in his pocket and said, "I'm in."

World's Fair Coin

❧ ❦

Late Sunday, Elinor returned to Pelican. She thanked her friend Muriel for another safe ride. She gathered her valise, her purse, and her book and stepped out of the car. Their predictions about the upcoming week at school and their laughter echoed in the dark alleyway behind the Nettestad home.

Elinor hiked the narrow brick sidewalk that led to the back door of her rooming house. She was on the lookout for patches of ice, but the path had been cleared for her.

She slid her key into the lock, opened the door without a sound, carted her suitcase and purse upstairs to her room, and threw them on the bed. She unpacked. Then she settled at her dressing table and automatically picked up the boar bristle hairbrush.

Staring into the mirror, she thought about the past weekend. She got it all done. She had finished the Christmas shopping. She'd even wrapped the gifts before hiding them in the den closet. She had sent her "old friends" samples of her homemade fudge. She packed boxes to California, New York, Massachusetts, and Washington state. And one to Irene in Illinois.

There hadn't been much else to do on Saturday night, and she needed some time with her mother. She hated to broach the subject of visitors on Christmas. But it wouldn't be the first time the Landgrebes had company on the holiday. Anyway, Trudie had nodded at the news. She smiled when Elinor revealed her plans to break up with Darrow. Then she had looked at Georg with raised eyebrows when she announced that Beat would be joining them.

⇒> <⇐

Beat heard the rumor at supper Monday evening in the galley. Amid all the clanking of dishes and the yelling for seconds, he heard it. Damn!

The uniforms the Navy had promised the men wouldn't be ready for the holidays, and he knew Elinor loved those bell-bottom outfits. Now he'd have to appear in his civilian rags. And with that new haircut the Navy seaman had hacked out.

He finished his meal quickly and dashed back to the barracks. Once in the head, he stared at the mirror and winced. He tried combing his hair with a part on the opposite side. It made no difference.

He and Mac had to study after supper. Code practice on the machines. Then battery work in the lab. When he dragged himself back to his bunk, he grabbed another textbook. He planned to put full effort into schoolwork now. No more Boston weekends.

He opened the book. A couple of the fellows in R-17 were wrestling and the gang had gathered down the hall to rubberneck and to offer their advice.

He heard the racket from far away but he remained on his slim cot, lost in thought, wondering how the whole Christmas break would turn out.

Whether she'd find time for him.

Who else might be hanging around.

Too Much to Think About

December 1942

Monday eve—

My sweets,

You can know for certain that I will be home just as quickly as I can. I want to see you waiting for me, smiling. That's my one wish now. To hell with school and everything.

What did the fellow from Pelican—Mr. Five by Five—bring you for Christmas? From him, I mean. I just want to get a general idea of what you might like for Xmas from your guy in Boston. And I'd hate to duplicate anything that you already have.

That next week sounds wonderful and please don't get the idea that I want to spend a lot of time with my friends. The only thing I want is to be with you—all the time—as much as you can spare. The time we spend together will have to hold a lot of memories for me. I've got a lot of things ahead—work, travel, and experiences. So let's spend a lot of these very precious hours together. When we're together again, all

the nights that I've spent in Boston dreaming
of you, being all yours, they'll not have been
foolish.

> Sweet dreams, my Bunny,
> Yours,
> Beat

616 Indiana Ave.
Coeur d'Alene, Idaho
December 12, Monday nite [wrong date]

Dearest Elinor:

Still kind of a hurt down inside - - - anyway I haven't heard from your end like you promised - - -

I still am determined not to wait until summer, too far away and things too indefinite between you and me.

If I sent you some money think you could come out and see me for a few days during Xmas vacation - - - working awfully hard again and am lonesome for you. I have been very good, I honestly wonder some times if it pays - - - How about you? Been good - - - true - still in love with me? Who you writing to? Stringing anybody along - - - How about marrying me, I'm still waiting - - You know, Elinor if you really cared you could marry me out here. It wouldn't be bad waiting for you to finish teaching knowing that we belonged to each other.

You're going to regret waiting much longer Bun.

Good nite Bun.

Still, lovingly your
Walter

P.S. Are you wearing my ring Bun?

from Bob F.
Philadelphia, PA
handwritten Dec. 23, 1942 in green ink

Dearest Elinor,

Darling I can't live without you. I only hope that this catastrophe is over very soon. I love you so much Honey. Whenever I look out the window I always keep thinking of you as you were sitting beside me on the train. You're more beautiful than the sun itself. Your eyes are like moonbeams. Your hair shines like gold in the soft moonlight. Your lips are like soft pillows of moonlight. Darling, will you Marry Me. Honey, I love you with all my heart and soul. I sent you something you'll like. Tell me in your letter that you love me, Darling, and say you will marry me. I miss you so terribly much. Send me your love and say you'll marry me. Merry Christmas and Happy New Year to you, Darling.

From your sweetheart,
Bob

(P.S.) Too far away but still love you with all my heart

Five Days

December 1942

It SEEMED LIKE THE longest train ride he'd ever taken. He spent some time in the smoking car. He paced the length of the train several times before settling back into his seat for a nap. He mulled over the letter she wrote him about Minneapolis. She said it wasn't a good idea.

"Damn!" He remembered her excuses. "Is Walt around again?"

When Beat returned to Fargo on the *Hiawatha* on Sunday, December 20, he'd been gone five months. He had just five days to show her he loved her.

She was waiting at the depot, bundled up in her coney coat, and he couldn't stop grinning. He saw her from the window of his car, grabbed his duffel, and came to a standstill. The women, exiting the train car before the men could leave, poked along. Beat clenched his teeth and tried to smile.

When released, he ran through the crowd and scooped Elinor up in his arms. She giggled.

When he set her down, she threw her arms around his neck and snuggled into him. "Cuddle up," she whispered. "That jacket is so thin and you look so cold."

"And you look like a baby bear in that warm coat," he laughed.

"Let's go home and get you warmed up," Elinor suggested with a laugh.

Because her parents were out of town, Elinor and Beat spooned on the sofa until sunrise. With the first shafts of gray light through the curtains, Elinor stood. She finger combed her hair and laughed at Beat. "C'mon, sleepyhead," she crooned. She stretched.

Darrow followed suit. He stood, slipped into his woolen jacket, and pecked her on the cheek.

"I'll see you tonight then," Elinor said as she walked him to the door.

Beat had family and friends to visit, but every late afternoon and evening were reserved for Elinor. She cooked for him. And after supper she played Christmas carols and popular songs they liked. They walked downtown to movies. They visited Gene's, the Aquarium, the Powers Café, and the Metropole. It took a few hours to reacquaint themselves, but the liquor helped.

"Hon," Beat asked on Monday, their second night together, "I know you couldn't make it to Minneapolis. I understand. I've only got five days here. Three left now. Is there somewhere else we could go? You know. To be alone?"

Elinor raised her eyebrows. "Beat, I have to be here this week. It's almost Christmas and there's still a lot to do to get ready for the holidays. I have several church services, too. I need to practice."

Beat grinned automatically.

"It's okay, sweetie," he cooed, even as he was thinking about the cost of getting home for these five days. He had to remind himself that he hadn't come home just for sex. He came to see whether Elinor had any feelings for him at all. Or whether she'd just been stringing him along, like her other "old friends." Now he wasn't sure. Again.

⇒   ⇐

On Tuesday, Beat took Elinor for a dinner at the Comstock Hotel. When they were seated at the bar in the most romantic space in town, he smiled, pleased with himself. "Bourbon, neat," he ordered, and as an afterthought, "a grilled cheese sandwich."

"I'll just nibble at your dinner," Elinor suggested. "I'm not that hungry."

He ordered her a Tom Collins, her current favorite, and a grilled cheese sandwich of her own.

Beat showed her a few snaps of his Boston adventures. There was a shot of Johnny McCall and Beat at Harvard. There was one of Beat in his new uniform. A picture of them from the newspaper after dinner at the home of Schlesingers. No pictures were allowed of the Island. War secret.

Elinor leaned over their table to listen to Beat's tales of life in Boston: the November fire when he carried out bodies, the big ships at the wharves in Boston, the blackouts. The crowds of people in a metropolis and the rich ones that invited servicemen for dinner. The shows on the weekends. All the stars seemed to route their travels through Boston.

"Not much happens in English classes, Beat," Elinor murmured when he slowed a bit. "I go to school and at night I grade papers."

"No big news, Bunny?"

"Well," she hesitated. She swallowed the last of her drink. "Remember, before you left for Gallups? When we introduced a few guys from your gang to Irene? Well, Irene dated one of them a while." Elinor looked into her lap. She whispered, "She's staying with Aunt Dorothy in Illinois this holiday."

Beat squinted at her.

"My father's disappointed. And a little angry."

"But it's nothing I did . . ."

"True. But, to say the least," Elinor added, "you have to be on your best behavior around home."

⁂

Elinor met him at the door on Christmas Eve. The Landgrebe home was full of the holiday. Piles of cards arrived daily, dropped into the mail slot on the front porch. The family tacked the cards on a stand-up, three-section, double-sided corkboard constructed by Georg just for this purpose, and, when that was full, they tacked cards around the doorframe. Former parishioners in town to shop dropped by for coffee and a little something. Pastors visited with the Bishop while together they planned the coming year in their parishes. The Landgrebe girls helped serve, kept the house clean, and kept up with the baking.

"This must be what Grand Central Station looks like," Elinor thought, as one group departed and the next arrived. Her parents were delighted with all the action. They had always managed a busy parsonage.

On the front sun porch, Georg and Trudie had set up their traditional German village scene on a table posed in front of the window. Despite the news from Europe, Georg was not afraid to admit that he was German. He knew the German people weren't to blame for the mad man leading them.

Right after Thanksgiving they had begun to settle miniature paper houses and a church on a fluffy sheet of soft cotton. More cotton from the medical supply, along with a few pinches of glitter, added heaps of snow to the scene. Then came the lights in the houses and six-inch high evergreens standing beside them. The church, of course, had windows that were lit. Busy glass people dashed around, running errands just before the holidays. A few strolled into the church. As a backdrop to the scene, Georg had devised a board which Trudie covered with deep blue fabric. There were pinpricks in the material where petite stars, electrically charged, glowed.

Beat surveyed the scene again as he passed through the sun porch. It was cool out there, and he was nearly ice from his walk to Elinor's place.

"C'mon in, Beat," Elinor said. "You look frozen. I'll warm you up." She took his hand and led him into the living room.

A four-foot tall evergreen tree took center stage on the corner table where Georg usually kept his smoking equipment. The fresh fir still smelled of forest, for the family had put it up that afternoon. When the children were young, the tree was put up by the *Weinachtsman* while the family was at church. Now that they were grown, the entire family spent Christmas Eve afternoon decorating, preparing for the arrival of the Christ Child.

This year's tree was covered with glass ornaments and tinsel, some electrical colored bulbs, and a shiny star on the top. Underneath the tree, on a sheet placed there to protect the tabletop, the family set wrapped gifts for each other.

Heaps of Christmas sheet music lay in disarray on the piano top, alongside a pretty glass angel with her mouth open, tuning up. A pile of a dozen songbooks of Christmas hymns like *Stille Nacht* and "O Little Town of Bethlehem," Trudie's favorite, rested on the music cabinet next to the piano.

Elinor played a while for Beat while he sat, warming up, on the horsehair sofa. He leaned back and shut his eyes. His breathing slowed, and his face relaxed. The recital ended with "White Christmas," their new favorite song. Elinor joined him on the sofa. He took off his jacket then and put his arm around her. She noted that he was wearing the same clothing he had worn to the wedding on the day she met him, the day he'd walked her home in the snowfall. Just a year ago.

"What are your Irish Christmas traditions, Beat?" she asked.

"I guess we don't have many," he replied. "Not like your family anyway."

Georg plugged in the tree lights and turned off most of the house lights. The family gathered around and admired their work.

"The best tree I can remember," Trudie laughed.

The tinsel twisted and glittered. The glass balls hanging from the branches were old family treasures: balls with stripes, golden or silver teardrop-shaped ornaments, and glass icicles that sparkled with the colors of the electric lights. The star on the top of the tree was a bit bedraggled from spending so many years in one attic or another, but the lights were sparse toward the pinnacle of the pine and its age wasn't obvious.

When everyone had gathered, Georg told the story of the candles that had set a tree on fire in some church in the district. "Wasn't a fresh tree," he ended, shaking his head. "But their ushers had pails of water ready. Only the tree burned."

Beat noted the pile of packages under this tree.

"C'mon, Beat, I have something to show you." Elinor grabbed his hand.

She turned on the lights in the kitchen and took him down the steep steps, into the basement root cellar. Before she turned on the lights in the storage space, a sweet aroma, the citrus bite of the Florida oranges and grapefruits packed in green strips of cellophane and trucked to the frozen north, surrounded them. When Elinor flipped the light switch, the scene came into focus. The fruit sat, glorious in their bright tropical peels, in a box in the corner. On other shelves in the storage room Trudie had stored the *lebkuchen* and *springerle*, spicy German cookies which the family expected every Christmastime.

Elinor flipped the light switch in the root cellar again, and they stood in the dark. She moved closer to Beat and put her arms around his neck. He leaned into her.

"Bunny?" Her mother was at the top of the stairs. "It's time for church."

When Elinor and Darrow arrived at the top of the stairs, Trudie was scowling.

They all piled into the Pontiac and drove to the new church. The Landgrebe girls had chosen their outfits carefully. Even though the church was always cool, they would remove their coats and sit fashionably in their pew.

Elinor wore a black dress with silver buttons on the bodice and a white crocheted collar at the neck. Like the fashion of the time, it nipped her waist nicely. The square shoulders were supported by pads. She arranged a white cashmere sweater, knit by her mother, over her shoulders. Elinor's large brimmed hat and short veil shadowed her face. The large white rose which decorated the millinery tilted as she looked around the nave. She took her white gloves out of her purse and put them on for services.

The candles glowed. The girls' eyes sparkled.

Unfamiliar with church services, Beat observed the activity from the corners of his eyes. He bowed his head when the others did. And Elinor shared her hymnal with him when it was time to sing.

The family party followed the service. "Come, girls," Trudie called. "I need some help." And a feast appeared on the stretched-to-its-limit table in minutes.

"C'mon," Elinor invited Beat to the table, where they sat side-by-side. He wasn't sure about the routines there either. There hadn't been many family meals at home while he grew up. So he kept a watchful eye on the others around him. When the family bowed heads, he followed suit.

"Bless this family and this food," Georg began the blessing. "Even though we are separated at this holiday . . ."

Beat kept his eyes closed through most of the prayer. It was a long one, though, and he found himself peeking at Elinor who was eyeing him, too.

Then Georg carved the turkey. Everyone started talking as the dishes were passed around the table. Beat relaxed and enjoyed the feast. Elinor watched her mother and father and thought about Beat's imminent departure. Midnight would find him boarding the train again.

The spread was the best one could expect in wartime. Trudie had saved her coffee and sugar ration coupons, and it showed in the delightful offerings: turkey, mashed potatoes and gravy, sage stuffing, beans picked from the Landgrebe garden and canned last summer, a loaf of homemade bread and some jelly, too. There were pickles, and, of course, coffee. The pumpkin and mince pies had been squirreled away, on the cool porch, saved for later.

After dinner and dishes, the girls joined the men to open gifts. Elinor sat on the doily which rested on the arm of the horsehair sofa, just beside Beat, who sat on the prickly part. Mickey took the piano bench. Yupps sat on the floor. Georg and Trudie sat in their chairs.

The tree glowed, and the angel on the music cabinet continued her silent praise.

"Well, let's get started," Mickey laughed. "I've made something for each of you and I want to see whether you like it or not."

Elinor leaned over and whispered in Beat's ear, "I hope you like what I got you, too."

He smiled at her. "I'll love it just because it's from you," he declared.

When it was his turn, Beat proudly presented his gift to Elinor. He sat up and, holding his breath, waited while she untied the ribbon. She began to loosen the paper.

Beat fingered the coin he kept in his pants pocket, his gold 1939 World's Fair coin, proof that he'd been there. He remembered the "Pageant of the Pacific" on Treasure Island, so close to the new Golden Gate Bridge. He and Bruns had shared a mix of memories from that train trip across the country via cattle car.

Beat excelled at poker, though he rarely joined in the games on the Island. He had hated to gamble that memento. But he had been desperate. And how he hollered when they played the last card!

Beat held his breath as Elinor lifted the lid on the box. He wanted her to like the watch better than whatever gifts she'd gotten from Walter, Dale, Phil, Bob, Johnny, and some unnamed male teacher in Pelican. The competition was stiff.

Elinor swiftly unclasped the Elgin watch she had gotten from her parents for college graduation and stuffed it into Beat's pocket. "Oh, Beat, I love it!" she exclaimed. She wound and set her new watch.

Beat put it on her delicate wrist.

Georg caught Trudie's eye and raised an eyebrow. Trudie looked into her lap.

Yupps handed Mickey the next gift to unwrap.

She shook it by her ear, and hearing nothing, began to unwrap the ribbon. "What is it?" she squealed.

The cuckoo chirped, announcing the time. Nine o'clock. It was then that Elinor noted that the hands on her new watch hadn't moved. She unsnapped the latch, removed it from her wrist, and put it to her ear to see whether she could hear any ticking. Everyone stopped talking to give her a chance to listen closely.

"Beat?" she asked as she handed it to him.

He listened. He shook it a bit, then tried winding the delicate timepiece again.

When the hands on the watch still hadn't moved, Georg, who set his clock by the Greenwich time signal transmitted daily on the radio at noon, tried resetting the time. No luck.

Darrow stared at the floor.

"Mickey, open the one in your lap." Yupps, always the peacemaker, grabbed the next present, ready to pass it to his father when Mickey was finished, and the unwrapping continued.

Darrow wiped his sweaty palms on his pants. If only he could take Elinor to Crescent Jewelers to pick out a perfect watch. All the shops in Fargo were closed. He had no money, anyway. He had to catch a train in a few hours. Christmas Day. There was no recourse.

Then he remembered his salesmanship text. He put on his best smile, pretending confidence. "I'll get you another one. In Boston," he apologized in his girl's ear while her father unwrapped a present from Trudie, a new tie.

Elinor laughed, "It's okay, Beat. It might just start working on its own one day."

"Will you still wear my Sigma Chi pin?" Beat whispered while they waited for the pies to be cut. He noticed that she had put her Elgin watch back on for the time being.

"Of course. I'll even wear it with my pajamas," she replied. Elinor patted the pin on her left shoulder. Then she handed him the largest piece of mincemeat pie.

The family gathered in the living room after the meal. They sang all the old familiar carols while Elinor accompanied them. Beat didn't know all the verses, but he did his best to go along with their holiday ritual by humming when he couldn't find the lyrics in the songbooks. Ching, purring, curled up in his lap.

Too soon it was time for Beat's midnight train ride back to Boston, the boat taxi to Gallups, and the final and most difficult weeks of study. Then shipping out to God knows where. Off the beach and into the war.

Beat set Ching on the floor with a final scratch behind his ears. He stood then and shook hands with Reverend Landgrebe.

"So, it's time to leave us?" Georg asked Darrow. He met his daughter's eyes then and said, "You two must have things to talk about."

When Darrow shook hands with Trudie, she said, "We pray for our American troops, and we'll think of you as you get into the war."

"It's after eleven, Beat," Elinor whispered. "Let's hope the car will start."

The two of them walked to the back door where Elinor grabbed the keys to the Pontiac from the hook. Beat's duffel was in the back seat already. The two drove the few blocks downtown in silence. When they arrived at the depot, Elinor turned to Beat.

"Beat, I'm truly sorry to see you leave this time. We always have such fun together." She removed her woolen gloves as she spoke. She turned toward him.

He had slid over on the seat during the drive. His arm was around her shoulders. "You can't be as sorry as I am," Beat whispered in her ear. He leaned toward her. Their lips met. Elinor felt a shiver go through her, even though the car heater blew warm air at the two of them.

Darrow touched her gently, and she fell into his embrace. Time stood still. Until the whistle of the arriving train entered Elinor's consciousness.

"Oh, Beat," she gasped as she sat up, buttoning her silver buttons. "There's no time left for that long chat."

Happy Christmas?

Duty to Country . . .

1:20 A.M.

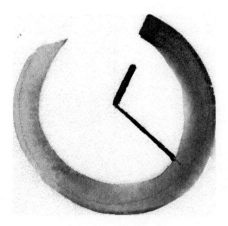

Sitting at her father's desk, Elinor sighed as she remembered that Christmas. Just two years ago.

It hadn't been the ideal visit, the one she had been dreaming about. She and Beat had had some fun times, but she remembered many of their arguments, too. Petty spats, really, when one looked back on them.

Elinor packed the Christmas letters back into her storage box.

Her parents must have been disappointed. She and Beat hadn't had that long talk. And she had promised her mother that she'd break it off.

She hadn't even had time to think.

Bravado

December 1942

5:45 AM. THE WIND, wet and cold, snapped at him as he stepped off the pier at India Wharf. One by one the other radiomen from Gallups Island entered the open-air water taxi, some slipping on the icy deck boards. They stumbled to vacant seats. The craft filled quickly with mariners returning after liberty. She rocked and lifted with each surge of the Atlantic, dancing with high seas.

The sky, an icy haze after yesterday's storm, began to color in the eastern horizon, even as the sliver of moon peeked out momentarily overhead. Some of the men had been up all night. A few had bunked in the Buddies' Club, the Seaman's, or the YMCA after hanging out at the bars or entertainment centers developed for the servicemen in the area.

Darrow silently counted to ten, in a hurry to get back to school before muster. A late arrival meant being disciplined at report mast and receiving whatever restrictions that would entail. He knew he was in trouble. That damned train had arrived too late to catch a ride to the island last night.

They began the trip across the bay—six miles to the Island. Six miles of watery hills and deeper than usual valleys. Beat shivered, his damp woolen dungarees cold on his legs. He pulled his uniform pea coat tighter. Brand new and it was not enough to warm him. The large lapels meant no buttons at the collar. Cold air seeped in around his neck.

Just a mile out, and the men aboard joked about the seas throwing them around. A couple of the newest recruits looked green around the gills.

"Hope the Army holds off their bombardment training until we get there," one of the guys called out, and a few laughed. For weeks the radiomen on Gallups had been on the lookout as ammo hit the water from the Devens Army base on a nearby island.

"Those fellas should be training all day and night. They'll never bag anything at the rate they're going," shouted a guy from R-16, confident in his own skills. At least, he hadn't been thrown out of the Gallups training program yet.

"Won't be long for us, fellas," another shouted to his classmates aboard. Just a few more weeks and his class would become actual radio officers on real ships, taking supplies to desperate troops in one battle or another.

"Aw, they don't start until daylight. We'll dock by then," the Navy ensign in charge replied.

The ocean, their enemy this morning, blustered. Beat licked his chapped lips and tasted salt. The men gingerly balanced their bodies with each wave, trying to move with the swells and dips of the old carrier boat.

And getting in before daylight? It looked like they might not make it this time, in these seas.

Most of these seamen were tired. Some, like Beat, had gone home on liberty. Others had spent their liberties in Boston. Word had spread that Dorsey's orchestra was in town, and many of them had squeezed into a show. Some were satisfied with drinks at their favorite hangouts. A few had girlfriends in port.

The icy spray into the taxi kept most of the fellows awake, if not completely alert. They turned their attention from their weekend memories to the tossing seas.

Although his liberty had served as a respite from study—music and drink, seeing Elinor and old friends—Beat was looking forward to school again. He started to organize his thoughts.

The first code class of the morning. The radio theory class on inductors, resistors, and circuits. His mind cleared.

Darrow eyed the submarine nets and hoped their taxi wouldn't be held up, waiting, while another ship came through into the safety of Boston harbor. But if a ship had been damaged—and they'd seen a number of torpedoed ships slide into safety lately—the sailors always deferred respectfully, no matter how miserable they felt. They prayed that they wouldn't have to navigate the seas on a crippled ship, or worse, one day.

The Navy pilot in charge turned the taxi toward the pier. The seas pitched and foamed around the crowded boat. The ocean roared.

"Don't ram 'er in this time," someone yelled to the Navy pilot.

The seamen laughed.

Not long ago the pilot, bringing the boat into the Island, crashed smack dab into the pier. That, of course, became fodder for a running joke. These Merchant Mariners, many of whom had been rejected by the Navy, relished the sight of a guy in the Navy uniform slipping up.

Staring into the chopping seas, Beat focused on his dreams of future heroic exploits, his part in this damned war. He knew the risks he was taking—sitting duck on the high seas, atop armaments and ammo. Or, worse yet, aviation fuel.

But he had always yearned for adventure and travel. Soon he'd get his fill.

There Are Such Things

December 1942 – January 1943

Sunday, December 27

My darlin',

Our train was late so we'll be going to report mast sometime tomorrow. We just registered at the Seamen's Club, took a shower, shave, and it feels as if I'll be able to like the city again.

   We had a couple of those days when one or the other of us was just a little provoked at the other, but the other times, we were laughing and happy together with nothing between us but knowing we loved each other. I'm terribly in love now, and it's all your fault, darlin'.

   As I said before, sweets, the five months that we were apart, I was really good. You were good, too, and that is so good to know. Of course, I don't like to think of you going out with any of the fellows. You promised to tell me about the times you go out. Please don't kinda overlook that as you did before. You see, sweets, I'm a fellow who doesn't want to have anyone put something over, no matter how small. Who knows what an Irish sailor with money in his pocket and a good grouch on will do?

All that about a bank account was hooey, hon. I owe some money on the leave, but that's the last thing that I want you to think about. Owing the money will keep me well in check for some time to come.

I hope you write me oftener, sweets, 'cuz your letters really help me to feel so much better. You probably don't know what I mean, but when everything goes right for me, 'tis 'cuz I'm feeling happy and purposeful. When I don't get a letter for a while, it worries me some. I let my studies go, 'cuz they don't seem to be fun, and sit down and write you a letter (and you'd much rather that I didn't write some of those letters!)

Tomorrow with the classes, detail, report mast, chow lines, bugles, musters, etc. there will be the life of before coming back to me again. Right now it doesn't appeal to me—but definitely! But it will be great to see all the fellows again and get into radio lab. Soon I'll be a real radioman!

My love to the family.

Yours forever, Bunny,
Beat

Sunday evening

My darlin'

They're playing "White Christmas" now. My stomach just aches. That two-ton heart is with me. We had a really swell Christmas—one that I'll never forget. We were just on the way to beginning a great lot of fun when I had to leave. For the next few months, your pictures and letters will have to keep me happy.

March is the month we'll all be working toward now—getting our tickets, no more school, real officers, maybe a leave, and an assignment to a ship!! All I've got to do is work hard, concentrate for a couple more months. Honestly it sounds great. Now to do it . . .

I miss you, Elinor,
Beat

⤳   ⤲

Monday

Right now I have 29 minutes until lights out. Yes, I'm living by the bugle again. The Island looks very bright indeed. From now on in, the days will mean just one closer to seeing you—and for a longer time this time.

USO

Jan. 1, 1943

My darling,

Honestly it's the pen—not the results of a New Year's celebration! My evening started not too well. At six o'clock your time I put through a call to you. At 7:45 I gave up!! I wanted to talk to you, hear you, and know that you are all right. And to wish you a really happy new year and tell you how much I miss you already, how much I love you, want you, but –

We had a swell time. In a big city such as this, lots of things can and do happen to make a night very memorable. 'Twas a good thing I was a good boy. It took a lot of dreaming of you to do it. There you were—sitting at home, knitting by the Xmas tree, the radio playing. What else could I do?

Our song, "There Are Such Things" is played quite often now. The song is perfect. The title is the part I believe. Funny how something like that can make life so much more livable. Just as I write this, a second class Navy signalman is playing it.

You know, sweets, this life has grown rational again—yes already. A few days on the Island, a night in town, a hot dog and coffee and a letter to you. No real worries. Just a feeling of contentment. It's not such a bad life. A fellow is treated according to how he acts, and I've no complaints (except these pens. They dig into this paper when I push upward!)

You see darling, I'm taking up right where I left off—continuing to be all yours. You try, too, hon!

Yours,
Beat

UNITED STATES ARMY
Sat., Jan. 2

Dearest,

There are so many things I'd like to say to you. If we could only have had a few more days, we really could have finished our "chat." Before that last eve, things were kinda up in the air. Then we finally got over all our petty little arguments and found that happiness together that we used to have.

That first morning—I saw you first—my heart almost stopped. For a little while I just wanted to holler out. Then, getting back a little sense, I hurried over, and you were so soft and warm and lovely. There was what I wanted, would always want.

Ed could hardly eat when I told him the story of the Christmas watch. He was embarrassed just thinking of it, he said, as I should probably have been. But I knew that it would run when fixed a little.

We should have a ring, shouldn't we? I've always thought that, but there are a few reasons why not. First I want to wait and get the best—a beautiful one. You can pick it out with me, but right now, we couldn't do so well. Besides, you're wearing my pin and, hon, I'd wear a ring—yes, even that—for us. The reason that rings never did appeal to me—well, I've seen some fellows' faces cut up from them. Had a good cut on the chin once myself. Some fellows wear them for that reason only. But I wouldn't. Besides I don't plan on being in any fights. I'm not living in Fargo, fending off the would-be suitors now.

You'll like this. Our platoon is spread out somewhat. One of the fellows that lives in the next barracks was over to have some of my real American cheese sandwiches the other night. He went in my locker to get something, stopped dead and let out a yell. Then he asked me if the picture were "Elinor." They all kid me about My Darling Elinor. And when I smiled and said, "Yes," he complained that I'd been holding out on them. He called all the fellows over to see you. They all agreed that you were the best in the barracks, Mike saying, "I've seen a lot of beautiful women in the best places in New York and she's really the best." He was very sincere, too, and, of course, I agreed with him. Not all of the fellows had seen your picture, 'cuz I don't parade around with it, but they all have now, and I'm kinda glad you're two thousand miles away.

This is what bothers me sometimes. They say, "Didja get a letter from Elinor today? No? Well, there's a second looey in there now, Beat." You see they know that the Army school is there from reading the *Forum*. And when they read the *Fargo Forum* with that inflection in their voices, it's a riot. The *Forum* is quite silly when they read it—somebody's cattle stolen, a party at Mrs. Whozit's tonite, toxin tests for all cows, grain up two points. But we have fun.

Miss me. Wear my pin.

Yours, forever and ever,
Beat

January 2, 1943
evening

Dear Bunny,

This is something—one of the biggest thrills of my life. When we had missed our boat and had a few hours to wait, we walked down into the yards. There we saw a huge 7000 ton capacity ship. There were seven of us and we wondered just how we would get on to it. They're repairing it now. A ladder stretched up the port side about midships. Ladders hold no terrors for me and nerve gets a person a lot of places. So I walked in the yards, past workers and up the ladder. I waved at the others and they came aboard.

The first mate is a great guy and gave us the run of the ship. We saw everything we wanted to. Until a person gets aboard one, it just can't be imagined how huge they are. Take an hour to walk around it on the catwalks. They're insulating it, putting ¾ inch bulletproof steel on the shack and bridge, and putting all the lifeboats in shape. It's a ship that's a cinch to be going to Russia.

On that ship, with my hands on the 50 caliber machine gun, my eyes through the cross-sights— that's what I'll see more of soon. And the months will fly by then. Lots to do and keep one's mind off things.

We had a good laugh at this. Right outside the radio shack a lifeboat hangs. And a couple of rafts are poised to fall into the water at the touch of a lever!! The equipment is RCA and the shack is clean and decent. Sleeping quarters are next to the room. We all wished that we could be out on it, taking our first trip. It won't be long now until some of us will be . . .

It was just the biggest thrill to feel my feet on a deck, almost as if I belonged a little. And seeing just how I'd live. But a few good tastes of that life will probably leave me with an urge to find something else to do. As long as I'm on my own I can afford to gamble and try things out.

Beat

Back to School—Pelican Rapids

The New Year

"SEE YOU TOMORROW," IRMA called. Ginny and Elinor waved. A couple of other teachers chatted together as they passed by the girls on the sidewalk. Their laughs echoed in the wintry air.

"I think Mrs. Larson was nearly asleep when Mr. Shipp called her name," Elinor spoke softly. She didn't want to be overheard when talking about a co-worker.

"Did you see the way she jumped and then came around so quickly? And Mr. Five By Five? Poor Leonard. Christmas must've been hard on him." Ginny sounded sympathetic.

The leaden winter sun had listlessly dropped over the horizon during the faculty meeting. No one had noticed with the flickering fluorescent lights glowering over the room. When Elinor and Ginny had exited the building, the world went suddenly dark. The merest sliver of a moon rode the early January sky, offering no assistance on the darkened paths to the downtown cafés. The girls walked side-by-side, close, whispering. Their breath steamed in the cold January dark when they laughed. Their feet scrunched the snowy crystals underfoot.

Elinor and Ginny, Pelican's home economics teacher, left school together most days now. As was their habit, they stopped at the post office on their way to dinner at a downtown restaurant. Elinor loosened her gloves and unlocked the door on her mailbox. She looked around to see Ginny fiddling with her key. Elinor slipped Beat's latest letter and one from her mother into her purse. The girls tightened their scarves again and slid their fingers back into their woolen gloves.

Then they dashed into the Pelican Café where the single teachers who roomed in the town gathered most Mondays for supper. The window of the café which had celebrated the holidays with snowmen and stars and gingerbread boys taped to the glass, was now clear, polished to a shine, and waiting for the next theme, probably Valentine's Day in a few weeks.

Elinor shivered in the blast of warm restaurant air as they blew in the door. She blinked at the bright lights.

The waitress nodded their way as the girls entered. Her gait as she marched around the tables and booths in the café matched the rhythm of "G. I. Jive," which was playing in the jukebox. The smell of French fries hung thick in the air. The second waitress stood at the counter monitoring the malted milk blender, hips moving to the music as she watched the ingredients spin in a silver container.

Elinor and Ginny settled into a booth and arranged themselves on the wooden benches. They slipped out of their coat sleeves but wrapped their coats around their shoulders, prepared for the vagrant winter air that would sprint into the café every time the door opened.

The waitress, the one they saw most Monday nights, delivered their coffee. She didn't slap menus on the table or recite the special of the day. "Tomato tonight." That was it. The girls laughed at her good memory and each ordered their usual, a cup of soup.

While they waited for their meals, Elinor took Beat's envelope out of her purse. She unfolded the stationery and began to read. Ginny opened her envelope from Charlie.

Elinor looked around the café as she snapped her purse open and slipped out her glasses. She put them on and squinted at the stationery. Her eyes fell back on those lines in the text. She parsed the paragraph. She hadn't misread anything. She quickly tucked the letter back into its envelope.

"Everything okay, Bunny?" Ginny asked. "You look so glum."

"Kind of sad that Christmas is over, I guess."

"It's back to the old grind, Elinor," Ginny laughed.

"It sure is. Same old boring meetings. Back to grammar lessons and essays. I think the German students forgot every single thing we've covered." Elinor sipped her coffee.

"It'll come back again. To all of us, Bunny. Takes time." Ginny laughed and turned to her letter. Elinor opened the one from her mother, and the girls read a while in silence.

Ginny got a letter every single day. She wore an engagement ring with a diamond one entire quarter of a karat straddling a golden band. She directed wedding plans that were already well underway, summer nuptials. "Ooh, listen to this!" Ginny read from her letter.

Elinor leaned in. She couldn't help it. She smiled. Ginny's beau sounded like quite a guy. And Ginny trusted him completely.

"Now, what's the news from Gallups Island?" Ginny asked.

Elinor slid the letter from Beat out of its envelope. She scanned it to find something romantic. It read mostly as a diary entry. His adventures. Business. Not a thing about how pretty she was. Or how he wanted her. Though she knew he did. Well, she thought he did.

"Well, not much, I guess. He just writes about how happy he'll be when he's off to war. And when this war's all over, he'll find something else. He's so restless."

"Oh, Bunny," Ginny consoled. "I remember how excited Charlie was to enlist."

"But, listen to this, Ginny. Here's what Beat wrote: '. . . a few tastes of that life,'" Elinor looked up. "He means on the sea," she explained. She went on. "'. . . will probably leave me with an urge to find something else to do. As long as I'm on my own I can afford to gamble and try things out.'"

"He loves adventure, Elinor."

"I guess so." Elinor folded the letter and set it on the table. "Doesn't want to be weighed down, I guess."

The waitress delivered steaming bowls of tomato soup to the table, along with a small bowl of saltines.

Ginny went on, "Beat's restless. But so are you. He wants adventure, experiences—just like you do. So why don't you both get it out of your systems?"

Elinor leaned back into her seat and stared at the cars on the street outside the window. She did a quick inventory of her Christmas memories. A broken watch. Beat promised her a new one, but she had taken the broken one to Crescent Jewelers just in case. He was so broke that she had to loan him money for drinks. He tried so hard, and she appreciated the effort. But she remembered their quarrels, too. There were more than she wanted to admit. The last day and night felt like old times, though, as they warmed to each other again.

"There Are Such Things" played on the jukebox. The noises of the café seemed to disappear. What was it about Beat that made her so mixed up? Like those milkshakes spinning in the blender.

"C'mon. Let's eat." Ginny's voice snapped Elinor back to the present.

She put Beat's letter back into the envelope. She tasted the corner of a saltine. Her eyes met Ginny's. She turned to her soup.

She lifted the spoon and stared at it. Such a cheap old thing. Tin or something. "One day," she confided to Ginny, "I'm going to have nothing but silver—real silver—flatware. Diamonds and furs, too."

"That'll be the day," Ginny snickered.

The girls had a good laugh together. After that, they had nothing to talk about. Their spoons dipped rhythmically into their soup bowls, each girl in her own universe.

Ginny turned around in her seat to talk with one of the teachers in the next booth.

Elinor sighed. Beat was great fun, but she didn't want to be tied down anyway.

After the soup was gone, the crackers nibbled, and the coffee sipped, the girls bundled up to face the January cold again. They pulled their galoshes back over their heels. Then they buttoned their woolen coats, popped wool hats on their heads, pulled long wool scarves around and around their necks, and then slid their fingers into woolen gloves. Complaining about the routine they had to follow in winter, they exited the café.

"I'm sure he loves you," Ginny said. "In his own way." Her breath steamed around her mouth.

"Well, I'm not sure I care," Elinor responded. She shivered in the bitter January air. The sky reflected the snow, glittering with icy stars.

"Why don't you go to the Nettestad's and get to work on that muffler you're knitting for him?" Ginny pointed down the road to Elinor's place. "If you stay in Pelican this weekend, we can have a knitting club. I'm working on a sweater for Charlie. I don't know whether he'll need it. We don't yet know where in the world he'll be sent."

"A knitting club? I'll think about that." Elinor sighed. Ginny was always so cheerful.

The girls parted with a hug at the corner of Second Street, and each set off for her own room.

The wind chased around the corner, swirling some of the newest snow from the piles by the road into the air. Elinor held her coat closed, her shoulders pressed up around her ears.

She plodded down the sidewalk and across the street. The wind whipped at her coney coat. The moon sliver winked behind some clouds.

Beat's letter bothered her. He wanted adventure. But wasn't that what she was after, too? Ginny was right. Elinor stumbled as she crossed the last street. Those piles of snow by the curb were simply dangerous.

Tonight, before bedtime, she would write to Beat. She'd tell him about the men in her life. Her dates. Aubrey. She'd start with their meeting last weekend.

Beat could have all the adventures he imagined. He wasn't as important to her as he thought.

Back to School—Gallups Island
January 1942

Sunday (1-3)

My Bunny,

It's four o'clock back there and I can just imagine you're getting ready to go back to Pelican to teach. Not too happy to go, but just going. And the wolf patrol will be there to meet you. And I don't blame 'em a bit. Hope the prizefighter—what's his name again?—still has all that confidence. Mr. Five By Five? Say hello for me, hon?

How I'd love to hold you tonite—feel your hair and have you laughing—kiss me—then have you slap my face!!! My God, I'll never forget that swat!!! Almost floored me for the count. Hope you didn't mean it, darlin'.

Yours,
Beat

Gallups Island
Tuesday eve (1-5)

My sweet,

School is going along quite rapidly now. They pulled a class out early again. So there's something cookin' somewhere. In a few more short weeks we'll be in there, too. Today, we had a big thrill in class. Yeah. What a thrill. The chief was sending us regular mobile service traffic. Then he slipped in a tape with an SOS and sub warning on it. We really worked to get the information on that. Some day we'll hear those in a different spot! Hope I'm not on the sending end.

And you needn't worry about my weekend. I've got $2.70 and owe $12.00 yet, and we don't get paid again until the 20th. Guess I'll try to find something really "free" to go to.

Don't work too hard. And try to be polite to all the dates you turn down. Must hurry to chow now and then back for four hours of study. And you think you've got it tough. Try studying on your bed sometime with your feet off the floor, back bent, no light, smelly, stuffy and hot air. That's my study hall.

Hi to the folks and family. This doesn't include that persistent Aubrey!

I'll always love you, darling!

Beat

Thurs. (1-7)

My Sweetheart,

A proposal from Bob. And then you had the eyes of Texas upon you. Aubrey is his name? That noise you just heard was the applause you so richly deserve for the speech to the Texan with the cute drawl. I just looked at your letter and you did use "cute." And he's right. Fargo hasn't many girls like you.

We're really in the most interesting part of school so far. We're learning call signals. We have learned all distress, urgent and warning signals, etc. Here's a new one—SSS repeated three times means a sub is sighted but hasn't attacked yet. XXX means an attack is underway—a fight. SOS is sinking. That's when we run to the lifeboat, climb in, grab an oar and get away. When out of range of the sinking ship's suction, we grab the 50-watt emergency set and transmit SOSs and position. Radiomen are seldom lost, as they have learned how to take care of themselves. You can bet I'll know how!!

FLASH! Just raced over to the port windows. It's pitch dark, a natural thing. Toward Boston, over the ocean, we saw a lot of flashes, followed by explosions. Then a couple of planes flew over and there were a few depth charges about a mile out from the Island. Then a lot of powerful searchlights went on and the water was as bright as day. There were a few more explosions and then all quiet. Nobody knows what's up.

Maybe you'll read about it. It just adds to the excitement of this place.

Must clamber into bed soon, say a prayer for the boys on Guadalcanal.

Beat

⇒ ⇐

Bay State Club
January 10

My darling,

Another peaceful Sunday morning and missing you like mad.

I've got a call in now that should catch you at home—about 12:30 there. All the arrangements were made an hour ago before I checked my coat or had my coffee.

I love you, Bunny—
Beat

To Make a Phone Call

January 1943

IT TOOK A STRONG man to make a phone call. A guy with nerves of steel.

First Beat headed to the nearest hotel lobby, a place with a bank of phones for fellows like him. He walked through the crowds of servicemen and lined up at the desk. Sometimes, when he was lucky, the lines were just long. Most times they were out the door.

When he got to the front of the line, he registered with the desk clerk who kept a record of names, in order. He had to speak loudly, precisely, because of the noise of the crowd in the lobby. This desk clerk had to get the name straight to call it out later.

Some of the clerks were accurate with their predictions of how long it might be to get a call through. Two hours. Four hours. Once it was thirteen hours because a ship had docked and the sailors had lined up at the phones just before Beat's arrival. Other clerks just stabbed at a guess. A serviceman couldn't estimate how many names, how many pages, were on that list. The list to make a simple phone call.

If a guy needed change, he had to negotiate that at the desk. If they didn't have coins for the phones, he had to barter with the other servicemen standing around or dash to a nearby shop.

Then it was the wait. Beat looked around the lobby. Chances were there were no places left to sit for a while. If the desk clerk were accurate, there might be time to grab a bite to eat in a local dive, somewhere close by. But if a fellow missed his turn by being out of the lobby when his name was called? He'd have to start over again.

Mostly Beat bought a newspaper or magazine and leaned on a wall, reading. Or he took out his notepad to write a letter home. Sometimes he felt too restless even for that. Eventually he got a seat somewhere, maybe in the hotel restaurant if he had enough spare change to buy a Coke and a chair for a while. Aimless hours. He chatted with other servicemen and gathered the gossip about the war to pass to his buddies later.

He paced to try to work off some excess energy. He thought about what he wanted to tell her.

Then his name. He was sure he'd heard it. "Darrow Beaton." His chance at a phone! He would leap to the phone bank and check in. He grabbed the available black handset and said a quick prayer.

The operator would pipe up, "Number, sir?"

He'd yell, "Fargo North Dakota 6835." Then he'd take a breath.

"One moment, sir."

He'd drop a few coins into the slots at the top of the pay phone. He held the phone in a death grip and rehearsed his message while the operator dialed.

He heard the clicks in the phone line, each connecting to another city on the route. Chicago. Click. Minneapolis. Click. Fargo. Click.

He heard the phone ring. Her phone. In Fargo. He would try to calm himself. He swallowed. Cleared his throat.

The phone rang again. And again. He wanted to shout her name. She'd answer then. Seven rings. She can't hear the phone. Ten . . .

No answer.

He stared at the instrument in his hand for a moment. Cursed.

Had the operator dialed her number right? He'd hang up the phone and leave the hotel. He'd stride up and down the main drag, searching for the nearest bar where he would order a few drinks to settle his nerves.

Later he'd simply write, "Tried to call you last night."

Telephone Center, Boston Common, Boston, Massachusetts, where operators help service men make their telephone calls. The center is operated by the New England Tel. and Tel. Co. with the cooperation of the USO-Greater Boston Soldiers' and Sailors' Committee.

Telephone Center postcard

Be Good

January 1943

Sunday again from the **Bay State Club**

My Bunny,

No one was home, so I had to be satisfied just to think that I had tried to call you. The call went through about one o'clock Fargo time, but they told me that no one answered. You're probably in Pelican by now. Maybe you're writing to me right now. If only I could be certain of reaching you at Nettestad's right now, I would call.

I just got back from seeing Woody Herman, the player of blues music. The program is tops and from here they go to Hollywood to make a movie or two. Remember the time in Chicago when we saw Eddie Duchin? They had one number when the lights were turned low, bluish? They played "Stardust" in just such a setting tonight. I was in such a dream thinking of you beside me that I almost took Ed's hand to hold! And what would he have thought!!

As Ed and I go down the busy streets here,

we often see some pretty nice gals. And Ed always says, "Hmmm." Other compliments follow. Then I tell him over and over that he'll never tempt me from the straight and narrow. None can compare to my Bunny. He grins and agrees with me 'cuz he's seen your picture. And he just kids me about stepping out. He'd be the first one to be mad at me if I should. He's dancing now, having his kind of enjoyment. He suggested as we entered this place, "I'll be dancing for a while, so you write Elinor."

Guess what, hon? My watch just stopped on me all of a sudden. Just won't run. So I'm sending it to Mom to have her get it fixed for me.

Tonite we're to sleep at the Milk Street Police Station again—just a couple of bums, eh, honey? They have a very clean place, though, and wake us in time to walk the four or five blocks to India Wharf. It's free. What more could a sailor want?

My regards to Mick, the folks, Ginny, the team, and all of 'em back there in the West.

And all my love to you, darling,
Forever and ever,
Beat

Monday eve (1/11)

Honey,

As you say in your letter, during the five months we were apart, we both sometimes wondered if it were really love. And at other times—a picture, a letter, music, or some little thing meant everything. We settled things during my leave. There are no limits to my love now, no wondering if I'm going to be a sucker and hurt. You know that until these doubts are gone, there can't be a real—a complete—love. I believe in war marriages. Especially ours!!

You mention that Ginny was quite jealous of the nine-page booklet, but that you're quite jealous of her day-by-day letters. I'm sorry, darling, but this school has to come first so many nights a week. Not that I wouldn't like to write you. If I had written to you all those times when I thought about it, I wouldn't be in the upper 10-15 of this class. In fact the upper seven that have failed only one test. Maybe Ginny's guy isn't as busy as I am. Probably.

March is creeping up on us, sweets. We have so much to look forward to.

Yours forever,
Beat

Jan. 14 (Thursday)

That muffler will come in quite handy, darling—
and every time it keeps me warm, I'll think of
how warm you make me. Right now the wind goes
in the open part of my coat. I've got that as
a good reason for not going to Boston on my
leaves. The scarf measurements sound right to
me, so I hope the four-inch stretches go by
pleasantly.

⟫   ⟪

Sat. aft. (1-16)

My hon,

All afternoon we've been talking and listening
to recorded music on the radio. Benny Goodman
is on now and Peggy Lee is singing "On the
Sunny Side of the Street." We've talked radio,
women, marriage, music, etc. We heard your
Ella Fitzgerald earlier this afternoon. Now
Peggy sings "Why Don't You Do Right?" Brady and
Hittson just groan and jump all over the place,
and Hittson just remarked for my benefit, "You'd
never think anybody like that could come from
SOUTH Dakota." They know that I'm from North
Dakota. It usually ends up in a wrestling match.
Right now, I'm too interested in the music and
not the remarks of these swing addicts.
    All the time you're reading this you should
be eating your dinner. Or maybe you don't get
your mail on the way to dinner any more? Anyway,

you'd better stop and eat sompin' now just in case you plan to read this at one sitting!

Yours forever,
Beat

❧   ❦

Thursday, Jan. 21

My sweet,

We razz the Bostonians about their famous winters. The radio last night told of -51° in Minnesota!! Our weather up to a week ago was rain and fog—freezing in an icy coat on everything. Now we have some good gales and cold weather, but it's nothing like North Dakota. But, darling, the muffler will keep me warm. How's the knitting coming?

Your weekend sounded O.K. Maybe Aubrey is too persistent, but I won't worry about it as long as you tell me all about it. About Walt—well, there just isn't anything to say, darling, that you don't know. You quote him as saying that I "couldn't appreciate you enough." You'll have to decide that one for yourself.

Hope your play was a lot of fun for you. The parents' party sounded as if it had been. Card playing is all right, but, as you say, it is quite boring most of the time. While here, the most fun I get from cards is watching the fellows play. They win and lose real money every night for a week after payday.

Tell me just what the latest clinic appointments

have told you. Let's try keeping me up to date. You know, Bunny, I'm very much interested in all of that business. The doc's orders for ten hours sleep a night sounds like good common sense. Now all you have to do is learn how to get to bed on time. Right?

If you think of me every time you look at your watch, you'll still not think of me as often as I think of you—'tis all the time that we're not studying and a lot of the time when I'm supposed to be studying!

Yours, forever,
Beat

Sat. aft.

My darling,

Jim Smith, a very quiet and smart fellow, lived in San Diego before coming here. When talking of home, he says that it has gone to the dogs since the war started. The town has become quite notorious because of the various training camps near there—Marines, Navy base, Merchant Marine and Army—yes, and Coast Guard. What makes the town a little worse is the number of defense workers. Places to live are hard to find and quite high. That's just what he says, and it makes not too much difference whether or not you go there this summer—just as long as I know where you are and can get to you.

Last week I got two big boxes of food—from my sister in Washington and from home. So, as I write you, I'm eating gingersnaps. As soon as I rattled the paper, the five fellows in the card game at the other end of the barracks were here to get some.

Chow will blow soon and I hope 'tis good. We had cocoa last night!! And they have meatless Tuesday so that the services will have enough meat. Now the Army, Navy and this place also have meatless days. Fish. And none of us like this Eastern stuff. But at least we're sure of not getting any of this Boston horsemeat. We have had it a couple of times. It's tough!

Suppose Walt will be seeing you soon—this week, hmmm. I know you're old friends and all. All I ask is that you don't make any more of these "old friends." How about that?

The big guns are practicing again on the forts around us. We watch the huge spouts they make out in the ocean. This afternoon a target boat went back and forth about a half mile from our barracks windows. We watched machine guns and 3-inch guns pepper it. Every once in a while they open up with ack-ack guns. Just now two big shells were shot out. They shake our building a couple of inches. One of the chiefs who was torpedoed at Murmansk commented, "You guys'll get all of that you want some day. Just pay attention to radio now." What a future!

My hair is grown out so that I can comb it.

Love me as I love you,
Beat

Sunday eve.

Darling,

Tiger, a friend from Detroit, is spending his last night on the Island. The fellows got up a party. I contributed a pound of American cheese, a box of gingersnaps, a loaf of bread, a jar of peanut butter, and everybody pitched in with other food. Tiger just couldn't get this stuff. We'll really miss that Polack.

We're going to be the senior platoon beginning a week from today. In the dim, dark past I remember some of the fellows that were my bosses. They gave me many valuable tips, the essence of which is just plain "work, work, and work." That's what I'll tell my boys, too, and hope they do it.

You're in Pelican now after seeing the folks again. The weekend was probably quite eventful and pleasant for you. Tonight I'm blue—yes, a whole lot. Seems as if the time we've been apart has been years instead of weeks. The leave just made me sure that we are meant for each other forever, and now we can't be together.

Your guy loves you,
Beat

Envelope to Pelican Rapids

Wed.

My darling,

The superintendent bit our class hard today. But the hardest to take is Brady's dis-enrollment. Now, you can see that they're playing for keeps here. Brady's a fellow that lets little things slip, forgets small responsibilities. He and the others got quite a speech on this and were told that the fellows they put out of here have to be dependable to the nth degree. One mistake may mean losing many lives; one or more slips and a ruined campaign. He gave me his set of notes. They're perfect. Add them to mine and I have the best notes in the barracks. We'll miss these fellows and profit by their example.

My receiver is in great shape. For a while after fixing it, I couldn't get a sound out of it. By experimenting, etc. I found a blocked grid. Now I've got a real set and by hooking up to a loud speaker, I get a lot of volume on my programs.

The draft board sent me my 2-B classification. Now I'm set for six more months and after that will be permanently 2-B.

Our platoon is in the middle of an epidemic of measles. About 15 fellows have had them in the last week. Last night four fellows entered sick bay. Hope I'm immune!

Tonite I've got to study antennas, wave lengths, procedure, and practice sending. When I finish studying, I'll take a shower and relax for about fifteen minutes before taps, answering questions on detectors.

I love you, darling,
Beat

＊＊　＊＊

January 30, Sat. afternoon

My darling,

Not many of us stayed aboard this weekend, so we'll probably get a lot of sleep. There's really nothing in town for me except a headache on Sunday morning. And you were wondering at Xmas if I were going to be an ol' drunk some day!

My, my, sweets. Fact is that the stuff seems to be the last desire of my life except when with some fellows once in a while. We like to sit in a nice place, have one or two and talk. You needn't think that Beat will ever become an habitual!

Last night we were listening to Balboa, South America, on our receivers. They have a regular BAMS broadcast at 11:00 GMT, 7:00 our time. Three of us had it fairly well tuned to their press and picked up all the sub news. Besides SOS, XXX and SSS calls, we had a really funny one. A ship off the coast of Brazil had sent in an SSS—sub sighted. The sub had fired 3 torpedoes at this ship from about 1000 yards—point blank range—and had missed with all of them! Then it came up all the way, followed the ship, and apparently in disgust submerged and went away. Of course, all the fellows in the watch standing room got quite a bang out of that.

Tonight I picked up Bogota, Columbia, an Argentine station, a Swedish station, one from Hawaii and many BAMS broadcasts.

Hope you're being good as I am on this Saturday night. You owe me a letter, Bunny!! In fact, one or two. C'mon and catch up! My best to the family, Ginny and the team.

Love,
Beat

January 31

Dearest Darling,

This morning I went to Catholic mass with the fellows here. Our sermons always tell of the perils of the deep, warn of sins. This morning's was a very vivid one. As I knelt there, I had all my future before me, and it's going to be good if I do everything right.

The fellows are back from town, the ones that didn't have enough money to stay another night. And they razz me about writing you like this. They tell of this or that "deal" they had last night and say, "Beat, you're wasting away while she isn't wasting time at all." They bring up the fact, as the priest did, that we'll soon be at sea with nothing to do but wait for port (or one of those new super subs to get us). Sometimes after you mention going out with Walt or someone, I wonder a little if they're not just a bit right.

Yours, forever,
Beat

⇒   ⇐

Monday eve
(2-1-43)

My sweets,

Hope to get a letter from you tonight. The mail hasn't come through yet 'cuz of—a military secret. But the nets were closed for most of the day after a—limped in pretty well crippled. We saw her and predicted she would sink before she reached the nets, but she went on into the harbor.

I just today got some pictures from home. Notice, please, the picture under my arm. At the time I was on my way downtown Fargo and then to "my girl's." Remember that day? You wrote, "I love you, Beat" on that picture. As I write this, I'm looking every now and then at that same picture and remembering the times we spent together. Seems a long time ago now as I sit on this bunk, the fellows talking, radios playing and study piled up ahead of me.

Beat with photo under his arm

Must close now to go watch standing. I'll write more if your letter comes, right after a very warm shower. Here's hoping the evening ends well.

For now, bye, sweets,
Yours,
Beat

9:40 NO LUCK. Guess I'll forget to look for news until Thursday or later.

February 3 (Wed.)

My darling,

You should have seen me this morning, darling.
We had more instructions in the rubber suits.
They're compulsory equipment now. We had races
today, timing how long it takes us to get in
them. They're a lot tougher to handle than
regular clothes! We learn a lot of tricks that
save seconds—and probably lives someday.

   Bob Dodd and your old pal, Bob Olson, really
got a spread in last Sunday's *Fargo Forum*. They
deserve it for all they're doing. Makes my feet
itch—I need to get into the action, too.

   Three more fellows are leaving tomorrow,
mostly because they can't get code. Our bunch is
cut down a whole lot now. All of us that remain
dig into the Q and A whenever we have a spare
moment. Did I mention that eleven of us were
all set to gain two weeks on our class—move to
R-18? We finally let sentiment stop us. Most of
our friends are here. So we voted to stay.

I love you, darling,

Beat

Thursday (2-4)

My darling Elinor, alias the "ogre,"

My, my, you really gave the class a going over. Now you might know how one of our chiefs feels when he passes ten or fifteen out of a class of seventy or more. But, then, they don't have to worry about the failures crying on their desks.

Say! That muffler really seems to be dragging, darling. A little here and there and a thought of me while working and soon Beat will have it to remember my sweets every time I feel it. But don't let it interfere with your work, hon.

You said in your letter that it seemed that I didn't like the idea of your going to San Diego. I'm not exactly for it, but you've certainly got every right in the world to do what you want. My description of the place is the one a fellow that lived there gave me. I passed it on for reference material for you.

This weekend I'm going into Boston, mostly for a decent haircut. Maybe I'll look up some things for my officer's uniform. Just a weekend to lose a little energy by walking, losing some sleep and running around. As for drinking, I won't be doing any—positively. On Sunday I'll catch a boat back to the Island and dig out my books.

All yours,
Beat

Sat. 1:00 A.M.

My Sweet,

I saw Henry Busse and his orchestra about six o'clock to seven thirty—and I must not forget that Sally Rand was in the show—bubble and fan dances and all (she stinks). The music was good and everything was swell.

Tonite we ended up at the Tic Toc. It's a really classy joint—as classy as Boston has. Eddie Thurman's all girl orchestra was there and gave a coast-to-coast broadcast while we listened. All night I had three drinks and a heck of a lot of fun. The girls (four of them) are from Wellesley. They wonder how I can stay on the Island for a month with Boston at my disposal.

I still don't know what you did last weekend, darling, but I'm trusting to fate that you didn't see Walt. If you did, you and Mick and the gang probably had a little celebration of your own, a good-bye party. Probably Mickey has gone to the West Coast.

Last Saturday—the whole weekend—I sat on the Island wondering what you were doing. Maybe you were out with Walt. I'd kick that thought out of my mind, then remember that you two had gone out together before—when I was away. He always does his best to build me up (##@S X) and it kinda gets a guy. But then what has Beat got to offer from this long a distance? Only my love and faithfulness and that is not always enough, I know.

Today we had seven photos taken for passports,

seamen's papers, insurance, etc. So you see that we're on the verge of sompin' again! They told us to go ashore today and have the photos in Monday morning. We just obey them and hope for the best.

Right now, I feel a whole lot better for telling just what I've been thinking. We always tell each other all and try to understand. No matter what happens, Beat will always be that way. Must get a few hours of sleep, darling.

G'nite—
Beat

Wed. (February 10)

My darling,

After last weekend's bustle and anticipation, we were informed Monday that we will graduate near the end of March. The last three weeks that we spend here will be devoted to school, shipboard, and government exams. You see that we will be busy.

I'm on a committee of six in charge of all "relationships," money, etc. for our class banquet. Our platoon split wide open—two real cliques—a while back. I'm the guy that's got to get each side to give in to the other. Guess they think I'm not prejudiced. Hence, the "relationships." We'll have a big party and a lot of fun if we can get these two outfits together. Let's hope, hmmm?

My watch has been on the bum for some time. Last Saturday I sent it home for repairing—pretty soon we'll both be telling the time of day! I'm so glad that your watch runs all right now.

Monday I climbed into my rubber suit in 37 seconds. By the time we leave we're supposed to do it in 30. We have a lot of fun laughing at each other as we hurry. Such remarks as, "The water's up to your knees," "the lifeboat is pulling away," "you're a dead duck now" go flying around. The suits make a fellow look like a man from another world, but they save a lot of lives.

Time seems to drag now but by keeping myself

busy, I forget it. We'll be together in a few weeks now, honey. Be mine as I'm yours.

I love you, Bunny,
Beat

⇒   ⇐

Thursday evening 1615
February 11, 1943

My sweets,

We've had some inspectors from Washington here the last two days. You should see the spreads they impress them with—chicken, turkey, salads, cocoa, etc.!! How these new 'boots' will be let down when the inspectors leave!

This weekend I'm on a real detail. I've got to look up some deals for the banquet. They've piled a lot of work on me 'cuz I just "waste" my weekends anyway, they say! Jan Savitt's and John Kirby's orchestras will be at the RKO, real jam sessions. That's the way I'll spend Saturday night. Then out here for some studying. Wonder what you'll be doing.

I love you, as always,
Beat

Friday evening
2/12/43

My darling,

Probably you won't be able to appreciate this type of fun 'cuz you've never met a real bunch of rebels. Today is Lincoln's birthday. We Yankees have been singing "Happy Birthday, Dear Abe" all day. The boys with the drawl are darn mad. So, you see, the Civil War is still being fought.

You'd be surprised how little we think of home now. Guess we're just ol' servicemen now, taking what comes and liking it. They keep us busy most of the time, and, darling, I'm actually happy when I'm learning radio, code etc. It is all leading to the day that I'll be on my way across. And that's something that I've wanted to do ever since seeing both oceans and most of the country.

Feels good to get out once in a while, doesn't it? You should do it once in a while. Relax and have some fun. I trust you and know you'll be good. All I ask is that I hear of the times you go out and a few laughs about 'em. Have you been telling me all, sweets? (Go ahead. Smile.)

I love you, Bunny,
Beat

Bay State Club
Sunday 2/14

My darling Frenchy—

Now I must tell you about my weekend. You've seen these agencies in movies—people sitting on benches, waiting for jobs, etc. The places we were at were exactly like that. Such a mob of people! We went into private offices and talked to the fellow that books the shows. We've got a real stag show lined up for the party. Piano player for the whole evening, dinner time and all. A good M.C., a fellow with a lot of jokes. Then we have three gals and they guarantee to give the boys a darn good show. Altogether it will run over $100.00. But that's what the guys want.

The various times that I've been in the Cave, etc. I've talked to bartenders, bouncers, parts of the act and all. All we know is first names but we act like old buddies sometimes. The last place I went last eve was the Cave. Outside the door was a line waiting for people to leave. I walked by them—a gob! They kidded me, "Where do you think you're going, sailor? They're filled up." At the door was a husky Swedish fellow. He saw me, opened the door and said that Jackie was in the dressing room, just finished his act. This Jack is the midget strongman—too short to get in the Navy. So I ended the evening in there. I like to remember the look of amazement on that line of gold braid and their debutante dates.

This afternoon I'll be on the Island and

I'll really give the Q and A book a beating. My income tax is in the way, something to settle, so I wrote Interstate Seed to see how much I made (and spent).

The first thing I'll do when I go aboard today is take your picture out, feast my eyes, and plant it on top of my locker. Honey, the studying goes quite easily with you to look at when I want to relax.

Yours, always,
Beat

Love

Valentine's Day 1943

LATE SUNDAY AFTERNOON, WHEN she returned to Pelican after a weekend in Fargo, Elinor discovered a few surprises. Valentine cards crowded her box at the post office. And florist-wrapped vases full of flowers waited for her at her bedroom door at the Nettestad's.

Elinor laughed aloud as she unwrapped the flowers and filled the vases with fresh water. She opened each envelope and savored each message.

Then she arranged the valentine cards (from Bob, Dale, and Clarence) right next to the dozen red roses from Johnny. From Leonard, the persistent "Mr. Five By Five," there was a Shakespearean verse along with a vase of bright spring flowers. He'd smirk at her tomorrow at the faculty meeting, cagey Casanova, anticipating her thanks. And what a surprise! Even Walt had sent a bouquet of carnations and daisies. She had brought the heart-shaped box of chocolates from Aubrey back from Fargo with her.

Elinor arranged the valentine offerings on her dressing table. She stood back, appraised the grouping, and shook her head. She tried moving the roses to the back of the display but decided, when taking the long view, to return them to the front. She thought about all these "old friends." She wondered what they were doing on this Valentine's Day.

Ginny stopped over, as they had arranged, to pick Elinor up for supper. "Charlie sent me a romantic card," she announced, waving the envelope before she spotted Elinor's collection of flowers and cards. "You got so many!" Ginny exclaimed as she stuck her nose into the roses. "Mmmm. Wonderful."

Elinor grinned. "Try a chocolate." She opened the box. Her men had remembered her. She giggled, then sobered. "What would Valentine's Day be like without the war?" she wondered aloud.

"Perhaps all your men would've been around, bumping into each other awkwardly at the Nettestad's door," Ginny smiled. She removed her winter coat and threw it on Elinor's bed.

The girls reminisced about the old days when there was no war. Couples could see each other on Valentine's Day, go for a Coke, or dinner and a movie. Was there ever such a time?

"I would love to have a Valentine's Day again with Charlie," she mused as she reached into the box of candy. "We had so much fun before he enlisted. What if he doesn't return from this war? Or if he's badly injured?"

"Don't worry, Ginny. He'll be back and life will return to normal. You'll see."

Ginny shook her head. "I hate this war. It's ruining all our fun." She settled herself in the wooden chair in the corner.

Elinor finished getting ready at the dressing table. She moved her roses to the side, then squinted into the mirror past the rest of the flora to see Ginny's reflection. "I'll be ready in a jiff," she said.

"You have so many boyfriends," Ginny sighed. "Did you know? Charlie's my first real boyfriend. We met in college."

"And in June you'll be married. Exciting!" Elinor brushed her hair back behind her ears. She set the brush on the dressing table.

Ginny nodded. "He thinks he'll have a short leave then. I hope it all works out."

"You'll never have to teach again, Ginny." Elinor powdered her nose.

"That's for sure. I'm worried, though, Elinor. Do you know what I mean?" Ginny averted her eyes. "The wedding night. I'm not experienced."

Elinor looked at Ginny's reflection in the mirror. "Well, you're not expected to be. Experienced, I mean. Only men can get experience. You know how it is."

Ginny looked up. "Are you? I mean, have you ever . . .?"

Elinor laughed. "Oh, Ginny, think about it. Wouldn't it be something if a gal could experiment a little beforehand . . . try 'things' out? If a guy can, why not a gal?"

"A gal could get pregnant."

"Maybe." Elinor turned from her mirror to look at her friend. "Not me. I can't carry a child. My health, you know."

"Yeah. You spend a lot of time in the hospital. Or home in bed."

"Anyway, I guess I'm like a guy. They can't get pregnant either."

Ginny laughed.

Elinor turned back to the mirror. She applied a layer of Courage, her red, red lipstick. Then she rubbed her lips together front to back and side to side.

"I should think about this. Trying things out. I could experiment, I suppose." Elinor turned toward Ginny. "Now don't you tell anyone I even said that," she laughed.

"Oh, I wouldn't. My lips are sealed, Elinor." Ginny sighed. "Do you think you'll marry some day?"

Elinor looked closely into her mirror. She blotted her red lipstick with a single square of toilet tissue. She kept a stack of them in the only drawer of her dressing table. "Maybe one day I'll be married. Right now I don't want to be."

She turned back to Ginny. "You know, I don't think I'd make a good housewife at all. Can't have children. Anyway, I want to get around and not tie myself down."

Elinor smiled, staring at the floor. A faraway look glazed her eyes. She grimaced as she raised her eyes to Ginny.

"My prospects aren't too great, either. Walter? He just wants a cook. He'd be a cheap husband. And you know I'm more about glamour." Elinor stood up, reached her right hand to the back of her head, smiled and raised her eyebrows at Ginny while she swiveled her hips.

The girls laughed.

"I'm stalling with Walt." Elinor sat down again. "Johnny just thinks the world of me. But he's a teacher. Sweet, but predictable. Not a lot of excitement in that quarter.

"Beat's fun, and he says he wants to marry me, but my family . . . And, anyway, he has all these other adventures planned. On the world's seas, I guess. And they don't include me."

Ginny stood up and walked over to the bed. She picked up her coat. "Gee, Elinor . . ."

Elinor took a few last swipes at her hair. "Anyway, I'd like to have adventures, too. I just can't figure out what girls can do. Without being seen as naughty, I mean. Or overpowering somehow."

Ginny nodded.

"Maybe the WACs or the WAVEs are for me. I need to check them out after this school year is over," Elinor went on.

Ginny snapped her purse open. She dug out her lipstick and applied a bit, using the compact she kept in the zippered pocket.

"Things are changing in this war. I may get my chance," Elinor continued. She set her hairbrush down. "The Fates haven't decided what to do with me yet."

"What's your plan?"

"Can a gal have a plan? Aren't The Fates in charge? Clotho spins the thread of life, and Atropos cuts it eventually. But Lachesis plans a person's destiny. She's the one I'm having trouble with. I don't want to sit around waiting for her any more."

Ginny nodded. "But . . ."

"Lachesis gives the fun to the men, darn it all. And why," Elinor continued, "do you think these female Fates can't think up something more adventuresome for us women?"

Ginny shook her head. "I have no idea."

"There must be something I can do to shape my own destiny!" Elinor stood at the mirror. "This war isn't helping either."

"It's the times we live in," Ginny offered.

"I want to wander around a bit after the war—if this war ever ends— and see what's going on out there." Elinor moved the vase of roses to the back again on the dressing table, and walked to the door to grab her coat from the hook. "There's a big world out there somewhere."

"But I thought good girls, preachers' girls, didn't . . ." Ginny paused and took a breath. "Wander, I mean."

The girls leaned in toward each other, eyes locked.

"Girls don't even like sex when they're married, I've heard." Ginny tittered.

Elinor slid her arms into the lined sleeves of her prized coney coat, then pulled a scarf from one pocket and bundled it around her neck. The other pocket held her tam.

"I think I might be frigid, Elinor, but I don't know how to tell. I've never done that with a boy. And it's just a few months before we're married." Ginny stood up to put on her coat, too. "What if it doesn't work with Charlie?"

"Well, you won't see Charlie until the wedding anyway. You won't have a chance to experiment. Don't fret. I think you'll be surprised." Elinor hugged her friend.

"I have to check over some tests tonight," Elinor eyed the stack in the corner on the floor. "I suppose we'd better get going. I wonder who else will be stuck spending Valentine's Day at the Pelican Café."

"Leonard, probably."

The girls laughed.

Ginny continued, "Say, how about next weekend? We could have the first meeting of our knitting club. Are you staying in Pelican?" She was nearly finished with Charlie's sweater.

"I've given up on Beat's muffler," Elinor admitted. And she was glad. Why should she go out of her way? He hadn't even remembered her on Valentine's Day.

The girls grabbed their purses and pulled the straps over their shoulders. Elinor opened the bedroom door, and the two of them headed downstairs where they slipped into their galoshes and then their gloves. Exiting from the warm front hall, they faced their frigid world.

Anxious to Get Moving

February 1943

Wed. 4:45

My darling,

Your letter of last Sunday arrived, and I feel
so like a heel! But usually a heel has some way
to excuse himself. Maybe I can excuse just a
wee bit of it, sweets. Darling, we are so very
busy now. Try to understand this. It's not a
line at all. We have school all day. Must go
to night classes on D/Fs [direction finders] now
and my detail as one of the senior platoon is
to proctor a hundred men in a code room after
night class. All my spare hours such as this are
spent in studying. I want to make a real success
of this work. I'm honestly sorry, darling.

   About the Valentine. Doggone it, darling. I
wanted to call and all but things just didn't
work out. Another thing, darling, is that every
little thing I've been and will be doing has
to be rationed. We've got so many things to
buy—uniforms, emblems, banquet, seaman's paper,
passports, etc. I see my way to getting a ticket

home and a good vacation with you. Beat's not in the $500.00 a month bracket yet! It's an awful excuse, and I realize it now, but I'd much rather buy the flowers for you when I'm home. It just gripes me, hon, not having sent a valentine to you. But, I tell you what. At the first time we get together, I'll give you a great big hug and kiss to make up for it. All right? I think so.

The WACs and WAVEs? I feel that there are a lot of men just sitting around doing nothing, so why should women have to get into a war as yet? I know how you must feel at times. It made me feel so "no good" at times. But let me do all the war work for both of us.

As I mentioned before, we are busy. The government men looked us up, took new fingerprints, pictures, etc. The reason is that we are pushing just a lot harder than former classes on certain new subjects—all more or less new and secret developments. That's about all I can say about it. If we're sunk, we just scuttle the equipment if we have it on our ships. It's a cinch we could never build one. And don't say a thing about all this even though it's not important sounding to you. O.K.?

Yours, always,
Beat

Thurs. eve

My sweet,

A great day! My dress blue officer's uniform is here. I pick it up tonite. My clothing allowance is gone and probably a chunk of my next check, but it's sure worth every bit of it!! I'm only going to be in Boston once more before going up for my license and for the banquet this coming Friday eve, the 26th.

The muffler is nothing to feel so badly about. The weather is pretty swell here and, anyway, I'd never really planned too heavily on it. I'll be looking forward to seeing your blue and white sweater—form fit, I hope!

G'nite,
I love you so,
Yours,
Beat

Sat. aft.

My Bunny,

A big thrill for me—putting on a real shirt, clean and white. It made me feel shivery all over, 'cuz it was such a decided change from these heavy, woolen blues. I'm looking forward to inspections from now on 'cuz I can put on the shirts.

 We have our party this coming Friday evening. The fellows will really kid me. They've been trying to line up dates for me, just to hear me laugh and wise off to them about the best woman in the world back home. So I'll be thinking of you, wishing you were here so that we could go out together as the other fellows and their girls will. But such is my luck, hmmm.

Yours always,
Beat

Sunday eve (2-21)

Sweets,

A really wonderful day! We sat on the dock all morning and afternoon, Bob Mirvish and I, without our shirts. They'll never be able to say New England has tough weather to me any more. We felt so good that studying was fun. After concentrating for a half hour or so, we'd talk about shipping out—a great life, just looking for a bird, a stray ripple, sitting in the sun with the phones on, waiting for land to come into sight. We had some good laughs out of it. He is a fellow that plans to be a novelist some day. He joined this service to get material and have radio to pull him along a few years.

One night as I lay in my bunk after taps, I began to think of all we've learned here. Education. A funny word but so darn vital and important in all of our lives. Thinking of you and your work, I thought to myself, "Does Elinor realize the job she's doing?" You have to think of the whole of the world to realize just how we have come forward in the past centuries. And you're doing your part to keep up that level of intelligence and culture. Ever think of it that way? I think you're doing such a swell job of it. I realize, too, that it's very hard work.

Did you ever stop to think just what the country and world will be like after the war? From the economics that I've studied, I think it over and shudder. What a turmoil it will be when all the guys go back to fight for jobs, armed with ratings as mechanics, machinists, pilots, radiomen, etc. What I wouldn't give for a college degree!

The new *Lexington* launched a couple of months ago and fitted near here. Went out the other day. She's a beauty and huge. One can't imagine how large until it's seen. We left classes for a while to watch her go through the channel. The old Navy chiefs wanted to be on her. They looked so darn lonesome. But age has them beat out of active service.

Going to drop to sleep soon.

Pleasant dreams, Bunny.
Beat

Tuesday eve (2-23)

M' sweet,

The 164th really did grand work, didn't they? Guadalcanal is ours. And to think that those guys are from North Dakota! Mickey must be so proud of Bob now. Makes me feel so darn left out. I hope some day soon that I can be a real vet, through some good action.

Now it isn't as it was six or seven months ago. We really are close to that day when we'll be on a ship and on a constant alert for subs and planes. They say fellows with poor nerves have to take a long rest after a trip. As we say here, "It couldn't be any worse than worrying about the exams!!" So I know I'll be all right. Still no sign of "nerves."

We've got a couple of the French warships here in Boston. They seem to be on training runs or calibrating the D/Fs. Don't quote me on this but watch the European front soon. Just what we've seen lately corresponds to what happened before Africa's invasion. Hope I make it in time.

G'nite, my darling. Think of me this Friday eve. I'll always love you and be

All yours,
Beat

Sat. evening (2-27)

My darling,

Our party is over—and how I feel! It would take me forever to tell you of all the laughs and fun that we had but I'll tell you of the most important things.

The officers and all of us were feeling darn good as we had a regular smoker meeting for an hour prior to the dinner. There was a bar set up—all kinds of liquor. The braids are swell guys. They acted just like one of us. Shop talk didn't last long. We had them telling all about their lives and their work on the Island. We got so many new things from them in the way of things to come for Gallups Island—real stuff to talk about!!

You'll like this, honey. We picked up six of the French sailors from the *Fantasque*, one of the French ships that ran out of Europe. The guys had a wonderful time as we have three fellows who speak French fluently. When asked for their home addresses, they said with a sad look, "What address? We have no home, no family, no country. We don't know if anything is left there." They sang songs for us. We all sang the French national anthem. They'll never forget the way we brought them in and entertained them. The Boston papers covered our party as did the W.S.A. from Washington and lots of pictures were taken.

The whole evening went along through dinner and the floorshow with a spirit that only a group of fellows can have—just spontaneous all the way. The officers' speeches were riots. They gave us a big hand for the party. They all agreed that we did know how to put on a party.

Ed and I went to the Cave for a few more drinks. That's when we ended the evening—but well. We got into an argument with a couple of Navy guys, and before I knew what was happening, this guy lays one on the left side of my face. Ed says he hopes he never sees me get that mean again. Guess I really got mad, 'cuz the next thing I remember is sitting on him, beating his head on the sidewalk. A crowd gathered, as we were on Tremont Street, one of the main streets. We didn't want to get in trouble with the Shore Patrol. So Ed and I ran for a while and then to bed. But this morning my face and eye were swollen way up. Really makes me look cute! Oh, yeah. What a party, as I said before!

We came back on the early boat and slept in as most of the class is AWOL. That's enough of Boston for me!! All we do is study and get out of here now. This study has started to work on us. Johnny was heard talking in his sleep the other night, reciting code and saying, "Little white men every place didahdidahdidah."

Darling, I came home prejudiced last time, but it wasn't really my fault at all. You wrote me twice in the last month and a half before I came—one only a note saying that you'd meet me. You'd been out with some of the guys. We just had a little misunderstanding, but it came out all right.

Tomorrow's the last day of February. Mmmm.

We'll be together so soon, now. There won't be any studies to worry about. We'll just relax and have that long talk you mentioned in your last letter.

Be mine, darling,
Beat

Sunday

Darling,

I'm as happy as can be—fat lip, black eye, and all! Just realizing that we'll be together so darn soon—really together. Oh, darling. I'm so darn anxious to get through here and come home to see you. We'll play with that wildcat your family loves so much, have coffee, go to shows, go to the Comstock and sit at our favorite little table in the corner. I'd like very much to meet Ginny and the gang at Pelican.

We'll be cramming every night this week, just as you probably had to do last week. My, but they must expect a lot from you—six weeks tests, rationing, and regular school work, too. But I hope that you and Ginny found time for that long talk she wanted. As you said, and I agree, she must be quite a gal.

We're having a big storm today. After writing you this afternoon, I went down to the canteen. We got down there and found one of the munitions barges on the beach! If it had gone up, there just wouldn't be any Gallups Island tonight!! All the boats were held up until it calmed down some.

We're all going to take a shower and shave and listen to "Inner Sanctum" in tonight's blackout. Too bad we couldn't spend this blackout together. But such is war, darlin'.

Yours,
Beat

Saturday, March 8

My sweets,

Going to take some time off from the studying.
What a wonderful grind this is! Most of the
time this weekend is being spent on diagrams
and problems for good reason. All of us need
practice in those things. A week off and some
small point is forgotten.

Darling, what arrangements could you make on
a Friday to meet me in Minneapolis? What time
could you get there and what kind of connections
could you make from Minneapolis to Pelican? If I
should happen to be checked out in time to get
there on a Thursday or Friday we could spend
some time there.

Gee, what'll we do all Friday night, Saturday
and Sunday?! My plans would include the Jolly
Miller and Andrews Lounge. A huge, soft double
bed. Sleeping late in the morning. Maybe we
can call it our second honeymoon—or a pre-
honeymoon. Just loving each other, living
together, catching time. I'm going to get off
that rather distracting subject or there just
won't be any concentration for study!

Johnny won $31.00 last night. A couple of
fellows lost $70.00 and $96.00. They played 'til
three o'clock in the head while Noe and I sat
in a corner firing questions and answers back
and forth. We're convinced we spent our time
much more profitably.

I love you,
Beat

3-9

My darling,

What a horrid person I am. Really, darling, your letter scares me. I'm really not the terrible person you painted. It hurts a little to think that you might think so. I've gained the respect of all the fellows and the instructors because I try hard here at school, and now I'm an old soak, etc.!!

Which reminds me, honey. Many is the time I've stayed aboard weekends—more than 2/3 of the leave I've had has been spent here. Could I be such a terrible runabout and footloose typical sailor? I haven't been anywhere near high since I've been here in Boston. That's the truth, darling.

About that poor sailor that I beat into insensibility, Ed says—and the guys laugh—"Beat doesn't do things halfway. That gob was the healthiest six-foot guy I ever saw. And was he mean and cocky." Have you ever seen me try to start a fight? No, and no one ever will. Remember at Xmas, the fellow calling at your house? I knew at that moment that I wanted to swing on him. Beat knew it wouldn't be the right thing to do.

Many are the times I've settled arguments peacefully 'cuz I know that's the proper thing to do. It saves friends and recurring troubles. This time I was grinning at a mad sailor, doing my best to kid him along. He thought I was yellow and said so. But he's one of these guys that thinks he's getting a "soft touch." One of his long arms hit me on the cheek, raising an eye and lip.

Now answer this honestly to yourself. Would you, if you were a man, run or stand there arguing? With the guy swearing and calling you yellow? Well, my natural instinct from many a lesson was to show him just how yellow I was. I proceeded to do so, and he got me quite mad by pulling a lot of dirty tricks. That was the end of the mess. Doggone, I thought you'd get quite a laugh out of thinking of me with a black eye.

Seriously, I had to laugh out loud when I read of your fear of my temper! It seems almost unbelievable that you could dream that one up.

⇒   ⇐

This has to be told, I suppose. Yesterday we took our school finals in theory. The tests lasted all day, and I wrote you soon after 'cuz I felt quite confident that I passed them all. Passing these tests means getting out of here a week earlier than the fellows who fail. This afternoon the marks were read. Doggone if I wasn't one of the ten lucky fellows! So my studying paid off, didn't it, sweets? The hours will be busy 'til I'm through my government exams. Spare moments I'll write you and hope to get letters from you to relieve a tired mind.

⇒   ⇐

After quite a few sad attempts, a lot of adventures in dark alleys, false tips, passwords, etc.

I'm glad to tell you that I made good on that unfulfilled promise to find some silk stockings. My New York, Philadelphia, Brooklyn, Springfield, Washington and Hartford agents were unable to produce, as stores just don't see these priceless bits of women's wear. But I finally made connections for the two pairs of 9 ½ longs (doggone you'll just have to roll 'em, sweets!). They're black market specials from last weekend. A fellow got them for me in the Dead End section of Manhattan. He asked me to look them over. All I could say was, "Just how the hell would I know if they're any good or not, whether the shade is right or wrong, etc." So, we'll take his word that they're good. They were mailed yesterday afternoon. You should get them soon by first class mail, darlin'! Look out for the wolves, for sure now!

⇛   ⇚

Monday 4:45 (3/15)

My sweets,

This morning after all my study and worry, I took my shipboard exam. From nine to twelve I answered questions, pointed out parts, operated and practiced maintenance work for three different chiefs. They gave me "excellent" in all my work, the best grade and one rarely given! I wasn't at all nervous. A secret of passing is to act confident, and I did. So, now I'm all set for sending and receiving finals on Wednesday and up to my government exams on Thursday. Worrying about that won't start 'til tonight when I start working toward it and doing my ten hours of "extra" study for Saturday night.

Darling, it would be perfect if we could meet in the Cities for our first weekend, but I'm not certain when I'll be leaving. If they have me stay over a few days, it might work out. You'll know as soon as I do, darling. Why couldn't we spend a weekend there, anyway? Or you could get a Friday afternoon free and meet me on the Northern Pacific at Detroit Lakes. We, then, could have all the rest of Friday, all Saturday and a lot of Sunday all alone—no one to bother us—just you and me in love. That sounds all right to me, darling. You'd have to decide, of course. I'm going to have a lot of money this time, in direct contrast to last time. Just think of the fun we could have!

Yours, always,
Beat

USO
Thursday
3:30 P.M.

My darling,

Maybe you can guess why I'm in Boston, writing you from the Buddies' Club. If you can't, m'sweet, I'll enlighten you. Five of us came in as the "guinea pigs" of our class. My head was full of radio—problems, diagrams, theories of this and that, etc. So we passed sending and receiving fine!

I whipped through Elements 1, 2, 5, and 6 in record time—with sweat and worry showing in every move I made. But you've got a radioman for a guy now!! Yes, darling, I passed the government tests. One of the fellows missed. One other hasn't arrived here yet, but the three of us are really happy!!

The last few days I've been a bundle of nerves. Every spare moment in a book. When I relaxed, I was helping one of the fellows in shipboard or telling a guy how to send. To tell you the truth, I was quite an old grouch when I got off in my corner and someone would interrupt my study. The late hours didn't help any either. But today I am a new man. When I go back to the Island tomorrow, I'm all done with study as far as the school is concerned. All I'll do is coach the others as much as I can. And sleep.

Whether or not I find that fellow (or gal)

with a "C" card, you can know, darling, that
Beat will be out to see you as soon as possible.
How long does it take to walk from Fargo to
Pelican?

Your guy,
Beat

We Need to Have a Long Talk

March 1943

GINNY, IRMA AND ELINOR had dashed out of the dim school building, into the bright spring sunshine. The air was crisp, still cool, but the days had lengthened. The snow piles diminished daily and oozed liquid, spreading puddles across the sidewalk. Elinor knew she'd have to be on the lookout for those in the morning on her walk to school. They'd be frozen again, treacherous. But for now, the girls, laughing, walked right on through the water.

They unwound their scarves. The warm wool draped loosely down the fronts of their coats.

"Spring is just around the corner," Elinor sang. It was something her father often said, optimistically predicting the end of a long winter. Or the end of tough times.

Irma joined Elinor and Ginny once in a while for their evening meals, when her husband worked late. As the girls entered the Uptown Café, they removed their purses and then those heavy winter coats. They threw everything into a pile on one of the seats of the booth. Then Irma and Ginny climbed into one side of their booth and Elinor sat with the coats opposite them.

"I believe we're early tonight," Ginny said.

"We are! So we'll have extra time to talk. I have a few things on my mind." Elinor checked her Christmas watch. She had taken it to

Crescent Jewelers for repair right after the holidays. Although Beat had sent her a new watch, paying it off last month, she preferred the sentiment of this watch, a gift he offered when he was so desperately poor. It was, after all, the best he could do.

The place wasn't too busy, the jukebox quiet between songs. The smell of hot beef sandwiches, the special of the day, hung in the air. A waitress arrived right away to take their orders. She plopped three glasses of water on the table.

"I'm having a salad tonight," Elinor declared. "Chef salad for me. With a Coke."

The waitress noted the order on her green pad.

Ginny duplicated the order exactly.

"Ditto," Irma piped in.

"Three chefs and three Cokes," the waitress echoed. She wrote out a check for each of them as she bustled toward the kitchen.

"Any new wedding plans?" Irma directed her question to Ginny.

"Nothing since yesterday." They were waiting to hear what Charlie thought the possibilities were for a leave in June. "It's probably too soon for him to get an idea," Ginny explained. She moved the salt and pepper shakers to the end of the table.

The waitress set the Cokes on the table. The girls unwrapped their paper straws and settled them in their glasses.

"I have news," Irma looked into her lap. Elinor and Ginny turned toward her. "I'll be retiring from teaching at the end of this year, girls." She looked at her friends and blushed.

"Oh, Irma," Ginny exclaimed. "When are you due?"

"In the fall. Early September."

"No more teaching for you then. Lucky!" Elinor reached across the table to pat Irma's hand.

"Oh, Irma," Ginny cooed, "I suppose you're hoping for that first son?"

Elinor sipped her drink thoughtfully. She heard Ginny and Irma chatting about boys' names. Someone dropped a nickel in the jukebox. Tommy Dorsey's Orchestra played "I'll Never Smile Again."

She heard her father's voice, his words. What had started as a conversation had ended in an argument. "Bunny, you mustn't have anything more to do with him! Or with his friends."

She had always believed her father. Now she saw his point. And she had promised. It wouldn't be hard now.

Elinor brought herself back to the present as the song ended. "Such good news." She smiled. "I want to have the shower for you. Some time in May, before the school year rolls to a close?"

"What's happening with Beat?" Ginny directed the question to Elinor.

"Well, you know he's done with Gallups. First to graduate, and he's proud of the license he got. He's coming back to Fargo for his break. Then off to war. To deliver arms and supplies to the guys who do the fighting."

"I'm so jealous! I'd love some time with Charlie. Just to talk and straighten out our plans." Ginny put her head in her hands, elbows on the table, and sipped on her straw.

"So, I suppose you'll have a big time when he comes," Irma sighed. "Movies and drinks and time to talk." She looked at Elinor when she said, "Romantic times?"

"Romance isn't in the cards, Irma. Not with Darrow anyway."

"What's up?" Irma said.

"He'll be here during school. Not a lot of time for me to visit. Essays and papers. You know." Elinor ran her finger around the rim of her Coke glass. "If he can find a way to get to Pelican, he says he'll visit."

"We'll get to meet him then?" Irma asked.

"I need to have a long talk with Darrow," Elinor sighed. She straightened up in her seat. Her lips pursed, she said, "There are a few things that are bothering me, and I need to air them." She pushed her hair behind her ears.

"Oh?" Irma turned toward Ginny.

Ginny leaned in.

Elinor took a deep breath and continued. "Well, he got soused at their Gallups graduation party. You won't believe this. He beat a Marine up on the streets of Boston."

"Oh, my gosh!" Irma nearly yelled.

"Beating up one of our troops? He needs to focus on the enemy." Ginny unfolded her napkin and set it on her lap.

"Yeah, he needs to save his energy for the Japs," Irma chimed in. "Why fight our own men?"

"Bunny, he's not for you. He can be such a jerk," Ginny said. She turned to Irma. "He forgot Valentine's Day."

Irma added "And your parents aren't that fond . . ."

"That's putting it mildly. I won't continue seeing him." Elinor unfolded her napkin, too. "Anyway, he doesn't have a car." She spread the napkin in her lap. "He won't have a way to get to Pelican, even for a short visit."

"It's a ways from Fargo to Pelican and with the gas rationing . . ." Irma murmured.

Men in the field needed all the fuel they could obtain. Consequently, there was a limit to the number of gallons every household was allowed. "A" stickers qualified for just 4 gallons a month. "B" stickers for war workers and servicemen meant ten gallons. Rev. Landgrebe had a "C" sticker in the windshield. He could have whatever gas he really needed, but he used this permit judiciously. Gas was expensive at 19 cents a gallon and Georg wasn't one to waste gas. He certainly wouldn't be loaning his car to Beat!

"Yeah," Elinor faced her friends across the table. "I've heard there's a war on. Anyway, it's not my problem. I don't care if I ever see him again. But if he gets here, I'm going to be prepared to have that long talk with him."

"You'd better have notecards, Bunny," Ginny said. Her eyes were serious. "You've tried for that long talk before. Whenever you see Beat, you forget all about that talk. This time—notecards."

Stateside?

March 1943

GI Grads
Darrow is sixth from the left in the second row from the top.

Thursday 7:10 A.M.
March 18

My sweet,

Six fellows are going in on the boat this morning. They're all dressed up and more worried than I was even! Just as I wrote that, they left with our cheers and hopes for success ringing out. We really hope for each other and are so happy to see a fellow come through.

Beat's got a confession to make. My quick trip to New York last weekend after graduation was a celebration. You won't be a teeny bit mad at me, darling? Please? The story starts at the Stage Door Canteen when I met two privates in the Army. We got along swell while we ate. This one tall, dark and happy guy is an Irishman from Frisco. When the dancing began, his eyes lit up and he said, "Say, Beat, haven't you always had the ambition to dance with a chorus girl or actress? Here's our chance. What do you say?" The gal is in the show "Sons of Fun," another Olsen and Johnson hit on Broadway. She is too nice lookin'. There is no more to the story, as soon afterward I leave.

This weekend you can think of me on my way home in a big berth sleeping and dreaming of seeing my darlin'. Not a single beer all the way home, not a drop of anything. The fellows I'll be coming home with live out West—Colorado, Montana, and California. We'll probably be talking over old times and radio and the coming weeks months and years. We hang together now as we never have before—during the day, at chow, at shows, in Boston. We're trying to have all the fun we can before we leave each other. My address book holds some names that are going places in this ol' world— not radio especially either. And I don't mean by going places that they'll be traveling a lot. That's just understood that we'll be doing some traveling. You know how much I'll dislike the travel!!! OH, yeah!

Know what? I could have had a job in Alameda, California as a chief op on a training ship.

The ship is at the school for deck and engineer officers there. My pay would have been $197.00 a month, and I could go ashore two nights of three. After about one second's thought, I told Mr. Grant that I'd like to try the ocean to see just how I can make out at the big job! There were also training jobs in New York and Baltimore that Lt. Grant filled from our class. The fellows that are just a wee bit afraid of the sea or the job out there grabbed them up— but quickly. Beat'll take his chances out there and hope that he's learned enough or can pick it up.

Yours forever,
Beat

Problems and Promises

March 1943

THE SIDEWALKS HAD BEEN shoveled after Tuesday's big snowstorm. But the snowplows had left the corners piled with snow. In order to cross the street, a pedestrian had to climb a snowy rise, slide down to street level, then scale the elevation on the other side to arrive on the sidewalk there. The storekeepers hadn't been out yet to carve pathways into the snowbanks for those who walked. They probably hoped for a quick spring melt.

Ginny and Elinor had stopped to collect their mail on the way to the Uptown to have a bite to eat and to read the letters where the light was better.

"I'm not sure how to handle things," Elinor confided as she and Ginny slid into their booth. "Beat's coming home on leave, and Johnny's coming one of these days, too. And if they come at the same time . . ."

Ginny giggled at the prospect. "Such problems."

The girls took off their wraps and settled in. Ginny opened her envelope from Charlie. He wrote much the same thing daily, but she knew he was thinking of her.

The waitress arrived and the girls put in their usual order: soup and a sandwich, coffee to drink. Pie? A laugh before the "No, thank you."

Elinor had a long letter from Beat, as well as one from her sister. She opened up the letter from Gallups Island first and read.

The coffee arrived at the table. Elinor thanked the waitress. The girls continued reading and rereading their letters. Neither looked up. Neither noticed the others coming into the café or the jukebox belting out Peggy Lee's "On the Sunny Side of the Street."

"That does it," Elinor thought. She gulped her coffee and tried to concentrate on the note from Mickey. But her thoughts kept wandering back to Beat's letter. She picked it up and read it again.

She stared out the window into the waning sunset.

"Bad news? You look upset." Ginny interrupted Elinor's thoughts.

"Once again I see that my father is so right. About Darrow."

The soup arrived. "Sandwiches will be here in just a minute." Their waitress bustled away to the next table.

"What do you mean, Elinor?" Ginny took a sip of her coffee.

"You know, I hope Johnny does arrive when Beat does," Elinor replied. "I want Beat to be knocking on my door when I walk out with Johnny. I'll tell him to get lost in no uncertain terms."

"So . . ."

"He's been out dancing with Broadway stars. You know? On his trip to see his sister, he veered to New York City for a fun time after he passed his tests. His favorite big city. Went dancing. And listen to this."

Ginny was all ears. She leaned toward Elinor.

Elinor set her cup down with a clatter. "He could've been sent stateside. To California, no less. Here's what he wrote: 'Know what? I could have had a job in Alameda, California as a chief op on a training ship. The ship is at the school for deck and engineer officers there. I told Mr. Grant that I'd like to try the ocean to see just how I can make out at the big job. Beat'll take his chances out there and hope that he's learned enough or can pick it up.'"

Her right hand flew into the air.

"For crying out loud!" Ginny sat back in the booth.

"I couldn't believe it either."

The girls each took a gulp of coffee.

Elinor snorted. "He won't be happy until he has an adventure on the high seas. Until he plays his part in this darn war."

She stuffed the letter into its envelope and back into her purse. She sampled her soup and nibbled at her sandwich. "It's a good thing I'm breaking up with him."

She took out the letter from her sister. An invitation to San Diego. California would be some adventure!

Leonard swung through the café door. His face lit up when he saw Elinor there. He sashayed over to the booth and stood beside her. She smiled, a tight grin. "I hear we'll be coaching together," she said.

"Right after Easter," he acknowledged. "We'll have to meet once in a while to make plans. Maybe Saturday mornings over coffee?"

Elinor nodded.

Leonard spotted a couple of male friends and joined them in another booth.

Elinor turned to Ginny again. "Anyway, Johnny . . . Did you know he gave me an engagement ring? I tucked it away, but now I'm thinking about wearing it."

"Atta girl!" Ginny cheered.

The Invitation

March 1943

Point Loma, Calif.
March 22, 1943

Dearest Elinor,
I received your letter today, and I'm going to
try to answer your questions.

Living conditions aren't nearly as bad as
everyone makes them. It is practically impossible
to get apartments, but there are lots of sleeping
rooms. A person can always take a sleeping room
until there is an apartment available.

The food situation is just like it is at home,
except for candy, and meat (we can get plenty
of it, but not as much variety). The only place
I've seen lines are theaters. Maybe some of the
restaurants during busy hours—because of the
shortage of waitresses, not food.

Jobs are more than plentiful. There is an
awful shortage of civilian help. I don't think
you'd like the war work. There is so much red
tape—school, training etc., etc., etc. However,
there is plenty of civilian work.

I sure hope you come, Elinor, and I more

than pray you'll stay. We could have scads of fun. Really. I've been helping our landlady pick oranges and lemons today. I can only imagine your blizzard. I know you'll like it and I could like it 100 times as much if you were here.

I do miss home terribly, but I am glad I came. Kid, please, please join me. Please. Don't worry about the money. This week my check was $40.80, and living (with car fare, lunches, meals and rent) is about $12 a week. Not bad at all, and you know how I eat.

Glad to hear of your decision to marry Johnny. I'm sure you'll never be sorry.

Take good care of Ching, and keep me posted on local news scandals and all that stuff. I'll be waiting for a letter.

Loads of Love,
Mickey

Just 24 Hours

March 1943

Tuesday eve
(3/23)

My darling,

For the past few days the office has been acting awfully suspicious. What with calls to NY, Washington, Frisco, etc. we just were left to wonder. On the trips to Boston we've noticed an increased activity in the shipping business. This morning eleven new merchantmen were at the docks—appeared overnight!! Right then and there we decided that that's where we were to end up, we first few graduates who were so suddenly rushed to town for our final papers.

So all day long I've signed papers, taken oaths, rushed from building to building and waited in lines. All the while I felt let down, wondering about those darn ships. My papers include a passport; seamen's papers; a Coast Guard, Navy and Army pass to any ship of our country; and a commission as a radio officer.

When I finished, I rushed back out here and

they told me at the commander's office that I leave this Saturday to see my girl for two weeks. Then I am to report to Seattle, Washington. Oh, darling, you can't know how it hurt to think that we couldn't have our long-planned leave together. Tonite would have been my night to cry, 'cuz I know it would have made me awfully blue. You'll be seeing me out in Pelican next week some time.

Be mine and plan on a swell time,
Beat

Later!
Are ya all ready to do a little lovin' with a very willin' radioman, a guy what has been savin' every little bit for ya? I'm expecting to see you in that "would have been" muffler of mine.

The guys gathered around here about ten minutes ago. Noe and I began talking and soon everybody began to gather. They're going back into the things we've done. They just had a good laugh over our Tennessean. While we were at the class party, we were served soup, of course. The fellows near him told him the food hadn't arrived. That the soup was all we were going to have. We all had a good laugh remembering him as he squawked about paying $8.00 for a meal, only to get soup. He's a genius at radio, but he swears that he'd never had shoes on until he came here.

We're going to miss each other. Some of the fellows are tops—college fellows and really ambitious. Noe is the guy I'll miss most of all, the screwy Frenchman. He's a genius at radio and we have fun just talking and being together.

I must close. Gotta get into this bull session that's raging all around me.

Beat

Fabric sparks symbol, signifying a radio officer, enclosed

Friday eve
(3/26)

My sweets,

Only 24 hours—less!—and I'll be on my way home!
My train connections will be a mystery to me
until tomorrow. Just as soon as I possibly can,
I shall call you at Pelican and come out to
see you. I'm just so anxious to get going that
I could shout. The papers are full of your big
snowstorm.

Last night a gang of us went ashore for a
last look at Boston. We had a swell time. We
saw Bob Chester's orchestra, Jack Duranty, Dixie
Dunbar, and the great stinko, John Boles. We
went to the Cave where we dedicated "There Are
Such Things" to Elinor. The fellows slipped it
over on me, and I loved it. I thought of you,
about as happy as I can be when we're apart.
We said our good-byes to all the people there
and at the Buddies' Club. They've treated us so
darn well during our stay here. Maybe someday
my ship will "put in" here in Boston and I can
see all the places again.

I've been getting addresses, sitting in on
bull sessions, dreaming of you, taking code,
loving you, checking out of two more departments,
missing you, picking up my last few belongings,
wanting you. You see! I love you, dream of you,
miss you and want you.

Be loving you in person soon!

Yours, always,
Beat

Radio Op Beaton in uniform

from the **Graystone Hotel**
in Detroit Lakes, MN
among the ten thousand lakes

Modern, fireproof, European plan
A coffee shop famous for fine food

Thursday 3:30 P.M.
(4/1)

My darling,

Must let you know that I enjoyed my stay in Pelican—stiff back, farmers' stares, meat loaf and roast beef suppers and all.

You really are so darn happy and 'tis fun just to be with you.

These last two days have been the kind of days I've wanted my leave to be—just a perfect time with you. We have many more ahead of us in the next few weeks. Beat will never forget them.

I'll love you always, hon,
Beat

DETROIT LAKES, MINN. *April 1* 194 *3* No. *000000 3/4*

BECKER COUNTY NATIONAL BANK 75-1576/9
OF DETROIT LAKES

PAY TO THE ORDER OF *Miss Elinor Sandgrebe* $ *∞*

A million days of happiness & no →DOLLARS

FOR *Fun*   *D. R. Beaton*

And this isn't an April Fools' joke either.

April Fools

From the **Grand Recreation Parlors, Inc.**
billiards—bowling, lunch counter

620 First Avenue North
Fargo, North Dakota
Dial 7558

Sunday eve 4/4
9:00

My darling—

I borrowed this stationery at the Grand (as
you can see). Filled my pen at the post office.
Turned on a light and borrowed this table at
the YMCA.

As you have mentioned, we really haven't
known each other so long. But I've been in love
with you for many, many months. As with you, I
have had little worries and doubts—moments of
wondering, as any guy in love.

This time we've had many serious moments—
speaking of Walt, etc. You've been darn swell—
fulfilled that hope and prayer of mine that
you were what I hoped you were, a really good
girl—my girl—forever. There's not a thing wrong
with the world any more except our having to
be apart for a few months 'til the war is over.
Those months will be so much easier to spend
knowing that you love me, that you're doing
things you've always wished to do and that we're
both being good for one another.

Your Dad didn't seem angry with me. I sincerely
hope that he isn't, but darn it, honey. I'd just
like to stay by you 24 hours a day. It's so hard

to leave while you're beside me in a dark room, a soft davenport to sit on. But dads don't seem to understand.

I'm not sure that I'll be out tomorrow eve. I've got a few things to do, people to visit, etc. I think that I shall be through in time to catch a bus. If I'm not, I'll be out Tuesday for certain. Let's have another swell week together, hon. I'll always love you, be good for you, and look forward to our next leave.

G'nite, darling—
Yours, forever,
Beat

It's Final

April 1943

THEY SAT IN THEIR corner of the Aquarium. She sipped her Tom Collins. Beat ordered yet another bourbon. He had lost count. The fish in the big aquarium behind the bar swam lethargically from side to side in their oversized tank.

Earlier in the evening the room had been crowded—noisy, even. Some of Beat's buddies and their dates dropped in, so they all drank together for a while. The conversation was mostly about the war. Beat bragged about joining the Merchant Marine, made it sound like it was a better choice than the other services. He didn't mention that the Navy and the Marines had rejected him because of his eyes and flat feet.

But now, after midnight, the bar was settling down to murmurs. There was just one fellow at the bar, whining about his life to the bartender who polished the glasses and nodded while he gave the room the once over.

The lights low, the colors in the room dulled with cigarette smoke. A few couples snuggled at small tables. The men looked splendid in their uniforms, mostly Army in town these days. Beat had on his Merchant Marine duds, his hat on the floor beside his chair. He worried that he'd spill or burn a cigarette hole through it if he left it on the table.

The jukebox played intermittently. Someone walked over, deposited a nickel, and "Stardust" whispered in the background. Lovers whispered, too.

Beat lit another cigarette. When the tip flamed, he leaned back in his chair. Smoke curled into the air as he exhaled.

The bartender arrived with Beat's bourbon and set the glass on the table. "Anything else?" he asked.

"Not . . . not just now." Beat slurred. He looked over his right shoulder at Elinor and smiled. "Bunny?"

She shook her head. She smiled at the bartender, too.

Beat stood as he felt in his pocket for a coin. He walked a nickel to the jukebox and pushed the button. "There Are Such Things" drifted around the room.

Elinor sipped her third drink. Beat was able to inhale liquor without much damage, it seemed. But she couldn't be pie-eyed tonight. Her parents were due home from their trip out west.

Beat returned to his chair and sat, resting his arm on the back of her chair, settling his hand on her arm. She put her head on his shoulder while their song played. She snuggled into him, and he brushed her hair with his lips.

"Remember?" Beat whispered.

Elinor remembered that Beat had once talked about getting married in June.

"I hate it that you have to go," she whispered.

He laughed. "That's why war is for men." He straightened up as the song ended.

Elinor glanced at her watch.

Beat's leave was almost over and she hadn't yet asked the question. It was burning in her now. Or was that the alcohol?

She sat up to look at him. "Why didn't you take that job in Alameda, Beat?" she asked. A simple question.

He turned to her and pushed her away to look into her eyes. She smelled the bourbon. She turned her head away.

He snarled, "And sit on the beach while the others get into this thing? Look like a 4F, like Wal—ter?" He said Walt's name in a singsong voice. Beat could be sarcastic, so needlessly sarcastic.

"I could've come to California to visit you, though, honey." She tried to touch him, to lean in again toward him.

He stamped his cigarette out in one of the empty shot glasses on the table. "You sure about that?" he responded, moving away from her.

"I know a few things about the men you've been seeing while I've been in Boston." His eyes scalded, accusing her. Of what?

Her voice pleaded. "Beat, what are you talking about?"

He laughed, his voice, now raised, along with his hand. "I have spies, gal." He slammed the table with his fist. The glasses hopped up and settled back down on the table.

He leaned toward her, nearly yelling now. "I know you've been dating Walter and Johnny. And Dale's in the picture, too. You act like they're just 'old friends', but they are more than that."

"Beat . . ." A picture flashed across her vision. The Marine in Boston just a week ago. She shrank back into her chair.

Beat lifted his fist toward her face. "You thought I would kill my opportunity of doing something in this war?" Glass shattered somewhere in the bar.

"Beat?" she repeated.

The bartender moved around the bar, closer to their table.

"Goddamnit! You are serious about no one, Elinor. Walter has told me everything. Your affair with him. How many of the others?" Beat stood up.

Elinor's hands flew to cover her face. What was he saying? Right here in public? What had Walter been saying?

"You can't believe Walter!" Elinor wobbled just a little as she stood. "Darn it, Beat. You still don't trust me." Her voice was too high, too loud. It rang in her ears.

As she straightened up, she managed to unhook the Sigma Chi pin from her blue suit jacket lapel. She slapped it into his hands. Beat stopped short. He threw the pin on the table and looked at the red dot growing on his palm. He wiped his hand on a paper napkin.

Elinor glared at him.

He bent his head over the table. She saw that he was trying to hook the latch on the back of the Sigma Chi pin. "How about the watch?" he sneered, as he looked up at her.

Elinor was stunned. Emily Post said that the gifts men gave a girl were theirs to keep.

Beat leaned heavily on the small table, which wobbled. A glass tipped. "Damned pin," he muttered, as he stuffed it, still unlatched, into his pocket.

The fog in Elinor's brain cleared. What was she thinking? She didn't want a reminder of him anyway.

She unclasped the latch and dropped the watch on the table. He grabbed it and slid it into his pants pocket with the pin.

"Let's get you home," he snarled, turning toward the door.

It was then that Elinor noticed that all the conversation in the bar had stopped. The jukebox had run down again, too. She felt eyes on her. She straightened her shoulders and raised her chin.

Beat threw a couple of bills on the table. "Let's go," he said. He grabbed his hat and her arm, and they negotiated their way out of the silence in the bar and into the cool Dakota night air. The door slammed behind them.

Elinor wished she had brought her coat. She had worn the suit without a wrap because his darn pin looked better that way.

She opened the car door and arranged herself. Hugging the side, she stayed as far away from Darrow as she could. She shivered. The smell of his bourbon nauseated her. She held her hand over her mouth and nose.

The two-minute drive from downtown Fargo to her home felt interminable. Now she grasped the veiled threats in her father's sermons. She sensed eternal hell.

The old car careened down the darkened streets of Fargo. With a skid they came to a halt over the curb in front of her home. Beat looked at her, but she refused to turn her head his way.

"Damn it! Look at me," he shouted.

She bailed out of the jalopy and slammed the door. She stood on the lawn as Beat roared down the block and out of her life.

She glared after the silhouette of Bruns's car as it disappeared around the corner. The cherry-sized brake lights barely blinked when the car slowed for the turn, and she noticed that Beat had neglected to turn on the headlights.

Elinor straightened her purse strap over her shoulder and turned toward the house. It was dark, according to blackout rules. No porch light shining these days. But she spotted the dim glow of the fluorescent desk lamp. Her father always left it on to guide her in.

We're Through, Through, Through

April 1943

"Good work, Landgrebe. Those kids really looked fine yesterday. Fergus doesn't stand a chance with you and Leonard coaching together."

Elinor smiled, then looked at Ginny who laughed and rolled her eyes. Elinor raised her eyebrows as another group of teachers passed by, offering praise for the girls' baseball team. When they were alone again, Ginny sang, "Measured from head to toe, he's the same from side to side," and the girls giggled.

Elinor hadn't chosen to coach with Leonard. He continued to write flowery love letters. He fussed over her when she was out with a migraine. "I just wish he'd get the idea. I'm not going to fall in love with him," Elinor sighed. "But he's a nice enough fellow, a good friend."

Ginny got up to put a nickel in the jukebox. Elinor knew what was coming. Leonard tolerated his nickname with good humor. "Mr. Five by Five."

As Ginny plopped back onto her seat, the waitress arrived. With the spring-like weather, Elinor decided to have a picnic. She ordered a hamburger with fries. Ginny, nearing her June wedding, didn't want the calories. She tried a salad instead of the usual soup. The waitress sped off to the kitchen with the order. "Hold the soup," she called as she neared the kitchen.

The Uptown had a jolly feel to it, despite the less than cheery war news. Easter decorations, bunnies and crosses on strings, attached with transparent tape, danced in the front windows whenever the door to the restaurant opened. Daylight lasted longer now. The sun still glittered in the big front windows at suppertime. By 6:00 there wasn't a seat vacant in the place.

The jukebox, crowded with nickels, cranked out tunes one after another. "Spring Will Be a Little Late This Year" and "You'll Never Know." Then "GI Jive." Laughter bounced around the room. Someone started clapping with every chorus of "Jive."

Ginny settled herself, her purse by her side. Elinor checked again. Her mail was safely tucked into her purse. It was no one's business. She'd read it later.

"So, where is Beat? What a surprise to see him in Pelican!" Ginny's eyebrows lifted. "He made the trip after all."

"He's on the way to war." Elinor was succinct.

"He's cute, Bunny. Confident. I can see why you used to like him." Ginny continued. "A bit cocky, though, I think."

"That's putting it mildly." Elinor straightened her mouth into a frozen smile. "He's on the train heading to Seattle now. To his first ship. "

"How was the weekend?" Ginny asked. Her brow wrinkled as her eyes squinted at Elinor. "Did you . . . ?"

Elinor stirred her coffee to cool it, then thought of ordering a Coca-Cola to go with her picnic fare. She called the waitress over to amend her order. She turned to Ginny again and spoke in an undertone. "Well, it's over. I won't be seeing Beat again."

"That was the plan, wasn't it? To break up?" Ginny set her letter from Charlie on the table.

The waitress arrived with the Coke. Elinor unwrapped her straw, stabbed it into her drink, and took a big sip.

"So you had the long talk?" Ginny nodded.

"I just got fed up. I told him I wasn't sitting around waiting for anyone, especially someone who would find new girlfriends all over the world."

"So, you've . . ."

"Someone who could've worked in Alameda, for Pete's sake. Close to home," Elinor interrupted.

The waitress arrived with the girls' meals. "Good eating!" she called as she waltzed away to get the next table.

The girls looked at their orders, unusual for them. The iceberg lettuce salad with a few carrot slices and a glob of French dressing. The hamburger, steaming in its bun and the crispy fries clumped on the plate. Elinor grabbed the salt shaker. Her meal definitely smelled better than Ginny's salad.

Elinor lifted the top of the bun and squirted ketchup onto the patty. She swirled some around the pickles and then slapped the top back on. She stared at her plate.

"I gave him his Sigma Chi pin back. That darn Christmas watch, too. Now that it's running, it's worth something." She chomped a big bite out of her hamburger.

"Good riddance!" Ginny reached across the table for a French fry. "It's about time you did this, Bunny."

"Yes. We are through, through, through." Elinor piled a few fries on her saucer and passed them to her friend. She leaned over, elbow on the table and her right cheek on her fist.

"Did you need the notecards?" Ginny laughed.

But Elinor simply stared at her Coca-Cola glass and sighed. As she began to pick at her salad, Ginny watched her friend. Elinor's hamburger sat nearly untouched on her plate.

Ginny picked up Charlie's letter. "Well, let's get off that topic. It makes you glum, I see. No mail today?"

"A note from my father," Elinor replied. She cracked her purse open and slid out a single envelope.

How could she tell Ginny that Beat continued to write? A little white lie wouldn't hurt. She had, indeed, gotten a letter from her father. She simply neglected to give a full inventory of her mailbox.

The girls ate and read their mail in silence. The jukebox played "Pistol Packin' Mamma."

As the last French fry disappeared, Ginny came back to the present.

"I must admit that I'm glad. About this turn of events. That you've dropped Beat, I mean." She piled her dishes on the table. "Finally. He always treated you like . . . you . . . Well, like he owned you or something."

Elinor had pushed her dishes away, too. Now she tapped the fingers of her right hand rhythmically on the table, starting with her little finger and ending with her index finger. She repeated the drumming movement several times, unconsciously, and then reached for her purse. She unsnapped it and stuffed the envelope back in.

Ginny continued, "He had some kind of a hold over you, I think. I've not been able to figure out why you liked him that much."

Elinor stood and pulled her purse strap over her shoulder. "I'd better get to work on those papers," she explained. She wondered whether she had said too much.

Mata Hari

April 1943

AT MIDNIGHT, WITHOUT A sound, as Mata Hari might've done, Elinor slipped off the daybed. She had decided to go ahead with the clandestine operation.

The rest of the family had gone up to bed early. With Mickey's expected arrival from California and Yupps's return from the seminary this coming week, the family would be together once again for Easter. Preparations had already begun.

Elinor scouted around the downstairs. She walked through the archway into the front hall, then into the living room. She heard nothing from the second floor. Even Ching had gone to sleep, curled up on the horsehair sofa. She ducked through the kitchen and slipped furtively back into her space. The desk lamp, with the red—dim— button pushed, barely lit her father's papers. The rest of the room lay cloaked in darkness.

Elinor massaged her temples. She glanced around the shadowed room again. Goosebumps prickled on her arms. She felt so vulnerable and wished more than ever that the den had one more door. She crept to the other side of the room to secure the door to the kitchen. Anyone could come into the room through the archway from the front hallway, but at least now only one entrance remained open to invasion.

Perhaps she had seen too many spy movies. Or heard too many things about spies in the wars. She tiptoed to the coat closet. She found her suitcase just where she had left it. She pulled it out, set it on the daybed, snapped the latches and opened the lid.

Had she made too much noise? She froze and listened. Nothing. Elinor laughed at herself. Mata Hari wouldn't have suitcases that snapped open. And she'd have had secret pockets in them.

Elinor lifted out the three essays she had stowed there, her cover for the cache of secrets she'd carried. She checked over her shoulder for any intruders. With Irene back from Aunt Dorothy's place, nothing was safe any more.

She wondered whether Mata Hari ever had doubts. Films, of course, showed the accused spy as courageous and confident. In real life, though, she must've had moments of indecision—or misunderstandings. Whether or not she could be proven a spy for the Germans in the Great War, she did, after all, manipulate a number of men.

The removal of the essays had exposed Elinor's pink angora sweater which lay, folded, in the bottom of the suitcase. She picked it up and carried it to the desk. In the dim glow of the lamp there, she unbuttoned the cardigan.

She heard something then, a soft movement. She covered her secret with the wool and stopped again to listen.

Ching padded into the room. He stared at the daybed. Seeing Elinor's things in his resting spot, he mewled softly. Elinor smiled in relief. She moved the suitcase a few inches to the side. Ching jumped onto the bed. Elinor scratched behind his ears and waited to hear his purr. He curled into a ball and settled in, haunches resting against her luggage.

Elinor turned back to the desk. She pushed her hair behind her ears and moved into her father's roomy desk chair. She heard a click and froze. She shut her eyes to listen. It was just the house settling into the gloomy night.

She knew she was too jittery. But this was her secret. She hadn't told anyone, not even Ginny.

She had hidden Beat's letters in her purse as they arrived in her mailbox in Pelican, uncertain whether to open them or not. The last time she had seen Beat, he was roaring off drunkenly in Bruns's car. It was over.

The sweater on the desk lay partially open, exposing the evidence. Elinor settled lightly on the edge of her father's chair, willing it to keep quiet, scarcely moving. She slid the cover sweater open and fingered the mail she had concealed there: a telegram, a postcard, and three envelopes.

Elinor slid open the desk drawer that held her father's letter opener. She ran her finger down the metal blade and back again.

Beat frightened her. He had actually raised his fist to her face. And he had embarrassed her in front of everyone in the Aquarium that night by accusing her . . . of what? Infidelity? Of an affair? With Walter? For Pete's sake!

Elinor shook her head. A simple question had set Beat off into a fury. Why on God's earth would anyone want to continue with a man like that? She put the opener back into her father's drawer.

She walked into the kitchen and turned on the faucet, then filled a glass with water and returned to the desk. Although the sheer numbers of Beat's letters drove her crazy because he expected an equal number in return, they were interesting to read. She set the glass of water down on the desk.

Perhaps he was apologizing. He certainly had had too many drinks that night. He was out of control. She reached for the letter opener again.

He could be so sweet. In so many ways he seemed like an innocent kid. That Christmas watch, for instance. He had absolutely no money. Yet he figured out a way to get her something special. And he was willing to risk his prized World's Fair coin in a poker game.

But he had taken his Christmas gift back.

His accusations had slashed her. He could be snide, brutal. Part of that came, no doubt, from his years of leading a gang, notorious in town. He knew how to bully "his" men into following him. And, it couldn't be forgotten. A member of Beat's gang had caused all this family trouble. The Landgrebe secret. They were all just beginning to mend.

She set the letter opener down on the desk.

Better to go to bed. She picked up the letters, then stood. She'd throw them out at the bus depot as she returned to Pelican. She located her purse on the end of the daybed and stuffed them inside. She snapped her bag closed, set it back on the floor and moved the suitcase back into the closet. Ching jumped off the bed and retreated.

Pressing the black button, Elinor shut off the desk lamp. The room lapsed into darkness. She stepped toward her bed, threw the covers back, and then turned toward the desk again. She stood there, frozen with her inner debate.

He was a man without a home. Without money. Without strong family ties. Yet he was trying to better himself. He worked while he went to college. He had to put in long hours at the seed company to keep himself fed and housed besides. And now, unlike Walter and the other 4-Fs, he had found a way to help out the country. He was working hard to become an officer, too.

And Beat was handsome, especially in that uniform. He could charm her, even if she resisted. My god, they'd done things together that she never thought she'd do.

Even though he was certainly rough around the edges, Beat had so many qualities that shined through. Like one of those rocks she used to discover as a girl. She would find her father's hammer and crack them open. They glittered in the sun, jewels, really. A surprise if you only considered their outsides.

Maybe he was apologizing in these letters. Maybe he'd even changed plans. Alameda.

"I'm not tired anyway," she thought. "I can't sleep." She flipped the light on again. She picked up her purse and found her mail. She would never know unless she read his letters.

The cuckoo popped out and sang twice. Elinor picked up the letter opener.

She began with the telegram which had been delivered in an envelope to the rooming house while she was in class. She stabbed the opener into the envelope, slit the top, and pulled out the Western Union. Montana. So what?

Next she stared at the downtown photo of Seattle on the colored postcard. Beat was on the coast, and soon he'd be at war. He had remembered to greet her parents and Irene. Brother. He should remember them! He was going to have to make it up to them all one day.

She should suspend this right now. Beat was dangerous.

But the telegram and postcard were pretty noncommittal, perhaps his way of saying good-bye.

He had scribbled a message to her on Western Union message paper while the train rocked down the tracks. So he was thinking of her even as he was leaving her.

Elinor slit open the envelopes from the Mayflower Hotel, one after another, and pulled out the stationery. She laughed at the paragraph about her photo. The Charming Beat again. She'd write him a note, too. She could give him the news about Irene's return. And Easter if she wrote after next weekend. And she'd say good-bye, too.

She saved the longest letter for last. Elinor scowled as she read it. What on earth? Had he lost his mind? Or had she? Maybe she had missed something. Maybe this was some kind of code.

Just Awaiting for a Ship

April 1943

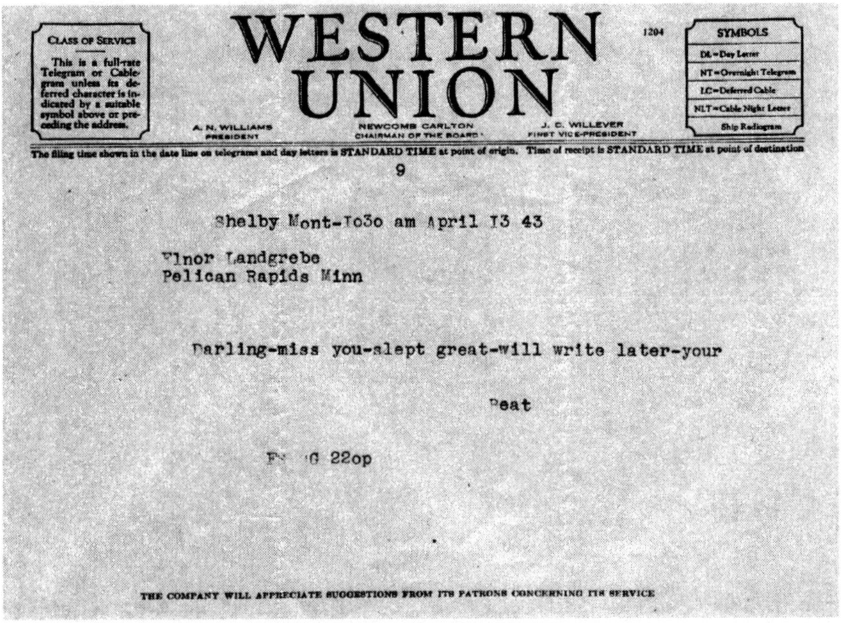

CLASS OF SERVICE
This is a full-rate Telegram or Cablegram unless its deferred character is indicated by a suitable symbol above or preceding the address.

WESTERN UNION

1204

SYMBOLS
DL=Day Letter
NT=Overnight Telegram
LC=Deferred Cable
NLT=Cable Night Letter
Ship Radiogram

A. N. WILLIAMS, PRESIDENT — NEWCOMB CARLTON, CHAIRMAN OF THE BOARD — J. C. WILLEVER, FIRST VICE-PRESIDENT

The filing time shown in the date line on telegrams and day letters is STANDARD TIME at point of origin. Time of receipt is STANDARD TIME at point of destination

9

Shelby Mont-Io3o am April I3 43

Elnor Landgrebe
Pelican Rapids Minn

Darling-miss you-slept great-will write later-your

Peat

F G 22op

THE COMPANY WILL APPRECIATE SUGGESTIONS FROM ITS PATRONS CONCERNING ITS SERVICE

Telegram from Shelby, MT

Hotel Mayflower
The charm of yesterday—The
convenience of today
Fourth Avenue at Olive, Seattle
4-14

Hi darlin',

The best hotel in town—at least as far as
I've gone! I'm rooming with Bob Paulson of
Minneapolis. We've got two big double beds in
a huge room. $2.00 each, a night. We might move
some place else over the weekend to be nearer
to the work we plan to get.

The city's really bustling—cool—crowded—
pretty swell, so far. You'll be glad to hear that
whiskey is rationed. Yes, one quart a week!! You
must have a license to get it at all. So, you
see Beat is going to be good, and I really plan
to be, darling. I told you that, and I remember
it. It won't be difficult.

Your picture was the first thing I unpacked.
As I put it in the center of our dresser,
Paulson said, "Jeez, Beat, I'm going to take my
gal down. She just can't compete with that!" I
talked him into keeping it there.

I'll write more tonight—
Your guy,
Beat

Hotel Mayflower

My darling,

I've a confession to make. I haven't been back to the hotel since I last wrote you. Well, Beat was just five hours in Seattle when he had a job. The company we work for is a huge milling concern. By the way, the job is handling flour. A large Russian freighter is loading right beside the building where I work. She's well-armed and the Russians take good care of her. Paulie and I worked from 3:00 to 11:00 P.M. The job pays well. We work the same shift every day (no night life at all). During an eight-hour shift, I lift between 60 and 80 tons of flour in 98 lb. bags! That's what I like about the job. 'Tis really tough.

Tell all your 4-F friends that it's almost a good feeling to be one. Although we're really in the service, we both agree that 'twould be all right to float around at these high wages. It's murder in comparison to the poor soldiers, sailors, etc. Something should be done. I mean it!

I'm all yours every bit, darling.

Beat

[handwritten on torn Western Union message paper]

Darling,

The snow-capped mountains are just ahead. You can't imagine the beauty of them, appearing from nowhere as we ride along on this parched prairie. We're in Blackfoot, Montana now. Glacier Park is a half hour ahead. Seattle is at the end of this run.

While eating dinner the train came to a sudden stop. I do mean sudden. We piled out and I ran up forward. In the middle of our track was a huge rock. It had rolled down one of the mountains. But for a section crew working near, we probably would have hit it and I'd have finished my meal about a half mile down a steep hillside. The crew heard it fall and stopped our train. Then they worked over an hour getting it broken up and clear of the tracks. The passengers all had a romp in the snow. The Ice Follies gang is aboard, and they really had fun getting each other soaking wet. I watched the crew work and almost wanted to jump in and help—but . . . So, we're on our way trying to catch up some of the time we've lost.

Last night as I waited for sleep to come, I had the feeling that I wanted to ride forever. Every time I get on a train, I'm going some place either strange or home. All the while I'm there, I have to settle down and live as if I belonged there. Then suddenly I must wake up and be off to start over again some place else! That thought takes all the sport out of this traveling, and I used to look forward to every new place. Maybe after a few weeks I will begin to like Seattle—then go out to sea!

Maybe you can capture that feeling. It's hard to put into words. Maybe all this just boils down to the fact that at last I feel that I have my own home some place—more than a Dad and Mother and brother. When I think of home 'tis always you.

We talked all of our problems and worries out—not a single quarrel! There isn't a doubt in my mind about things now. You're the only girl that fits into my arms now. You belong to me.

I'll always love you, darling,
Beat

Dying to Tell You

April 25, 1943—Easter

"I'll meet the train, Dad," Elinor volunteered. "You look tired, and I'm wide awake."

"Let's go together, then, Bunny," Reverend Landgrebe suggested. He put down his pipe. "I'm anxious to see her, too."

Her father sat in his usual place in the living room, reading material in hand. He looked on the corner table for his tobacco can. He collected his pipe and his box of wooden matches.

It was eleven. The family had gathered earlier in the den, as they did every evening, to listen to the latest on the Scott—somber news on this chilly, dark night.

Elinor couldn't imagine putting her head on a pillow after hearing about the desperation in the world. What kind of an Easter would this be? Even with the good news factored in, there was enough evil to give her bad dreams.

She decided to stay up to try to write a cheery letter to Johnny. She settled at her father's desk, found some blank onionskin in the stationery drawer, and filled the fountain pen. But she couldn't think of a thing to write. She couldn't shake the images.

More than 56,000 Jews killed in the second uprising in Warsaw. More than the population of all of Fargo, even with the college students counted. The Nazis were still in charge there.

Elinor tried to counter that image with one of the Allied bombing of aircraft factories in Bremen. The Luftwaffe would be hurting with

115 planes destroyed. But even that good news didn't shake the picture of the Warsaw ghetto and all those human lives.

Or the brutal fighting in the Pacific. Even though our men flying out of Guadalcanal shot down one of the Japanese heroes. She imagined Yamamoto falling from the skies. It was surely an occasion to celebrate. But what about Mickey's Bob? Was he okay?

This war was interminable. And way too huge to comprehend.

⇒ ⇐

At just after two on Good Friday morning, Elinor and her father motored to the station. In her excitement, Elinor couldn't keep herself from tapping her foot impatiently as they got close. They parked the car and then strode into the station where they checked the timetable on the chalkboard.

Georg nodded, pleased. "Just like the old days, Bunny. When the trains were infallibly punctual."

They exited the depot and stood in the crisp spring air. Georg began pointing out the stars.

"They look the same in this hemisphere," he noted. "But for our men down south, the stars are different."

Elinor felt herself bouncing on the platform, as she waited for the lights of the Northern Pacific. Movement helped keep her warm in the chilly air.

"Think of all the people on this earth who are looking at the sky tonight, Bunny," her father continued. "Some are looking at the beginning of a new day. Others the heat of noon."

Elinor, still now, remembered all the "old friends" she had. She wondered which ones sat in foxholes and which ones were flying toward a target. She remembered her Navy friends and thought of them sailing over the deep blue oceans of the world. Elinor sighed, her breath a fog of icy stars in the cold Dakota air.

A group of people came out of the depot and crowded onto the platform. Elinor edged closer to her father. They caught the sound of the locomotive's melancholy whistle. The crisp prairie air carried the whispery moan across the town.

Elinor squeezed her father's warm hand. It wouldn't be long.

Her father glanced at the big depot clock which supervised the railroad yard. They stood under the lights and stared down the track. Elinor ran her fingers through her hair. She straightened her skirt and grinned at her father. His face was lit with energy and his blue eyes sparkled.

The light on the engine came into view. They could feel the rumbling announcement of the wheels braking. The train screeched to a stop at the station.

Elinor laughed as the familiar combination of steam and oil reached her nostrils. "Mick's here, Papa!" she screamed.

The two of them ran through the crowd, down the length of the platform, looking for Mickey.

"There!" Georg pointed.

They ran back toward a car that was just unloading passengers.

Women exited the train, holding the hand of porter at the steps. Most looked like they'd been asleep until the last moment.

Mickey, however, scampered down the train steps, ignoring the outstretched hand of the conductor. "It's so good to be home," she breathed as Elinor hugged her. "Dad, I'm so full of coffee I don't know if I can sleep." Mickey hugged her father and kissed him on the cheek.

They gathered Mick's luggage, packed it into the trunk of the car, and the two girls rode home, chattering, in the back seat with their father chauffeuring the large vehicle.

"So how was the trip?" Georg loved hearing about the trains. He had a pastor's pass which allowed him free rides on the Northern Pacific. When traveling by train to the parishes that needed him, he would use the time on the tracks to prepare. He carried a regular briefcase full of files and information. He packed his clerical robes in the suitcase he carried in the other hand.

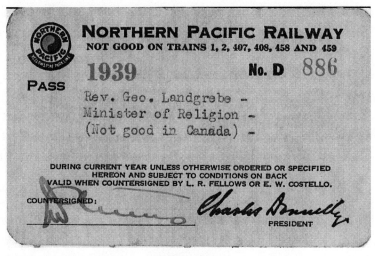

Railroad pass

"Comfortable, Dad. It wasn't crowded at all. I had a berth, so I got in all my sleep."

Elinor could still smell the smoke on her sister's clothing. She winked at Mickey. The girls knew when they had to tell half-truths, little white lies, to keep their parents happy.

≫   ≪

Saturday began bright and warm, a perfect day for a walk downtown. Snow melted everywhere and puddles stood in the low spots along the sidewalks. Right after breakfast dishes were done, Trudie added the yeast and a pinch of sugar to warm water to start a batch of rolls for Easter dinner. Georg finalized his sermon with intermittent breaks with his pipe and his thoughts. Mickey and Elinor announced that they were going downtown to do some shopping.

On their hike, Mickey told Elinor about San Diego. "To be honest, it's hard to make ends meet, kid. Betty and I are struggling. It's not the easiest life. Then, who has an easy life these days?"

Elinor nodded. They stepped around a big puddle on Broadway as they neared downtown. "Almost as big as the Pacific Ocean," Elinor joked.

Mickey laughed. "Speaking of the Pacific, how's your love life?"

"Well, now that you're home, I'll tell you everything. I've been dying to tell you."

Mickey pulled her purse strap up and moved closer to her big sister. "Details, kid."

"I think I wrote you that Beat's done with his training at Gallups Island. He knows that I've been seeing some of the 'old friends' I have here. Beat got Walt's address and they've been writing. Walter told him that he and I were having an affair."

Mickey laughed. "You with Walter?"

"Beat and I broke up during the leave. He said I have too many men around me and that I'm not true to only him. But he goes out on the town all the time in Boston, so he is with other girls. From Wellesley and like that."

"Bunny, did you remind him that he's been seeing other women? Or did you just let him make you feel guilty about your other men?"

"I didn't have a chance Mickey. He was so busy accusing me, I just wanted to get out of there."

"Bunny . . ."

"And he had a chance to work in California. Alameda. Training radiomen. Living in California, not going to war."

"California is getting crowded, kid."

"Well, that's when we broke up. At least I think we did. It's the strangest thing."

"What do you mean?" Mickey stopped to look at Elinor. They stood in front of Todd's Tavern.

Elinor stepped over the litter of cigarette butts and a couple of empty bottles on the sidewalk. "We quarreled. He took me home. That was it. The end." She motioned for her sister to move past the place. The girls stepped quickly.

"But he's still writing to me. Says it was a great leave. That we didn't have even one quarrel. Do you think he might've had too much to drink and now he can't even remember that we broke up?"

"Well, if he did, Bunny, you'd better watch out," Mickey warned.

"I gave Beat back his Sigma Chi pin and the watch he presented to me for Christmas. He must remember that we broke up when he sees those."

"You don't want to be with someone who lets himself get that far gone." Mickey turned to the door of Leeby's.

When the girls stepped into the store, they stopped again for a moment to breathe in the smell of sausages and cheeses. Then they proceeded to the cheese counter to pick up the Limburger their father had ordered.

They decided to purchase a Whitman's Easter Sampler box of candies for their mother, too. It wasn't too much and they could afford an extravagance once in a while. A person couldn't tell what was inside by the box. They hoped it held a couple of chocolate covered cherries, Trudie's favorite.

Then they continued down Broadway, carrying the packages, walking close together, past the six-story Black Building with its modern elevator. They stopped to look in the big window at McCracken Photography. They didn't know anyone in the photos there. Hall Allen Shoes had the latest in spring fashions displayed in their window. The girls ducked into the shop and browsed. "Gee, Bunny, shoes are getting expensive," Mickey complained. "I hope this pair will last a couple more months."

Elinor stopped at Crescent Jewelers and then Hoenk's Furs. She stared in the big glass windows. Impossible dreams.

"Bunny, you're stuck. You need a change. Why not come to San Diego this summer? There are a lot of men there, and you might find someone interesting."

"At least it would be an adventure," Elinor sighed.

As the girls strolled on down Broadway, Mickey glanced at her sister. A glint came into her eyes as she teased, "Isn't Johnny at Camp Roberts? And Dale is somewhere in California, I think."

Elinor had to grin. "I guess, Mickey. But I keep thinking about Beat. Maybe he's sorry about the whole thing."

"Bunny, you're getting sentimental."

"But what if he was just too drunk? Maybe I misunderstood?"

"You know . . ." Mickey began.

Elinor interrupted. "He's far away now and in the thick of things. I feel obligated to write back to him now that he's writing to me again."

"What!"

"You know. Emily Post. It seems the right thing to do. In this war."

Mickey stopped there on the sidewalk and stared at her sister. "I don't think that's a good idea, kid. You're playing with fire."

"I suppose you're right," Elinor whispered. "But at the very least I need to explain about Walter."

"Just don't let Dad find out." Mickey shook her head. She reached into her purse for a cigarette.

Three blocks down Broadway, Elinor slowed to peek in the windows at the Dotty Dunn Hat Shop. She stared at the mannequin heads, posed with the latest in Easter bonnets atop their blank faces.

Mickey tried again. "I hope you'll join us this summer. We could have a lot of fun."

Without taking her eyes away from the window display, Elinor replied, "Maybe I could try out for something in Hollywood. Modeling or something different."

"Lots of opportunities. Hollywood keeps making films, even during the war. And, oh, Bunny, I've seen a lot of them."

Elinor grinned, thinking of it. The silver screen.

Doubts

May 1943

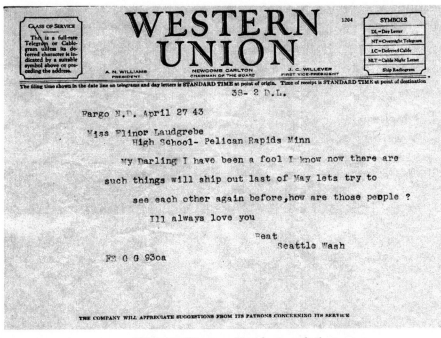

WESTERN UNION

A. N. WILLIAMS
PRESIDENT

NEWCOMB CARLTON
CHAIRMAN OF THE BOARD

J. C. WILLEVER
FIRST VICE-PRESIDENT

The filing time shown in the date line on telegrams and day letters is STANDARD TIME at point of origin. Time of receipt is STANDARD TIME at point of destination.

39- 2 D.L.

Fargo N.D. April 27 43

Miss Elinor Laudgrebe
     High School- Pelican Rapids Minn

   My Darling I have been a fool I know now there are

such things will ship out last of May lets try to

     see each other again before,how are those people ?

        Ill always love you

                              Beat
                                 Seattle Wash

FR C G 930a

THE COMPANY WILL APPRECIATE SUGGESTIONS FROM ITS PATRONS CONCERNING ITS SERVICE

Western Union—I've been a fool

Return address: General Delivery,
Portland, OR
Sat. morn 11:30
(May 1)

My darling,

Today after your TWO letters, it seems to me that all is perfect.

Beat is being good. You don't seem certain of that at times. Believe me, sweets, I'm not doing much drinking. This last week I've been just relaxing, slinging the bull with the fellows, having one now and then, but it's not anything near as bad as many of the nights you and I have had together—and you playing the organ in church a few hours later!

I'm honest enough to say that before this trip is over, I'll be sitting on my ship out there, and I'll wonder if you're being good. Any fellow has doubts about that. I'll read over your letters, tell all the other officers about you and our plans, be very proud of you as I see your big picture on my desk.

I realize the situation you were in, that you needed to see your 'old friends' and keep up morale and all that, and I really don't see how I could have been such a rough fool to the only woman I've ever loved—the only woman I've ever wanted to marry. If I could only prove to you that I've forgotten those 'old friends' and that I'm planning so hard, not for me but for you. No sacrifice is too great for me if I know you'll benefit by it and enjoy it—if you'll feel proud of me and love me every minute. Can you see that and believe in me once again? Time will go by quickly and we'll be together again.

You write that you wonder if the world will ever be the same again. Of course, the world is going to settle down again. We'll all live those very normal lives—the sort of lives that we used to hate at times because they seemed to be so dull and uninteresting. I must keep believing that. We all must, or there is no use fighting.

You're always mine,
I love you,
Beat

(return address: 105 Columbia St., Seattle)
Monday, May 3
12:10 P.M.

My darling Bunny,

Today I sent the pin, watch, etc. back to you
via airmail, special delivery. They would never
be of any use to me. You're the only woman I
can ever see wearing my pin, or our watch. They
looked so useless here in my drawer. Except
for the mood I was in at the time, I would
never have asked for the watch. It made me feel
awfully small when I knew that I loved you and
wanted you.

Now, there is no one in the world that
deserves to have them more than you. You'll
have something to remind you of me always, to
give you a bit of strength when doubts cross
your mind.

Let's hope that everything arrives in time
for the big shindig this Saturday. You can
find a prominent place to place the pin, I
know. And I'll be thinking of you as the hours
pass Saturday night, wondering how you look
in your formal, knowing how the students will
be admiring you. Thinking that you might have
a moment or two to think of me way out here,
listening to the Hit Parade and dreaming of you
as each selection plays.

You mustn't have any fears that I'll ever give
you a physical beating! Really, only a coward
would hit or hurt a woman. At times I've felt
as if I might, but there's something inside
me that somehow musters the common sense and

willpower. You might hurt me quite deeply but I'm certain that there are other and far more practical methods of dealing.

The fellows are in their bed and the light must bother them some, so I'll go to bed and think out all the plans for the hoped-for trip.

I'm all yours, always,
Beat

105 Columbia Street, Seattle
May 6, 1943 (Thursday)

My dearest Elinor,

I've really got the fever again as there are many really good rumors flying about what trips are about due. I want to do all I can so that I can in some measure believe that I'm doing as much as the next fellow, the guy on Guadalcanal or in Tunisia or in China. I want to be able to hold my head up after the war and say that I did my part. You really can't know how that ambition possesses me.

No letter for three whole days and no hope that one will come in the next two or three. That's my thought for tonight. You're "just too busy" or "there hasn't been time." It seems you're slacking off again. I hope that I'm wrong.

Thought of something funny. I'm really not "Flopsie" any more—quite the opposite. Damn it. It takes a couple of weeks or more to wear off a leave at home.

We were paid today and it really wasn't hard to take. I'm sending Bruns money for the car repairs and banking the rest. 'Twas nice of him to loan me his car for my Pelican runs.

You worry and fret about having to spend a weekend in Pelican. Did you ever stop to think of the freedom you really have now? There are many of us that are giving up much more than that. The only reason that I mention that is because it might help you to evaluate a bit more clearly just how lucky you are. I'm really not sorry for one bit of time I give up. A person just isn't supposed to have everything perfect these days. There are many sacrifices to be made before we can return to that "perfect" stage again. I'm turning into a Fulton Lewis, Jr. Oh, man! But I'm really quite serious.

Yours,
Beat

May 9, Mothers Day

Mah Sweet,

I bought a huge book today. It consists of
detailed maps, information on cities, ports,
etc. I got that old feeling again—just to be
on the move. It's crowding me again as it did
in those days Bruns and I planned our cross
country train trips with maps and notes laid
out all over his or my room. I'll be so glad to
get going now and to come back and figure out a
way to go a still different place.
    Maybe Beat's off your list again. No letter
today again.

2 A.M.
No letter tonight, after a long, hard night at
work thinking of you at Pelican. What a cruel
woman! So, Beat is going to have a few drinks
and sling the bull with Johnny.

                                    Goo-nite—
                                       Beat

Wed. aft. 4:00
May 12

My darling,

What a day! Paulson has a ship now. I'm the top man for a chief operator's job! There are two fellows ahead of me on the register, but they can't handle the whole set-up. They are looking for jobs as second or third radiomen. So, darling, any time now should find me going aboard my very own ship. Maybe tomorrow!

Paulson is just back and raving about his ship and the equipment. If I were a really lowdown rat, I could have had the ship. He was in the head, so I answered the call which was for either Beaton or Paulson. He was in Seattle first, so I told the ACA they were talking to Paulson. Then John and I got him dressed and rushed him over to sign on. Right now I'm green with envy. His ship sounds really perfect—a brand new Mackay machine.

Good ol' Steve. Bet you two had fun together talking over ol' times and things. Wish I could have been with you for a few hours that night—or all night.

Hope the shower for Ginny went fine. The concert tonight should be sompin' (Spring Social Event Number Two). If you could get through school as you hope in three weeks, you can take a rest at home with the folks. Get things ready for your trip. Jus' thought to myself, "Wherever the hell she's goin'." You see, every letter brings a new decision or idea from you.

When you finally decide (and it will most likely be the day you leave) let me know just where and when and for how long.

Your guy,
Beat

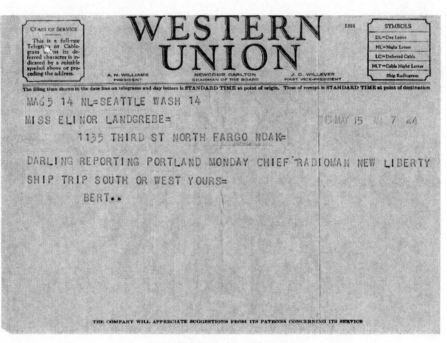

New Liberty ship telegram

"DARLING REPORTING PORTLAND MONDAY CHIEF RADIOMAN NEW LIBERTY SHIP TRIP SOUTH OR WEST YOURS BERT [sic]"

Friday, May 14

My dearest,

You're now reading a letter from the happiest fellow in the world! I've got a brand new queen of the seas for my ship. Honey, she's a huge Liberty cargo ship just accepted and O.K.'d May 8! I'm so excited that I'm jumpy. This letter looks it, but I really have a perfect excuse! I asked a few leading questions at the office here and the fellow finally said, "All I can tell you, Sparks, is that you aren't going to Alaska. You're going south and maybe west." So, I've got a good trip to hope for.

I just wired you and Mom. Before that I spent four and a half hours with a Navy Lieutenant. Before we go out, we have to report to them. He took me into a room with a big steel door. That's when I really began to realize why he had just sat and talked with me for two hours—about radio, sea, subs, etc. Anyway I know all the codes. I'll have all new equipment—at least three rooms for me—and I'm the top Sparks on her. I'm the big shot on a tough job—at last! I'm just plain shaking!!

I'm supposed to report on Tuesday. The ship is in Portland. My letters of introduction to different people read, ". . . to extend to Mr. Beaton all the usual courtesies of the port." Hope those courtesies can take care of me.

The fellows don't know it, but I'm going to be awfully sorry to leave them, especially Johnny. We spent a night just eating, seeing a show and not saying much. Paulson is going out tomorrow night. He's on a three trip Liberty ship and has it swell. John should have a ship any time, as he's number one on the chief operator's list. So, to another place, more new friends. Then leave there, too! What a hell of a life for a guy!

It's getting late. There are many things on my mind tonight. I want to lie here for a long while and figure things out. There's this business of secret codes. It's quite a load on my mind, believe it or not. It's just having it given to me without warning—and on top of the rest of the job, too! But by tomorrow I'll have this ol' Irish mind cleared up, things in their right notch.

Your letter full of doubts has me grinning. I've hurt you and I'm sorry about that. I'm sincerely sorry. Honey, you're my future happiness. You're my insurance against a lonely, useless, unhappy and tired future.

All yours,
Beat

Sun. eve 9:10
May 16

My sweets,

I was up at nine this morning, packed my clothes, books, etc. into two sea bags and my suitcase. That's a big job. So many things to fold, arrange and cram into a small space. We took them to the station and checked our bags through on my ticket. Now all I need do is get that noon train tomorrow.

I'm going to attempt to call you tomorrow night from my hotel room in Portland—if and when I get one. Our birthday is tomorrow. Bet your birthday is very happy. Mine won't be so very, I'm afraid. I'll be on a train after rushing around all morning—ride for five hours—hop off and try to get a room and locate my ship. Will be the only good happy moment of my birthday to hear your voice again.

Life kinda seems a mess now. After I get past these first few days and get settled again, it won't be bad. I'll just remember in these lonely hours that someday we really shall be living our lives together.

I'll always love you,
Beat

St. Andrews Hotel, Portland
Monday eve 6:00
May 17—
Our Birthday

My darling,

Here I am! My company is really good to me. I called in and they had a guy come down and take me over here to a reserved room. Guess rooms are awfully hard to find here, as in Seattle.

    I've just placed a call to you in Pelican and they say it will be about two hours. This time I'll wait 'til tomorrow morning. I'm just not going to give up! It's going to be swell to hear your voice again, and I've got to hear it!

    Guess what! Johnny and I had parted. I felt tough. Almost as empty as when I say good-byes to you. I was in the room getting things ready. In walked Johnny and he handed me his assignment papers to a new tanker, and it's here in Portland! He'll be down tomorrow night; and, if possible, I'm going to meet his train. So, all I need to make me feel perfect is your saying, "I love you, Beat."

With all my love,
Beat

That's me. Look how lucky you are!
   "Particular people choose the St. Andrews for a quiet night's rest in a downtown location"

May 17
Monday
9:00 P.M.

My darling,

You needn't wish me a Happy Birthday. I'm the happiest fellow alive! You sounded so very good—so much mine. And as I told you before in a couple of letters, there might be a chance of a long layover. There IS!! Guess we're really going places because she's getting the works in armament, etc. They say she'll start loading about May 27, and that should last ten days. You could go to San Diego to see Mickey via Portland!! You promised me a birthday present. Well, honey, this is it. We've got to get together for the sake of, let's say, morale.

It's easy making a phone call from the hotel. I took a long bath and had just finished shaving when your call came through. There I was, all soap, a towel around my neck, shirt off, hair mussed and your voice saying, "Is that you, Beat?" And I felt tops. If only we had television!

Quiz program no. 1,665,089,436:

1. I'm not sure just yet where you should write

me. You'll know in due time—about five minutes after I know.

2. The things I don't wish to take with me will either be sent home or checked at my steamship company here.

3. There are a lot of ways that I could tell you where I'm going—by letter, wire, phone call, etc. But I probably won't know myself!!

4. As for how long I shall be gone—ditto number 3!!

That's all tonite. Send your inquiries to
D.R. Beaton (Captain Quiz)
General Delivery
Portland, Oregon
Prompt answers assured!

An Evil Attraction?

Monday, May 17, 1943

"HAPPY BIRTHDAY!"

Elinor held the phone away from her ear. She laughed, even though the movement of her head drew new twinges at her temples. "Is that you, Beat?" she interrupted the song. "Happy birthday to you, too. Happy twenty-second."

"I'm calling you from my hotel room. Sweet deal here, honey. I just asked the desk to put the call through. Then I bathed and started to shave while the operator went to work." He laughed. "Of course, the connection came through before I had predicted, and here I stand, with lather on my cheeks. I'm a soapy mess right now."

Elinor glanced around the hallway in her rooming house. "Are you naked?" she whispered.

Beat laughed again. "Good thing we don't have TV, honey. I have a towel around my neck, though."

Now it was Elinor's turn to laugh. "I wish I had a TV."

"Have you ever seen TV, Bunny? I saw a set at the World's Fair."

Elinor put her hand to her forehead, to compress the pounding. "Thank you for the pretty birthday card, Beat. It arrived on the weekend," she managed.

"Hey, Bunny, I have an idea." Beat was talking fast as the three minutes were clicking away. "The ship won't be leaving here for a while. Maybe if you are coming this way to see Mickey . . ."

She heard the excitement in his voice. A couple of drinks, too. "Bunny, this ship is something else. You've got to see it to believe it."

The migraine—such a birthday gift—was taking hold of her skull. "First I have to finish the school year. Then I'll figure out what I'm doing." She covered the mouthpiece to silence a low moan that escaped.

"I thought you might make a stop in Portland to see my ship. On your way to California. I could put you up here overnight and we'd have a chance to try again." He spoke cheerfully. She knew he was trying to convince her to try. To try something outrageous. Again.

"Well, I have finals to give and grade. The Glee Club concert. Graduation. And then I still have to pack up." She leaned against the wall.

"I would love to see you again, Bunny. It's the only thing that matters to me. Before I ship out, you know."

She knew. Into the war, the danger, the battles. Elinor remembered Emily Post's decree to be especially kind to our brothers in arms. Hospitality to the uniform. In black and white. "Give what we can in whatever way we can to every man in uniform because we have no other way of taking a personal part."

"Maybe," she started. She thought about their last night together in the Aquarium. She sighed. "I don't know, Beat," she added.

"I'm going to send you instructions," he continued as if she had agreed to this preposterous plan. "Where to go once you get off the train in Seattle. Be watching for them."

Mickey called Beat an evil attraction. Indeed, Elinor found it hard to resist him. Sometimes they drank too much. Way too much. And Beat always knew where to find hide-outs where they could be alone.

"I'll keep an eye out. But I can't promise . . ."

"C'mon," Beat laughed. "I hope to see you soon, honey. We can have some more fun together."

And then the operator cut in. "Your three minutes are up."

"Bye, Beat," Elinor whispered. She couldn't stand the noise—any noise—any more.

He yelled, "Try, honey."

And the phone clicked. She settled the handpiece into its cradle and walked her drumming head upstairs to her room. She moved one step at a time to avoid jiggling her head. Her knuckles were white as she grasped the bannister.

She took a double dose of Anacin and arranged her body carefully into her bed. She closed her eyes. Her fate. Another unpredictable migraine. She would have to call for a substitute. Again.

The aura flashed through her head, bold and jagged shapes which interrupted her vision. The pounding began, now in earnest. It wrapped around her head, grasped her face, twisted her brain. Along with the jagged lines and the bright designs that wobbled now under her eyelids, she heard Beat's voice. "Try, honey."

She'd leave her trip to the coast to The Fates. If Beat were still in Portland when she went to see Mickey, she'd stop in to visit. She would return the Sigma Chi pin and the Christmas watch. She would break it off once and for all and then continue down the coast to San Diego.

She rolled to her side and moved her wastebasket closer. She had remembered a towel. She was ready for the vomiting.

She lay there, in her private battleground. Her thoughts twirled into nightmares. A girl during wartime couldn't make plans. If she thought she was in love and she planned to settle down, well. Bad news. She might end up a widow. Or taking care of an invalid the rest of her days. Elinor leaned over the wastebasket.

A girl should just have fun. Who knew how many days anyone had left?

But first. The obligations. Johnny was due home any day. There were still papers to grade. Then finals. The end of a school year. All the ceremonies. The faculty meetings. And now Beat had inserted himself back into her life and was pressuring her, too.

The jagged lines moved across her vision as she wrestled with her future. In minutes her thoughts were no longer clear. The pain was excruciating and took her full attention.

Don't Worry About Expenses

May 1943

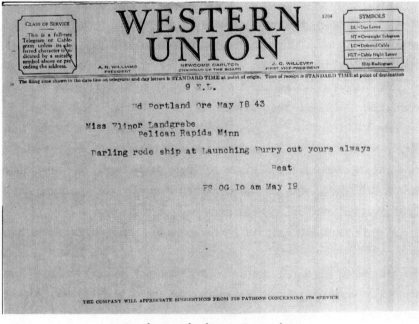

Darling rode ship at Launching
Hurry out yours always
Beat

Tuesday evening
May 18

My darling,

Today was tops in thrills for your guy. I moved in here this morning about ten and then I left for St. John's where the ship is. All together I made buses for about an hour to get out there. I talked to the guards at the gate. They told me my ship, the *James Oliver*, was due to be launched in 25 minutes! I really high-tailed it for Way 11. Grabbing the first cap I saw there, I showed him my pass and asked for the chief guard. I found him and he put me aboard six minutes before the champagne bottle was broken.

Yep, honey, I rode my ship down into the water amid all the cheering, whistles, etc. And, darling, don't think I wasn't thrilled! Maybe you'll see it in a movie. There were cameramen there.

So, we were picked up by tugs and put into line at the outfitting dock. That's where guns, radio equipment—well, everything—is added, down to the mattresses, etc. To see what my ship would be like when finished, I went aboard number one in the line. Honey, if I could only tell you how perfect it is. My equipment will be brand new—a huge Mackay Coke machine. (That's what we call the radio at GI because it looks like a darn big Coke machine.) The men were working on it and they were glad to see me. I helped them with a few pointers. Yes, at Gallups Island we learn every part of that very same piece of equipment.

My cabin is maple-finished and large. There's a shower bath close by. My bunk has sides on it; she'll roll around, you know. There are plenty of drawers for clothes. A closet is set in the corner. Two portholes let air and light in. Oh, darling, it's homelike already. What you would probably call sun porches are on all sides of my shack and quarters. The decks are gray steel and quite roomy—sun baths for me! Officer's mess is a big, clean room. Looks O.K. I'm happy 'cuz it's 10,884 tons, too. After one trip I can become a full grade lieutenant with two full bars, you see, because it's the largest of the ships, and I'm chief operator aboard her. Happy Days!

They say at the yards that she'll be ready to go about May 26th. Then we load, etc. You can't imagine the hundreds of workers, the massive steel structures, the huge yards, the sight of the eleven ships in all states of structure. The sight is quite shocking, surprising.

Many women workers do their bit, too. Most of them do clean up work at the outfitting dock. They figured I was a boss or sompin' 'cuz of my khaki pants, white shirt, and leather jacket. They'd all smile and work harder.

This weekend whenever I can get the call through, you'll be telling me all. Sit down now and rehearse a nice long speech—folks or no folks!! How's about, "I love you like mad, Beat, etc. etc." I'm just going to listen 'til I drop from sheer joy!

Your guy,
Beat

Hotel Benson
R.K. Keller -- W. E. Boyd
Managing Directors
Portland, Oregon

Wednesday 5:30 (5/19)

My dearest Elinor,

Maybe you wouldn't realize it, but Beat's got a job—a tough job—one that requires much work, education, worry, and guts. It's a real man's job. Most of the time I'm a clear-minded, cool-headed, calculating, thinking and serious man. But when I sit down to write you, I forget all these things. I forget about being grown up. I just relax and have fun. I kid along, sometimes almost childishly, and I feel a whole lot better for feeling very young again! Soon again I must begin acting very grown-up, always doing and saying the right thing to people, putting a serious look on this face that would much sooner smile.

If you're coming out (as I hope), you'll be making a lot of plans this weekend. You get out here, and I'll have money to give you for your trip and stuff all the way through. Don't worry about expenses. Just get the heck out here and see your Beat. It's your turn to do the planning, rushing around, sacrificing and traveling, now.

I'll meet your train. You'll have the time of your life, sweets!

Until later tonight,
I love you, darling
Always,
Beat

Wed. eve

My dearest,

Your swell letter came tonight. I picked it up not long ago. What a birthday present you got from Mother Nature! Poor you, darling! If I'd known, I'd have wired a few cartons of Anacin and a couple of cases of bourbon.

You should be proud of me!! You said you were. If you could see the ship, you'd realize what a responsibility I do have. Usually these ships carry two, three and four operators. Because we are educated to the auto alarm and all its workings, we are able to take the whole job over. Auto alarms are set to go off on a certain series of dots and dashes. They are radio receivers and have a complicated mechanical addition that counts seconds, dashes, dots, etc. It takes a brain just to understand them, let alone know all the other equipment. I'm bragging again, but it feels good!

You'll hear all about my quarters, mates, etc. for certain. You'll hear all—be damned the military secrets. Guess you wouldn't remember much and besides you won't meet any Japs!

Dale seems to want to hear from "cute and witty" you so you'd best make him happy. I really haven't much to say on that sort of thing. Let's just skip it, hmmm?

I positively don't want you to go to the U.S.O. in Fargo. So you probably will!! I was at the canteens at the colleges during my leave. Sales of contraceptives really are booming.

They're not nice guys. At least I know and you know what they're looking for.

Guess maybe both of us have been around a little and had awfully cheap fun. But when a person finally falls in love, those things are forgotten. There's only you in my mind.

I still love you. Now it's your turn to try to do a few things for me.

Yours forever,
Beat

Hotel St. Andrews
Friday evening—
May 21

My darling Elinor,
Please rush through school. Don't waste a moment at home and come here. Catch a Northern Pacific all the way through—or Great Northern. Leave on a Friday and be here Sunday morning. If I should be shipped out, I'll wire your train. If that doesn't reach you, there'll be a long note here at the St. Andrews Hotel and a reservation for you, as rooms are darn hard to find. Call me collect some morning. I'm always here until noon Fargo time—and later. Two hours to put a call through, remember!! That way would be quicker than wiring. Let me know what's up. Don't hold me in this terrible suspense!

I'm not certain, but I think this is Johnny McCall's last night in Portland. They may sail any time between Saturday and next Wednesday. That's how secrecy is maintained. The crew just doesn't have a chance to tip anyone off!!

Maybe you should rest for a while when you arrive. I'll be on the ship during a lot of the day, and you can just sleep all you wish. Then we'll try some of these nightclubs I hear so much about. I'd be the proudest gold braid in the world—you with me in a fine place.

Ich liebe dich, mein schatz. (I remembered that from a letter of long ago.)

All yours, now and forever,
Beat.

Hotel St. Andrews
Sunday afternoon 2:00
May 23

My darling,

The call didn't go through Friday eve. I'm on the run so much now that I can't find two hours to sit and wait! I've given up the hope of seeing you before I leave. Now I'm the one that's mad because you teach school!

By the way, you were out very late last Friday. Later than we ever got by with! After that call hadn't gone through, John and I went down and caught a taxi to his ship. On the waterfront it's pitch black. We had to identify ourselves about ten times before we were aboard. At that time they were "filling." We went through the ship's passageways, lit only by a red light about every forty feet . . . Spooky! I sat down at his equipment and tuned in seven different stations on a low frequency band. Took code. We talked radio, Navy stuff, etc. We planned to meet next morning. John didn't call, so he's on his way!!

Since all this came up and I came through O.K., I've got an expense account—cab fares, equipment, stamps, tips, etc. go on it with no questions asked. Tomorrow all of us ship's officers go aboard and make out inventory sheets—ask for what we need—down to a thumbtack, even. I'm going to get all the extras I can—even ashtrays! So, to spend a sunny Sunday aboard

the ship—in a crowded, hot room, guarded by six
sailors . . . What a life, honey!

Your guy,
Beat

P.S. Hope your exams go well, darling.

Hotel St. Andrews
Monday (5/24)

My darling—

What a life! I'm worn out every night. I just droop to sleep. The government examiner was aboard and we had to go over every part of the equipment—even specific gravity readings on the small A batteries. The stuff passed fine. All I'm worried about now is finding that I forgot a book or sompin'. I'm going to check thoroughly tomorrow so that I won't leave Portland without anything.

We're taking a trial run tomorrow about 120 miles or so. I'll be aboard for all the company bigwigs and their families to look at. They always are fascinated by the bridge and Sparks' equipment. Maybe there'll be a pretty daughter!!! Anyway, I'm going to get a lot of code, check my batteries and get used to everything.

You seem to be doing a bit of running around! Two parties last Thursday alone. What a social climber you are! The navy blue hat with the white tassel sounds very much like you. Bet it's as cute as all the rest of your hats—or is it you that makes them look so good! Bring it along when you come. I'll promise to rave about it.

Plans: You leave Fargo Thursday, the third, and arrive here the fifth. I'll be at the station. Then we'll go to wherever my ship is and locate ourselves. When I leave, you'll have a ticket for San Diego and you can hustle down there. When I wire my new address, answer by

wire, either Yes or No to this plan. Guess it
wouldn't pay to call you at home this weekend.
Someone might (mis)understand what's about to
come off.

Yours, forever,
Beat

Summer Plans

May 1943

"THE USUAL?" THE WAITRESS asked. "It's chicken noodle tonight."

Elinor nodded. "And tuna salad."

"Same," Ginny added.

"Ding!" The insistent bell rang from the kitchen.

The waitress turned on her heel, still scribbling their orders on two guest checks. She darted off to grab the meals for another table.

Ginny and Elinor had arrived at the restaurant just in time to claim their favorite table—the one tucked into the back corner where they could gossip more freely. The place was nearly full, busy with chatter and music. The jukebox played "I Don't Want to Walk Without You." The fry cook, at her small kitchen window in the back of the restaurant, rang her bell again and shouted, "Order up."

The girls had settled onto the wooden benches of their booth, arranging their sweaters and purses beside them. Elinor moved the sugar dispenser to the end of the table and Ginny slid the salt and pepper shakers over. Their vision clear, they were ready to talk.

Sunlight streamed in through the restaurant glass, past the cut outs of tulips and daisies that now hung there on threads attached with transparent tape. The buds on the neighborhood trees had begun opening. Robins strutted around, gathering nesting material and snapping half-frozen worms from the cold soil. The world was awake and bustling.

"Ding!" More meals ready for delivery.

Elinor looked across the table at her friend. "It's wild here. Busy tonight. Maybe we should've gone to the Pelican."

"Well, we're here, and we got our table, Bunny. It's noisy tonight, so no one can overhear us. Anyway, the jukebox is better here, don't you think?"

Elinor nodded. "Just a few days left, Ginny. I'll be happy to be done with this year of teaching. There's too much going on right now."

"These extra duties." Ginny laughed.

"The prom. What are you wearing?"

Ginny moaned, "Same old formal. I wore it in high school. You know. That dusty rose thing."

Their glasses of Coca-Cola appeared on the table, and, before the girls could thank her, the waitress charged down the tight aisle between the booths and the tables.

Elinor lazily unwrapped the paper from around one end of the straw. She blew on the open end, shooting the wrapping at Ginny. The girls giggled.

"I can't imagine planning a wedding while you're teaching." Elinor shook her head. "There's just so much detail in a wedding if you do it right. According to the book, anyway."

And then Ginny opened up. Wedding planning was her favorite topic. She hoped that Charlie would make it home for the celebration. The Army didn't plan around the soldiers, after all. What if he didn't make it, didn't get the leave as expected? The girls agreed that that would be unimaginable. But the odds were that he'd be there.

Ginny took a breath as the sandwiches and cups of soup arrived, then added, "I can't think about it. How's the glee club coming along? Will you be ready for the spring concert?"

Elinor nodded. "I think so. It's just that we haven't had that many rehearsals. The baseball team gets preference in this crazy extracurricular schedule of mine." She stirred her soup and stared as the steam rose. "I can't remember what teaching was like before the war . . . when we didn't have to take over the extracurricular duties of the men who've left."

"It's exhausting all right," Ginny nodded. "Summer plans? Have you settled on something?"

"I'm thinking about going to the coast. To visit my sister in San Diego." Elinor took a bite of her tuna salad sandwich.

"Isn't that close to Johnny, too?" Ginny leaned in, smiling.

Elinor blushed. "Well, seeing Johnny is part of the plan. We can have some fun before he heads to war."

She didn't mention the possibility of sitting at the soda counter in California drugstores, waiting to be discovered.

Both waitresses were flying in and out of the door to the kitchen, racing from one table to another. Kitchen smells, mostly sizzling burgers and French fries, invaded the place with every swing of the door.

The waitress appeared with the final total on their checks. The girls signed and stood up. They each left a nickel on the table for the good service.

While they had been eating and chatting, the warm spring sun had set. The girls slipped into their sweaters. Early May evenings brought a chill to the air. They swung their purses over their shoulders and waved good-bye to friends.

As they exited, Elinor turned to Ginny. "You know, I've been thinking. I might stop in to see Beat on the way to California . . . if he's still in Portland when our gig in Pelican is up."

"But why, Bunny?" Ginny stammered, her eyebrows lowered. One hand raised, she stopped short on the sidewalk. "You've broken it off. What are you thinking?"

Elinor continued walking and Ginny quickened her pace to catch up. They stopped under the streetlight that marked their diverging paths home.

Elinor turned toward Ginny. She pulled her purse strap tightly over her shoulder. "I have to have a talk with him. He sent me back the Sigma Chi pin and the watch—"

"But, Elinor . . ."

"He keeps writing to me, and now he's sent these things back to me. Can't you see? I have to make it very plain to him. We are not a couple." Elinor grimaced. "I need to give him back his damned pin. And that watch. And, Ginny, I won't need notecards this time." She smiled. "Then I'll go to see Johnny."

A Bad Break

May 1943

Pelican Rapids, Minnesota
Study Hall—Thurs. (5/27)

Dear Elinor,

Just ten minutes left and the kids are still coming and going. Happy days, tho'. This is my last one for Pelican Rapids. You surely planned it grand so as to get out of that. Mr. Shipp has had your study hall. Mrs. Johnson has had the last two classes in the day and a couple days the soph. classes met. But I don't know the arrangement and Alice took care of the Juniors. Now, you see, you really weren't important at all.

Your exam schedule is: Eng. XI at 8:00 Monday, English X at 10:15 Monday and German Wed. AM at 8:00. I have no exams Monday so should there be any reason for your not being here (and I hope nothing but laziness) I could arrange to police your darlings for you. Just let me know if I should.

You took a good week to be in the hospital if

you had to choose one—as the weather has been so miserable. Am wearing my coat today.

After I finished talking with your mother last night, I remembered I forgot to ask about Johnny. You got a bad break on the time he was able to be here.

Be seeing you—
Love,
Irma

There was an insured package. Am not sending it. Hope that is O.K.

General Delivery
Aberdeen, Wash.
May 25, Tuesday
[9:30 PM postmark]

My darling—

Beat was scared!! But good, darling. There hasn't been a letter since last Saturday. None today. As I walked here from the P.O., I wondered about it. Then the girl told me there was a Western Union call for me.

I rushed up here and got the telegram from Irene. Then I placed a call to your home. By that time I was shaking—every thought in the world crowded in. Maybe that clot had moved. Maybe you might be seriously sick. Even . . . But I just couldn't think any further.

The call took only ten minutes to go through to Fargo, a real miracle. Irene was her same old self. I got mad and shouted for her to quit fooling. I wanted to know where and how you were. Finally she told me you were all right again. That you'd be okay soon and be able to finish school.

Honey, I felt relieved!! At that time our ship's clerk came in. He looked so startled when he saw me that I had to laugh. I told him what had happened in the past 15 minutes. We both agreed that things happen fast nowadays.

That definitely ruins our plans for meeting, doesn't it?

We tie up at a dock downtown tomorrow. I'm moving aboard in the morning. I've packed all things that won't be of use. I'm sending home my blue uniform, winter underwear, a lot of heavy civvies, etc. It's too warm to wear them out here, I guess. Thursday we go to Aberdeen, Wash. We'll be there Friday afternoon, I imagine.

The skipper is giving me all the code books first thing in the morning. I'm going to do all the decoding and be the first to know what's what aboard the ship. We've got a good crew and a good trip ahead.

Be a good little patient, darling. Get well real soon. I love you so darn much. I'd hate to lose you. There just wouldn't be a world left for me. So, be careful, darling.

Your guy, always,
Beat

What Day Is It?

May 1943

SOUNDS TIPTOED INTO HER unconscious. She could discern muffled footsteps, soft voices. The too-familiar smell of antiseptic enveloped her. Elinor knew where she was without opening her eyes. She felt for the edges of the narrow bed and then hugged the pillow. She would face the world later.

"Bunny?" She heard her mother's voice.

Elinor tipped her body toward the sound and squinted one eye open, a narrow slit. She was practiced in not letting in too much light at once. One glittery light could trigger the pain. Her eyeballs still felt like hot marbles.

She tried to smile at her mother, but found that smiling took too much effort. "Mother? What happened?" Elinor felt her mother's warm hand on hers.

"You're okay, Bunny. They did the cleansing. But then you . . ."

"Why am I here then? Am I okay?"

"You'll be fine." Trudie squeezed her daughter's hand. "This was a really bad headache, Bunny," her mother explained. "It came on right after your D & C. You've been pretty sick for four days already."

"Oh," Elinor wanted to sob. "Mother."

Trudie leaned over her daughter. "The doctors have done everything they know how to do. Strong drugs . . . to give you some relief."

Elinor moaned. She couldn't help it.

"We're in St. Luke's," her mother continued.

Elinor opened her other eye. She raised herself a bit on one elbow and tried to focus. The window shades had been pulled. She searched for her mother's face in the darkened room.

The door to the room opened in a burst of light and a nurse peeked in. Elinor averted her eyes and lay back on the bed. The nurse's white-capped head disappeared when she spotted Trudie in the chair by the bed. Elinor waited as the door closed slowly, relieved at the renewed darkness.

"What day is it, Mother?"

"It's Thursday morning. May 27. Sunday is Decoration Day, Bunny."

Thursday! In a moment of lucidity, Elinor remembered Pelican. Her classroom. The end of the school year. "Did someone call the school?" Elinor tried to sit up.

Trudie grabbed a second pillow and fluffed it up. She set the pillow on top of the one already on the bed. Elinor leaned into them.

"Your father called, and everything is taken care of."

With a deep sigh of relief, Elinor whispered, "Thank goodness."

There were such teacher shortages during the war years that others from the faculty would have had to take over for Elinor in her absence. "I wonder who I'll have to thank this time," she sighed.

Trudie got up to find her purse. "I've brought you your mail. When you can read again you might want it." Her mother spoke from the corner of the dark room.

"Something from Darrow?"

"And Dale, I think." Trudie sat again beside Elinor's bed. She set the envelopes on the bedside table.

"Can I go home tomorrow? Perhaps Dad would drive me to Pelican Sunday? I have to finish out this school year."

Elinor touched her forehead. Still tender but no longer throbbing. She felt a jiggle of queasiness in her stomach, though, as she moved her aching body.

The nurse reentered the room, this time with a tray on which lay a large white pill and a small glass of water. She stood by Elinor's bed, waiting for a chance to dispense the medicine.

"Don't worry, Bunny. We'll figure out a way to get you back to school. Your father is heading to Bismarck and then Minot. But Johnny's in town. He might drive you."

"Johnny's here?!" Elinor fell back onto her bed and covered her head with one pillow. Her voice, muffled, wailed, "Has he seen me like this?"

"He's been at the house a few times, waiting for your return. Worried. You know how he is. He'll be so glad to hear that you're feeling better."

"Oh, Mother, I can't see him like this!"

"Well, there's not much time left. I think he leaves soon for duty. Somewhere. You know they can't tell us. In case we're spies."

Elinor drew herself upright again as the nurse handed her patient the white pill. "To relax you," she advised. "Drink as much water as you can, Elinor."

Elinor did as she was told, but she knew it would take a much larger pill to relax her. The end of the school year. Grades and good-byes. And here was Johnny, just when her systems had collapsed. She remembered the pleas from Darrow. He wanted her to come to the coast. It was all too much pressure.

"Could I have several of those?" she asked the nurse. She would have smiled but she felt that her face would crack.

The nurse scowled.

Elinor swallowed the pill with the water. Then she carefully rearranged her tired body back onto the mattress.

Hurry!

May 1943

Aberdeen, Wash.
Friday, May 28
11:00

My darling—

We docked this morning at 9 AM. The trip up was rough but a lot of fun for me. So many new things to learn. Of course, we were blacked out. That deck is really hard to get around on when it's pitch black!!

We'll be loading XXX and XXX and XXX. I'm one of the very few on board who knows where we're going and just about when we'll be back. I'm happy, so you know it won't be Alaska!! 'Twill be some time before we're through the entire trip though.

We shall be leaving here about June 10 for San Pedro, California. That's really a part of Los Angeles. So about June 7 you start writing General Delivery Los Angeles. That's only 125 miles from San Diego. Guess what I'm thinking?

I'm a long way from a night at Gene's or a

piano solo at your home or a show or a long
walk—all the things I want so very much. You
can see why it is bad business to even think
about such things now. In the long days ahead
I'll remember many, many of the grand times
we've had, and I'll be planning toward the next
times we have together.

Your picture is on the bulkhead right over
the front of my bed. You rock back and forth and
it's fun to watch you. If you don't get seasick,
why should I?

> All my love, darling,
> Yours, forever,
> Beat

SATURDAY NIGHT
EIGHT O'CLOCK

MY DARLING,

HOW ARE YOU, SWEETS? I'VE BEEN CHASING AROUND
THE SHIP FOR A COUPLE OF HOURS. THE CADET AND I
SHOWED THE CAPTAIN'S DAUGHTER AND SON THE WHOLE
SHIP. THEY REALLY HAD PUZZLED LOOKS ON THEIR
FACES WHEN I SHOWED THEM THE INSIDES OF THE
TRANSMITTER AND AUTO ALARM AND THE DIRECTION
FINDER AND FATHOMETER. (BY THE WAY, IT WAS A
DISTINCT PLEASURE. THE GAL IS ABOUT 20 YEARS
OLD AND A HONEY OF A BRUNETTE.)
    I GOT MY 'ZOOT ZOOT' TODAY—THE RUBBER OUTFIT.
IT'S A HUGE AND CUMBERSOME THING, BUT IT MIGHT
COME IN VERY HANDY SOME DAY. WE'RE GETTING GAS
MASKS AND WHISTLES SOON. WE HAVE TWO FLASHLIGHTS
FOR SIGNALLING IN THE WATER AND A KNIFE FOR DUTY.
WE WILL GET THE EMERGENCY RATIONS OF CHOCOLATE,
HARD TACK, ETC. BEFORE WE SAIL. THIS IS SERIOUS
BUSINESS JUST ALONG THE COAST HERE, BUT WHERE WE
PLAN TO GO, IT WILL BE SLEEPING IN CLOTHES ALL THE
TIME WITH EVERYTHING READY TO GO AT ANY TIME. WHAT
A LIFE THAT WILL BE FOR A POOR NORTH DAKOTAN!
    THE LOADING IS GOING ALONG ALL RIGHT. WE'LL BE
READY TO SAIL ABOUT JUNE 8 OR SOONER. WE'VE GOT A
DARN VALUABLE CARGO. IT'S HIGH IN MONETARY VALUE AND
A LOT HIGHER IN VALUE TO THE GUYS WAITING FOR IT.
    HOW DO YOU LIKE THE TYPE? I'M GETTING USED TO
USING THE THING AGAIN. THE CHIEF ENGINEER AND I
HAD TO TRADE MACHINES. HE COULDN'T FIGURE OUT
WHY THE GUYS HAD GIVEN HIM A MACHINE WITH ALL
CAPITAL LETTERS! SO I INFORMED HIM THAT I HAD
BEEN LOOKING FOR THE ONE WITH THE CAPITALS.
    HONEY, I HAVEN'T HAD A LETTER FROM YOU IN SO

MANY DAYS THAT I'M ALMOST USED TO NOT GETTING THEM. THAT'S THE WAY IT WILL HAVE TO BE FOR A LONG TIME, SO I MAY AS WELL GET USED TO IT. BUT WHY START BREAKING ME IN SO EARLY?

IN ABOUT FIVE MINUTES THERE WILL BE A PROGRAM OF CODE ON THAT I'LL CATCH. IT'S ONE OF THE TYPES THAT I MUST CATCH FOUR TIMES A DAY AT SEA. IT'S ALL IN CODE GROUPS—NUMBERS AND LETTERS IN GROUPS OF FOUR OR FIVE.

(HERE'S MY PROGRAM!!!)

BACK AGAIN.

MY CALL TO YOU LAST NIGHT WAS QUOTED AS A THREE HOUR DELAY SO I HAD TO REFUSE IT AND COME BACK ABOARD. SUCH IS LIFE. IF I DECIDE TO GO TO TOWN TOMORROW, I'LL TRY AGAIN. GUESS I'D BETTER CALL PELICAN FIRST AND SEE IF YOU ARE BACK IN SCHOOL.

YOU KNOW, DARLING, I STILL KNOW NOTHING ABOUT THE REASON OR REASONS THAT YOU WERE IN THE HOSPITAL! YOU MAY BE THERE YET FOR ALL I KNOW, AND IT BOTHERS ME NOT TO KNOW JUST WHAT IS WHAT. IF THINGS WORK OUT BY SOME MIRACLE WE COULD BE TOGETHER A WEEK FROM TONIGHT. THAT IS A REALLY GOOD THOUGHT. THE TRIP WON'T SEEM SO LONG IF I'VE SEEN YOU JUST BEFORE LEAVING. OF COURSE, I REALIZE THAT THERE ARE A LOT OF THINGS THAT COULD HOLD YOU UP, ESPECIALLY SINCE THIS HAD TO HAPPEN. BUT, DOGGONE IT, I CAN STILL HOPE, DARLING.

I'LL ALWAYS LOVE YOU,
DARLING—

YOURS,
Beat

Sunday night, 2015

My darling,

I didn't know when to call you or where you'd be on Sunday afternoon. So I decided to call you in Pelican tomorrow night and find out whether or not you can make it out to Seattle by this coming Saturday. The clerk and the ensign have their wives here, so we could make a foursome. And I can take you aboard the ship and show you what makes one go and all. The skipper gave the clerk, ensign and me permission to bring our wives aboard. Then you could see how I live and all my equipment and the ship's officers' salon and the whole works. You'd even get a good look at the cargo and probably make a good guess as to where it is going.

I could tell you right now where this ship is going. If I did and it got out, I'd come back to this country and find a two-year sentence in the Federal Pen awaiting me. We can't even tell the people in town what the name of the ship is. We don't have a bit of identification on the ship. We don't even use the American flag until we get outside of the coastal waters.

The entire population of this town knows that there is a new Liberty ship out here at port dock. They all gawk at us as we walk down the street, and today the ensign and I heard a couple of gals say as we walked by, "They must be off that big ship out at port dock." Cars and people can't get very close to the ship—about three blocks away—but all this Sunday afternoon they have driven cars along that highway and parked and sat looking at that "huge ship."

The food is great. All the coffee, sugar, butter and meat and potatoes, etc. that a guy could want. We have a menu every meal and have a choice of what we want. Last night we had to make a tough decision—fried pork chops or Virginia baked ham. The cadet and I decided we'd have both—and did! A fellow cleans my quarters, makes the bed, changes towels, etc. every day. I'm glad I'm an officer.

Be mine and try your hardest to come out. If not here, California.

> I'll always love you, Elinor,
> Your guy, always,
> Beat

Monday afternoon

My darling,

I just got two letters—one May 20th, the other May 29th. You were quite sick, weren't you? I don't know yet what 'twas all about, but you can tell me this Saturday.

Good news for us, but, of course, not for the war—the loading is going a bit slower than expected. They lost about 14 hours due to a whopper of a storm last night. We don't expect to leave until about June 10 or later now.

I mentioned in last night's letter that I didn't want you to mention my ship's name or even a ship. Really this ship is on something secret. We could load in 1/3 the time in a regular port. Now you guess why we came in here! Please don't say a word about things and don't mention San Pedro, either. All right? It's more important than you or I may think. I'm beginning to think in terms of real secrecy now as I learn more about this life.

This Saturday—It's all going to be too good to be true!

Hurry out!

Yours,
Beat

Monday evening

My darling,

WELL!!!!! What an intelligent telephone conversation we had. The line was really punk and I'm only hoping that you got all the instructions that I gave you in good order. I sent you a telegram right after I called and gave you all the dope that I could.

When you arrive, go to the Travelers' Aid desk in the lobby of the station in Seattle. I may leave a note or telegram in their care for you. Grab a taxi over to the bus depot and there's a bus at eleven o'clock in the morning that arrives in Aberdeen at about five in the afternoon. Go to the Morck Hotel here in the city and they are all ready to take care of you as my wife. They'll also be able to contact me in case you arrive or a wire comes for me. They have my phone number and can send a seaman from the Coast Guard base here to get me downtown in about a half hour. You'll always have a lot of gentlemen ready to carry your bag, etc. Hurry as fast as the trains and the buses will carry you. We'll have at least five days after your arrival, and maybe more before this loading is done.

The rain has stopped and we have actually had a look at the sun.

All the arrangements are made on this end. Now all I must do is wait for you. Hurry out darling, 'cuz time isn't too long.

Good night, honey. I love you-
Beat

On the Rails

June 1943

ELINOR TOOK A DEEP breath as she started up the stairs leading into the train. The steps trembled with the vibration from the engine, which pulsed on its track, ready for the trip west. Beads of moisture from the steam on the metal caused the steps to feel slippery. Elinor gripped the porter's hand tightly.

He greeted her, "Morning, Miss." He took her valise in one hand and helped her steady herself with the other.

Elinor's legs shook as she tried to hurry. She wondered whether she was really well enough to make this trip so soon after the hospitalization.

She entered the car and looked around. The seats were nearly filled. These days there were so many servicemen traveling around the country. Wherever she went, by bus or train, there they were, heading to or from somewhere, maybe on their last visits home before shipping out or on their way to the war.

But, despite the crowd, this ride to the coast could be a relaxing diversion. After all, school was out, over, done. No more Pelican. She had resigned and they were probably happy enough to see her go. She had taken up so many sick days, and the other teachers must've resented having to dash into a class of hers on a moment's notice to take over. She imagined her Norwegian friends attempting to teach German.

Elinor smiled. The thought of the adventure ahead cheered her. Who could predict what might happen in San Diego!

The porter turned her over to the conductor, who took her valise.

Elinor flashed a smile toward the porter as she showed the conductor her ticket. He took her in hand then, nodding in the direction she was to go. They walked past the passenger seats in the car, then sidled down a narrow hallway.

"Here you are, Miss," the conductor nodded again, as he opened a small door to her very own compartment. He set her dainty bag on the floor. Elinor barely had time to tip him before he rushed off to help another passenger who was waving a ticket.

She examined her small space. Her own miniscule sink folded out of the wall. A private toilet. Even a seat by her window. She could keep an eye on the country as it flew by. The bed section would fold out of the wall to meet the seat—a perfect spot for sleeping. She wondered how soon she could ask for her bed to be made up. She was so tired.

She settled her purse on a small shelf. She set her bag, containing her nightgown and a change of clothes, on the floor by her seat. She pulled out her current book and set it beside the bag. Then she sat herself down in her tiny palace, waiting for the rumble of the solid steel wheels. She remembered other trips she had taken when she had to sleep in her seat. After that migraine, her father wouldn't allow her to take any chances. He contributed the extra money she needed for all this luxury.

Her darling father. He hated to see her go and had agreed to this trip reluctantly. As long as she was with her sister, he would feel okay with the situation.

Little Mickey, nicknamed after a mouse, had launched out on her own. She already had a swell job and a busy social life. She'd have a place for Elinor in San Diego. The two of them could squeeze into the apartment together with Betty, and there was a chance that Elinor could get a good job. The word was that the jobs paid more than teaching. It was crowded on the coast, but that didn't matter. Elinor looked forward to meeting people.

The train began its slow pull away from the depot. Elinor spotted her father one last time, standing in his Sunday hat and looking soberly at the train. She waved, but he didn't see her. He was turning to leave as Elinor's purse tumbled from its shelf. She grabbed for it, caught it and set it on the floor. Then she stabilized herself in her seat and watched from her window as her hometown disappeared into the prairie.

In no time, the train picked up speed as it moved more smoothly along the tracks. The rumble of the wheels lulled Elinor.

What lay ahead? Well, geographically there would be prairie stretching along for miles, then some mountains, and the ocean at last. Minot, Shelby, Spokane, Seattle. California and Mickey would be the second leg of the journey. Her father didn't have to know that she planned a quick stop to see Beat before the last leg of the journey, down the coast to San Diego.

"I hope Beat's still there when I get to the coast," Elinor thought. "We need to have a long talk."

Beat. She'd have to be strong. To plan what she was going to say. She needed a wartime strategy of her own. How does a girl break up with a guy when he's about to head into the Pacific? Nothing in *Etiquette* about that.

She rehearsed. She could do this without notecards.

She would tell him that they simply could not be a couple. He was the wrong fellow for her. She would point out that she hadn't written much to him. That was a message. Her life wasn't as free as that of a sailor, a drunken sailor with women in every port. Her life had responsibilities. And she had her parents to think of. Parents with good reason to resent him.

She had packed the Sigma Chi pin and the Christmas watch in her purse. Returning them would finalize things once and for all.

She remembered the 1942 meeting at Casablanca. The Allies had gathered to plan European strategy. They watched each other warily, she supposed, but at the end of the meeting they shook hands. The two Frenchmen hated to do it, but the rest made them. A team had to stand together.

That's what she planned for her meeting with Beat. They'd discuss this logically, shake hands, agree to be friends, and that would be the end of this attraction they had for each other.

The train glided along. Elinor stared out of her window. The early prairie grasses reminded her of her childhood home in Elgin, west of the Missouri River. She remembered all her "old friends" who were now spread around the entire world.

She reached for her book and held it while she continued to stare at the prairie. Memories floated through her mind. Schooldays. Church services by the thousands. Their sweet collie, Laddie, who had once herded a group of circus horses home to the parsonage. She smiled. She opened the cover of her book. She thought about the nights the family made candy—taffy and fudge—for friends. Her family was so loving and close. She thought about Beat's childhood. He really hadn't much of a family to fall back on. He had been out and on his own for a long, long time already.

The late morning sun was bright in her window, too bright for reading. Her eyes still ached. She couldn't concentrate. Maybe a rest would be better. She closed *The Robe* and set it on the floor. She leaned her head on the backrest of her seat.

She imagined Beat meeting her at the train station. He would run up to her, catch her in his arms. Smiles all around. A kiss or two. She sighed.

No! She would have to be strong. She would plan every detail as she crossed the continent. Time to memorize those notecards.

About Nine Hours

June 1943

Monday morning
June 7

My sweet,

Well, you almost did us up!! Up until about three minutes ago, I was in doubt about seeing you for one second in this burg. Just now the stevedore captain gave me the final word and said that we would miss the two o'clock high-water. We shall have to wait for the high-water at three A.M. Tuesday morning.

Now, all you've got to do is get on that first bus from Seattle so that we can see each other for some time anyway. We can spend most of the day and night together—until twelve tonight anyway. That gives us about nine hours.

We're going to be awfully lucky to steal these few hours together during this time. Doggone, I can't take a chance of not being on this ship when she sails. I'd never be able to forgive myself for missing this chance to

really get into the war—and also get a nice,
long trip with free room and board and a hell
of a good wage!

SEEYOUSOONDARLING--------

Ship Movements for the *James Oliver*
7,176 tons, built 1943

June 1943 to October 1943
Manifest of the first voyage of the *James Oliver*.

Departure	Convoy	Arrival
June 16 San Francisco	independent	July 17 Hobart
July 20 Hobart	independent	August 23 Aden
August 23 Aden	independent	August 30 Suez
September 17-18 Port Said	independent	September Alexandria
September 19 Alexandria	GUS.16	October 15 New York City (Hampton Rds.)

Aberdeen, Washington

June 1943

JUST A HANDFUL OF passengers rode the bus from Seattle to Aberdeen, so they had plenty of room to spread out. There were a few sailors, a lonely-looking girl, and an old couple, returning from Seattle, probably from seeing someone off into the war. The old woman kept blowing her nose while her husband patted her shoulder.

Elinor claimed a window seat. She settled her valise on the shelf overhead. Her big bag already sat in the luggage compartment. She had watched the driver slide it into place in the bowels of the big silver vehicle. Elinor set her purse in her lap.

She waved at Albert from the window. He smiled back, and she blew him a kiss. She was glad he had been around and available for carrying her luggage from the train station to the bus. Her "old friends" could always be counted on—and it was nice to have someone left in the States.

The Trailways bus took off in a roar and a black cloud of diesel exhaust. Elinor leaned back into her seat. Now she had just the last 100 miles to travel, motoring to Beat's ship. Five hours of highway and bus stop layovers. Her book was in her big bag, so she spent the travel time staring out the window.

They took on a few more passengers at Tacoma, and then the bus settled back into its routine. Elinor stretched out. She leaned into the corner by the window and shifted herself. She put her legs up on the empty seat next to her, her feet on the armrest. She made her purse into a pillow and settled it underneath her head.

Olympia was a surprise. It came up so quickly. Maybe she had dozed a bit. There was the usual exchange of passengers, and then the final leg of this jaunt. She was sure she could smell the Pacific, even through the cigarette smoke circulating in the air of the bus.

When she exited in Aberdeen, she gathered her luggage around her and stood in the station. She combed her hair with her fingers. She smeared fresh Courage on her lips. Ten minutes passed, and still Beat hadn't arrived. She snapped her purse open and found the telegrammed directions. The Morck Hotel. She supposed she'd have to take a cab. "Heron and K Street, " she directed the cabbie. "The Morck."

She stood outside the hotel and stared at its four stories of tan brick. A doorman rushed to her side and grabbed her bags. She pushed her hair behind her ears and followed him into the lobby. She stepped to the desk and announced, "I'm here to see Darrow Beaton?" She coughed a little and hid her left hand from the clerk.

"Certainly," he replied. "We've been expecting you." He handed her the key and directed her to the third floor, to Beat's room. The bellhop balanced her luggage, and she followed him to room 314.

She was ready. Notecards weren't necessary. And she'd let him know just how much trouble she'd had just to get here to this out of the way dump of a town. He could've met her, for Pete's sake.

When she opened the door, she found an empty room. Beat had left no luggage, no shaving equipment. There was an empty bed, now made up, a desk and chair, and a bathroom. She walked to the window and looked down on the street.

"For Pete's sake," she thought as she stared at the busyness of midday Aberdeen. "He's either forgotten. Or he's left already."

"Everything okay, Miss?" the bellboy wanted to know.

Elinor smiled. "It's perfect. I'll just be here tonight, and then I'm on my way to California."

She dug into her purse to find a tip.

She stepped into the bathroom and ran the warm water. "All this trouble for nothing," she thought. "And Beat's sailed."

She soaped her hands and considered her next move. She would have to find the train station to continue her journey to San Diego. She rinsed. She could hang out at the depot tomorrow. Tonight—well, she was going to go out on the town. She dried her hands.

She hoisted her big suitcase onto the bed and opened it. Then she snapped her purse open and removed the pin and the watch she had kept there to return to Beat. She packed them deep into the suitcase and then checked that the latches of the suitcase had fastened.

Now, with the jewelry stashed, she had more space in her purse. And she had time to rearrange the lipsticks, her wallet, and her comb. She had left her Fargo keys at home. She parked the ticket to San Diego in the inner pocket. More than twenty hours, not including any station stops. She sighed. She should never have taken this detour.

She settled the suitcase on the floor again and stretched out in the double bed for a rest. She let her tired head sink into the pillow. California!

Elinor's eyes slowly closed, and California came into view. She saw the sun on a warm beach. Girls in sunsuits or bathing suits, their navels covered, naturally, lay near the blue water.

And in her dream, billboards—with her face dominant—floated.

She had surprised them all when the agent found her in the drugstore in Point Loma, of all places. Not only was she good looking and movie star material, but when she sat at the baby grand and played for the production company, the producer himself jumped up with a pen and a contract in hand. Why, Elinor could do things that Peggy Lee didn't know how to do. Elinor strutted in furs. Her ears dangled diamonds. She stood in front of a microphone, ready to belt out "It Had to Be You."

The sound of the doorknob turning woke her from her reverie, and Elinor sat up quickly.

The door opened and Beat entered the room, laughing, "Bunny! I can't believe my sore eyes!"

She rubbed her eyes. Then she had to laugh. He was there, after all.

"I'm sorry I couldn't meet you, honey. I was delayed with another last minute inspection." He pushed his hair off his forehead.

"I thought you'd left," she said.

"C'mon, you have to see the ship."

"But I should put on something more suitable!" She noticed that Beat was dressed to the nines in his Merchant Marine officer's uniform. Chief Radio Officer Beaton. He held his hat by his side.

"No time now," Beat laughed. "You look fine to me."

"In this old traveling suit?"

"Let's go. You look just like the girl I love, whatever you wear," Beat said as he kissed her cheek.

Elinor jumped off the bed, slid into her pumps, grabbed her purse and followed him out the door.

They walked to the wharf, where Beat proudly ushered her aboard the *James Oliver*. When he introduced her to the Captain as "Elinor Beaton," she felt her eyebrows arch upward at the combination of names. She shifted her left hand behind her back as she shook the Captain's hand with her right.

Beat took her to the radio room, his shack, right away. He showed her the big Coke machine, his Mackay radio. He demonstrated getting messages, and she tried on his headset. Then she toured his room, located right next door. The alarm would wake him for distress messages, and he could jump up and be at his radio station in moments.

He showed her the bed he'd sleep in and the small library he would oversee. She could imagine his life now. The war seemed closer all of a sudden. Beat put his arm around her. She turned toward him as he turned away to take her to the officers' mess right down the narrow passageway.

"You know," Elinor said, "Dale was in Fargo to see me. He was disappointed when I took the train to the coast and left him there. He thinks you owe him a day."

"Sure." Beat wasn't listening, but she continued.

"I'll probably see him in California anyway."

Beat opened a door and they looked into the salon. The officers ate there, away from the crew. "All the food you could ever want, Bunny," Beat bragged.

They stopped by the Master's quarters, though they didn't knock on that door. She noted how close Beat's room was to the Captain's.

"That reminds me," she whispered, "why did you introduce me with your last name?"

Beat smiled. "The captain assumes I'm married. I guess I've talked about you a lot. So I'll let him keep thinking that. It got you aboard at the last minute, at least."

Elinor jabbed him with her elbow. "You rat. He probably won't let you off the ship into port if he thinks you're married and wanting to play around. Ever think of that?"

They both laughed then.

They toured the decks and Elinor saw some of the materiel that had been loaded onto the ship. The *James Oliver* rode low in the water due to the extra weight. These days, all the ships steaming into the war, carrying supplies or men, were overloaded and in a hurry. Our troops in the Pacific were waiting for ammo and equipment and even food and medicines.

They skipped the climb down to the black gang in the engine room. Elinor's heels couldn't make the trip, and Beat wasn't anxious to disturb the engineers there unless he needed to. They were already on duty, preparing for the 2 A.M. high tide ride out of the bay.

They ended up back at the radio shack. Beat sat at his desk and sorted through some papers. He was nervous about forgetting something that he'd need on the long trip ahead. Elinor leaned on the Coke machine.

In a while, Beat looked up, and his eyes widened to see her there. "Sorry," he said. "Did you notice that they even gave me two rolls of transparent tape, Bunny?"

Then in a flurry of activity, Beat organized his desk again. At last, he suggested, "Dinner? I've got a favorite place. We can get a couple of drinks there, too." He stood and straightened his back.

She smiled. "Sure. Sounds good."

He took her hand and led her from the ship and down the gangplank.

He stopped her on the pier and they looked back at the *Oliver*. "Some ship," he grinned.

They continued back downtown, to the bar. They didn't speak much as they strolled along. Elinor wondered how many other dates Beat would take, in different places around the world, to his room.

They found a little booth in a corner and sat across from each other. Elinor fidgeted with her napkin. She spread it in her lap and looked up at Beat.

They each had a drink. Beat was unusually quiet.

Elinor said, "The *James Oliver* is quite a ship, Beat. I see why you got so excited to be assigned to her."

"Yeah." A single word reply.

They stared across the table at each other. She smiled. He smiled. The waiter delivered dinner and refills on their drinks.

"So . . ." she tried again.

He looked into his lap.

"It's a big job, Beat, keeping that ship afloat."

He looked at her and nodded. "I'm not sure about this, Bunny," he started.

She eyed him. "Everything okay?"

He pasted on a grin and straightened his shoulders. "It's gonna be fun!" Then he picked up his glass for another toast to the trip and he downed the bourbon in one fell swoop.

After another drink, the two of them walked to the Morck. They took an elevator to the third floor, to the room. Beat sat on the bed. Elinor sat right beside him.

"So this is your last night in the States?" she asked. She turned toward him.

"We're leaving at 2 A.M., Bunny. High tide. So I have to be at the ship before midnight." He looked into her eyes. "I won't be back for months."

She wished she hadn't packed the watch. She had no idea what time it was, how much time they had left together.

"This is good-bye, then," she sighed.

He leaned toward her and kissed her gently. "I'm glad you came to see the ship," he said. "And me. Thanks."

"Beat . . ." she started. She leaned back to have a look at him.

"Bunny," he interrupted. "I want you to write to me, even though I can't get your letters until we get into port. And, you remember, my letters will come to you in clumps now. I'll mail a batch to you from every port."

She nodded. "Beat . . . could we . . ." she tried again.

"You didn't write very regularly while I was at Gallups. And Walter . . ."

"Don't start that again!" Elinor stood. "You rag on and on about Walter and me. But you know the situation. My parents love him. I don't. We are just 'old friends,' Beat."

"C'mon, Bunny," Beat tried to cajole her into sitting again. "I'm sorry I mentioned Walt. Sit by me."

"You continue to bring Walter up. You've been seeing girls. I know you've been dating. In Boston. Probably here, too. How can you criticize me?" She walked to the desk.

"C'mon, Bunny. I don't want to fight again."

"Can you understand how tired I am of your needing me to be 'good' when you are out with others? A sailor with a gal in every port?"

"But, Bunny," he tried to explain.

"Beat, I don't want to. Not tonight. I'm not in the mood."

His eyes downcast, he was quiet for a few minutes. "All right, then. Have it your way. Damn it, Elinor."

Elinor sat at the desk until her breathing settled. She knew if she said something more, she'd regret it. Beat would be in the war zones soon. Respect for the uniform, she remembered.

They stared at each other a while. Beat mumbled, "Shit" and "Goddamnit" a few times. She turned her head. She waited for him to apologize. Or to defend himself. To tell her that he could never date another woman.

Instead, he picked up the latest *Time* magazine and a newspaper they had purchased on the walk to the hotel. He reached the crossword puzzle to Elinor. Then he turned to the front page and the editorials.

Elinor wasn't sure what he expected. She wondered what Emily Post would suggest for this situation.

She began to doodle beside the puzzle. She looked up once in a while to see Beat avoiding her, too. So, this little affair of theirs was really over. No notecards needed.

After a long time, Elinor stood. "I'm so tired tonight, Beat," she said, "after that last big headache and all this traveling."

"I guess that's it then."

"Beat . . ."

"Bunny?"

"It was good to see your boat."

"Ship. Anyway, Bunny, it's okay. I am not in the mood for anything much tonight either. And it's getting late." He folded up his reading material and, leaving it on the bed, walked to the desk.

She turned toward him.

"I'm sorry." Elinor heard a tear in her voice. She cleared her throat. "It just didn't work out."

"Yeah. And you had such a tricky time getting here, too," he said. "We never had enough time together, did we? To really know each other?"

She thought about unpacking his jewelry to return it to him. But it seemed like a kinder thing to do after the war, when she returned the others' engagement rings and trinkets.

He walked to the door. "I'll come to see you when we get back," he added as he opened the door. "And I'll write." He straightened his shoulders.

"Me, too," she promised.

He laughed. "Sure."

"I'll look for your letters, Beat. I always love hearing from you."

The door closed as she was talking. And then she was, with no reason, in tears.

The following morning, Elinor was up early. She dressed in her comfortable traveling suit, gathered her valise and her suitcase, and checked out of the hotel. She caught a cab for the short ride back to the depot. There she'd catch a train south, and it wouldn't be long before she'd be in California. Well, a little more than 24 hours. But the time would fly. Getting there would be a dream come true!

Elinor checked in with the station agent who took her big suitcase, tagged it, and piled it on a baggage cart. Then she sat on a wooden bench in the brick station, waiting for her connection.

Trains came and went, mostly freight trains destined for ports along the coast. The depot was surprisingly busy because it was a connection from Chicago to trains heading down the coast.

She waited. She tried once more to read the book her mother had given her for the trip—*The Robe* by Lloyd C. Douglas. But there was so much to see in the bustling depot that she kept popping out of the first century A.D. to watch. Military men lounged on other benches. A dispatcher sat at the telegraph in the back room. The agent in the window sold tickets and tagged baggage as new arrivals lined up. Porters lugged luggage, and large crates stabilized on wagons passed by the station windows periodically. Everyone bustled. It made her tired to watch all the action.

The aroma of summer sausage alerted her to the fact that she hadn't eaten much for breakfast. A fellow sitting on the bench beside her had opened his brown lunch bag. Elinor looked up at the station clock. It was getting on to lunchtime already. She checked the schedule again and determined that she had enough time to grab a sandwich in the café across the street. If she hurried, she might beat the crowd. She grabbed her valise and her purse and book and cut across the street for a quick bite and a necessary cup of coffee.

When she returned to the station, there were no seats left on the hard wooden benches. She stood with many others along the brick wall, her valise by her side and her purse over her shoulder.

She rued the moment she had thought this detour was a good idea. How had Beat convinced her to rush out of her hospital bed and into a train headed toward him? And then the hot bus ride to get to the ship before it sailed. Now she had an overcrowded train ride ahead of her. She had given up her comfortable Pullman car for this? Darn!

She could have been arriving in California today if she hadn't stopped to see Beat. She was in a hurry now to get settled, to unpack her things, in Point Loma. The trip couldn't go fast enough.

She used her linen handkerchief to swab the beads of sweat that had settled under the hair on her neck. She thought about Beat with cool ocean breezes blowing his way. He would be out to sea already, perhaps steaming away in the direction of San Diego, too.

She wondered what had happened last night. And then she wondered why she cared.

And what had she accomplished anyway? She still had the darn jewelry.

California!

June 9, 1943

"KID!" ELINOR HEARD MICKEY, shouting from somewhere in the crowd. A hiss of the steam released from the train. And then a cacophony of noises filled the air.

She stepped further out onto the platform. People swarmed past her. She squinted into the sparkling California sky. Crowds of servicemen milled around, waiting for buses to take them to the naval base. A sailor leaned on a post. Smoke rose into the air from his cigarette. A nice young Navy ensign stepped out of the crowd and asked if he could help.

"I'm joining my sister," Elinor answered with a smile. She cut her way through the crowd. Her sister's voice had come from that direction. But Mickey was so short, hard to spot.

Elinor set down her valise as she spotted Mickey running toward her, waving her arms. The girls hugged and laughed.

"So good to have you here. Really here. I've been so lonesome, Bunny." Mickey hugged her big sister again. "How's the family? I miss everyone so much."

The two of them gathered Elinor's suitcase from the Red Cap. Elinor hefted it while Mickey balanced the valise and Elinor's book. They pulled their purse straps over their shoulders and staggered toward the bus stop to sit on a bench there. They had to make a couple of connections to get to Point Loma, but Mickey had plotted the route.

"It's so beautiful here, Mick," Elinor said. "It was cloudy in

Washington. And still cold at home." She smiled into the sunshine. "You know . . . Spring in North Dakota . . ."

"Tell me about the trip."

"Crowded with servicemen coming down here. To the naval base. And you know how I love those Navy uniforms! We had a lot of fun in the dining car and in the lounge, to say the least."

"The trip isn't too bad between here and home. How about your head?"

"Well, Papa made me take a Pullman. He thought I needed peace and quiet, and for a little while I really did. You know. Things on my mind."

A flock of seagulls landed close by, and Elinor studied them. "Maybe with no more school, there'll be no more migraines. A girl can hope," she added as she looked back to her sister.

"I'll take you to see the Pacific on the weekend, kid," Mickey said. "It's just beautiful. Peaceful. And so huge you can't believe it!"

"I saw a little salt water in Aberdeen. Have I told you? I stopped to see Beat."

"Bunny, what were you thinking?"

"Just for a few hours. Beat showed me the ship. A brand new Liberty. Huge!"

"When does he leave?" Mickey scratched her head in the heat.

"He's gone already. Somewhere in the Pacific."

"Good riddance. So how's Beat?"

"Quiet. A bit nervous, I think."

"Ready to go to war?" Mickey unsnapped her purse. She fumbled around, looking for a cigarette.

"Yeah. He's so proud to be the one and only radio officer on board. He has to be at the radio for messages every six hours. And when the ship is in enemy territory, he'll have to be on watch around the clock."

A bus rolled up to the curb. Elinor started to rise, but Mickey shook her head. It wasn't their ride. Several other people climbed the stairs and disappeared into the bus.

Elinor settled back on the bench and continued, "We had only a few hours together. Not a great visit. I wanted to have a long talk. And to return the jewelry he gave me. But I couldn't break it off just before he leaves."

"Oh, Bunny," Mickey sighed. She dug into her purse to locate a matchbook. "You get too sentimental. Emily Post doesn't know everything. You've got to let him know."

Elinor rearranged her purse in her lap. "I just couldn't."

Mickey shook her head. "I thought you broke up in March . . . when he took the pin and the watch. Wasn't it over then?"

"I thought so, too. But then he started writing again and he sent the jewelry all back to me."

"Think of Papa." Mickey popped the cigarette between her lips and struck the match. "He's not fond of Beat, to say the least."

"Yeah, I know. But it's too late to tell Beat now. Anyway, last night with him was so different. He just mostly ignored me. He had his head full of thoughts. Maybe some other gal he's met. I'm sure it's all over and done with."

"Where's he headed?" Mickey released a stream of smoke into the clear California sky.

"Who knows? He has only a general idea. He gave me a code sheet, the names of the places he might go, each one attached to the name of a person."

"I wish I knew where Bob is now, what he's doing, where the 164th is."

"I'll show you the code when we get to your place. It's secret, and I can't lose it."

More people began to crowd the area. Baggage lay piled up behind the bus stop benches. A second bus arrived and about a dozen men with duffels leapt aboard.

"They're going to the Naval Base," Mickey explained, nodding toward the men.

"I feel like a spy, carrying a code," Elinor whispered. "I wish the guys could write more about the war."

"All that censoring," Mickey agreed. "I've gotten some pretty shredded letters, with all the important stuff sliced out."

"I'd love to hear about it. It's hard to imagine from here—the actions of the Japanese in those islands or the Germans in Africa. But the men would be heading for jail if they said the least thing."

"Well, one day," Mickey stopped to take a drag on her Lucky Strike. "One day we'll have a chance to catch up. To find out what they really faced. If they'll tell us. Men who go to war keep a lot of secrets, Bunny."

"They say we wouldn't understand. I suppose not," Elinor said.

The bus arrived and Mickey stood. Elinor jumped up, too. Mickey took a last drag and looked at how much was left of her cigarette before she threw it underfoot and stamped it out. They picked up the luggage and lined up to board the bus. To Point Loma.

Then, somehow, Elinor hoped, to Hollywood.

DARROW R. BEATON

WEST COAST BOUND	EARL
EAST COAST BOUND	HARRIET
UNITED STATES BOUND	AL
ENEMY ACTION	HANK
INVASION	GORDY
HAWAIIAN ISLANDS	LORRAINE
MARSHALLS	JIM
NEW CALEDONIA	JACK
FIJIS	BETTY
AUSTRALIA	HELEN
ESPIRITU SANTOS	JOYCE
GUADALCANAL	NAOMI
NEW GUINEA	GARY
TRUK	PAUL
CAROLINES	LEO
KURILES	WAYNE
PHILLIPINES	VIC
WAKE	AUDREY
MARIANNAS	NORMA
BOUGAINVILLE	NORMAN
RABAUL	HONS
PANAMA CANAL	LANNY
GIBRALTAR	SWEDE
ENGLAND	LARRY
FRANCE	SI
BELGIUM	RUTH
NORTHERN EUROPE (SCANDINAVIA)	DOTTY
ITALY	FRED
SOUTHERN EUROPE	BILL
MEDITERRANEAN SEA	EDDIE
EGYPT	HARRY
INDIA	PETE
SOUTH AMERICA	ITCH
SOUTH AFRICA	LARS

BE GOOD TO THIS, DARLING. IF YOU WISH TO SPEAK
OF ANYONE WITH ONE OF THESE NAMES, AND DON'T MEAN THE
CODE, USE THEIR LAST NAMES WITH THEIR GIVEN NAMES AND
I'LL UNDERSTAND.

Beat's code

On the Sea

June 1943

Author's note: The following letters are typed in regular font, using both upper and lower cases. The actual letters were typed on the mill and are all in capital letters. They're typed on sheets of onionskin paper, lightweight so they could be airmailed.

Thursday morning

My darling,

I told you that I would quit the sea at Pedro if I got even a tiny bit seasick. I've really weathered all the weather and not felt even the least sick. Guess it's the old boxcar days that make this seem like sissy stuff!! The ship is rolling from side to side and I'm sitting on a rocker chair without the roller wheels. Every time the ship rolls one way or the other, I roll with it and the typewriter gets either closer or farther away.

We're hugging the coast pretty closely. Our ship's compasses are way off and we plan to calibrate them in Pedro. I'm on the radio beacon direction finder, the D/F, in the chart room a lot of the time. All the way down the coast it is foggy and I have to keep them posted as to our position in relation to the station that we are approaching or leaving.

We had test firing for our aft guns yesterday afternoon. The ensign had to fire them for the first shots. There is a chance that they will explode and kill someone, so he has to take the responsibility. The big guns make a terrific noise and a huge flash and splash out in the water. The 20 millimeter AA guns fire a shell about ten inches long and one inch across. Every third shell is a tracer and it is a pretty sight to see them go up as far as three miles—a whole string of tracers and in between each of them, two non-tracer shells. Now for something to shoot at to find out how good we are!

What a time I had decoding a special message. I picked up our secret war call on the program, the only ship to be called. When I got through decoding the thing, we are now heading for San Francisco. About two hours later, I sent a code D message to them, telling them that we were on our new course, to have a pilot boat ready to meet us at a certain time tonight. And my message went over the ether without a hitch—the very first that I have officially sent over the air!!!! What a thrill it was. It went over the international distress frequency for a while, so stations all over the world were listening to me. It was a hell of a lot easier than sending to one of the instructors at school.

If I'd missed that last message, I would have caused at least three hours' delay and many dollars in cash to the company—and maybe held up a convoy. So, I'm darn glad that I got it and everything went well. Heck, the skipper himself doesn't know where or why we are going now!

We had general quarters a while back. Every gun was manned and uncovered and ready to fire in less than two minutes—pretty good for a surprise drill. Of course, I had to come in here and get my equipment ready to send out a report of the trouble that we supposedly encountered. It was fun!

We've picked up the pilot that I wired for and we're on our way near the Golden Gate Bridge. Soon we'll be in Frisco and if I get a chance I'll wire or phone you tonight.

Your guy,
Beat

❧   ❧

I really am not worried about you or what you do any more. You'll do just as you please. I think that you always have and always will. While I'm way out in the ocean, I want you to feel free to go out and feel very free to tell me all about the dates you have had.

I imagine that I shall be going out a couple of times myself. When we come in from a long trip, I want to meet someone to talk to and someone who knows the city that we are in. It's almost a necessity in a strange place to have a date if a fellow wants to go to the best places. That's what I want—the very best places, the places that people talk about.

Friday night (June 11)

Hiya, Nuttie!!

I tried to call you before I came back aboard tonight, but it seems that the charms of San Diego had you in their throes. Anyway, I spent over an hour trying to find you. Give me an "A" for effort. I might have known that you would not be home. You'll be there when I call in about six or seven months, won't you?

I'm on my way and I know not where. At least I'm not able to say in this letter. 'Twas a lonely sight to see the old Golden Gate Bridge go by and know that it would be a long time until we saw good ol' America again. But you may be sure that I'm in this thing all the way.

We're outside and in the Pacific proper now. The pilot may drop over the side at any time, so I had better hurry. He'll mail this for me.

I love you so much that it hurts to be leaving you for so long—

Yours, forever,
Beat.

From D.R. Beaton (R.O.)
SS James Oliver
Alaskan Transportation Co.
Pier Seven
Seattle, Wash.

Somewhere on the Pacific
June 16, 1943

My darling,

I thought of you in San Diego when we passed
by there.

It's always cool out on deck. There's always
a breeze blowing. Not so in my shack. There are
always batteries on charge and the consequent
heating of the charging resistors in back of
the Coke machine. But I'm used to it and I sit
around in only a pair of trousers and drink
water all the time. So life flows past.

I'm soon to be initiated into the Pollywogs
for crossing the equator for the first time. That
should be quite a riot with the crew we have
aboard this ship.

I'm in charge of the library and I'm going
to be a regular bookworm before I come home.
So I keep busy, as I am now, with the phones
tuned to 500, nothing coming in and having to
find something to keep my mind off the boredom
between BAMS broadcasts.

I love you!

June 22
HOT afternoon

My darling,

You think that it is hot back there in Dakota
or San Pedro! Every move down here brings out
a flood of perspiration. We lie out on deck for
a while every day after dinner. Then we hurry
through another shower. Since I last wrote you,
I've been reading all the best books that I
could find here in my library—and doing some
studying (review) for that next license. The
books that I have read are:

Native Son	Richard Wright
Strange Woman	Ben Ames Williams
War on Saturday Week	Ruth Adam
This Is for Always	Gladys Taber
Kipling's Short Stories	(guess who!)

The fellows are getting tired of me coming
out on deck to sit with them, a book in my
hands, ready to read as soon as the conversation
lags a bit. I'm going to continue to read a lot
and help the time pass a bit more quickly.

Every night I manage to catch a bit of news
from the States and I type it up and post it in
the two mess halls. The crew goes for that. We
are all awaiting the news of the invasion as it
may have an effect on our ship.

Perspiration is running down my face in
little rivulets as I sit here typing. The port
is open and the fan is going top speed. These
batteries on charge make it so much hotter in

here, and then there is the added concrete wall about the bridge and the radio room that soaks up the heat. That wall is supposed to be able to stop machine gun bullets and I'm quite thankful that it is there. But it is HOT!

In the evenings it is cool out on deck with a breeze blowing. Flying fish play and once in a while we see a big fish jump out of the water or turn its stomach up. We all sit there and think how perfect it is and in the same breath wish that we were sharing it with our wives and sweethearts. Some day, I would like you to see how really beautiful this ocean is at sunset and then during the time the moon first appears over the horizon. We have a long shimmering path of yellow moonlight across the dark blue ocean, truly beautiful.

By the time this is mailed, I will have traveled over 16,000 miles. One of my favorite songs used to be "Don't Get Around Much Any More."

Beat

July 2, 1943
2100

My darling Elinor,

I was painted and had a good time being initiated
into the "shellbacks" last week when we crossed
the equator. That Sigma Chi initiation and "hell
week" are mild in comparison to the Navy and
Merchant Marine crews' ideas of a good time! I
was the first to go through because I had to get
back up here for some work. In the afternoon
I got a chance to watch the others go through
the same things and maybe a little more as they
had many new ideas popping up all day. I won't
have to go through that again anyway.

   Since I last wrote you, I have read Steinbeck's
Grapes of Wrath, *Into the Valley* by John Hersey,
Rebecca by DuMaurier and *Way of the Lancer* by
a fellow named Boleslavski. So I'm keeping up
on my reading.

   All day with the static and dahs and dits
has given me a good start towards a headache.
Remember me in your dreams.

                              Yours, always,
                              Beat

July 13
[postmark Aug. 3]

Dearest Elinor,

As I lie trying to go to sleep, I often think
of you and the times we've spent together and
the other things that have happened in the last
two or three months (re: Walt). No matter what
you may say, I know you, and I know that you
aren't changing overnite. After all why should
you for one guy? Especially a fellow who isn't
home over 15 days a year.

The thing is that I now see your viewpoint—
the one I had when I met you. I see no reason
why we can't act grown-up about certain things.
We both can have a lot of fun and when we
possibly can be together, we shall. That's the
way I want it to be and I feel that it is the
way you have always wanted it.

There'll never be two better lovers that you
and I when we are together. Outside of that,
we can both do what we wish. After a couple of
months spent in experimenting around Seattle
and Portland and Oakland, I find that a guy can
be happy with more than one gal. I feel that
this will save you and me a lot of trouble when
we meet again. I will be just as happy to see
you and laugh at your stories as you will be to
hear mine and laugh. We can have that same old
arrangement that we had when we first met—"the
ideal arrangement." Just so you don't carry that
idea too far and go marrying one of the blokes
back there!

We have been out thirty-two days from Frisco,

so you can imagine what the main topic of discussion is now—plans for the port! I'm going to get me a couple of big beers and mail this letter and find a quiet place where there is dancing and mixed drinks. Oh, honey, it sounds great!

Bye, darling. I love you as always—
Yours,
Beat

ONE DAY OUT OF PORT
JULY 16, 1943

Hi, Sweets,

We had a darn good time last night. We were all sitting on the edge of our chairs for about seven or eight hours. I finally got an all clear from Australia. Yes, there's a war on and I'm just beginning to find it out.

It's going to be a relief to get this stuff off my mind for a day at least. It's been my job for 24 hours a day for 32 days straight. No Sundays off or anything. I'm darn tired and stale on radio right now. This little time spent among people again will fix us all up, I know.

I almost forgot. Don't forget to thank Dale for letting me have a day or two of your time. I'm sure that he didn't really miss you for that short time and what the hell—

Bye for now, m'sweet. I'll be thinking of you and wondering about you, wondering if you can picture me in the middle of the night with only a pair of pajamas and bedroom slippers on, listening to the earphones dit and dah and taking down all the stuff. And I think of you back there with a lot of nice things to do and I sometimes wish that I could trade places with some of those guys back there. But you may be certain that that thought doesn't linger long! It's fun out here, too.

All my love, darlin',
Beat

Indian Ocean
[postmarked Nov. '43, delayed in arrival]

Dearest Elinor,

How's my darlin' these days? Whatever you're doing, you are having some sort of fun anyway, if I know you. If you are still in San Diego or Frisco, there should be plenty to keep you busy for a while. Did you see Dale out there as you planned?

We have had some excitement in the past few days, but it isn't the kind we want. It is all "shop" excitement, and has to be treated with seriousness. We will be right in the middle of it soon, if we aren't now. Ho hum, something to break the monotony a bit is all right!

For some fun last night we tied a can of sardines to Pete's long fish line that he is trailing about a half mile behind the ship. He had quite a job pulling in the line and then he was the object of the whole crew's laughing. Poor Pete!

Yesterday I read an article that had as its main point the fact that men are now governed by women—that women want security and tend to influence their men not to take chances that were once taken to get ahead. It started me thinking (it's printed in a *Readers Digest*) and I've been thinking, "Is that what I'm letting myself in for?!!?" If it is, there is no woman worth having—or is there? We have had discussions on it over our coffee at night. Of course, you know which side I have to take when I debate with two married men. And the arguments that I made were so good that it made me think even more about it!

Well there's a news broadcast in a couple of minutes and I must get this out of the mill before then. I hope Sicily has fallen by this time. I hope, I hope, I hope.

As always,
Your guy, Beat

July 20, 1943
[Hobart]

My darling,

Leo, the clerk, and I met some nurses that he
knows and we went to a dance last night and
then over to the big hospital and had a late
lunch. We had them in stitches and they made
us laugh, too.

Last night we had our usual troubles of a
port. Paul called me out of bed to go down to
the city jug with him, and we took some sidearms
along. They had a couple of our guys locked up
for some funny reason and we brought them back
to the ship. This town is full of fights. In
three nights I've seen over a dozen fights and
most of them were big gang fights with over 25
guys in them. I'm still in one piece, darling.

The weather here has been cold, and the
people who live here are continually shivering
around the streets. We wonder why they don't
put more clothes on, but they seem to like to
shiver. In their best pubs the climate is almost
as cold as outside. There is no heat of any kind
so we all wear our coats and sit around smoking
and drinking.

In a few months I'll be dragging home and
we'll have a big celebration together. And it
should be a good one, darling, because I'm
saving up for it. There are so many interesting
things that I have to talk about, things that
will interest you for a moment or two anyway.

(letter continues into next day)

July 22

This ship is bucking just as a bucking bronco does. One of our A.B.s [able bodied seamen] was on a ship that broke in two in these waters about six months ago. If I send out an SOS tonight it won't be because of the enemy but because of one of the peacetime reasons for a ship to go down. She seems to be all right so far, but one can never tell about one of these quickly built ships, the boys say.

I'm looking forward to a letter or two from you over here—about 22 days from here. For now, it's good night, and all my love, darling,

Yours, forever and ever,
Beat

July 25, 1943
GOING WEST!!!!
Mailed August 23rd
[postmark November 11]

My darling,

A quiet Sunday afternoon—and I mean quiet. We
came out of the storm about four hours ago, and
all is perfect right now. The boys have been
taking a real beating topside the last few days
and nights. They have all kinds of equipment
for that kind of weather so they got by all
right. Sometimes when I got up for some of my
watches at night, the huge waves lit up with a
phosphorous. My antenna was a streak of white
light at times due to the friction and some of
nature's own phenomena.

Wonder just what you are doing for yourself
these days. And what do you do at night? Oh,
man, that's silly to wonder about that!! Just
let the boys know that some day they may have
to give you up for a few days, because I'll be
coming home and I don't want to waste any of
the few precious days that I'll be having in the
States. I imagine that you and Mick gave the
Marines a whirl while you were in San Diego—or
was it a sailor or two?

Maybe I've never thanked you for something
that you did rather unconsciously for me. If
it hadn't been for you, I imagine that I would
have waited for the Army to grab me as so many
other fellows did. I'm glad I knew you and that
you were right behind me, helping me with some
encouragement when the work was the hardest.

Some day, darlin', I'll try to repay you for all the good things that you have done for me.

You might say that we're in the position we were when we first met. We had fun until I was fool enough to fall in love with you. I know that you wouldn't sit around waiting for anybody any more than I would sit around. All we can hope is that we don't lose that something that we always had when we were together.

That blinding trust that I once had in you has been replaced with a rather different feeling, I must admit. For all I could imagine, you may be married to somebody by the time I come home. You write such grand letters, but I'm maybe a bit more cynical about them than the ordinary guy would be. I would want nothing more in the world than to have you for always for my own. I'm not in the habit of being hurt twice by the same means, though, so I'm just hanging on and hoping that when this is all over and we're ready to settle down, we'll somehow end up together. I guess that I'll always be somewhere for you to fall back on if other plans go wrong, but if you have other plans that don't include me, I'm a good loser, too.

I suppose that you are the old faithful writer—once a month at least. At least, I hope that you are that good. Give my regards to the boys back there and wish them luck. We'll all be over here before the war is over.

All my love, as always,
Beat

Home Again

August 1943

As the Great Northern rattled into Fargo, another train heading the opposite direction on the next track lumbered by. "On the way to war," Elinor thought. She sighed. The men with her on this train were heading home for a leave, finished with training on the coast.

"Far-GO," the conductor called as the train came to rest at the depot. "Far-GO."

Elinor stood and tried to straighten her skirt. After three days of making connections and traveling, she was a bit frayed around the edges. She located her valise on the rack above her head, then pulled her purse strap over her shoulder. She left her book on the seat. Someone else would find and enjoy *And Now Tomorrow*. Elinor didn't have room to store it at 1135.

She looked forward, however, to a lot more space than she'd had at Mickey's place in San Diego. The den in her parents' house seemed spacious by comparison. And she couldn't wait to stretch out in her own bed again.

Mickey rushed into the car, toward Elinor, arriving from the smoking car at the last moment. The girls waved good-byes to the men they'd met on this trip, nice fellows who would probably write and expect mail wherever they were sent in the world.

Elinor double-checked. No one was at the station to meet them. Their folks were in South Dakota tending to a problem in some congregation. Elinor had written to Walter, but, since he wasn't there, he must be traveling or at the farm.

The girls waited for the baggage cart. When it arrived, Elinor hoisted her suitcase to the floor beside her. She looked at all the luggage she had—the valise, the suitcase, her purse—and sighed. She pulled the purse strap over her shoulder, lifted the suitcase with her left hand, and grabbed the valise with her right.

Mickey grabbed her suitcases, too. They stepped out of the depot and aimed themselves north on Broadway toward the Landgrebe home.

"I was sure hoping that Walter . . ." Mickey suggested.

Elinor was lost in her own thoughts and didn't hear her sister. So what had she accomplished by rushing out of town? As she dragged herself down the sidewalks of Fargo, she took stock. She had quit teaching. That was a relief. She hadn't had a single migraine since she left Fargo. Another good thing. She had seen California at last. She and Mickey had met a few men and had some good times. Those were the positives.

But fate had let her down. Where were the easy jobs, the ones with good pay, for women? The coast was like an anthill, with people crawling everywhere. Too noisy. Too crowded.

Now she was too broke. She hadn't been able to get into LA enough to look for work in Hollywood. A gal needed money to get to the glamorous jobs.

She needed to take charge of her life. She was finished waiting for The Fates.

All Guns Are Manned

August 1942

August 27

We are in bombing range of German planes now
and all guns are manned day and night. There
is a constant watch during certain parts of the
day and night that I must keep. This is a great
life, darling, and I'm learning a lot about
things besides radio, things such as history
and economics, subjects which I always was darn
interested in.

➵ ➴

September 3, 1943

My darling Elinor,
I'll be seeing Ruth the first thing after I get
back, so you can tell her that. You have her
address someplace there as I gave it to you out
at Aberdeen. [refer to code] Why don't you drop
Pete, John, Frank, Ann and Gloria a line, too?
I did from over here and I hope that they get
them all right.

I can think of a lot of things to write, but

I'm sure that you would only worry a bit, and it isn't necessary at all. We'll pull through and with flying colors, too.

There wasn't any mail from you over here. I have had only the one letter from you since we left the States and that was dated June 16. I'm sure that you aren't at fault. It's just that the Navy mail department can't keep up with us! I'll mail one of these today, and the other will be left with a Sparks on another ship here to be mailed a few days from now. That way I hope that one of them will get through.

The guy who loves you,
Beat

Restless

September 1943

"DAD, HAVE YOU HEARD what the Red Cross is doing these days in England?"

Elinor and her father sat together, as they had so often done, in the living room on Sunday afternoon. The Sunday *Fargo Forum* had been divided up and they sipped coffee as they read.

"Mmmm," he muttered. Was he listening?

"Maybe I could get around in a Clubmobile in England, cheering the boys up with coffee and doughnuts. I'd talk to them, keep their spirits up."

Her father sat up in his chair. He put the paper down and looked at his daughter.

Elinor went on, "They have a better reputation than the other services. Clubmobile girls are selected. Interviewed, even. Not many of them get in. One out of every six. It says here that the service is for good girls who want to help out."

Georg picked up his pipe and held it between his teeth. He snapped a wooden match in half as he tried to light it. The second attempt was successful and he began to draw on the stem of his pipe, all the while looking at Elinor.

"The girls of the Red Cross aren't mannish at all," she continued. "And they aren't out to find men to marry. They're respectable gals, Dad."

Georg removed the pipe from between his lips. "Bunny," he started. Then stopped.

"I've been reading articles. In *Life. Ladies Home Journal*. The girls are older. Like me." She knew she was talking too fast now. "They don't take everyone who wants to get in. They want college graduates. Girls over 25. Single gals."

Georg set down his pipe.

Elinor went on. "Sounds like it's something I could do for this war."

"So these girls," her father tried to understand, tried to slow her down, "go to war? What do they do there?"

"Their job is to provide recreation. To be a listening ear. And they use their college educations, Papa. Their talents are put to use."

"What is it they do?"

"They drive around in buses, with music piped out of them. Listen, Papa. This is what it says: 'They deliver gum, candy, doughnuts, and coffee to troops freshly furloughed from the front lines.'"

"The front lines? Too close to the war, Bunny!"

He reached over and picked his pipe up again. He puffed on the stem to keep it ignited. He set the pipe back in the copper ashtray.

"So you want to help out. Mm-mm." He leaned toward her. "Perhaps the Red Cross has something for you, Bunny."

Elinor grinned. She would apply tomorrow. On to England! To doughnuts and music and conversation with the men.

Her father continued, "Maybe something here in Fargo. There's a Red Cross station here, too. They wind bandages, I believe. Bunny, there are many ways to support our men. The Clubmobile is just one of them."

"Papa, I'd like to try it."

"Doughnuts?" Her father actually smiled. He chuckled as he popped his pipe back into his mouth. He lifted the *Forum* to cover his face, and Elinor knew that he wasn't reading. She watched the smoke curl into the air while he pulled himself together.

He soon placed the paper on his lap. "Bunny," he continued,

"you have many talents, talents more important than handing out doughnuts."

She thought about that. She could speak German. Not needed in England. She could play piano. No pianos on the front, just piped in music. She knew literature, but it was hard to imagine talking to the men about Shakespeare or *Wuthering Heights*. She had the wrong talents for war.

"Would you have to pass a physical exam to get into this Club? In addition to the other requirements?" Her father met her eyes.

Damn those everlasting migraines! They limited her everywhere she turned.

Elinor stood. She walked into her father's den and entered the closet. She located her pink jewelry box and sat on the daybed. As she browsed through her treasures, she wondered whether that was all there was—a gal's choices. Marriage.

Or what?

On the High Seas

September 1943

September 17, 1943
[Port Said]

The rest of the trip will be much easier than the last few days and weeks were. We are practically in, no matter how many subs Mr. Hitler has out. I'm listening to some of Mr. Hitler's music now—Austrian waltzes. He has some of his favorite announcers talking in English, Italian, Egyptian, etc. telling us how they are winning the war. It is a grand feeling to know that I am at least out here and in the war, feeling at last a part of it all. And, somehow, it has been a bit of a let-down from the romantic Irish dreams that I once had about it all. It is really just a job and nothing more.

Time seems to stand still here and the world goes on and on and a fellow begins to realize that the world will go on whether or not he is alive. And one begins to wonder just what has been gained from life so far. It seems that whatever I can make out as having been gained leads me to you every time. I want to live the rest of my life with my Bunny somewhere waiting for me, smiling and loving me. It won't be so tough if we give each other a few chances, darling.

> Good night, my darlin'—I love you,
> Beat

September 25th
Sicily

My darling,

We are expecting to be in the States before New Year. If this ship is turned over to the British, I'll probably take a leave. On the other hand, if she remains in the American Merchant Marine, I'll re-sign articles as soon as I can. And that will mean no leave probably. Even after the five months spent in hell-holes over here, I want to get out as soon as possible again. There are so many things to see and do over here where the war is and where history is being made. I'll be darned if I'll feel right sitting back there in the States again after seeing some of the war and hearing about a lot more. After all, there is a war on. Have you heard, darling?

You may want to hear where we have been after trying unsuccessfully to decode the famous Beaton code. We went to Hobart, Tasmania, Australia. It's an island south of Australia and quite a place. It took us 32 days to make the run, unconvoyed. We were right in close to Tahiti, Guadalcanal, etc. One ship was sunk in there and I met a fellow in Hobart who was on a ship who did some fast sending. They had a running gunfight with a sub about 30 miles from us. Every time he broadcast a position and course, I would dash in to the mates and we would change course to get away. But he always seemed to turn the same way. They finally got away at dark.

From there we went to Aden, Arabia, through the Australia Bight and the Indian Ocean. It was another 34 day run without convoy and not uneventful. Some ships were sunk and others had good scares. Yeah, GOOD ones.

We went to Suez, Egypt from there and discharged the cargo after some delay and a start through the canal. After that we were ordered to Port Said and then over to Alexandria, Egypt. We picked up our first convoy out of Alex and have come past Crete and Malta. We stopped at Malta for a while for air protection. We still have to go to Cape Bon, Algiers, Oran and the Rock.

As far as action goes, there were plenty of times when I had plenty of business in here—and not loafing either!! We have seen some of the war first hand. There were German planes over Suez, Aden, Port Said, and Alex. One was shot down outside of Alex. It got so that I couldn't tell the crew what was going on outside the ship until the trouble blew over. They all packed their bags and didn't do their work as well. The "black gang," the crew in the engine room, especially got up in the air, and I would, too, if I had to work down where they do. Oh, yes, there are quite a few mines in here. We missed a couple by about 15 feet yesterday and today. The escort explodes them and they make a geyser about 300 feet in the air. I'd look pretty riding one of them, wouldn't I?

We still have the dear old North Atlantic to cross, but it doesn't seem near as tough as it may have last year before I shipped out. At the conferences they tell us, "The Germans are still getting their quota of XXX ships a day. It's as bad as it ever was." So, I guess it is a bit tough yet. You'll know that I made it all right if this is mailed.

We have seen a lot of the world and know that there is a war on. We have been in all the zones of the war except Russia. Now I know why veterans of the last war don't like to talk about the war. It just isn't interesting second-hand.

I have to be in here a lot of extra hours now. Most of the ships in this convoy carry three radio officers. Two, at least. At the conference at the Rock I'll probably get some new hours. The ensign, Skipper and I have to go ashore in every port to get instructions for the next part of the trip—convoy conferences.

The blackouts over here are real ones. New York is the best I have seen in the States, but it is daylight there in comparison to these cities over here. They are pitch black. You can't see each other when you walk side by side.

Taxes, etc. will take a lot of money from us, but we know where it is going and every cent of it is worth it. I've seen ships come overloaded down with tanks as we were, and then be converted to hospital ships to take the maimed and dying soldiers back to the States. We are lucky, Elinor.

Just got a message on the BAMS program. Seems that there is a German raider (or raiders) in these waters somewhere. The other night we heard about it on the air, and now we are here. He has got some ships through the narrow spot in the Mediterranean. He has moved farther westward, now, and we'll feel better when we get by. The Berlin radio makes quite absurd claims on shipping losses through here. I hope they're absurd, anyway!

I hope that this letter doesn't stink of "the great hero act." We have had some scares. We just tighten watches a bit and seem to come through all right, as you would do if you heard that there was a burglar loose in the neighborhood. I have no gray hairs or wounds to show my children. So, you'll just have to be content to say that you know a guy who isn't a hero.

Love, always darling,
Beat

❧   ❧

Last night I was in here twice and got my two late programs. This morning I couldn't remember having been here and when I looked at the log, I had a good laugh. It was a mess of scribbles, and at the end was a long sweeping stroke as if I had gone to sleep right here. I made the schedules all right, though, with some quick check-up work. I'm awaiting a program now before I turn in.

❧   ❧

It just seems to be an awfully empty world right now. No letters from you for weeks at a time. None of our favorite songs on the air any more, and one look out at the sea makes one realize just how far apart we really are now.

❧   ❦

As soon as I get back, darling, I'll wire you and give you time to straighten out your affairs somewhat so that I can get a date once in a while. And maybe I'll get some of those letters I hope you have written and find out if you are teaching—what kind of a job you have back in Fargo—whose wife you are—or what. Right now I'm in the dark about such things! A guy gets awfully lonesome being over here for so long.

❧   ❦

October 4th
Atlantic

My darling Bunny,

We're almost home! And after five months of self-restraint, isn't a fellow allowed some kind of allowance? I hope that you have been having fun while I have been gone. I have been out myself and I have had passable times with some grand gals. It's very possible to go out with others and still know where the old heart stays, isn't it? I guess that the war is going to last for a few years yet, and that will mean that we shall be apart most of the time. But it doesn't mean that we have to forget each other or that we have to restrict ourselves to each other.

Guess that a bit of time in the States won't be complete without some time spent with you.

I know that I want to see you, and I have to, to make up for that day and night in Aberdeen. I guess that I was rather a wet blanket, hmmm, darling? But there were a million things on my mind then as we were just getting ready to sail and all. This time there won't be any of that beginner's worrying and I'll be an old-timer.

Yours, Always,
[no signature]

October 8, 1943
North Atlantic

Darling,

Here it is an early, cold, rainy morning on the broad ocean, and we are only a week out of the States. I have some good music on the radio from Boston—"You'll Never Know," "Don't Get Around Much Any More," "Sweet Eloise," and others. They bring back memories!

Assuming that operations go according to plan, this ship will be back in the States a week from today. Back in the States and civilization again! I've been thinking about signing off in order to assure myself of a leave in Fargo. Maybe the next trip will be a long one and I might be sorry that I hadn't come home. It all depends upon what you are doing and how things go at the pay-off.

Yours, always,
Beat

Mackay radio message

October 9
from the *James Oliver*

Dear Miss Landgrebe:

There's a certain seaman which would like to
see ya, very much pretty soon, huh. Coming in
after a trip of five months gives me a backlog
of dates with you—ration coupons saved up, so
to speak. Well, darling, I want to cash all of
them in and borrow on the future books through
1,000,000 if I have to.

Just what we shall do for excitement is
up to you—you'll have to name it, as I must
admit that I won't know my way around the old

town with all the servicemen there. Maybe we can sneak into the Comstock early and get our favorite corner—or make a booth in the Aquarium—or have our private table at Gene's to hear the latest in women's orchestras. Wherever it is, I shall be happy just to have you sitting across from me or beside me where I can hold your hand.

We are in a bit of a blow right now and this old typewriter just tips up and down making this job a bit tedious as I have to wait until it is down to strike a key! We really know the North Atlantic now. She's a bit tougher than a North Dakota blizzard, only we don't have the snow—just the salt spray which is much worse. And here I roll, thinking of you and the good old level feeling of a prairie under me again. Doing my best to talk myself out of staying with this ship, darling, but don't know a thing as yet—a day in port and I shall know for sure what is what—and I kinda hope that it means a trip home to my darling—and I hope that you aren't teaching this year, but working in Fargo—yes, even with all those wolves!

Your guy,
Beat

October 15, 1943
New York Bay

Dearest Elinor,

Well, we are just about in and everything's all right. We can't see the skyline as yet as there is a lot of fog. How glad we are to be back again in the States! I hear "Pistol Packin' Momma" is a hit piece now. What the heck is the country coming to!

Italy, Sicily, Suez, Hobart and Oakland seem a long way now, but we have been in all of those places in the past five months. It hardly seems possible that we have been around the world.

I'm hoping to get some mail today. The fellows who have made this trip before say that they got a stack of mail here, so I can hope anyway. And there had better be at least one from you. That would make two you have written since I left the States, and I don't think that it would have been too hard to squeeze in!!

There are a lot of subs around here, but we haven't been bothered much by them. Right now we have two blimps, some Catalinas and about 8 destroyers and some Corvettes around here. And I can remember when we went all the way from Frisco to Aden, Arabia and didn't see one plane or ship of protection. That is 15,000 miles filled with reports, too. But then we haven't got a Navy big enough to follow all of us around, and, besides, it lends that bit of adventure to it!

Hoping to see you while I'm in the States, darling.

Bye now, and be good,
Beat

Broadway!

October 1943

THE METAL FLAP ON the Landgrebe mailbox clanked as the mail slid through the slot in the porch door.

Irene heard it first. "MAIL!" she screamed as she charged through the house. It was mid-afternoon, the final mail delivery of the day.

Elinor and her mother were in the basement workroom when they heard Irene's call. They had planned the day for sewing a winter dress. The morning had started out warm and sunny, a gift, a surprise, before the refrigeration that was sure to come. The frost from last week had only made the day more perfect. Elinor found it hard to imagine that winter could be just around the corner. But, knowing Dakota seasons, she had gotten to work.

They had laid out their supplies and organized things for efficient production: Pins. Spools of thread. Buttons, rescued when dresses and sweaters were thrown in the rag pile. Scissors—both regular and the heavy black-handled pinking shears. Pictures of the latest styles that Elinor had cut out of the Sears catalog, the *Ladies Home Journal* or *Good Housekeeping.*

The black treadle Singer sewing machine had thrummed rhythmically much of the afternoon. Trudie's short legs tired before all the seams were sewn. So Elinor and her mother took turns cutting out the fabrics and piecing them together with pins, and then stitching the seams on the old machine. They chatted as they worked.

"Dotty Dunn has the cutest styles in the window right now, Mother.

There's a winter hat there that I've tried on twice. A small hat, just a little netting and a beautiful velvet flower. Black."

"Bunny, it sounds perfect for this dress."

"But I think I'd better imagine which of my old hats I can remake to match this new dress," Elinor said after removing some pins from between her lips. "I'm not making a lot of money these days."

"How's your job going at Kresge's?" Trudie asked.

"Not much money. But I get to meet a lot of people. And the pressure is off," Elinor sighed.

"Not so many migraines, then," her mother agreed. "That's good news, Bunny."

Elinor slipped into her new dress so her mother could pin the hem. They had fashioned it from a dove grey tweed. It had the requisite tighter waist and narrow skirt. They had added a band of black wool at the short-sleeve hems and on the front overlap where the buttons would be sewn. Elinor had chosen special buttons at Kresges—shiny black stone instead of the less expensive Bakelite ones.

She smiled as she looked into the floor length mirror in the sewing room. "Pin the hem a little higher," she directed her mother. "The style, you know, *Mütterchen.*"

Trudie turned the hem just one patriotic inch and inserted the pins. "Just think of the fabric we used to waste with those three inch hems!" she said.

They heard Irene's mail call. Elinor checked her watch. The day had passed so quickly! She slipped out of her new dress and back into her housedress. She folded the tweed carefully and found a needle and thread for the hem.

Now bleary-eyed, Elinor and her mother climbed the narrow basement stairs to take a breather with a cup of rejuvenating coffee and their afternoon mail. Elinor carried her new dress to the living room and set herself up for hemming after her coffee break.

Before settling down, she opened the back door and stepped out on the porch to savor what was left of the afternoon.

"Mother, you won't believe what we've been missing," she called back into the house. Her mother, carrying two cups of coffee, hurried to join her. They blinked into the sunshine and sipped. They breathed in the smoky trails from the incinerators and the moldy dampness of the soon-slumbering earth. The busy voices of the children in the neighborhood gathering the crisp leaves into jumping piles in back yards filled the air. The children's cries of delight, as they ran into their small mountains, echoed up and down the block.

Elinor laughed when she stepped down the back porch steps. With a hose running slowly, her father, in his Sunday hat, stood watch in the back alley at his fiery incinerator. "Papa, come in for coffee," she called to him.

Her father turned toward her and pointed at the smoke still rising from the smoldering incinerator. He shook his head and waved. The garden hose in his right hand, now watering the sedum, was ready to douse any errant sparks. Georg was probably mulling over a sermon while he burned the leaves from his back yard apple tree and the old elms in front of the house. The acrid incense from the many Fargo fathers at their alley incinerators penetrated the air over the town.

Gardens, picked clean before last week's frost, lay fallow. Elinor spotted a few apples that delayed the ultimate, clutching their boughs. The rest had been gathered into bushel baskets and stored in the basement. Depleted tomato stalks drooped in the black dirt of the garden. An empty garden meant food for the winter.

Indeed, squash, Pontiac potatoes, onions, and canned tomatoes, beans, peas, and corn packed the cold room in the Landgrebe basement. Pickles fermented in a large ecru crock, the ceramic lid held down with an enormous picklestone. A few plump pumpkins, raised for Thanksgiving pies, rested on the floor of the cold room. The coal room by the furnace nearly burst with the latest delivery from the Edison Company.

As they had done for decades, the family had prepared for the coming season. They hoped for a modicum of comfort when snow blanketed the prairie.

Elinor stepped back into the house. She refilled her coffee cup and walked to the dining room table where Irene had stacked the envelopes.

"Thanks for bringing in the mail," she called to Irene. She sat at the table.

Irene returned to the dining room and grinned at the attention. "I got nothing," she said, shrugging.

Elinor organized her letters into a small pile. She found one postmarked New York City. She studied the handwriting. So Beat was back in the States. She put his envelope at the bottom and read the others first.

"Bunny, look," her mother said, joining her and reading the family mail. "Hall Allen is having a shoe sale. Perhaps we should go. Just to have a look around."

"Sure," Elinor replied absently. She skimmed through her letters. Clarence and Dale again. Not much new. They still loved her. Still hoped she was waiting for them. Little did they know how boring her life had become. How she envied the men and their adventures all over the world.

And here was a short note from Johnny. "Not much time to write," he said. "Things look bad in the war over here." She wondered where in the world he had been sent.

Elinor's adventures in San Diego had ended when Johnny and Dale left. There were no jobs that were intriguing enough. Or that paid enough to keep a small room. Well, not both a room and meals. Mickey put in her forty hours to keep food on the table, and the girls slept in the same twin bed. Elinor contributed from her savings, but they still couldn't make ends meet. Everyone sacrificed for the war, but this was too much!

Elinor had heard the stories of how women were being treated in their new jobs, too. Sure, there were a few Rosie the Riveters, but most of the gals were handed brooms or worse. They were the clean-up gangs in the boatyards, the assistants to the men. Or, if they had a position, they had a lot of guff to take from the male contingent, the men too old to go to war or the 4Fs, as the women learned their new roles.

Besides, there were no agents in Point Loma. Although Elinor imagined modeling or a role in the movies, she could only afford one daytrip to L.A., not long enough to even get acquainted. Her California adventure had ended. Her parents, wary of the news coming out of the war, were delighted to have their girls home again.

Elinor rearranged herself on the chair at the dining room table to read Beat's letter. She pushed her hair behind her ears. Of course, first thing, he scolded her. `I have had nine letters from you in exactly five months,` he wrote.

She felt no need to write regularly. She had climbed out of her hospital bed to get to the coast to see him. He didn't arrive, as promised, at the bus terminal. And when they did get together in the hotel in Aberdeen, his reception had been lifeless.

He admitted it. He had dated others. Mr. Flopsie.

She remembered how he had introduced her as "Mrs. Beaton." What an embarrassment! Just who did he think he was?

"I didn't get a single letter," Irene reiterated. She moved into the kitchen to pour herself a cup of coffee, too. "Again."

Elinor heard the jangle of the family phone. But Irene got to it first. She would, the rat! Did she have a sixth sense? Irene seemed to have the uncanny ability to predict when Ma Bell might ring, and she stood ready at any time to be the family secretary, handling phone messages—not always accurately.

"Elinor, it's for you," Irene screamed into the phone. "LONG DISTANCE! It's one of your boyfriends."

Elinor dashed into the den and grabbed the handpiece from her sister. She put it to her ear. "Hello?" she answered.

"Pssst!" She heard her mother's usual warning. "Long distance!"

Elinor heard the static, a click, then Darrow's voice. "Bunny!"

"Oh, hi. Where are you?"

"We just got in. I'm in New York. The big city. I didn't think I'd find you in Fargo. Back from the coast, I see. How are things?"

"The same. Boring, actually. We're all well. You?"

She looked around, locating the members of her family. Her mother was in the kitchen, tidying up after their afternoon coffee break. Irene? Elinor pulled the phone cord around the corner to the stairway. Of course. Perched on the steps. Elinor signaled with one hand to shoo her snoopy sister away.

Irene scooted upstairs to her bedroom, but Elinor hadn't heard the door to the room close. She retreated to the den and pulled the long phone cord as far into the room as it would reach.

"Oh, Bunny, it was quite a trip. Around the world! Can you believe it? And I'm still alive. No seasickness either." He took a breath. "I didn't know where to find you. What are you doing in Fargo?"

"No jobs on the coast for me. And it's expensive. Just to stay alive."

"Told you so, didn't I? Miss me?"

"Well, your letters kept me up to date. It's surprising how many got through."

"The code?"

"I finally caught on. You really get around!"

"I've decided to stay here while they upgrade the ship. We're really going deeper into the war on this next leg, Bunny. They're adding armaments and more protection to the *Oliver*."

"I thought you were . . ." New York? Elinor pushed her bangs back.

"I can't come to Fargo. No time this time."

"Oh, so . . ." Hadn't he promised to come home to have some fun after this first trip? When he finally had some money? And his first leave? She was ready for a little diversion.

"Any chance you'd come for a fun time in the city? We could go to a show or two, maybe a ball game. Oh, Bunny, this place has everything!" She had gone to Aberdeen. She was finished with all this running around.

Elinor twisted the stiff phone cord around her free hand. "Are you kidding?" New York City? "Beat, don't be silly." It seemed obvious. What could she ever tell her parents?

"Well, I thought you might want an adventure."

Elinor recognized the slur in his voice.

He continued, "It's okay. I've met some nice girls around here, and they'll help me pass the time. Before long I'll be back on the seas in the Jimmy *Oliver*."

Elinor sighed. Of course he had other girls. Didn't all sailors? Girls in every port?

Anyway, there were no travel options for a single gal. A teacher. A preacher's daughter. A girl with no logical excuse to travel to New York City.

But . . . New York City. Shopping. Nightclubs. The theatre. Stars!

Her father would be fit to be tied that she had even spoken to Darrow. Thank goodness he was occupied at the incinerator.

The time was nearly up on the three-minute phone call. A girl needed time to think!

"I've picked up a few trinkets for you. From Egypt, the South Pacific. Interesting stuff, but you might not like it."

"Thank you." They were talking fast now.

"Guess I'll mail them to you, then."

"I . . ."

"Bye, Elinor," he mumbled.

"Bye," she shouted as the phone clicked.

Elinor set the handset into its cradle. She looked at the kitchen clock. She felt certain the operator had cut them off too early. Next call, she'd attend to the second hand on that clock, the one her father set daily using the Greenwich Mean Time signal on the radio at noon.

"Who was it, Bunny?" her mother called from the kitchen.

"Just an 'old friend.' Nothing important," Elinor responded.

She plopped onto her daybed. Ha! He wasn't coming back to Fargo. So much for Beat's promises.

The lonesome whistle of the train cut into her thoughts—the Great Northern pulling out of the station, she supposed, taking a crowd toward one adventure or another.

She Usually Won at Tug-o-war...

4:00 A.M.

ELINOR JUMPED WHEN THE cuckoo chirped. Four o'clock and she still had a stack of letters in front of her!

She leaned back in the desk chair. She swiveled it to face away from the desk.

Ching's front leg twitched in his sleep. She stared at him, so sound asleep on her daybed. She hadn't slept that soundly for weeks.

She turned the chair and looked at the letters strewn on the desktop. She fingered an envelope.

She and Beat had played at tug-of-war. She supposed she tugged as hard as he did. She had exaggerated her dates with "old friends," and he had countered by bragging about his adventures around the world. And his dates with other women.

Elinor reached over the desk to turn off the lamp. It flickered, reluctant to darken. She tipped her head back, then rolled it in circles to stretch her neck.

She and Beat really didn't know each other. They hadn't had enough time to build a relationship before the war marched into their lives.

'43 was the summer of her big dreams. California . . .

She sighed as she stood up to stretch. She pulled her sweater back up over her shoulders.

What would her parents have thought? They didn't know about the times she and Beat had been together—in Minneapolis, Chicago, Sauk Center, Aberdeen. They wouldn't have believed it of her. They thought of her as their sweet girl, not a woman with passions, a woman with dreams.

A traitor to the family.

Life was like one of those eddies in the water, sucking her down, draining the energy right out of her core.

Elinor sat back down again. She flipped on the light. The white button. Three blinks and it lit the pile of remaining letters. With a sigh she returned to 1943. The end of October.

Setting Sail Again

Late Fall 1943–April 1944

October 18, 1943

Dear Bunny,

Maybe I'd better explain why I'm not coming home, darling. In the first place, I don't like this cold weather. And where I am going it will be good ol' summertime again.

Now, I'm getting this ship overhauled as far as this department goes. I'm getting all kinds of priority equipment. I just tell them the name of the ship, and then they do all they can. All my requisitions are going through without a hitch.

Then, I want to be out here instead of sitting "on the beach" for so long. I want to get into all I can before she is over. You see, darling, these campaigns are planned a long time ahead to give all the ships time to get there and assemble, etc. We are going to load a cargo of stuff. I think that I'll quit smoking this trip!

I want to see you so darn much and you can't

come. It's something that I won't get over
until we are out at sea again. Then, a bit of
excitement and the feeling that there just isn't
the least chance that you can come to me will
gradually make me feel as I always do at sea. I
live the sea then and forget all about the good
things which happen back where people laugh and
have fun. And I'll be looking forward to your
letters and our time together when I get back
next time.

You'll be hearing from me every once in a
while and I hope to hear from you, too.

Yours, forever,
Beat

Oct. 21

Darling,

After battling for the third straight day with myself, here I am again still with the ship. I could still leave at any time for home and you—and God only knows just how much I want to do that. Everything reminds me of what a fool I am for not going home and seeing my girl again.

What I can't figure out is why you didn't want to come to New York. I know that the trains are no fun these days, that you have just returned from the West Coast, that you are just loafing around and having a nice life, that Mick is with you, that there are friends around. What I can't figure out is why you wouldn't give them up for a while to come and see me.

I've been hounding the company offices and the general delivery offices day and night all by myself, but no letters come. I've given up now and I guess it's for the best.

You say you've been going out with some "old friends," so I guess that I may feel at liberty to do so, too. I have met a swell gal here. We went to shows and a few of the places around here the past few nights. I'm going up to Boston to see Libby, one of my old girlfriends, again. Got a swell letter from her the other day and talked long distance to her last night. We'll think of you at the Cave up there either tomorrow night or Saturday night. Or both.

So, for now, darling, 'tis bye and all my love to hold with you for another 4 to 9 months again.

Beat

We're at an Army dock now and will be leaving soon. They really have changed this ship in a lot of ways. They put escape panels in all the rooms. They are made of plywood and cut through the steel bulkheads so that a man may kick them out in case the door is jammed in the torpedoing or bombing. They put two in the radio room so I have two to work for. Whenever we hit an emergency, the Navy radiomen in my crew have to call if I'm not on watch and I take over in here. They have guns to man right outside here. And I'll have to help them some, too. They have a lot of new blackout lights in, mounted about two feet off the deck in all the passageways. They give off a red light that enables one to see where to walk after the sun is down and the ship is blacked out. Last trip we just had to stumble around in the dark. They also put on another lifeboat transmitter and two more life rafts and some guns (and I can't say what kind or how many). We had some old timers come aboard and walk off as soon as they saw what work is being done. Now, if I were an old timer, I'd probably do the same thing. But what would you want with an old timer?

[no date]
Darling,

There haven't been any letters from you here in New York since that first one, so I guess you must be busy with a job by now.

I'm forwarding some stuff to you which I hope you will like a bit. The perfume is the real oil and has to be diluted about ten to one with alcohol and is a popular and darn expensive stuff, darling. The necklace is pure silver and was made by hand by Egyptian labor—darn good work, but maybe a bit gaudy for you. The cross is for your dad. It's from Jerusalem and made from Mother of Pearl.

So, I'm going. Too bad we couldn't get together this time—But—

'Tis all for now, darling,
Your guy,
Beat

D.R. Beaton (radio officer)
SS James Oliver
c/o Fleet Postmaster
80 Varick Street
New York, N.Y.

James Oliver
November 1943-March 3, 1944
Manifest for the second voyage of the *James Oliver*

Departure	Convoy	Arrival
November 4 NYC	NG.396 Guantanamo	November 11
November 12 Guantanamo	independent Cristobal	November 16
November 18 Balboa, Panama	independent Noumea	December 17
January 13, 1944 Noumea	independent Pearl Harbor	January 30
February 23 Ahukini	independent San Francisco	March 3

November 7, 1943

My darling Elinor,
Here I sit already so hot that I can just imagine how it will be soon. We are running around in T-shirts and light trousers. That's my type of life in exchange for missing a North Dakota winter—and I can't say that I'm a bit sorry!!

Last April was the last time that we were really together. Aberdeen was just a tired meeting for a few hours. I could live on times such as we have had in Chicago and Pelican and Fargo and Moorhead and Sauk Center.

Remember that time in Chicago? I remember calling you from Minneapolis about fifteen minutes after I had passed my final physical and begged for a waiver on my one bad eye. I knew the waiver would go through as I had kidded them some on knowledge of radio. And then I heard you on the phone and I couldn't go home. I just had to come down to the Windy City to see you and we spent almost all of your money, remember? We saw the Dodgers and Durocher and had some good times downtown there. Next time we shall have much more fun.

You mentioned in one of your letters that you would like to wander around a while after the war. We could have a lot of fun that way, looking up old friends and seeing the country all over again. And, darling, if I ever come into New York again, I hope that you can make the trip here, because it is one place in a million to enjoy.

Beat

November 9, 1943
AT SEA

Hi ya, Sweets,

Sitting here on watch having just had a look at a piece of land which was going by—or was it we who were going by?! Anyway, it looks like a good place to live in comfort and peace. And it hardly seems possible that we are already discharged and loaded and out again on another trip. And already so far from the good old States and any contact at all with you and the family. But here we are, and it is quite easy to believe if one goes to the porthole and looks out!

You never did tell me if Johnny went across or not and where Dale is now. I remember that you thought John was going over and that Dale was supposed to be stationed in California for some time. I'm just curious, darling, that's all. They seem to be pretty nice guys and I always like to try to keep track of everyone. Just a salesman's habit.

You'll be seeing Walt, I suppose, as you are so close to each other back there. Won't you say hello for me sometime? That 4-F back of his seems to be bothering him a lot these days, doesn't it? And he seems to be making some money, too, which is a good thing, I guess. Dear ol' monya.

The weather is warm and makes me remember the day you and I spent at the lakes just before I shoved off for this outfit. I went swimming in the afternoon and that night we got pie-eyed and we were traveling down to Pelican. Remember? And you had everything timed so that we would miss "those people" but it didn't work out so well.

The Xmas card was picked up in Alexandria, from an old Greek stationery store there. The old guy liked us and we talked about the war there for quite some time one night. The blackout is perfect there. We stepped out of the store and couldn't see anything for about 15 minutes as we struggled down the streets. I saw the New York blackout and the new version called a "brown-out" and laughed as I thought of some of the other places over there where a real blackout is something like habit to the people now.

Well, this is all for this time. Be mine and wait for me a bit longer. I'll be there some day.

Beat

November 12

My darling Elinor,

I'm about as stiff as a guy can be without
having a drink. We've been rooked into lifting
weights and all of us started off too fast! Last
night Leo and I were walking on deck and some
of the crew were around the bar lifting. One of
the fellows lifted all the weights at once, and
then they started to kid me. You know, telling
me that I was a passenger without a muscle
and all of that. So, I went over without any
warm-up and out-lifted all of them. The good
old Y training is just how I did it. They won't
razz me any more, but I feel like hell today.
And, darling, don't tell them, will you? They
would have me then.

    We celebrated Armistice Day in port for a
half day with shore staring at us but no shore
leaves granted.

                    Bye, darling. I love you
                                          Beat

NOVEMBER 14, 1943
AT SEA

MY DARLING,

HOW'S MY DARLING?! JUST READ THROUGH ~~SOME~~ SOME OF YOUR LETTERS WRITTEN WHILE I WAS GONE LAST TIME, AND I HAD TO SMILE AT SOME OF THEM, DARLING. YOU REALLY DONT TRUST ME, DO YOU? EVERY LETTER IS GIVING ME HECK FOR SOMETHING--LIKE NOT WRITING, GOING OUT WITH GALS, BEING CYNICAL, HAVING A DRINK, ETC. BUT, DARLING, I HAVE TAKEN ALL OF YOUR ADVICE AND I'M GOING TO LIVE JUST AS YOU WANT ME TO--NONE OF THOSE THINGS FOR ME THIS TRIP--I'LL ONLY BE LIVING FOR THE TIME THAT I CAN BE AT HOME AND WITH YOU AGAIN. O.K?

STILL LOVE ME, DARLING? BETTER, 'CUS I'LL MAKE IT JUST AS MISERABLE FOR YOU AS I CAN!!! I'D HATE TO BE ONE OF THOSE GUYS WITH A BROKEN HEART, TRAILING AFTER A GAL WHO JUST DIDN'T CARE WHAT HAPPENED TO ME--NOW, WOULDN'T YOU FEEL AWFULLY SORRY FOR ME, TOO? SO, JUST CONFINE YOUR TIME TO KNITTING, ETC. AS YOU HAVE BEEN. THEN I'LL KNOW THAT I HAVE A FIGHTING CHANCE WITH THE

An example of a censored page; some lost a line or two or a word or two. There must've been something important in these paragraphs.

From now on, I'll number the letters for you. I mailed one already so that makes this number two of this voyage. Maybe you could do the same if it wouldn't be too hard to keep bookkeeping records for all the letters you write.

LETTER 12
December 1, 1943
Pacific Ocean

My darling Elinor,
Well, darlin' the month of December is here, and we still haven't gotten together. By the time we do, I guess we shall be the total strangers we were when we first met.

We met over two years ago now. Two years from this Christmas season. Remember? We walked home together. It seemed to be too good to be true at first that I was even going home with you! But we seemed to have fun together—the kind of fun I'd never had before with anyone. Things seemed to work out perfectly for us for a while, didn't they?

You were teaching, and we could get together only on weekends. And there were certain complications then, too—such as waiting until midnight to see you! I can laugh now, as I did then, when I think of Walt, "The Glass and Paint man", sitting there trying to outwit you. He did sit us out a couple of times, but we seemed to do all right most of the time, didn't we? Then he went down south and we were together all the time. We got to know each other a lot better and I knew then what I had imagined all along was the truth—I loved you and I was stuck for better or for worse. Only time can tell which.

The following spring and summer were perfect until I shipped out rather hurriedly. Since that time we have had about two weeks together, and they were all squeezed into the leave last March. We've had a day or two here and there twice, but they can't count really, as either of us had just traveled a long way and there was present a bit of irritability and tiredness. Taking all this time we have had together wouldn't make up over four or five months, I guess, but they were about the best I have ever spent and they will always be the ones that I will look back on and remember as the happiest of my life.

But times do change, and so do women, they say! We started having troubles and before long they had gone so far as to get out of hand for both of us. Up to this time, we haven't had that "long talk" you seem to want. Darling, I want a long talk with you, too, but I guess that I don't have the same things on my mind as you may imagine. Let's just concentrate our little time on building something instead of tearing down something that is already a bit worn out.

Before I forget it, will you promise to look up that guy Axel. Remember you met him in Aberdeen, Washington, when you were out there? He's on that list of musts which I gave you out there, and I want you to be sure to buy him a birthday present for February 6th. Make it any little thing and sign my name to it, will you? And stay away from Lorraine, too. I'll see her. [see code sheet]

I won at poker last night. It's the third night in a row. The chief engineer, Army Looey, first engineer, purser, two cadets, two mates and I meet just about every night to battle it out. So far, I'm ahead, but it is just because I have dared to gamble with a lot of money at once in a couple of crucial hands. So far I've been lucky and it will take a lot of poor nights to pull me down to where I started—at exactly nothing. I borrowed some money to start and the first night went ahead to stay. I guess that the fraternity taught me something after all! I'm getting rich.

Drop me a line, darlin', and I'll promise to write you.

Your guy, always,
Beat

Our Men, Good Men

December 8, 1943

THE WIND DANCED FROM the north, across the open prairie and into Fargo, north to south, whirling down the city streets. The gray sky hung low over the town, dimly lit as the invisible sun began its ascent. Cars parked on Third Street sat under a sheet of ice, a frosting of snow decorating their tops. The family rose warily in the eerie silence of the first winter snow.

Trudie slipped into a housedress and dashed downstairs to her morning post in the kitchen. She plugged in the Coffeemaster. Shivering, she turned on the oven to warm the room, then closed the door to Georg's study to keep as much of the heat as possible in the small space. As the oven heated, Trudie spooned a bit of bacon grease from the jar she kept on the stovetop into her fry pan. She cracked a couple of farm eggs, brought to them by former parishioners, into the bacon fat as it sizzled in the pan. The coffee pot began to percolate, and the family, smelling breakfast, began to gather.

Georg had followed his wife to the kitchen, but then continued into the basement to stoke the coal furnace. He opened the cast iron door in the side of the "octopus." The fire, banked overnight, lay passive, and now minimum heat circulated upstairs. Georg shoveled in fresh coal from the coal room—three precious shovels full from their winter delivery. He shook the grate to separate out the ashes and then added a few pages from yesterday's newspapers, which he lit at one corner. He turned the damper to let more air into the furnace, and the fire woke, roaring, yellow and red. It leapt at the furnace's mouth. Georg slammed the hot door.

He then danced upstairs and entered the kitchen. "What a lovely day, *Tay-Air-Oo,*" he laughed as he hugged his tiny wife. "First day of winter and we'll have heat in the house for a few hours. We can splurge once, even with coal rationing."

Mickey shuffled into the room, wrapped in a blanket to stave off the chill of the house. "Have you looked outside, Mother?" she asked. "Winter! And in time for Christmas." She opened the back door of the house, ducked outside, and returned with an icy glass bottle of Cass Clay milk. "It's freezing out there!" she exclaimed, stamping her feet, as she handed the bottle to her mother.

Trudie paused to hug her youngest daughter and then opened the refrigerator.

Heat hissed and rose from the heat register on the kitchen floor.

"And we'll stoke up our furnace for Christmas, too," Georg added. "Even during war, there are, after all, still days to celebrate." He looked out of the kitchen window. "I'm going to have some shoveling to do to get the car out this morning," he laughed. He and Trudie had plans to take their ration coupons to Grondahl's for a few special grocery items. It was time to start the *pfeffernüsse* and *lebkuchen*, Christmas cookies which benefitted from some aging.

Elinor buttoned up her sweater as she hustled through the front three-season porch toward the outside door. She snatched the *Fargo Forum* morning edition from the third step and dashed back into the house, slapping the snow from the newsprint. Shivering from the icy winter blast outdoors, she called to her parents, "I've got it! The paper's here."

She spread the newspaper on top of the tablecloth of the dining room table and turned the pages.

"Have you found it?" Trudie asked as she entered the dining room.

Georg picked up his cup and followed his wife.

Mickey was already seated at the dining room table, her hair bobby-pinned into curls, her eyes bleary. A coffee cup steamed on the table in front of her.

⇥   ⇤

Two days earlier, Mrs. Hinschberger had been over for a morning cup of coffee when her husband unexpectedly arrived at the back door. Georg had welcomed him in before noting the strain on his neighbor's face.

"Bess?" was all Mr. Hinschberger could manage. "Oh, Bess . . ."

Georg grabbed his neighbor's arm to steady him, and they both entered the kitchen where the women were chatting in the breakfast nook.

"Martin?" Bess was surprised to see her husband. "What's the matter?"

"We've gotten a telegram," Mr. Hinschberger stuttered as he felt in his pants pocket for his handkerchief. "A telegram. Just now, Bess." He pulled a folded yellow paper from his shirt pocket and handed it to his wife. "It just arrived," he explained. While his wife read the message, he dabbed at his eyes with his hanky.

Elinor hadn't been home, but she'd heard the news. The way the Hinschbergers held each other and sobbed. The way they called their son's name. The comfort—impossible— her parents tried to give them.

⇥   ⇤

"Here, mother," she said. "The notice is in the obituaries today."

"The Catholics will gather for a service." Trudie dropped into her chair at the table. "We'll have to go."

Elinor continued to read. "It says he was killed in Tarawa. Another one of those islands. There must be a thousand between us and Japan." Elinor looked up. "Must we fight for each? One by one?"

"Places we had never heard of before the war," Mickey added, her hands now wrapped around her warm cup. "Dots of land. Can they be worth all these lives?"

"Just think what our men are going through. They parachute behind enemy lines. Gil and Phil are trained to do that," Elinor continued. "In the daylight. Or in complete dark."

"Dale and Bob Flynn fly into enemy guns," Mickey added.

"Some of our boys deliver armaments. Sitting ducks on the oceans, waiting for the Japs to shoot them. Like Beat." Elinor shook her head. "Can you imagine crawling up beaches into gunfire?"

"Like my Bob? Too much to imagine." Mickey put one hand to her forehead.

"This too shall pass. Remember that, girls," Georg said, sipping his coffee. "It seems at the time that evil will win, but good triumphs over all. Remember the Great War . . ." He slipped into a reverie.

Trudie returned to the kitchen. She shut off the oven and opened its door to release the pent up heat. Then she dished up breakfast for her husband and herself.

Elinor followed to put a slice of bread into the toaster. "But our men," she started. "Good men. They march off and follow orders, even orders to march up hillsides when they know they'll be shot."

"And if they didn't, Bunny?" Trudie sighed.

"Our freedom is worth fighting for, I know. But I just don't want anyone I know to have to do the fighting." Elinor stood by the toaster, warming her hands and waiting for the bread to brown.

"We are lucky," Georg reminded the family, as he joined them, settling into his spot in the breakfast nook. "We have no sons in this fight."

"With Yupps at seminary. But the Hinschbergers," Trudie whispered. "Their son . . . *Ach!*"

"No brothers in this war, but we have friends, Papa," Elinor said. She turned to Mickey, who was refreshing her coffee. "Let's write letters to the men tonight," she suggested. "You write to Bob. And will you also write to Dale? I know he'd like to hear from us."

Mickey nodded. "Sure, kid." She refilled her cup. "We ought to, I suppose."

Elinor continued, "I'm going to write to Johnny first." She watched for her father's reaction before continuing. "And then I'll write to Darrow."

"Bunny . . ." Georg looked up at his daughter. He set his cup down with a distinct thud.

"Georg," Trudie interrupted.

Elinor turned toward her mother.

"It's time to forgive. A man isn't responsible for what his friend does. Darrow was in Boston." Trudie stepped toward her husband. She set his breakfast on the table in front of him. Then she sat down across from him and reached out to touch his hand.

Elinor's eyes followed her mother's movements.

"All our men need support," Trudie offered. Her eyes met those of her husband. "No matter what."

Another Year

December 7, 1943

Two years ago all of this started. But we have
come a long way since that day, haven't we? One
can just look around and know that the Japs are
getting the worst of it now. Yes, we own a lot of
territory now that once was Jap-held and looked
as if it would be so held for a long while.

❮ ❯

LETTER 15
December 11, 1943
Pacific

Darling,

One of the Navy boys is as regular as clockwork.
He feeds the fish just about every hour on the
hour. He is one of the boys who just can't
get over seasickness. For a while during the
weather, we could find quite an audience out
there helping him! It sounds kinda crude, I
must admit, but he is a good sport and makes
it a pretty good laugh for all of us. When we
get back to the States, he will probably be

transferred to permanent shore duty. It has happened to many of them.

The other day I decided with Leo that if the ship went to England or the Mediterranean on the next trip, we would stay with her. That night I had a dream. I was calling you and hearing you give me the same answers that I got in New York. I woke up quite mad and decided that I had better not take any chances on that happening again.

We have a good idea when we will be back to the States, but I couldn't say any more than that. Unless this ship has a European run for the next trip, I shall be signing off and coming home. It won't be too long now, darling, so don't be surprised whenever I call.

Yours, forever,
Beat

V . . . -Mail
Dec. 19
South Pacific [Noumea]

My darling,

I've already mailed some letters to you, but I'm not sure that they will reach you as quickly as one written on V mail stationery. They say that this is the mail that has the priorities on mail to the States and should reach you in about four or five days from the time of mailing out here!

We are loafing around, and trying to entertain ourselves in the town here. There is an officers' club here, and I plan to spend some time and money there as they have some American whiskey and beer.

When I look and see these men and women here working for the war, I feel a bit guilty when I think ahead. I'm going to be able to take a leave of thirty days when I get back. There are fellows here who haven't seen the States in over three years. They have worked hard all of that time. And when I think of the people back home and the way they are living, it makes the whole war seem very unfair to these men.

Beat

LETTER 17
December 20, 1943
SOUTH PACIFIC

My darling,

There are a lot of sights here and we are seeing them one by one. This is an island that you have often seen in tropical pictures, except there aren't any Dotty Lamours! The natives wear sarongs, some English clothes or nothing at all. They don't seem able to grasp what is going on around them.

They have a leper colony here and it is only marked by signs. The lepers live right in a section of the city here as the poorer class will live in the slums back in the States. We have been warned to stay away from there, and needless to say, I have done just that.

There is a Jap prison camp here, too. They don't look any too down-hearted about being prisoners and seem to be in good health. Before this war is over out here, the camp will be filled a bit more. It gives a fellow a funny feeling to get a look at them inside their fence. A guy can't hate them for some reason. Maybe some day I shall have a good reason to hate them as much as some of these men down here do.

Seeing these islands makes one more of my wishes come true. There aren't many more places that I really want to see, and before long I shall be seeing them, too. I do want to see Europe and Rio, and I'll be all ready to settle down back on the plains again with my gal.

Your guy, always,
Beat

To Elinor 439

LETTER 23
South Pacific
December 25, 1943

My Darling Bunny,

There will be no Christmas holiday here as
there will be in the States. Everything goes on
as usual but for some extra food. I visited the
ships and did some shopping and had turkey for
dinner and went to church last night. Otherwise,
the day is the same as any other.

Just had to laugh as I thought of the field day
you will be having today. That cat is probably
tearing the tree and all the presents down
again this year! Then with everybody trying
to catch him and stop him, he only goes more
wild and tears more down. It's a funny memory
to carry away from that wonderful evening last
year, isn't it?

The skipper, Pete, and I went to a show and
then church last night. After church we went
for a long walk in the hills around here, and
we were silent for the most part, just thinking.
I thought a lot about you and home. I thought
of some of the foolish things I have done since
leaving there and more of them that I had done
while still there. Now, looking back on the
last leave at Christmas, the year and all the
traveling around the world since, it just doesn't
seem possible that only a year has passed. If
all time can go so slowly, I shall be happy.
Think of the years we shall have after this is
all over!!! If they last as long, we shall have
a lot of time together, darling.

And, darling, I bought fifty more airmail stamps today, so you'll be sure to hear from me for a while yet. The Army gave us all the V-mail blanks we could handle, and they recommend them to us as the quickest way to get word home from these parts. I always am in hopes of getting your letters some day and reading them and knowing that you were thinking of me, too.

Yours,
Beat

Girls from left: Mickey, Elinor, Irene
Middle row: Yupps and Trudie
Front: Georg

Print the complete address in plain block letters in the panel below, and your return address in the space
provided. Use typewriter, dark ink, or pencil. Write plainly. Very small writing is not suitable.

No._____

From

To   MISS ELINOR LANDGREBE   D.R. BEATON (R.O.)

     1135 THIRD STREET NORTH   SS JAMES OLIVER

     FARGO,   C/O FLEET POSTMASTER

     NORTH DAKOTA,   NEW YORK, N.Y.

     U.S.A.   DECEMBER 31, 1943

[CENSOR'S STAMP]   [Date]

SOUTH PACIFIC

MY DARLING,

DON'T ASK ME WHY I'M SO HAPPY TODAY!! THERE WERE 47 LETTERS FOR ME IN TODAY'S MAIL AND FIVE OF THEM WERE FROM YOU, BUNNY. WE CAN THANK THE ARMY AND NAVY FOR SOME GOOD SERVICE ON THEM, AND I HAVE NOW RECEIVED ALL YOUR LETTERS UP AND THROUGH NOVEMBER 31. FROM NOW ON THEY WILL KNOW WHERE WE ARE, AND WE EXPECT TO GET OUR MAIL EVEN SOONER.

I HAVEN'T TIME TO ANSWER ALL THE QUESTIONS AND ARGUMENTS WHICH YOU SEEM TO HAVE PRESENTED TO ME IN SOME OF YOUR RAMBLING, BUT I SHALL ANSWER THEM ON OUR NEXT STRETCH AT SEA, DARLING. THEY ALL MAKE SENSE, AND YOU HAVE EVERY REASON IN THE WORLD TO BRING THEM UP. I STILL THINK THAT OUR LONG TALK WILL BE THE BEST WAY TO CLEAR UP ALL THESE DOUBTS IN YOUR MIND. JUST HANG ON AROUND HOME, DARLING, AND I SHALL SURPRISE YOU BY BEING HOME EARLIER THAN EITHER OF US THINK.

WE HAVE BEEN HAVING FUN DOWN N THIS PORT--I HAVE TO MEET A RADIO OFFCR. FROM A TANKER IN TOWN TODAY. HE WAS IN MY CLASS AT G.I. AND HE MET SOME OF OUR OTHER OFFICERS ASHORE YESTERDAY AND GAVE THEM A NOTE FOR ME. HE HASN'T BEEN BACK TO THE STATES SINCE SHIPPING OUT IN JUNE. WE SHOULD HAVE A GOOD TALK. I'M STILL PICKING UP SOUVENIRS--MAYBE I SHALL GET THAT STRAW SKIRT YET!!

WALT SEEMS TO BE IN THERE PITCHING WHILE I AM GONE--BUT HE ISN'T THE ONLY GUY WHO IS UNDERMINING GUYS WHO ARE OVER AND AWAY FROM IT ALL. WHT THE HELL, DARLING, ALL IS FAIR IN LOVE AND WAR--BUT IT TAKES MEN TO FIGHT WARS.

I'LL BE WRITING MORE FROM HERE IF I CAN--OR MAILING SOON FROM OUR NEXT PORT--I'LL ALWAYS LOVE YOU--------------------------YOUR GUY, Beat.

V...-MAIL

New Years V . . . -MAIL

LETTER 27
December 31, 1943
New Year's Eve
SOUTH PACIFIC

Bunny, darling,

The letters from the States made all of us happier. It seems that everybody remembered me at this time of the year, and it makes a guy feel pretty darn swell. The best part of it all, though, was hearing from you.

I am looking forward to seeing some of those more patriotic dresses—the ones that are going to be slimmer and tighter. I imagine that you will be able to show your patriotism to advantage, and there are quite a few who are going to be handicapped!

You will probably get more of these ancient history letters before I get back. People are writing that they get letters from July in November, so don't be surprised. You didn't seem to think that I had written, but I had, darling. So far I've done all right with you, writing—counting this—27 letters since November fourth. Betcha I write more than you do! And me with a job, too!

If I could only show you how little I worry about Walt! He doesn't give up, does he!!!! And one can't really blame him for proposing over and over again to such a gal as you, now, can one?

This church work you are doing or were doing has been keeping you pretty busy, hasn't it? Maybe you'll be glad to get back to teaching some time after a "vacation" such as this! With the choir, Luther League, playing the organ, drilling little kids, etc. you must find it a bit hard to squeeze in a date here and there! Keep it up!!

Yours, always,
Beat

LETTER 28
January 1, 1944
South Pacific (Noumea)

My Darling,

Seems that the New Year always makes a person
think a bit more than usual!

In the first place, it is hard to see these
fellows out here celebrating their New Year with
about a minute off work—just long enough to sing
a song and clap each other on the back. These
fellows have been here for a long time, and
there is no rest at home due them. But they take
it with smiles. They have adjusted themselves
to the inevitable.

I belong to a union, and I think that they are
good things. But since seeing guys in all the
different parts of the world working together
and not crabbing too much (just enough to make
them happy!), it is hard to hear about strikes
for higher wages back in the States. Workers
back there are thinking only of feathering
their pockets, thinking that the guy next door
is getting the bigger cut of the "sugar" which
the government is giving away during this
emergency. If they would only cultivate the
idea that they are all working together—some at
less wages, some at more, maybe they could get
the necessary cooperation to do a lot better
job and we would have an America that would be
united as never before.

So, I have made a resolution to do a bit extra
every day and not worry about it. There are
a lot of things I can do in this job to make

myself and the department more efficiently run.
I'm going to pitch in and really do my best and
a bit more.

                              Yours, forever,
                              Beat

No._____

From

To   MISS ELINOR LANDGREBE   D.R. BEATON (R.C.)
                                         SSC JAMES OLIVER
      1135 THIRD STREET NORTH   C/O FLEET POSTMASTER
                                         NEW YORK, N.Y.
      FARGO,

      NORTH DAKOTA,
                                         JANUARY 11, 1944
      U.S.A.   [Date]

[CENSOR'S STAMP]

LETTER 32   SOUTH PACIFIC

DARLING,

     WELL, WE HAD MAIL TODAY, AND I HAVE BEEN ANSWERING LETTERS TO ALL THE
PEOPLE--IT'S QUITE A JOB SOMETIMES. AND, DARLING, THERE WASN'T A SINGLE
LITTLE LETTER FROM YOU HERE. I KNOW JUST HOW WRITING CAN BE AT TIMES, AND I
SEE THAT FOR YOU IT IS SOMETIMES HARD TO SIT DOWN AND WRITE ABOUT WHAT YOU
THINK IS "NOTHING." "NOTHING" IS ABOUT ALL I'VE HAD TO WRITE ABOUT, TOO, AND
I'VE DONE MY BEST TO MAKE IT INTERESTING AND QQQ STILL ABLE TO PASS THE
CENSOR. FROM NOW ON, I SHALL CUT DOWN ON THE LETTERS AND JUST WRITE ABOUT THE
THINGS THAT HAPPEN--I'M SURE THAT WE SHALL BE HAPPIER AND HAVE MORE TIME ON
OUR HANDS FOR OTHER THINGS!! LET'S JUST WRITE WHEN WE FEEL LIKE IT, DARLING,
AND MAKE THE FEWER LETTERS LONGER. I LIKE THAT.

     I HAD A LETTER FROM MY SISTER IN PHILLY, AND SHE IS REALLY PROUD OF THAT
DAUGHTER OF HERS. MY BROTHER DAVE WRITES THAT HE HAS VISITED HOME AND ALSO
PHILLY TO SEE HIS NEICE--HE TRIED TO GET OUT OF THE ARMY AND INTO THE NAVY, BUT
NO SOAP. LETTERS FROM THE GUYS I WENT TO G.I. WITH ARE REALLY FULL OF THE WAR--
ED WILDER OF MINNEAPOLIS WAS ON THE FIRST SHIP INTO NAPLES. HE HAS HAD SOME
REALLY EXCITING EXPERIENCES--AND TOOK OFF THIRTY DAYS TO REST UP AND SPEND ALL
HIS MONEY!! WISH THAT I COULD HAVE BEEN ON LEAVE AT THE SAME TIME. AND THE
USUAL LETTERS FROM THE OLD GAL FRIENDS TELLING ME OF THE GUYS WITH WHOM THEY
ARE NOW RUNNING AROUND. IT'S GREAT TO HAVE FRIENDS, ISN'T IT!!

     I'M LOOKING FOR SOME NEW AND DIFFERENT SOUVENIRS HERE, AND I HOPE TO BE
ABLE TO GET YOU SOMETHING, DARLING. BUT #### IT'S BYE FOR NOW--THINK OF ME--
                                         YOURS, ALWAYS, Beat

V....-MAIL

V . . . -Mail

LETTER 36
February 3, 1944

My darling,

I shall never forget the night that I have
just spent. The view across the water with the
moonlight and various flashing lights made one
feel a bit small. Sitting out the early evening
and trying to watch movies on the decks of
various Navy vessels around us, we had the
experience of seeming to be in a ridiculous
position. Overhead, planes of all kinds roared
by. Harry James played his famous notes in one
of the shows. In another, "Johnny Come Lately,"
it showed Cagney saving an old lady and her
newspaper from gangsters. The moon was bright
when it did come out, and we sat out on deck
until we were very tired, just thinking and
wearing ourselves out for a good night's sleep.
But when we got up and decided to go to bed,
I couldn't think of sleep right away and here
I am, Bunny, trying to put some of this on
paper.

Sometimes I wonder just what you have been
doing now. I suppose that Walt is still seeing
you. I wonder if he doesn't get mad about his
brother being a prisoner and all. That would
seem a big enough reason for me to want to
get in, come hell or high water. My wish is
that this war will be over before either of my
brothers has to go over, but if they do, that
they do as good a job as the others over there.
Maybe Johnny has gone over now as he told you
he might. Phil is still flying the PBYs and Dale

is still doing his flying some place. It takes a lot of guys, and it sometimes seems funny that so many could be in fighting zones at once!

Beat

LETTER 40
February 8, 1944

My darling Bunny,

Right now I am on watch again. We found some
trouble with the main transmitter a couple of
days ago and I was busy with that for a while,
but now it seems to be O.K. again. Of course,
I don't dare test out here, but I'm hoping that
it is in good order just in case! I remember an
old GI classmate had the same trouble, and when
it came time to do the "big act" he couldn't
get any more than a peep out of the set!

In your letters, you seem more than anxious
to have that long talk with me, Bunny. Anything
you wish is O.K. with me.

Your description of the house during the
holidays . . . I could almost see myself there.
And don't think that that's easy when the
temperature is around 100 most of the time
here.

As for that visit to Todd's. This Monty must
have quite an orchestra to get you in there.
I used to go stag there with Bruns when we
couldn't wait a block to get a drink at the
Bison Tavern. But as soon as we were fortified,
we were on our way out of there—but fast. So
you'd better continue to take the gang along
when you go there. It's really not your sort of
place, darling.

My New Year's resolutions wouldn't fill very
much space, I guess. One, and I guess the only
one, is not to drink until I get back to Fargo
again. These pals of mine are tough guys with

a bottle, and one night with them in a good port was enough to make me swear off for good. Most of the time we have spent in port has been spent in places where there is no use trying to find a drink. And I drink only when it is served somewhat cleanly. You should see some of the dives that go as top-notch places in ports around the world! Todd's is paradise!!!

This evening I hope to make a bit more money at poker. I've really been lucky and the stakes have gone up with the guys trying to get some of their money back in a hurry. But they are only going in the hole more and more and I'm darn happy about it.

Yours, with love always,
Beat

February 11, 1944
Mid-Pacific

My darling Elinor,
Things have eased up with us, and I can now sit
here and listen to a broadcast station again
after dark. As I sit here, something somehow
demands of me to remember how darn lucky I have
been so far in life. Things could be so darn
much different with me, couldn't they? But here
I am alive, feeling great, working at a good
job, feeling as if I have a bit part in the war,
and looking forward to a leave at home. There
are luckier guys, I guess, but they can't feel
any happier than I do tonight.

Another thing that pleases me, but I'm sure
not everybody, is the fact that the invasion
has been holding off. If things are slow when I
get back, I shall go to the East Coast and try
my hand at a ship to France. It would be funny
if those plans should take away my long awaited
leave and leave me out at sea again about a
week after seeing the States! But we won't think
about that now, darling.

The second looey aboard has had some phenomenal
luck in poker the last few nights. He got a
letter a while ago, and he found out that his
girl is marrying some guy back in the States.
He considers it a good trade for the luck he
has been having ever since. Funny thing about
it—he always said, "I must be losing my girl,"
whenever his luck was good! Now it has come
true and we have all had a good laugh over it,
although I wouldn't put much on the chance of
catching him by himself laughing about it.

I hope to surprise you one of these days with a call from the West Coast. Be awaitin' it, Bunny, and give with the "welcoming tones" this time, will you? I don't want to think that I'm only going to be in the way when I do get there. That was the impression I got last time, so I easily made the decision to stay with the ship. I hope that I was wrong and that you really do look forward to having me home with you again.

Yours forever, Bunny,
Beat

LETTER 42
February 14, 1944
Pacific

Bunny,

We've developed a lot of "old salts" since
this trip began. All the Navy boys, or at
least most of them, are getting tattoos of one
kind or another. I suppose that they think
they will be tough guys when they get back
to Arkansas and Pennsylvania. Remember? And I
still haven't found a place that can take one
off without amputation! I'll keep on trying and
maybe someday I won't have to wear long sleeves
every time I come over to visit you!

My decision is made. I'm definitely leaving the
ship after this trip. And I'm definitely going
home for at least a week, no matter what. They
allow us thirty days, but my feet are already
itching to get to some especially interesting
places—and in time.

Yours, as ever,
Beat

LETTER 45
February 22, 1944
Outbound from Hawaii

Darling,

After sitting around Pearl Harbor and Honolulu for a couple of days, we were shoved over to another island in the bunch for twenty-four hours to take on a cargo for the States. Whereas Oahu is very civilized and densely populated, this island of Kauai is quite the opposite. We had some darn good times here in a town by the name of Lihue. Sounds like "la hooey."

There are real virgin jungles near the town and within a mile of our dock there. Pete and I took some long hikes through the stuff with our best jungle equipment and had a grand time wearing ourselves out. We climbed coconut trees as far as we could, picked them up off the ground, went swimming on a beach that is probably the best we have ever seen. There were so many different plants, vines, trees, bugs, animals, etc. that we had never seen before.

We almost missed sailing time, finding our way out of a particularly bad place. Anyway, we didn't end up the way a few others did here. A couple of the officers and some of the crew were carried aboard last night by their hardier pals. I saved myself a headache and I still have that New Year's resolution in the bag, darling.

Hawaii is really a paradise. The atmosphere, even with all the defense activity and the many servicemen present, is one of contentment and happiness. The feeling is most contagious, too, and everyone enters into the spirit of the islands. My time here won't be soon forgotten, I promise you!

We left about two hours ago. It's dark now. We have a cargo that makes a guy think just how lucky we are this time. We have had cargoes of everything tough that one can imagine this trip and now on the way home, they give us sugar! It can't blow up and it will float for a while even if we are hit.

We went from New York to Cuba and then through the Panama Canal. From there we headed for Noumea, New Caledonia. From there we were in on some good things, and they beat last trip "all holler." Right now we all feel more than a bit relieved that it's all over and that we are in good waters again and this is only nine or ten days of peacetime traveling to the States.

I'm afraid that I don't miss home as much as one would suspect!! Home seems to be no. 1 on our lists as long as we are leaving it for a long trip, but getting back nearer and nearer to it again, it isn't the first thing we think of. No, I'm afraid that it's the next trip and where it will take us and what sort of a ship and what sort of guys there will be to pal around with.

But, nevertheless, I'm planning on coming home this time. I don't want to go through that first couple of weeks at sea that I did last time. I was quite mad at myself for not taking a leave. I won't feel any guilt thinking of the servicemen overseas who aren't getting any leaves and are taking all the chances.

And just my own very biased ideas, but I think that this war is good for at least another two or three years. All the optimism there is comes from the States, not from the places near the front where opinion is made up of first-hand experience and changes as the daily happenings go, things that happen that you back in the States will not hear of until after all of this is over. So just sit tight, Bunny, and buy that war bond. Uncle Sam will need all the money he can get before this is over!

The boys are calling me for poker again. They still haven't been able to break me!

Yours, forever,
Beat

LETTER 46
February 25, 1944

Sweets,

Sitting here with the static beating a regular
tattoo on my ears, I suddenly got the brilliant
idea to read over some of your letters again.
Maybe it's just that I happened to get the wrong
letters, but in the three letters I picked up,
I'm branded for life—a cynic, unfaithful dog,
drunkard, etc.

Let's come to the charge that I have been
unfaithful. That's a nasty word even if it is
correct, darling. And I'd say that it is quite
impossible for either of us to fling it about
now. We haven't seen each other for just about
a year.

As to drinking, darlin'. I must admit that
not every guy goes around and gets a jag on to
call his gal. Most guys wouldn't dare call the
gal at such a time. But it so happened that in
New York I felt like hell. Right now I haven't
had a drink since December and I'm quite happy
to say that it hasn't occurred to me to drink
even when it was available in Hawaii. But I'm
afraid that you shall have to overlook a few
when I get home, Bunny!

Take my word now. And when we get together,
I'll prove to you how wrong you were. I'll always
love my little French gal.

Yours, forever,
Beat

LETTER 47
March 2, 1944

My darling Bunny,

This afternoon we ran into the first of the
Frisco weather. It began fogging up. Of course,
in that weather and so close to land there is
only one thing to do, and the mates immediately
got out the radio direction finder. Something
was wrong with it right away and they called
me in. I made a continuity test and found the
trouble in a relay that connects with the main
antennas through this room to the chart room.
After that it didn't take long to fix, but they
didn't know how to work the thing properly. They
told me to be on stand-by for the rest of the
time coming in. If it fogs up tonight there
won't be much sleeping for me, but it will be
kinda fun to come in blind!

On top of all that, I finished all the battery
super charges so that they will hold up while
in port until another guy comes aboard. Doing
that, I was a frequent visitor to the "black
gang" in the engine room, and that's a long
way down there, too, darlin'. Now things are
O.K. but for final O.K.s on my logs tomorrow by
the captain and Naval liaison officer. Then two
inspection men come aboard from the Navy and
the Federal Communications Commission.

We expect to be in around noon at the latest.
The boys on deck and in the engine room were
all laughing and playing at their work, just as
kids do on the last day of school.

My leave is all planned. I'm going to Seattle

for at least two nights and a day—business there to attend to. Then I'll be on my way to see you. Damn, isn't it going to be perfect, Bunny? Last night with nothing else to do to keep me busy I went into my sea bags again and repacked. They are in good order now for shipment.

Just to think that tomorrow morning will be the end of all this static and blackouts and rolling meals and sloping bunks and rotten ports and decoding long-winded messages about nothing for this ship and worrying about some little thing that may go wrong with the equipment if I don't "do that tomorrow" and just a million other things. A guy does need a rest and some time with people again. Especially his gal! Tomorrow night will find us talking to one another on the phone. Time will be flying now that we are so near to each other.

Your guy, always,
Beat

⤜   ⤛

March 3, early morn

We just finished our last poker game as a group. In the past few weeks I have been having some darn good luck, and tonight it was even better than that. So I made quite a hunk of change on the trip and it isn't too hard to take either! (And, of course, I would say that it was due to smart playing—if I didn't know better.)

Bunny—

Great country this Frisco—raining cats and dogs all the way in. As soon as possible I'll be ashore to get my mail off to you and ready a phone call. The States look wonderful!!!!!! The Bay Bridge was our first, and a good 'un, too. Be seeing you, Elinor.

Saturday nite
March 4th

Darling,

I hope that this will somehow explain why I haven't called yet. We went into this small town last night. There is one phone and the railroad depot closes at 11 o'clock. We all tried to place calls, but there was so much traffic waiting ahead of us in Frisco that all we could get out of the phone company was hopes. We finally gave it up and went out on an "invasion" of the town.

As things stand now, we are to be off the ship Tuesday afternoon. Then I'll battle for a seat on the *Beaver* to Portland and then a transfer there for Seattle. I have to spend about a half day there before catching a train for Fargo. And that run from Seattle to Fargo takes only one and a half days! I'll have a berth, and the porter will never get a chance to make it up. I'll be in the way!

Less than a week from now, and I'll be one of the happiest guys in the world. Be waiting for me, won't you, Bunny?

Yours, always,
Beat

March 4, 1944
Crockett

Darling,

We sat around the small beer hall for about five hours today. First we were promised that the call would go through right away, then it was a three or four hour delay. So we sat. And then one of the guys from the ship came in and told me that I was wanted back here immediately. I went through some work with the Navy department and then hurried back. Still only about an hour and a half from the time I had placed the call. They told me that you had been on the line. So I placed it again and waited until I did get you this time.

It was so worth it, darling. Just to hear you smile. I was so happy that you could hear me. It felt so darn good that I just couldn't think of much to say other than I would be home. And if ever anything were more true—even if I had decided to stay with the ship—after talking to you this time, I would never have signed on again. You sounded so very much like the gal I met two years ago last Christmas. You sounded happy and so full of pep and fun.

Your guy with love,
Forever,
Beat

March 8, Monday

I went out looking for some means of getting home. The busses are no good, but I tried them just to see what they would say. Then I tried the Southern Pacific RR to Portland. They didn't want to give me a break at all. So, on a hunch I called the Great Northern, still my favorite road. They were darn nice to me over the phone. Their guy is a Mr. Scott and he is going to fix me up all the way to Fargo with Pullmans. And he took my word for it that I would be there to get the reservation. It was pretty darn nice of the guy, and I told him so. It is something to make me believe in the human race again. So, darling, if things go well, I shall be on my way home tomorrow night at 6:30. And I'll be in Fargo Friday afternoon at about 3:55. Save me Friday night, won't you! I'll do my best to stay away from all my other gal friends back there.

Magnets

Easter 1944

ELINOR STOOD IN THE waiting room of the Fargo depot, dressed in her navy suit and hat, her coney coat slipped over her shoulders. She checked Beat's Sigma Chi pin. He was bound to spot it when he helped her with her coat, but right now it was out of sight. She twisted the Christmas watch Beat had given her, moving the dial to its place on her slender wrist. She noted the time. 8:27 P.M. The train had been delayed, but it was due any moment.

She hadn't expected the station to be this crowded. Some uniformed fellows sat in the side benches, rucksacks at their feet. One was asleep, his chin at rest on his chest. Another, right beside him, nodded at Elinor as he enjoyed his smoke. A few families, waiting for loved ones, crowded around the windows. They checked their watches regularly and chattered about the plans they had for the upcoming furlough.

When Elinor heard the whistle far down the tracks, she snapped her purse open, reached for her Courage lipstick, and began to retouch her lips. She smiled into her compact, stretching her lips to make certain they were equally covered. She had a tissue with her to blot the bright fire engine red she had applied. When she was satisfied, she put the lid back on the tube, tucked everything into her purse, snapped the clasp, and stood waiting in the shadows of the dimly lit station.

She heard the bell on the engine. It clanged steadily. The tracks seemed to hum as the Great Northern rolled into the station. The building vibrated in synch, and the air in the depot thrummed. So did her heart. She wondered how this visit would go. A year ago Beat had taken all her jewelry back. And in Aberdeen. Well, that meeting had been worthless.

Still, he had continued to write. And such interesting letters! He was the only officer among her cadre of "old friends." There was something about Beat—an untamed something—that intrigued her, even when the times they shared left a sour taste in her mouth. He was in touch with a world so different from her own.

The people in the depot, now alert, began to move. The servicemen stood. One leaned over to jab his sleeping friend. The serviceman who had been smoking stood and stretched. He dropped his cigarette onto the floor and put it out with a quick movement of his foot. He picked up his duffel bag and paraded toward Elinor. As he passed her, he winked. She pulled her purse strap over her shoulder and looked away.

The families at the window, now chattering and laughing, raced toward the door. Elinor stepped out onto the platform after they had crowded through. The night sky was cloudless, dark blue. Pinpricks of light glittered like tiny sequins sewn onto blue velvet.

Elinor heard the familiar screeching of brakes, a release of steam from the boiler, and, then joyous greetings all around her. "Over here." "So good to have you home again."

Her eyes scanned the passengers exiting the train, women first. In the crowd of men coming through the doorways of the train cars after the women, she spotted a familiar grin.

"Bunny!" He ran toward her, just as she had known he would. On the platform, beside her, he threw his bag down at her feet.

She was surprised at the magnetism she felt as he reached for her and took her into his arms. His lips met hers, and she became oblivious to the cool of the night, the crowds that swam around her, the entire bustling station.

"C'mon," he urged. "Let's get something to drink. I didn't have a drop this time on the trip out here."

Elinor laughed. "So you're being good."

She arranged Beat and his rucksack into the Pontiac. They drove to

Gene's where they settled into their favorite corner. Conversation could wait until the next day. Beat put his arm around his sweetheart.

She looked into his eyes. "Glad you came home this time?"

"It was a long trip. That snowstorm slowed us down in the mountains, and I wanted to get out and run alongside the train. I was sure I could beat it home."

Elinor smiled. "So tell me everything about your travels, Beat." She leaned her head on his shoulder.

He sipped his bourbon and told her about the war in the South Pacific. Elinor shuddered to think of the "old friends" who might be on those islands now. She shook her head to try to erase the images.

They ordered dinner and more drinks. After the place closed, Elinor invited Beat to her house where they sat side-by-side on the horsehair sofa. Beat slid his arm around her shoulders, and she relaxed into him. He smelled just right, bourbon on his breath and the odors of the cigarettes from the bar and the long train ride lodged into his clothing. Elinor lifted her head to look at him, to memorize him, and he lowered his to meet her lips.

It didn't take long to become reacquainted. Elinor was glad that she hadn't taken another teaching position for the year. She could be with Beat whenever she felt like it. He didn't have to hang around some little burg waiting for her school day to be over, and they wouldn't be forced to wait for the weekends.

In the morning Irene appeared at the bottom of the steps, dressed in her pink waitress uniform. She held the starched cap in her hand. "I didn't know you were here," she squawked as she noticed Beat asleep, his head in Elinor's lap, on the horsehair sofa.

Beat sat up in a daze. Elinor stood. They pressed their clothing with their hands to settle the wrinkles.

"I'll put on a pot of coffee," Elinor suggested, and they all disappeared into the kitchen to make breakfast for the family. Beat sat in the breakfast nook with a cup of coffee in his hands while Elinor fried some eggs. Irene handled the toaster. And in minutes there was breakfast for three.

"But you'll have to hurry," Elinor reminded Beat. "Dad and Mother will be back in town before noon, and how would it look for them to find you here?" She wondered whether the neighbors were up yet. It wouldn't do if one of them saw Beat slipping out of the house at this hour of the morning.

⤜   ⤛

One afternoon they drove Bruns's old car to the countryside. They parked in a secluded spot. Beat slipped his arm around Elinor's shoulder. She leaned into him. He nuzzled her hair and kissed her behind the ears. She felt the tingle sizzle up her back.

She looked at him. "Beat," she breathed.

"Bunny, I want to marry you," he said.

She smiled and replied, "Maybe after Yupps's wedding. There are a few things to take care of first." Then she reached for Beat's lips and they melted into each other. After a few minutes, the car windows had steamed up in the cool March air.

"You're always putting me off," Beat teased as he removed Elinor's coat.

"But, Beat, family comes first. Yupps is all organized for his wedding. Remember? After he leaves the seminary. And after that, we can see. If we still feel this way, and all . . ." she drifted off. He was kissing her neck, blowing gently in her ear, snuggling her hair with his nose. She almost lost control. Again.

"Remember last year at this time?" he asked. They both sat up.

"I do. You really hurt my feelings, and it's taken me a while to forget that." She looked at her wrist. "I have my watch to remind me."

Beat looked out the windshield of the old car. "I know. I was a fool."

"There are such things," Elinor reminded him, and they both laughed.

This visit there had been no arguing, just a whirlwind of fun. His leave was, indeed, perfect. But too soon, they were at the depot again. The sun had barely crawled over the horizon.

Chin up, she said, "See ya."

He straightened his shoulders, laughed and gave her one last peck on the cheek. He heaved his pack over his shoulder and strode up the steps and into his train car.

She stood on the platform, waving toward his car, toward the window where she—at last— spotted him waving. He blew her a kiss. She blew one back, then checked the depot to see if anyone had seen her. She didn't recognize any parishioners around the station.

The whistle blew and the train began its rumbling trek to the coast, delivering the men back into the war.

Elinor watched the train become a speck on the wide prairie horizon. Then she turned and walked to the parked car. She unsnapped her purse and found her linen handkerchief. She wiped her eyes, blew her nose, and then started the car.

When she arrived at home, she hiked upstairs to find Mickey. The girls went for a stroll around the neighborhood.

"It was such a lot of fun this time," Elinor admitted. "I could be in love, Mickey."

"Made a decision, then, kid?"

Elinor simply grinned.

"You know how Dad feels," Mickey reminded her big sister.

"Maybe. Maybe I don't care how Dad feels. This is about me. My feelings. Beat and I certainly do have fun together."

"Sounds like it." Mickey splashed through an early spring puddle in the middle of the sidewalk.

"Anyway, have you noticed what the 'responsible' daughters of the pastors in this synod do?" Elinor continued. "Martha Peter stays home to take care of her invalid parents. Or Agnes Hoeger. A broken love affair and she's heading to Africa somewhere to be a doctor to the natives."

"Yeah, well it's hard to be a female doctor in the United States," Mickey added.

Elinor took her sister's hand, "I'm determined to have fun with the days allotted to me," she explained. "After all, the world is in crisis. We don't know how long we'll be around. Or what life will bring. I'm taking charge of my life."

The girls walked along then, silent.

When they arrived back home, Mickey dashed upstairs to have a smoke while Elinor dug into her closet to find her lavender stationery. She grabbed a sweater, sliding into it, before settling on the sunny porch to compose a letter to Darrow. It was still cool in early April, even with the sun shining in all those windows. But the bright light was cheery after the gray months of winter.

As she started her letter, Elinor realized she'd been too joyful. Mickey, after all, had been without Bob for three years. No time on the beach for him. At least not this beach. He was stuck fighting in muddy foxholes in the Pacific, on one of those worthless islands after another.

Elinor set down her stationery and pen. She tiptoed upstairs, knocked on Mickey's door, entered and gave her little sister a hug. "Bob'll be back and we'll all have so much fun together," she whispered.

⤞   ⤝

When she heard Beat's voice again—he called Wednesday to tell her he was safely in Portland—she knew she was in love.

But it was Holy Week. Elinor practiced 'somber' when she looked into the mirror in the upstairs bathroom, and her eyes betrayed her. Maundy Thursday. Then Good Friday. She played for all the services. Such sad music.

And she sat, nearly bubbling with joyful memories, at the organ. *Freude.* It was wrong to be jubilant until Easter morning. She had been too lively for the Lenten season.

Remembering You

April 1944

April 5, 1944
Portland, Ore.
(handwritten on USO paper)

My darling Elinor,
There are many wonderful memories of our leave—
memories that will make the time go so very
quickly this time. The memories that stand out
above all others are not the ones one would
imagine. (I can recall those, too!)

But I like to remember you with me in the
Fargo Café, laughing and drinking Cokes. And
in a semi-dark room, you playing the piano. And
leaving each night having you throw me a kiss as
I closed the doors between us. And remember our
times together walking up and down Broadway?
We had fun during this leave, didn't we? I'll
probably never forget the time you went looking
for your Christmas Night perfume, your gift, at
Gene's! And another night your drinking a bit
too much . . .

My last look at you stands out the clearest,
though. You were waving at me, smiling, looking

so darn nice. And I felt all choked up. I spent
all the time from Fargo to here in the smoker
just thinking.

   We'll be married some day, Bunny. I'll always
be happy with that thought in mind.

Yours, forever,
Beat

Sat. afternoon
[handwritten]

My darling,

Yesterday morning I went the first thing to find out about a ship. Within two seconds of entering the place I had one. They really pushed it off on me in a hurry! She's one of the ten or fifteen brand new turbo-electric jobs that are the fastest in the world for their kind of ship, one of the very largest tankers in the world. I'm going aboard Monday.

So, Bunny, there will be a lot of stuff to square away and some new equipment to learn well enough to take over. I'm going to like it much better than the other ship as we shall get places quicker and not stay too darn long. As soon as we are all set, I'll wire you to write me.

SS (NOT USS) *Mission San Carlos*
c/o postmaster
San Francisco, Calif.

At the post office, I found a note from Bruns. So I called him and we got together. We had a few drinks, too. In this letter I'll put some of the covers we picked up during the evening. Needless to say, we both got a bit "high," but we were in bed at 1:00, too, after calling Mrs. Bruns to tell her we were O.K. I thought of calling you, but it would have been about three in the morning there, and I know how you like to sleep when you get a chance.

Time has seemed to drag so darn much. It isn't a week yet since I last saw you, but it seems years ago. I suppose it is the change from pleasure to business. There aren't too many laughs when I'm away from you. The ship and the coming trips don't appeal to me as they did before.

All my love, always,
Beat

Hotel Whitcomb
San Francisco
At the Civic Center

April 10-11

My darling,

You should see this ship. She's tops, darling, and makes the *James Oliver* look pretty dumpy! Bruns couldn't quite believe what he was seeing—my own private quarters are as large as your front room. It's huge—with a large locker (closet to you landlubbers)—a perfect desk for private papers, two extra large portholes. It is pretty darn swell. I'm already planning to turn part of my room into a gymnasium and it should keep me in good shape.

I called last night from the room here, but things didn't go very well. The fellows were here and you sounded so very different to me. You must have been in the same position as I. Tonight I'll call you again from a private booth.

During the day I browse through bookshops here looking for good books in subjects I like—becoming pretty much the "self-educated" type. So far I haven't been able to locate *In Bed We Cry* by Ilka Chase. As soon as I find a copy, I'll send it on to you, Bunny.

Good night, my darling—
My love, forever,
Beat

April 13, 1944

I was in Frisco this afternoon for requisitions and a wonderful letter from you, darling. After reading it, I wanted so much to call you and ask you to come right out and get married. It would be so perfect, honey. It's what I want more than anything in the world. But I remembered, too, how your family would feel. Yupps is to be married, etc., etc., etc. We should have planned things ourselves, rather than for everyone else. After all, darling, we are the ones who have to live these lives of ours.

⇛   ⇚

Tuesday night (4/18)

My Darling Elinor,

Another day and another fifty-cent piece earned. They had some sort of a breakdown in the engine room today, but they expect to have it fixed soon. It is some sort of a bug that is developing on these ships. It is a new system of engine power, and they will have to experiment before it is perfect. It isn't important but it could be some day, when it would count.

You wrote in one of your letters that you didn't like the idea of sailing on tankers. Old tanker men say that they are much safer than cargo ships. Flyers always say to stay away from them. But I say, "What is the difference? If a guy is going to get it, he will get it here as well as anywhere else." With a tanker, if you once get away, you are safe. A ship like this, of course, will be a real prize for anyone who gets a crack at it. Flyers in the RAF with whom I talked say that they always go for tankers first and the bigger, the better. Anyway, you can't scare an Irishman, especially one in the Merchant Marine!

I'll be trying to call you tomorrow night to hear your voice again, darling. That will make my third date since leaving you—all three of them for three minutes with you.

Listen, Bunny, you'd just better get all of that singleton life out of your system, 'cuz you're marrying me when I get back this time. There won't be any arguments or plans or anything. We're just going to get married and let things take care of themselves. I love you and you love me. That's about all people get married for anyway, isn't it? I know that it is reason enough for me.

Beat

D.R. Beaton (CRO)
Mission San Carlos
Pacific Tankers, Inc.
c/o Postmaster
San Francisco

Good-bye, Walt

April 1944

Elinor sat in her nest in the glassed-in porch, staring at the raindrops as they slid down the windows. When Walter drove his jalopy up to the curb and parked in front of the house, she jumped right up and composed herself. They hadn't seen each other for a couple of months, and there was a lot to discuss. Elinor hesitated at the porch door. She didn't run out to the car as she had often done.

Walter stumbled a bit as he exited his vehicle. He grabbed the side of the car to hold himself upright. His back again? Or had he been drinking? He looked up from the street toward the door of the porch and saw her staring at him. He smiled and waved. He reached into the back seat to grab something. Then he straightened his back and marched up the narrow stone sidewalk.

Elinor met him at the door. "Hi, stranger!" she smiled.

Walt wiped his feet on the doormat. "I brought you a surprise. A few things for the family. The rest are out in the car," he panted as he handed Elinor a heavy package.

"I'll get Dad to help you," Elinor said. She carried the package into the kitchen and set it on the counter.

Georg jumped out of his chair when he heard Walter's voice. He slid into his coat and slapped his hat on his head. Walter tipped his in deference to the old man, and they sloshed their way into the rain. The back seat of Walter's car held packages of pork from Walter's family farm. A ham, chops, and sausages! Reverend Landgrebe's eyes lit up.

"You'll have to join us for Sunday dinner one of these days," he said. "We can eat some of this sausage in one of Trudie's stews." He patted Walter on the shoulder.

"I remember her cooking," Walter crooned. "I'd like that."

Elinor waited as the men worked. They wiped their shoes on the mat as they reentered the house. With their hands full, they couldn't take off their hats to shake off the raindrops. Georg strode toward the kitchen. Walt limped along behind, his hat dripping onto his shoulders.

Georg made spaces for some of the meat in the refrigerator. The smoked items belonged in the cold room in the basement. The men traipsed downstairs with a couple of packages. Georg hummed, eager to arrange these sausages in the nearly empty space there. The shelves held a few jars of vegetables left from last summer's garden. Several potatoes lay on the cold floor of the room. One moldy squash sagged in a corner under the bottom shelf. Walter sneezed.

When Walter joined Elinor in the living room, the two settled down, as was their habit, on the horsehair sofa, where they made plans for the evening.

Walter complained about his back. He had hurt it mixing paint out west and then working on his father's place, the pig farm, during the busy season. When he moaned, under his breath, really, as he stretched his arm toward Elinor to move her closer, she stiffened.

After the energetic days she had just spent with Darrow, Walter seemed to have no life. And he'd been drinking. She could smell it when he came close. Medicinal liquor, he claimed, for his back.

They overheard the conversation in the kitchen, Georg telling Trudie about all the packages Walter had brought. Walter smiled. He knew the Landgrebes appreciated him. He leaned toward Elinor. She squirmed away from him. She rubbed her forehead.

"Headache?" he asked.

"No, I'm fine," Elinor replied.

"Well, let's hit the road," Walter suggested. "The rain is letting up a bit." They stood then and Walter helped Elinor into her coat.

She, in turn, helped Walt down the slippery porch steps. They got into his car and drove downtown in silence. The only sound was the windshield wipers scraping the drops from the window.

Gene's, usually a crowded place, perfect for lighthearted flirtation and some freedom from propriety, was quiet. Perhaps it was the dreary night. Elinor and Walter sat at a table in the front of the house and ordered a bite to eat and a drink.

"So, how are the plans coming for your brother's wedding?" Walter tried for a certain conversation starter.

"We're organized. We'll head to Iowa at the beginning of June." There wasn't much to add that Walter would be interested in. The dresses? The flowers? She sipped her Tom Collins.

"Have you heard from your brother yet?" she asked.

"No. He's still a prisoner, far as we know. Nothing new." He dispatched his first glass of whiskey and ordered another.

After dinner, they trudged between Gene's and the Fargo Theater. Elinor slowed her pace to walk beside Walter, who limped slightly and gritted his teeth as they moved along. Luckily, the rain had stopped, though the skies still scowled.

The theatre featured *Since You Went Away* with Claudette Colbert, Shirley Temple, Lionel Barrymore, and Agnes Moorehead, another war movie. But this one wasn't about the battles or the ships. It showed the home front and the sacrifices made by the women—the nursing of the wounded, women opening their homes as rooming houses to make ends meet, and women taking jobs to make what the men overseas needed.

Elinor had packed just one handkerchief and, before the intermission, she had to borrow Walter's. Having his stiff arm around her, she found, gave her no comfort.

Perhaps this mood she was in would become a migraine. Or "those people" would arrive off schedule. But she thought it had to do with that handsome Merchant Marine in the film, the one who lived through a sinking of his ship. He needed the sympathy and care of a woman to get well again. Elinor sobbed seeing him there at the Christmas celebration with the family, a new man, hale in body and healthy again in spirit.

Somehow, seeing this movie with a 4F seemed blasphemous.

They exited the theater in a heavy rain. "I'll pick you up," Walter suggested.

Elinor huddled under the marquee. Neither of them had thought to bring an umbrella.

Walter limped to the car.

When he drove up to the theater door, Elinor edged herself into the front seat, pressing her body toward the door on the passenger side. Walter's hat was soaked and his hair dripped onto his shoulders. He looked miserable.

The wipers whished back and forth. Elinor's side window and the fly window dripped with the rain.

"So Beat's been home?" Walter asked into the silence.

Elinor nodded. She blew her nose and sat up straight. They drove north on Broadway and turned on Twelfth Avenue.

"Your 'old friend' Darrow? And I suppose you went out with him," Walt continued.

"Why not? He has more life in him than some men."

"Your patriotic duty. To entertain the troops, huh?" Walter sneered.

"I have a lot of 'old friends' and you know that, Walter."

"He's a playboy, just trifling with you." Now he laughed at her.

"Well, he's off to war. He's not sitting at home, whining about life stateside. Have you heard there's a war on?" Elinor shivered in the cool car. She snuggled deeper into her coat.

"Cut it out, Elinor. You know. My back." Walter slowed for the turn on to Third Street. He glanced at Elinor. She wouldn't look at him. She stared out the window of her door, her fingers wrapped around the handle.

"Beat's got excuses, too. But he joined up." She spoke through her teeth.

"You can't be serious about the guy! A man with a reputation like his?" he snarled. "A gambler? A drunk—and before he was the legal age to have a drink? Before he was even 21."

"It's not your business, Walt." Her voice was cold, angry.

"He's a womanizer, Bunny. Irish, for Godssake. What do you expect?"

She felt herself hating this old man. How could she ever have dated Walter? Why, she was wearing his engagement ring. She was through pleasing her parents.

He parked his car alongside the curb in front of her house.

"What does your father think?" Walter challenged. Then, his voice, sing-songing, snide, he added, "You know, Elinor, Darrow's just stringing you along. He's a cynical smartass, and he's got you fooled."

"Stop it, Walter. You don't know . . ." She felt dizzy. She closed her eyes and saw a reddish color with big white explosions erupting at random. Maybe this was the beginning of a headache after all.

He laughed. "I'll bet you ten dollars he doesn't marry you. Or anyone."

Elinor twisted herself around to look at Walter. She glared across the long car seat. Then she twisted his engagement ring off her finger and slapped it into his waiting hand. She had nothing more to say. She reached for the door handle.

He wrapped his fingers around the ring and slipped it into the inside pocket of his coat. "So we're broken up again? What a merry-go-round! You'll be back when you need money. Or someone to run around with."

Then, just like in the movie, he grabbed her arm and yanked her closer. Hard. He pulled her face close to his. "Elinor, settle down. You aren't thinking clearly."

Without another word, she wrenched her arm free. She hadn't won all those arm wrestling contests with her siblings for nothing.

"Do you hear me?" Walter raised his voice.

Elinor pushed the car door open, scrambled out, and slammed it. She turned her back to Walter, straightened her purse strap over her shoulder, and strode, through the rain, across the front yard, up the six porch steps and into the house, toward the fluorescent desk light her father had left on for her.

Afraid of Marriage?

April 1944

April 20, 1944

I was surprised to hear that you and Walt had gotten together again to have that long talk. And at the same time, it was a great relief to me to feel that all of that is now over. Yes, Walt did look a bit dissipated when we saw him the last time, and, believe it or not, seeing guys of his age and condition scares me sometimes! That's why I'm quitting the stuff and getting plenty of sleep and good food at all costs. When he finally saw how things were, he just had to admit that he was more or less licked.

⇢ ⇠

You really sounded wonderful on the phone when you said in answer to my question as to whether you would marry me or not, "You bet!" That's all I need once in a while, too, darling, and I'll be able to go on like this forever.

April 24, 1944

My Bunny,

Well, we have moved again, and we are now in Oakland, Calif. at another shipyard for some more repairs.

The latest in the way of news from this part of the country is the argument about raising the school teachers' wages out here. There are big editorials in all the papers about it. And they all seem to agree that to keep any teachers at all they should raise their wages again to correspond a bit more closely with the higher living costs out here now. Just thought that you might be interested in a city where they really go to bat for the poor non-unionized teachers.

                              Yours, forever,
                                    Beat

Friday
(April 28)

My darling,

Here we sit in the shipyard and another shipyard ahead, just doing nothing because the dopes who installed the engines did it wrong some way or another. Not that it is the easiest thing in the world, but they could have done it O.K. in the first place after making mistakes on a couple of other ships just like this one. Anyway, coming back to the ship today and reading the paper with headlines "Invasion Ships Mass, Nazis Say" was enough to make me get anxious to get going again. The sooner we get going, the better chance we have of getting back sooner.

We all want to get off-shore again as soon as possible as we have been on the beach for so long now. I went up to the Mark Hopkins Hotel to the Sky Room. They have huge windows, and a person can look out over the whole Bay Area and see all the lights. We could see way out to sea from our ringside seat, and it turned out to be a rather moody evening for us as we were all thinking the same things—how much fun it would be to be out again and away from all the noise of the places around the States—way out there without a light, all alone on a quiet blacked-out deck, leaning on a rail, watching for falling stars, dreaming along with the moon, watching the phosphorous wash along the side of the ship, all alone with our thoughts.

Beat

Friday night
Frisco-Oakland

My Dearest,

Doggone, Bunny! There hasn't been a letter for over ten days now. You must be writing to the fleet P.O. and the mail still hasn't been delivered from there as yet. That just has to be it, as I know you are writing and I feel that you aren't sick, as I would've heard about it by now.

I'm in a screwy mood tonight. Feel all nervous and strung up for some reason. Are you out with somebody tonight? If ever I started to worry about your dates with these unexpected "old friends," I guess that I would be worrying all the time. You just know too many of 'em, darling. Maybe that's the hold up now. You just may be too darn busy and out of the mood for writing me, hmmm. Maybe a little coffee would help me, sweets.

But, my darling, I'm going to find myself weeping in a moment here. I miss all of our good times so much out here away from them just long enough to really get a long-range perspective. You don't know it, Bunny, but we've had a lot of long, serious talks during the time I spent away from you! Now who's crazy?

Yours,
Beat

For a person who very often writes, "Beat, there is absolutely nothing to do around here now that you are gone," you seem to do a lot! As soon as one leaves, there is another there. And, darn it, when we are married, I'm going to lock you up somewhere and keep all of these wolves away from you.

Oakland, Calif.
Sunday afternoon [4- 30]

My Darling Elinor,

I've never seen this much ammo go aboard any ship before, and all the officers agree about that. They have been bringing it in for days now and the boys are getting help from shoreside Navy gangs in getting it away in magazines. It is a major project! Many of the munitions factories have been closed down because there is so much of this type of ammo manufactured now that we could fight for the rest of the century and not run out.

So, my darling is afraid of marriage, hmmm? Well, Bunny, if you are always the way you have been during the time I have known you, I will be the happiest guy in the world. I can't think of one little thing about you that isn't just as I want it.

As to marrying a gal who can't have a little baby, well, if you're the gal, I love it. I still don't understand just what is wrong. I should know more, but I just hate to find out too much. I know enough of it from what you said to be afraid of it.

I miss you terribly, Bun,

Beat

Sunday evening
Still Oakland!

My darling,

You'd really have fun walking around the ship with me, darling. People don't realize how large one is until they get aboard. Start walking from forward back aft and it is a real job, honey. And all the quarters with private baths up in this section of the ship would make you realize what an easy life this is now! Why I have better quarters on here than I have ashore in the best hotels in town.

And as for food, well, darling, you can't beat it. Today's menu, for instance. For breakfast you have a choice of any dry or hot cereal you want; ham, bacon, or sausages; eggs any way; fruit juice or some sort of fruit; toast; milk or coffee. For lunch we had turkey or lamb curry after a course of cream of tomato soup with creamed asparagus, creamed cauliflower, baked potatoes; then ice cream and choice of milk or coffee. For dinner tonight we had pork chops or fried frankfurters with sweet green peas, creamed corn and fried potatoes and pudding and the usual beverages. All this, of course, doesn't include the butter and bread and as much as one could want! And the steward says as soon as we get going, the food will be even better! They always leave all the milk and coffee out at night with cold cuts of meat and liverwurst and cheese to make sandwiches. I only wish that you were here so that I could get you out to the ship for a meal. I'd be so very proud, darling, to have you.

You know, Bun, on this ship there is so much more to do that I'm a bit afraid that I may fall behind at times. They have so many more pieces of equipment aboard this baby that it isn't funny. And being the head of this department makes me liable for all of it. I can't expect any help from these other guys, as they know even less that I do! When I want to figure something out, I get out all my books and sit down by myself, do some experimenting, and it always seems to come out O.K.

I'm in a heck of a lonesome mood. These past few letters you haven't seemed so sure of my love for some reason, darling, and it is beginning to worry me a lot. You have been out since I left, and quite a few times, too. I'm more or less worried about all of this talk about the poor marriages, broken love affairs, etc. There doesn't seem to be a reason for any of that kind of thinking on your part at all. I wish that you could feel the same way I do about things.

Miss you so much it hurts,
But it hurts good, Bunny,
Beat

Inertia

May 1944

"I DON'T UNDERSTAND. EVERYONE seems to think that marriage is the ultimate." Elinor plopped down with Mickey on the bed that had been squeezed into the corner of the girls' upstairs bedroom. Mickey slept there. Irene occupied the cot by the window. In the crowded space between the beds, there was just enough room for an old dresser with a scratched, silvery mirror.

Irene had left with their parents to visit relatives in western Dakota. It wasn't quite noon on Saturday, and the weekend stretched out ahead of the girls.

"Want a piece of gum, Elinor?" Mickey asked. She held out a package of Beeman's.

"Where'd you find gum?" Elinor reached for a piece.

"I have friends in high places," Mickey grinned.

A piece of gum. Simple before the war. Now all the Juicy Fruit, Spearmint and Doublemint was shipped to the troops. With sugar rationing and the supply of latex from the Far East nearly dried up, good gum was getting to be nearly as scarce as a good cigarette.

The girls unwrapped the treat and popped the sticks into their mouths. Mickey took Elinor's foil wrapper. She opened the top dresser drawer and pressed the foil into the ball of gum wrappers the sisters kept in there, where it sat, along with pajamas and other lingerie. Saving aluminum. The gum wrapper collection would be big enough one day to contribute to a scrap metal drive.

The girls settled back on the bed. Mickey arranged a pillow and lay down, hands under her head. Elinor sat up to open the envelope.

"Promise you won't tell anyone?"

Mickey nodded.

Elinor released the letter from the envelope, but she didn't open it until she had checked again. "Promise."

Mickey sat up and crossed her heart, a childhood pledge. They both laughed.

Elinor unfolded the thin paper. Her eyes skimmed the page. She found the paragraph.

"Okay, then. Darrow writes, `Listen, Bunny, you'd just better get all of that singleton life out of your system, 'cuz you're marrying me when I get back this time. There won't be any arguments or plans or anything. We're just going to get married and let things take care of themselves. I love you and you love me. That's about all people get married for anyway, isn't it? I know that it is reason enough for me. If we are married, there won't be any of the silly little doubts in our minds about the other's sincerity and all, and things will be even better for us.'"

Elinor sighed. "Darrow's so sweet, Mick. We have good times together, mostly. Once in a while I think of getting married, having the life everyone expects a girl to have."

"Well, rule Darrow Beaton out. I hope you have enough sense to take him off your list, Bunny."

"But . . ." Elinor turned toward her sister.

"If he's proposing, get rid of the guy."

"Well, I hardly think he's serious, Mick. Don't worry. He loves the singleton life as much as I do."

"Thank goodness," Mickey exhaled as she lay back down on the bed. She fluffed up her pillow and rolled toward Elinor.

"Anyway, I want to do something with my life," Elinor continued. "What can a girl do, Mickey? Something besides marriage."

"Bunny, think of it. What woman would want to work? At what? There aren't many things women are cut out to do, kid."

"I could find something," Elinor sighed. "I'm sure I could. Anything is more interesting than being stuck in a classroom or in a darkened school all day."

"Well, when the fellows return from the war, they'll scramble to take their jobs back, the jobs women now hold. What then?"

"The same old thing. We'll all have to set up housekeeping again. Or be nurses or teachers or secretaries." Elinor closed her eyes and leaned back into a pillow.

"Or maybe go to Africa like Agnes to do what you want to do." Mickey grimaced.

"Well, I'm not going to be a doctor like Agnes. But I'm going to get around. Like Peggy Lee," Elinor whispered.

Mickey sat up a bit and raised one fist into the air. "You know what they say. 'Work like a man, but look like a woman.'" She settled her hand behind her head and leaned back on her pillow. "Things will return to normal after this war is over."

"That's my problem." Elinor got up. She walked to the window in the corner of the room, pulled the curtain aside and looked down into the neighborhood. "I want to see some more of this world. I don't want the world to return to the old way of things."

She let go of the curtain and turned to Mickey. "Women can do more than they give us credit for. What's wrong with a woman doing something a man can do? Being a lawyer, for instance. Or the boss of some business? How about being the principal of a school?"

Mickey giggled. "Bunny, get real."

"Why not? It makes me so mad, Mick." Elinor sat down on the bed beside Mickey again.

Mickey rearranged herself on her pillow. "I hope Bob gets home pretty soon. With the guys all gone, things are pretty boring here."

"Anyway, I'm never going to make a good wife. You know."

Mickey turned herself to look at her sister. "But Johnny would be a reliable husband. He'd help out when you're down with a migraine."

"Maybe. I wonder if any man would lower himself to doing

housework. Can you imagine Johnny—or any man—changing diapers?" Elinor stretched out on the bed beside her sister.

"Well, Papa does some things. He peels potatoes, Bunny. And he helps Mother at suppertime once in a while. But diapers? That's women's work."

"What would you do if you had a migraine for days? Think of it, Mick. It's not an option."

Mickey rested her head on her hand, elbow in the pillow. She looked closely at Elinor. "I guess I haven't thought about that, kid." She lay back down and sighed.

The girls settled there, silent for a moment.

Elinor changed the subject. "What do you think about Yupps getting married? It's funny that he's the first of us, I mean."

"Yeah. But he is ready. He'll be done with the seminary. Time to start a life. And you know that a minister needs a wife." Mickey sat up again. "What would men do without women, anyway?"

Elinor sat up, too. "How do women get along without men?" She shrugged.

"Yeah. I suppose I'll marry Bob when he comes home."

Elinor continued, "I read the other day that the guys—the 4Fs and the old men—make nearly $55 dollars a week. A woman makes about $31. For the same work, Mick. We can't stay even with expenses without a man to take care of us."

"It's rigged, kid. Face it."

Elinor put Beat's letter back into its envelope, which she tucked back into her pocket.

"But I wonder," Elinor continued. She pushed her hair behind her ears.

Mickey stood up. She reached into her mouth to remove her gum. She stepped to the dresser, stuck her chewed wad on the mirror, and grabbed her purse. She snapped open a compartment and reached for her half-full package of Luckies. She smacked the pack against her left palm, repeating the action until one of her cigarettes emerged. She nabbed it and held it between her lips while she returned the pack to her purse. She found her lighter and turned back to Elinor.

"You were saying?" she mumbled. She repeated her question as she removed the cigarette from between her lips. "You were saying?" She popped the Lucky Strike back into her mouth and lit her cigarette.

"I was wondering," Elinor went on, "why Papa blames Beat."

"You have yourself quite a problem, kid. You know why he doesn't like Darrow." Mickey turned toward her sister.

"How can he think it was Beat's fault?" Elinor stood and began pacing the cramped room.

Mickey sat back down on the bed. She crossed her legs.

"It was, after all, Irene's bad decision," Elinor continued as she stepped back and forth. "She knew what might happen if . . ."

Mickey exhaled before answering, "Well, she's fragile, Bunny. Nervous." Smoke curled into the air.

"I know. But how can we protect her from men who want something from her?"

"Men like Beat's friends." Mickey took a drag. "Dad blames Beat for introducing Irene to his friends. His gang."

"That doesn't make Beat the devil. He wasn't even there. With them. He wasn't even in the same state, for Pete's sake." Elinor turned to look at herself in the mirror. She reached for the hairbrush and took a few swipes. "Well, anyway, it's all over now."

"Those were long months with Aunt Dorothy . . ." Mickey stared at her sister. She put the cigarette to her lips again. "It was hard on Mother and Dad." Smoke rose into the air. "The whole family, actually. You know how it is when everyone in the church is watching you."

"I know. But Irene's problem is over and done with. And Beat? He's not so bad. Really! We had a great time together in March." Elinor turned toward Mickey. She leaned against the old wood dresser.

"Bunny!" Mickey stood. "Want to break Papa's heart?" She flicked the ash off the end of her cigarette into the ashtray she kept on the dresser. She turned to her big sister and gripped Elinor's arm. "Drop him, Bunny. He's trouble."

Your Guy

May 1944

May 2, 1944

They are taking all the magnetism out of the ship now with large cables strung around her, degaussing her. We anchor out tonight and tomorrow start loading. We are definitely taking on high-test aviation gasoline as our bulk cargo. It's hot stuff, in case you didn't know! In fact, as hot as they can make tanker cargoes these days. On our deck they are going to put planes and some landing barges, so we shall be well loaded down for something. I'm rarin' to get going, darling, and get back.

If you could only see all the good books we have now, all the very latest in hits! This second operator is well-read and we are sharing our books with each other. He's got Tolstoy's *War and Peace* and Ehrenburg's *Fall of Paris*. I'm going to struggle through Tolstoy. I've read some of his other stuff and I find it hard to stick to at times. But there is something one can gain from such works that makes it impossible to pass it up.

Yupps' wedding sounds like trouble to me! You and Mick already worrying about clothes! There is a lot of time yet, more than a month, so don't go wearing yourself out so early in the game. Take your time and have fun. I know it is the last time that wonderful brother of yours is going to be married.

➤   ◄

May 4, 1944
Frisco

Dearest Elinor,

About nine last night Butch came up and suggested going in to call our gals and the folks. We went to the Palace Hotel to place our calls, and they really gave us a bad time. It would take at least four hours and maybe more. A large transport got in yesterday with fellows from the South Pacific and they were reserving all lines for them. So figuring that a wire might take its place, we went to the Western Union and sent the usual nonsensical telegrams to you and our folks back home. It's so darn hard to think of things to say in 25 words!

This morning I was in Frisco and walked myself dead almost. But when a ship is new, and especially in wartime, it is hard to get things organized. It was a mad house all the way, darling.

I went into some bookstores, and I got, first, the book you have been writing so much about—*Signpost*. I hope to read it soon and let you know what I think of these terrible Irishmen.

I'm reading a book tonight that you wanted so badly when I was home. I wanted to read it first and see what could possibly be so important. It's Ilka Chase's *In Bed We Cry*. And this is a best seller, darling! They put the sexual urge above everything else, even love, Bunny. They openly, and frankly I must admit, tell the thoughts that go through the heads of people—people with no inhibitions at all. While the various characters are seemingly having a grand time with their passions, they are never really happy and sure of anything—never sure of each other. I don't like to think of your reading such stuff, Bunny.

The engineers came up here *en masse* to tell me the latest story. Something big is cooking. I shouldn't be telling you this, I know, but there have been battleships, cruisers, and destroyers, etc. out here in Frisco Bay for over two weeks. It is the first time since the war that this many Navy ships have been here at once. They are working all Liberties and slower ships with an unusual "urgent" on the orders. They are shoving off by the dozens for Pearl Harbor and an anchorage there until a large convoy is formed. The word is that all the transports with the troops (and there are over 20 of them out here now with men aboard), the tankers with our speed, and other fast cargo ships with munitions and tanks, etc. are going to leave the end of this week for Honolulu with the Navy ships. The rumor is that we are to go to the Philippines! From what I have seen here in Frisco with all the ships of our speed just waiting instead of the usual sailing immediately upon loading, it kinda looks as if some of the rumor boys may have something this time.

If I ever start writing about the convoy, you will know that we are in on something big, as they don't convoy in the Pacific unless there is something in the way of invasion coming up. And if I should accidentally say that I have been to a convoy conference, you will know it, too. It will be just my meat. We'll probably be fueling carriers or sompin' like that so that their planes can fly, and maybe going in with some of our load to help land-based planes fuel up. All this, incidentally, is pure conjecture and wishful thinking.

Have I ever told you my philosophy of this life? I've really never had occasion to think much about being dead before the end of the trip before, but on here we have a bunch of guys who are constantly talking about the chances we have of not getting back. On the old *Oliver*, we never talked about it except during some alert when we sighted danger. It is the philosophy of most seamen that someone is going to get killed, but he is the very last one that is going to get it.

That's the way I figure, too. Maybe this honey will go up in a cloud of smoke some day, but Sparks will be one of the guys who is lucky enough to get away from her in time. Maybe I haven't as much gray matter as some of these guys who call me crazy.

Be a good gal for this poor old war worker.
I'll be coming home soon with a full poke and
we'll be married and live happily ever after.

That nut, and yours, too,
Beat

May 5, Friday

Hi, my sweet one,

We are under the Oakland Frisco Bridge, and the trains go overhead, directly over the ship here at pier 26. The noise is terrific about every five minutes. Out on deck they have stowed all the planes and are now finishing up the work on the "ducks." The boys are making a lot of noise with their gear and big cranes lifting the stuff around and properly securing it there.

It is something quite new that tankers have taken deck loads. All ships are loaded way over the peacetime load limits now, so it is nothing unusual to see these ships way down in the water. The water comes over the decks of a Liberty, so I can imagine what it will do on here with no freeboard at all. It will be fun to try to get back to the mess room to get food. It is about a half block back there from here across a catwalk. That's what I call working for a meal!

≫   ≪

Getting to be an old man, I guess—gee, all of 23 soon! It's hard for me to realize that that is all I shall be. I feel so much older than that!

≫   ≪

My darling,

Here I sit enjoying my last cigarette aboard the ship until we are loaded and battened down again. They won't even let a guy smoke in the quiet and solitude of his quarters with this stuff being worked. Seems that there is some danger of an explosion!

Well, Bunny, the old baby surely goes when they open her up! I'm going to like to ride this baby. I guess that it's just the feel of movement that has gotten me into this enthusiastic mood, darling, but it is a good feeling to have again after this long period of lassitude.

I wonder what you'll think of this book. I'm sending it along to you. I imagine it's supposed to be some sort of a review of war psychology to the book, but I have read much better ones without the seemingly necessary unwed couple sleeping with each other. But I guess that that is quite necessary nowadays to make a good book. But who am I to be a critic? I've still got my first book to write. (Or have I? I've been doing quite well on these letters lately. But I really wouldn't claim to be an author on the basis of some of the silly things I have been forwarding to you.)

I left April third, if you remember. During that time you have seen men and been out more times than I was during the entire year without you. It sets a guy to thinking, darling. I wonder if you feel the same as I do about us.

Beat

P.S. Just thought of something that tickles my funny bone! The theme of this letter might well be "Have I Been Away Too Long?"

May 8, 1944
Avon, Calif.

My darling Elinor,

Well, things are looking better for us now. The old baby smells like a large group of filling stations. The gasoline is darn sweet and will make one drunk if too much of it is breathed. The boys are out on deck now checking the load for temperature, depth, etc. And Butch is getting a bit "high" from it. The ship moved again last night at about ten so we are at another dock taking on the last of our load.

The guys are constantly coming up here to ask me to put on some music so they can enjoy their coffee time or time off from work. There is a law on this ship that no radio equipment shall be used during the transfer of any high octane cargo, and I have to stick with it. I'm all for it, naturally, as it is much safer that way! But the guys are a bit disappointed and I have to explain to them. Things are O.K. then.

By the way, send along an invitation to Yupps's wedding, darling. I'd kinda like to be invited even though I can't possibly be there. It will be something good to remember some brighter day when we can all get together and go see Yupps preach, and sit in the front row, nodding our heads and saying, "Amen" to everything. I would so enjoy being at the wedding. I'd just like to be there and be near you, Bunny.

That package sounds darn intriguing, Bunny. From Johnny. You're too darn popular for a

guy who is going to be away from you for some
time!

Beat

⍟ ⍟

May 9, 1944

Your letters will be my only contact with a
world a guy just couldn't forget and a gal that
is all a man will ever want.

⍟ ⍟

LETTER 1
At sea
[postmarked 5/19]

My darling Elinor,

I was assigned to the ship on the 8th of April
and here we are just going to sea again. It
seems so different this time. I'm not looking
forward to any of those romantic places which
I had always dreamed about. I'm in love and I
have to leave my gal behind for no one knows how
long. But it gives one a kind of quiet thrill
to be out again on a good ship with a good job
and a good crew, I must admit.

    She's blowing and making quite a fuss outside
now, and it is quite a day for these first
trippers. Of course, we tell them it is like this
all the time—just wait until we get some rough
weather! They all look a bit green around the
gills, but I think they will be all right.

Two of the cadets got up in the middle of a good liver and onion dinner and walked out with their hands over their mouths. The steward's gang is a wreck and only about half manned. The gun crew is pretty short-handed, too. Up here, the Navy boy on watch is just getting over his "first attack," as he so pessimistically puts it. This is a heck of a rough day for the guys who are going to sea for the first time.

That screwball guy of yours,
Beat

May 10
LETTER 2

My darling Elinor,

A rough night it was! I was in for a night of
constant calls from the Navy boy in here who
wanted help. It was important stuff, so I didn't
mind, but right now I'm darn tired!

I had to take about an hour and a half of the
Navy boy's watch last night after I noticed he
was sick. We were working in here when suddenly
he ran out and across the passageway. When he
came back, I asked him what was the matter,
as he did look healthy enough. He told me that
he was just getting used to the swells and
would be all right after a bit. I advised him
to go back to the galley and get a box of soda
crackers and bring them up here to munch on
while he was standing his watch. This morning,
the second told me that he was much better
and it is expected that I shall have a better
night, sweets. The boys'll be gaining confidence
all along now. The sooner they can do the job
by themselves, the sooner I shall rest more or
less at ease regarding this department.

In one of my last letters from back there, I
heard that there's a good chance of that dream
of Lorraine and Earl being broken up for good.
[code] Not many of us thought it was such a
good match anyway, did we? In comparison, I
always thought that Helen and Pete much better
suited to each other than the aforementioned
twosome.

Well, it's just about time to have that dinner

date with the guys. Every time they come into my room, they purr and smile at your picture and hold it out in front of them and comment, "Look at this, will ya? And a guy like this gets her. Life can be tough, but it shouldn't be that tough for any gal with her looks!" Maybe I'd better hide that picture and just take it out in the solitude of a blacked-out room with all the doors locked, as a miser would over his jealously guarded hoards of gold. But I'm pretty sure that these guys won't be able to beat me home after this trip.

> Yours, always,
> with all my love,
> Beat

LETTER 3
May 11, 1944
Pacific

My darling,

The ship is rolling, and this mill is placed thwartships, so we have some trouble. When the ship goes too far one way, this mill doesn't have the power to pull the carriage along and we strike the same place three or four times without realizing it. Last time I fixed the typewriter so that it would pull almost uphill, but this one won't take the cure. So, you'll have to excuse some of this bad typing to faulty machinery, darling, and the rest to my own nervousness in trying to get down all the thoughts I get while I sit here with you.

In this outfit, the Merchant Marines, we don't go looking for fights, as we know we could be bested most of the time by better armament. We have some pleasure in getting things over to the actual guys who have to go looking for a fight. Sometimes, we are drafted to do some work on invasions, but they don't like to waste ships either, so they give all the protection they can to us through air and naval support. We never actually kill anyone right out. Sometimes I wonder how it would feel to know that one had actually killed a guy.

We have some interesting things ahead of us, I'm sure, and I hope that you can find some things of interest to keep you busy and happy while I am gone this time. I imagine that I would dislike very much to be in your place and have you traveling from me.

> I'll love you always, darling—
> Be mine alone, won't you,
> Your guy,
> Beat

LETTER 7
May 13, 1944
Pacific

Dearest,

It is now late evening, and I just came in from
a quick peek at the sunset everyone was raving
about tonight. It was truly beautiful and they
say that I must go out with them tonight and
see the moon, too—how romantic! It's the first
trip for all of these raving guys and I try to
tell them that I have seen it before. But they
insist. After seeing the scene, I'm always glad
they talked me into it.

   Suppose that everyone at home is watching for
the news of the invasion. I know that we all
are hoping that they put it off for a while so
we can get at least close to it when it starts.
It's just a dream I suppose, but we are all a
lot of optimists. It's going to be something
huge, and I can't help but think that peace will
come shortly after it starts. Then we shall have
only this theater to worry about. Let's hope
that things go just perfectly for the boys when
they hit the beach over there.

   It is dark. I have a small desk lamp on, and
the radio is playing static to me. The ship is
asleep and quiet except for the throbbing of
the thousands of horsepower pushing us along.
It's not the best atmosphere in the world for
writing a cheery, happy letter. Rather more of
a setting for the melancholy *Wuthering Heights*
sort of thing. There's a cigarette burning in
the ash tray, sending smoke up to be scattered

by the fan which is going this hot, moist night. The ports are down, the huge steel doors are closed about me. I'm quite alone with all of these dials, meters, trimmers, and gadgets, alone with my thoughts and my work.

And my thoughts, quite naturally, are about you. When there's no work or worrying to be done, my mind always turns to happier things. The happiest moments of this somewhat happy life were spent with you, darling, so I quite surely dream of more to come. I'm quite lonesome tonight, and I know there are many other fellows in my mood, too, scattered around the world. I can't be sorry for myself when I compare notes, can I!

Your guy, for always—
Beat

➤   ◄

May 16, 1944
Pacific port

Oh, yes, about that birthday present, darling. I've just had the best in the world from you— these three wonderful letters. If you think that they aren't enough, how about a new 1944 Buick Roadmaster, a console Scott radio or something little like that! No, darling, I would like another picture of you, one the size of the one I have here. And letters and a few snaps here and there. They'll keep me more than happy, darling, and I know that when you sent them along that there is some feeling with them. You just let me know often enough that you love me and I'll be the happiest guy in the world, Bunny. Tomorrow's the big day for us—our birthday, remember? I'll be thinking of you all day, darling, and of our wonderful plans for the future. I know you will be, too. That's more than enough for any guy's birthday, Bun.

⇘   ⇙

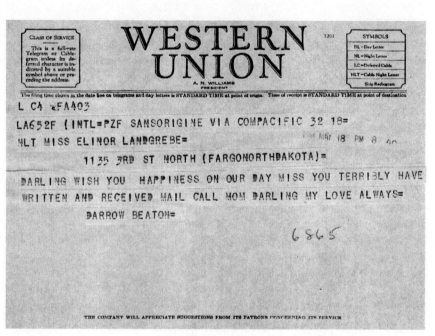

BD Telegram 1944

LETTER 13
May 20, 1944
Pacific, port
[handwritten]

My dearest Bunny,

The past couple of days have been busy ones for us. We're all making plans for a wonderful trip. There have been so many things to do that all departments have been overworked. About all we had time for was coffee time and movies at night. There is a lifeboat on my deck out here, and I invited all the guys up to watch the pictures. They were shown on the ship alongside of us for the Navy boys, but we "sneaked in" by watching from our balcony seats!

You're probably quite busy with Yupps' wedding, so don't force yourself to write. I'll understand, Bunny, really. Just give me all the news you have when you do write, won't you?

I miss you terribly, darling,
Beat

≫   ≪

May 23, 1944

After sitting up half the night with the skipper, I got all the final instructions and fixed the radio room up with all the necessary dope, then piled into bed only to be knocked out with all the bells on the ship going full blast. Dashed into the radio room and got things set up and then put on my clothes and got the other guys on their respective ways to battle stations. It gives one a funny feeling each time, and more so when it is in the middle of the night. But we finally got the all clear and today we can't find out just what caused the alarm.

⇒⊱　⊰⇐

May 27, 1944

My sweets,

Did you ever stop to wonder just when this war is going to be over? Guess most of us take it for granted, now, as part of our lives. It surely spoils a lot of wonderful times for all of us, doesn't it? For example, here I am, marooned out here thousands of miles from the nearest land and many more thousands from you and my home. A guy adjusts himself to it, but there is often a feeling of frustration at the way The Fates are treating him. These years should be spent loving you and having you close to me. We'd be living together, having fun all the while, wouldn't we? But the war is fought to preserve that sort of life for people like us. We'll see it through happily, won't we, darling?

I'll love you always, Elinor.
Beat

LETTER 19
May 28th
San Pedro bound!

Hi, sweets!

We just up and suddenly changed our minds about
going to the Panama Canal and to England by
way of Venezuela, and here we are on our way
home! Things happened all at once last night
right after I got into bed. They put me on the
air for a bit—quite a bit—and I had a hell of a
time getting through to Frisco in the static,
but I got our messages in all right. It's quite
unusual for a ship to break radio silence at
sea, and especially so at nighttime, so you may
know that we were under emergency conditions.
There is a chance that the boiler (one left)
will go out, and we would have to call shore
for sea-going tugs to take us in.

We had a conference in here to decide what to
do. The chief engineer, skipper, gunnery officer
and I got together and tried to work something
out. I convinced them that I had the equipment
to contact shore and that I thought there would
be a poor chance of a sub near us picking it up.
The engineer and skipper decided to make San
Pedro as it is much shorter than Panama and we
have to get to shore darn soon or go down!

We let it wait until this morning and then
I went on the air and contacted WSL in New
York with the information that I wished to be
forwarded to Frisco to the Navy Department. It
was coded, of course, and that took time, too,

with all of us adding and subtracting numbers, etc.

There was an animated and excited and interested audience present when I went on the air this morning early. Most of the guys had never seen Sparks go on the air, as in wartime it happens very seldom. At times they aggravated me, but I held my temper and it turned out to be fun. I'd tell them a lot of lies on what they were sending back to me, etc. They'd get worried and the story would be all over the ship in five seconds. The Navy radiomen are still wondering how I could do it with all the guys standing around me. They thought they would have folded up. I know I did sweat it out. But good.

I would just have soon achieved my ambition to see England and the Invasion. In fact, it is rather a let-down for me—a big one, too. But I can't do a thing about it out here.

Guess you know Los Angeles fairly well from your trips there this past summer, so it is no inducement to offer you. But, darling, I would like very much to know right now that you would come out to see me if we find for sure that we are to have time enough there. You would have to travel across the country to see me, and then have no purpose out here—I can see that, of course. How it would look to your parents. I suppose that I should know from experience better than to get my hopes up too high. We had such a grand time together at home that I think you may be more than tempted to come out for a while.

If you give me the necessary bit of encouragement, I shall sign off and we can have more time together. We could have some time in Frisco then while I waited for another ship to come along. We could be married during that time and have our future really set, Bunny—or are ya still afraid of this thing called marriage?

When I call, Elinor, I'm going to ask you if we can't get together. I know that there may be some people there to listen in while we talk, so I'll do all the questioning and you can answer in yeses and nos to let me know your thoughts. I'm getting all excited here, Bunny, and there's really no percentage in it, I guess. I'm afraid of the result of that phone call. Call it intuition if you wish. I'm only hoping that after calling you, this same feeling of happiness is present.

My love for always,
Beat

LETTER 21
May 29, 1944

Darling,

I'm just plain tired out—all the way—exhausted
so to speak. Things began happening last
night again. They radioed us late last night
for some more information, and I had to work
it out and get it through all of this static.
It was just plain murder and hard as hell on
the nerves. We have a new code book without
any instructions as to how to use it—just
a supplementary one along with the regular
books—and the stuff last night came over in
it. It took me about ten minutes to figure out
the method, and I was just plain lucky to do
it.

On top of all that, I'm the only guy the
old man will trust to take radio bearings.
Every half hour during the night I had Anacapa
Island, Los Angeles, and Point Loma on the air
and got a fix on them. You must have upset San
Diego quite a bit when you left—or before you
left—as Point Loma insisted upon coming in on
the port bow when she should have been on the
starboard quarter! We got some perfect fixes
on the ship and it made the old man happy.
We haven't had any sun for three days and he
hasn't been able to take a sight which he could
call reliable. The first few bearings we got
he wouldn't believe, but I finally convinced
him that we were here instead of there! He's
not drinking today, and he is as nervous as a
cat.

So we should be in this afternoon some time,
and I hope that I get ashore right away. As
soon as I can, I'll be on the phone trying to
get you.

                              Your guy, always,
                                        Beat

May 31, 1944
San Pedro

My darling Elinor,

Your wire was waiting for me this morning when
I went to the desk. It was good to have you say
you loved me and all, darling. Yupps' wedding
was scheduled for June first and if it had gone
off as we thought, we would be able to get
together for a while, darling, but June sixth
is quite late. We are going to be here until
about June tenth, and it just wouldn't make
sense for you to come way out here for a day or
two at the most and maybe get here to find me
gone already. It was a good try, darling, but
we'll have to wait now until I get back from
this trip to see each other.

So far here I have met many gals. Vince has
a way with the gals and always brings them
over to talk with me. Believe it or not, but
he has introduced me to four of the gals from
the movie *Cover Girl* already. They have a home
in Long Beach and are doing bit parts and some
supporting roles in other movies now. One of the
gals, Carol Sompin', is now on all the billboards
out here for Lucky Lager beer. She's cute as
hell. We spent two hours together last night
just talking about things. She likes to hear
about the places I've been and I enjoy hearing
about the movie racket out here. They want to
take us through one of the lots out here, and
I'm a bit tempted to go along. She's engaged to
a dentist out here in L.A. and besides you can
just imagine the Dakota Kid going home with a

gal in the movies, huh? She's been hoping to meet you when you came out and says that if you are as pretty as I say that she will get you a job out here! She made forty-five dollars yesterday in six hours just posing as a Ziegfeld gal in some scene!! That's the kind of job you would really like, darling.

When I talked to you on the phone, you sounded so good—the first time I ever really felt that you were happy to hear from me out there. When I get back next time, Bunny, please be ready to come to me. We'll be married and do just as you wish for a honeymoon and all.

Good night, Bun—my love always,
Beat

June 1, 1944
San Pedro, Cal.

My Darling Bunny,

When I got back aboard this morning, I found a letter from you and it has put me into a funny mood, darlin'. You were all mixed up about things again and wondering if you and I would be happy together. The war has interfered with us at every corner and other things have come up, too, to make it tough for us to see each other and have the time together that we really need.

As to the difference in ages, which seems to bother so many people, darling, I agree with you that we shouldn't let someone talk us out of our happiness because of the old story that has come down through the ages. Many marriage experts agree that the very best of couples find the woman from two to three years older than the man. At times it is so hard for me to realize that I am only twenty-three years old. I feel so much older than that and find my friends in the late twenties or early thirties. I've been around much more and seen much more than men many years older than I. I have a much broader outlook on life from all of that.

You make me smile to myself, Bun, when you ask me if I shall be running around with younger girls when we get a bit older. If the truth were known, you would be the one to be running around!

As to our capabilities to get along together, we know we can. Our every day companionship is perfect and we have fun and work together. Our physical life together is something almost too perfect. After marriage our physical union will be something we shall both appreciate much more than we have so far. We won't be afraid of someone coming along and finding out about things. We won't have to wonder if we are doing the right thing.

Hey, darling! The gunnery officer just came in with this news. The ship may be here for a month or more with some new repairs to be made! I'll let you know as soon as I really confirm it. Let's hope that this additional break for us works out and we do get to see each other, Bun. I'm praying with all my heart.

All my love, for always,
Dearest—
Beat

LETTER 30
June %, ")%% (?)
June 4, 1944
Pedro

My darling Elinor,

"Long Ago and Far Away" is now playing and it
certainly is all right, Bun, a fitting composition
for me to listen to this evening way down here
in California. Suppose that you are busy with
something or other today with the wedding so
close now. I'll call you tomorrow or the next
night and see how the things went, darling.
When it is all over, sweets, how's about a full-
length letter all about it? It'll be fun to
read of someone's wedding even though it isn't
mine.

You were remembering better days when you
wrote. We met right at the wrong time really,
just as the war started. We haven't lived a
normal life at all since we started going with
each other, and I'm truly sorry for that. Some
day we shall start out and do all the things
that people in love in peacetime do and enjoy
together. We do deserve some good breaks before
long. This war can't last forever.

My love, all of it,
Always,
Beat

June 4, 1944
San Pedro, Calif.

My darling Elinor,

We heard Roosevelt speak tonight while we were eating. His speech was all right. He mentions that there is still a long way to go, and how well we all know it, huh? But it won't last forever, and it will be worth all of it when it is at last over. Heard today that the Germans are increasing their toll of guys to go before the firing squads in order to get better morale from the poor war-sick men in their armies. They are ready to crack.

One of your letters makes me a bit mad and sad, Elinor. You talk about Marge and Luverne, and you mention that Marge gets around, and that you would like to get away from home for a while and "get around" too. What that means, I can only guess. If you do decide to take off and "get around" be sure to let me know. I'd kinda like to get around a bit more, too, if you are to do it. I've been happy until now thinking you were quite well satisfied to sit around there.

I know you got around in San Diego, and I don't really care about it, darling. As for me, I'm quite happy to live this life and sit around waiting and working for the day when we shall be able to "get around" with each other. I've tried more than once to get you to come somewhere so that we could have fun with one another. Then comes a letter from ya deploring the sad situation you find yourself in. What the hell can I say, Bun? So far, since our last leave, you are the only one to have a date or more. Sometimes I wonder if I'm the broad-minded type or just a plain fool. And when you write this nonsense to me, I really worry about you and me.

Does life get boring back there? Yes, I know it seems that way, doesn't it? Far be it from me to try to give advice which you should follow to a "T," darling. But may I offer some advice in the way of suggestions? Why not get a job— any kind and anywhere. It would take your mind off yourself. Why not get something to do that will really help the country now, Bunny? It is important at a time like this for everyone to be in there pitching. They announced the invasion over the German radio tonight, and if it is true, there will be a lot of work to do in the coming months for wounded and sick men. There are so many things you can do to really help and give you that peace of mind that is quite essential to living these days in a country at war.

Good night, my darling,
Beat

Wedding Day

June 1944

ELINOR WOKE BEFORE SUNRISE. She couldn't sleep with the to-do list bouncing around in her head. Yupps's wedding morning had arrived, the weather drizzly and cool for the season. Tuesday, June 6, 1944.

She heard her father and sisters waking upstairs. In no time at all they had arrived downstairs for breakfast. Irene plugged in the coffee pot, Georg hummed as he fried eggs for himself and Mickey, and Elinor toasted the last of a loaf of store bought bread. Mickey placed silverware on the table of the breakfast nook beside the plates she had set out. Because the wedding had become the responsibility of the groom's family, breakfast was a hurried affair. They ate quickly.

Irene set some toast on a plate, filled a cup with coffee, and padded upstairs to deliver breakfast to their mother.

Elinor followed her father into the den, while Mickey and Irene finished the breakfast dishes. "Dad," she reminded him. "We're going to need the car to run some errands for the wedding. I'll drive. Okay?"

Georg nodded as he dialed the Scott, twisting the knobs to bring in the news from the European front. "The keys are on the hook by the back door, Bunny."

Elinor wrinkled her brow as she smiled. She squinted at her father. He didn't often agree to let a woman take his precious Pontiac. She wondered whether he'd really heard her.

"We need to start early," she went on. "There's so much to do before this evening!" She began making up her bed, turning it back into the daytime sofa in her father's den. She slowed when she heard the emotion of the announcers coming from the radio. The voices approached hysteria.

Wherever Georg tuned, the intense energy of the commentator exploded into the room. Some of the reporters spoke loudly in order to project their voices over the action that fractured the air in the war around them. Elinor heard the whine of bombs and the buzz of airplanes. Georg turned up the volume on voices that he couldn't focus as well.

The big day—Yupps and Bernita's big day—had turned into a Really Big Day. The invasion! And not a moment too soon. D-Day, after all the waiting. After all the planning and predicting and editorializing.

"Mein Gott!" Georg settled on a station, then settled himself into his desk chair. He spread his maps on top of the papers strewn around there.

Elinor sat, riveted in place on her daybed, trying to absorb the details. She set the folded chenille spread in her lap.

The country had been waiting for this big push into Europe. Although an invasion had seemed imminent for a while, the exact location and date had been kept secret. General Eisenhower had even set up artificial infrastructure near other ports to deceive the enemy into thinking that those were places the Allies would be landing. And now the action was in progress along a 50-mile stretch in Normandy.

And, the radio announcer reported, 20,000 men had parachuted into France—behind the German lines—after midnight. It had been a gloomy night there, doubly black. And the men, including some of her "old friends," no doubt, had dropped down behind the enemy's lines. Who could imagine it?

Of course the Germans offered resistance.

The radio continued with more details. Soldiers rushing from their LSTs up Omaha and Utah beaches from the sea—156,000 men, their lives in the balance, risking everything for the country. Tears pooled in Elinor's eyes. It was hard to fathom the courage of these American men.

Georg jumped up and dashed into the living room. He snatched his pipe, tobacco can, and ashtray from the table beside his chair and carried the smoking equipment to his desk where he sat again. He located battle sites. Without moving his eyes from his maps, he stuffed Revelation into the bowl of his pipe. His aim off, he dropped a few tobacco flakes on his desk and distractedly brushed them away. He looked up long enough to strike a wooden match. Then he lit the tobacco and took a tentative puff on the stem of his pipe, eyes closed, as he offered a quick, private prayer to the Almighty.

Elinor imagined the battle scene—the weather in France stormy with high seas, a blessing for the Allies. The Germans had been sure a naval attack wouldn't be mounted with such weather.

"Thanks be to God," Georg whispered. He set his pipe into the copper ashtray and leaned over his maps again for a closer look.

Elinor stood up. "Let me see," she said. She set the bedspread on the daybed and leaned over her father's shoulder to view the maps. How close was this action to Germany? How much more territory did the Allies have to win to declare a victory?

The announcer continued, "5,000 Allied ships are trying to evade underwater mines and bombs from the air. The seas here are choppy and there is limited visibility due to the storms."

There would be too many casualties and deaths. Elinor didn't want to imagine it. She put a hand to her forehead.

Reverend Landgrebe offered a whispered plea. "Oh, Lord, the Almighty One, take these souls to your bosom as we hold their families in our hearts." Then he picked up his pipe and leaned back in his chair.

Mickey, with Ching at her feet, entered the den. "What's going on?" she asked. She joined Elinor and stood behind their father.

Ching leapt onto the daybed. He curled up beside the folded chenille bedspread. His eyes stayed alert, but his ears lay, flattened, on his head. As gunshots and bombs echoed around the room, he jumped down and slipped away into the house.

Elinor quickly got her sister caught up on the facts. "They've done it, Mick. The invasion!" She pointed out the locations on her father's maps.

"Oh, I know someone who will be so disappointed," Elinor whispered. She raised her eyebrows and nodded toward her sister. "He wanted to be there and he's stuck in California, waiting for his ship to be repaired."

Mickey nodded. "If this is the end of the war in Europe . . ." Her lips formed a straight line across her dainty face. "I know I'm dreaming. But when the darn thing ends in the Pacific, I'll see Bob again."

Elinor hugged her little sister. No one knew whether Bob was safe or what danger he might be in on one of those Pacific islands. The war was especially brutal there.

"If the war takes a while to wind down, you know who will probably be in the thick of things, too. The troops need aviation fuel and ammunition." Elinor sighed. "I suppose he'll be happy then, seeing action. I wish this were all over."

"Psst!" their father reminded them. He pointed at the radio. The girls quieted.

George Hicks, now reporting from the deck of the *U.S.S. Ancon*, described the scene. "You see the ships lying in all directions, just like black shadows on the grey sky. Now planes are going overhead. Heavy fire now just behind us."

As the news repeated, Reverend Landgrebe moved the dials on the Scott, sliding over the static. He brought in other stations and gathered the news from various connected corners of the universe.

The three of them sat spellbound until nearly mid-morning, when the Elinor checked her watch.

"Mercy! We'll have to rush," she said.

She and Mickey slipped off the daybed and dashed upstairs, whispering about the news, considerate of their mother in bed, recovering from the emergency gall bladder surgery which had altered the wedding plans, the location, even the date of the nuptials.

Elinor had lists of last minute errands to be run. With her copy of the 1942 *Etiquette*, she tried following Post's suggestions for "The Wedding of a Cinderella" on page 392. Certainly they were in no position, now rushing, to make arrangements for "The Most Elaborate Wedding Possible" or "The More Usual Fashionable Wedding." At least

Bernita wouldn't be a bride in "everyday clothes," which Post included in chapter 51, a section of the war supplement.

Post considered it a breach of etiquette for the bridegroom ever to give the wedding. Certainly even she would have surrendered in the Landgrebe's situation!

Mickey pulled Irene away from the mirror in their bedroom, where she had been primping. The girls located their purses. Despite the radio's continuing coverage, the wedding marched into the forefront of their minds.

The phone rang downstairs.

"Adolf! Adolf Hoeger!" Elinor heard their father's loud preaching voice. He muted his radio. "*Ja*, we've got the radio on. *Was denken Sie?*" A quick conversation. Then back to the radio as local announcers began to interrupt, listing churches which planned noon hour or evening prayer services.

"Girls," their father called to them. The girls dashed downstairs into the den. "We are going to have a prayer service at the church right before the wedding," Georg explained. "Perhaps just before Yupps' ceremony."

"That'll mean more people at the wedding, then?" Elinor started to amend her lists as she spoke.

"We have to include everyone, I think," Georg agreed. "I'll invite them to stay after the prayer service."

"More cake, then. And coffee." Elinor looked at her sisters. Who knew how many might be at a prayer meeting on this eventful day? "Just in case . . ."

The girls dashed around town. They ordered a larger cake from Quality Bakery to be delivered to the reception hall. They picked up corsages, Bernita's bouquet, and the carnation boutonnieres at Fargo Floral. With the downtown errands complete, the girls drove through a light drizzle to the church to arrange the fellowship room for a reception.

Old Mr. Westrick was already setting up the long folding tables and Elinor began planting portable chairs around them. Mickey dug through the cupboards, hunting for tablecloths, which she spread on the tables as quickly as they were set up. Irene found the large coffee pot. She filled it with water and coffee grounds. It sat, ready to be plugged in just before the wedding reception. Before long, the room was ready.

"C'mon," Elinor urged. "It's almost four. We have to get Mother ready."

The girls jumped back into the Pontiac for the quick ride from the church to their home.

Trudie had risen and come downstairs. She was now rummaging around in the refrigerator.

"Mother, let me make you a sandwich," Irene suggested. She helped her mother settle into the breakfast nook.

Elinor caught her mother up on the wedding progress, and Trudie shared the latest news of the invasion.

Just before six, the girls helped their mother into her corset and dress. Then Elinor guided her back down the stairs to the main floor where she settled Trudie into a soft chair in the living room. Irene brought in a cup of freshly brewed dark coffee.

The news bombarded the girls as they hustled between their bedroom and the single bathroom, preparing themselves for the ceremony. The sounds from the radio of planes overhead, bombs screaming, shouts, and confusion made up the background music for Yupps' wedding day.

Irene, Mickey and Elinor listened as they buttoned, tied, and zipped themselves into their best dresses. Then the three of them gathered in the small bathroom, sharing the mirror.

Elinor began a game. "Let's try to name all the fellows we know who have gone overseas. Who might be involved in the invasion?" The three of them quieted for a few moments. "Dale and Bob Flynn for sure," she continued. She applied her lipstick as she had a turn at the mirror.

"Didn't Gil train to parachute?" Mickey asked. "He's a sure bet."

"What about Phil?" Irene suggested and the girls nodded. They all had memories of Phil from their first parsonage in Elgin.

"Well, there's no chance for the men in the Pacific," Elinor added. "For Beat. Bob Bruns. Johnny. Maybe Melvin."

"And my Bob." Mickey tried to smile. "A bit of good news, I guess."

The girls straightened their skirts as they slid across the back seat and crowded into the Pontiac for the ride to church. Georg helped Trudie down the back steps and across the lawn to the car. Holding her right elbow, he eased her into her front seat as carefully as he turned the big dials on his Scott. Trudie leaned into the door's armrest as they drove slowly along the seven block ride to their newly built church.

Elinor watched protectively as her father shuffled into the prayer service with Trudie on his arm. They greeted parishioners along their path, stopping here and there to share news about the invasion as well as to give Trudie a breather. Toward the front of the church, they moved carefully into a pew where Georg arranged his delicate wife. Trudie sighed when her bottom settled on the wooden bench. Georg patted her knee as he sat down beside her. Their eyes met, and they smiled as they pulled a brown hymnal from the rack.

Reverend Keller, at the altar, bowed his bald head in front of the new brass cross nailed to the wall. He prayed his finest. For our troops, of course, especially the boys from Fargo. For those injured or killed. For all the souls, even the German ones. For the people back home and their sacrifices. For the weather in France. For General Eisenhower. For the women and children here and abroad.

Elinor glanced at Reverend Keller just as he stole a glimpse at his watch under the wide sleeve of his robe. The prayers would end soon.

When her father took the pulpit, he invited everyone to join the Landgrebes and the Lenths at the wedding following this service and then the reception afterwards in the basement of the parish hall.

As Georg stepped out of the pulpit, the organ burst into the "Star Spangled Banner." The congregants stood at attention. Their voices, sometimes cracking with emotion, filled the large room.

Everything about the wedding which followed the service was perfect: the wedding party dressed up and happy, the gold band Yupps added to Bernita's tiny diamond, even the never-ending sermons which made the legs of the bride and groom ache as they stood there in front of the altar. And at last, the march back down the aisle.

Elinor felt tears forming in her eyes as she and her sisters followed the bride and groom. Maybe, even in this age of conflict and war, there was room for love—and hope—after all.

The congregation filed through the narrow hallways and into the fellowship room, where they found the reception. The bride and groom and their four parents had already formed the receiving line, and they chatted with their guests as they shook hands.

"You'll never forget your anniversary," people told Yupps and Bernita, "on D-Day!"

Conversation around coffee focused on the war. Yupps and Bernita focused on themselves, laughing with friends and flirting with each other. They were ready to face the joys and adjustments of establishing a home together.

Georg and Trudie left as soon as the greetings were finished and the cake cut. They shuffled out of the reception hall holding hands, Georg gently guiding his bride back to bed.

When Elinor had a chance to sit down, she played piano for the background music. Her hands skimmed the keys, delicately broadcasting popular Hit Parade songs into the air, their favorites.

"When the Lights Go On Again," a good choice on D-Day. No more blackouts. No more bombs. No more of this damned war.

When Yupps, Mickey's twin, wrapped his arm around Bernita's waist, Elinor remembered Beat's touch, the way his kisses feathered up and down her neck. The way he had held her when he was home on leave. She licked her lips and played "Together." This time they hadn't had a single quarrel. They hadn't needed that long talk.

"There Are Such Things." People still loved, despite war. Men and women still found each other, sometimes across a country. Sometimes even when separated by an ocean. But love, even in these times of atrocity and barbarity, lived on.

If only Beat could pick up her message on his radio tonight! With her eyes closed, she played "It Had to Be You."

Glued to the Radio

D-Day 1944

June 6, 1944
San Pedro, Calif.

My Bunny Darling,

I've been glued to the radio all of this historical day listening for the big German push which I think is due very soon. I had planned a day in Pedro getting more things straightened out, but this is much more important to me. We'd have been in England and just about now if we had kept right on going. Damn the luck!

It's three thirty now and I can see you and the family getting ready for the wedding back home. It's five thirty now back there, and in less than two hours Yupps and B. will be married, or so close to it that he won't be able to get out of it!

Off to Hollywood again tomorrow. I'll see what I can do for you in the way of getting in pictures, Bun!

Your guy for always,
Beat

Even Good Girls Did It . . .

5:30 A.M.

ELINOR PRESSED THE RED button on her father's desk lamp. The space in front of her dimmed. She sat in the shadows.

What a turn her life had taken since June!

What a turn the world had taken . . .

With the boys closing up the European front, it couldn't be too long before the Pacific war would be over. Then the world would settle back to normal.

She couldn't remember what "normal" was.

Had she lost her mind in June? The other girls were doing it, too. Unchaperoned girls traveled all over the country to see their men off to war. They probably did things they would never do at home, too.

Maybe it was the uncertainty of the war.

But what she had done next still surprised her.

I Have to Go

June 8, 1944

"CAN'T YOU SEE?" ELINOR raised her voice. It was a plea. And a scream. She found herself standing, surprised at the extent of her anger. She marched to the kitchen, poured some scalding coffee into her cup, and returned to the dining room table. She sat back in her chair and set her cup on the table.

She needed to regain her composure. Anger, loud voices, even pouting had never worked with her parents. Besides, the stress might trigger a migraine.

"I have to go." She spoke calmly now, her voice controlled with effort. "I have stayed around home. I've taught school, even when I hated it." She spoke through her teeth, but she maintained her hushed voice. "I helped with Yupps' wedding, the new church. I've been the perfect daughter." She took a calming breath. "Now, it's time for me. And this is what I want."

"I don't see why," her father thundered. His right arm lifted into the air, like it did when he was making a point in a sermon. When his hand came down, it slapped the table. The cups jumped in their saucers.

Her mother shrank deeper into her chair. "We just got done with Yupps' wedding. And all that gardening yesterday. I think we all need to relax a while," she offered. "Perhaps it's this weather today . . ."

Elinor stood. "This is my life." She glowered at her father. "And I've made a decision."

Her parents stopped drinking their afternoon coffee. They leaned toward Elinor. The air hung hot and muggy around the three of them.

"Have you heard there's a war on?" Elinor continued. She sat back down and stared into her coffee cup. "Well, I want to see some of my 'old friends' before . . ." She looked at her mother. "Well, they happen to be on the West Coast." In the distance she heard the low growl of thunder. Elinor wiped her brow with a napkin and then pushed her hair back behind her ears.

"This is about seeing your 'old friends'?" her father was controlling his volume now.

"A single girl going to the coast to visit boyfriends? How does that look?" Trudie piped in.

Elinor felt an electric charge scattering through her thoughts. A migraine was the last thing she needed now.

She turned to her mother. "Beat will be shipping out soon again. He doesn't know how long he'll be gone this time." Another breath.

Her parents exchanged looks. Her father scowled. "Darrow?! So this is about meeting Darrow?" He pounded a fist once on the table as he spoke.

"Alfred's out there now, too. Maybe Dale, Johnny, some of the other fellows. And, well, I might stay out there anyway and get a job. There must be something a girl can do in wartime. Something besides teaching."

"Alone?" Her father stood, then sat again. "Are there rooming houses? What do you know about this coast? Good girls didn't wander around alone when I was a young man. Girls didn't live alone either."

"You need to adjust to the times," Elinor responded hotly. "Girls are doing all kinds of things now that they weren't allowed to do in your time. Why girls are even welding and building ships, Dad. And I could help the war effort in some way."

An atmospheric crackling, followed by thunder, rolled over the house. The three of them glanced at once out the window. Spring rains were what one hoped for after planting season, gentle droplets watering the rows of seedlings. But this was a downpour. The rain barrel would be half full in minutes!

"But, Bunny," her mother resumed. "*Good* girls don't run around unchaperoned. So many things could happen to you. We worry."

"Oh, Mother. That was in your time. Someone used to have to take care of the old maids in the family while they sat around in dim houses withering away. Thank goodness, today it's different. I can take care of myself."

"But we like it when you're around home," Georg interrupted.

"You already have one daughter to take care of the rest of your days, Papa. You don't have to worry about me. Wait a minute." Elinor stood and dashed into the den.

Georg and Trudie eyed each other, then glanced toward the dining room window, now streaming with water. Rain pounded on the roof above them.

Ching slinked into the dining room, his blue, blue eyes focused on Trudie. He wrapped himself around and around her ankles, until she leaned over to scratch behind his ears.

Elinor returned to the room with her copy of Emily Post's *Etiquette*. She rejoined her parents at the dining room table. "Listen to this."

She found page 351, dog-eared and familiar to her. She read, "The Vanished Chaperon and Other Lost Conventions. From an ethical standpoint, the only chaperon worth having in this present day is a young girls' own efficiency in chaperoning herself. The girl who has been trained to appraise every person and situation she meets, much as an expert automobile driver has been trained to appraise speed and distance, and to counter the probable impulses of other drivers, needs no one to sit beside her and tell her what to do. In short, the girl who in addition to trained judgment has the right attributes of proper pride and character needs no chaperon—ever."

She set the book, open, on the table. The Bible of manners. No one could argue with Emily Post. Then Elinor reminded both her parents, "I am twenty-eight now. I will take care of myself."

"Oh, Bunny," her mother nearly moaned. "The old rules have been useful for many generations. I don't know why so much has to change. It's this war. Everything is different now." Her hands flew to her chest and she held them there, crossed, holding her heart inside.

"Come now," her father cajoled. "You can stay here and find a good job for the war, Bunny. You have a home here and no expenses to worry about." He tried a smile. "Don't forget San Diego. That didn't work out for Mickey and you. What's to say that a trip out there again will be any different?"

"And Reverend Keller counts on you to play the organ in church on Sundays when you're in town." Her mother got up to refill her cup and her husband's. She called from the kitchen, "If you must go, why not take Mickey along?"

"Mickey doesn't want to leave right now. She's having fun. She loves working at Kresge's. And Bob is expected home some time this year. From the Pacific. And don't . . ." Elinor thrust her hands out, palms toward her mother, a policeman directing verbal traffic. "Don't suggest Irene. I'm old enough to know what I want to do. And to do it by myself."

Trudie returned with the cups just as the sky lit up around their home. For a moment they froze, waiting for the thunderclap. Then the house lapsed back into the bath of clouds. Trudie dashed back into the kitchen to find a candle and some matches. She set them on the table just in case.

"My life is certainly going nowhere, and I need to matter somehow," Elinor explained.

"You matter to us," her mother soothed.

"Then let me go without all this quarreling." Elinor found herself standing again. "I'm leaving whether you and Dad approve or not."

The lights flickered, then rallied.

"Let me see your book, Bunny," her mother proposed. Elinor placed *Etiquette*, already open to the section on chaperones, in her mother's hands. Trudie read the entire section silently while Georg waited, stiff in his chair. The wind wrapped around the clapboard house. Rain pounded on the roof.

Elinor's thoughts turned to Beat. They had arrangements to make. What if he called just now, in the middle of this? Would the phones even work in this storm? Her mother discouraged any phone calls or baths during an electrical storm.

"Georg," Trudie raised her head from the book.

Georg focused on his wife. "*Tay-Air-Oo-Day-Ee-Ay?*" he asked.

"I think Bunny's right. Post agrees with this idea of no chaperones. So different from our time. I was chaperoned until our wedding night. Remember, Georg?"

"1913. Not so long ago, Trudie." Georg nodded. "I remember well." He smiled at his bride.

"Our wedding night was spent in my home with the family all around. We had no privacy until the next day when we began our train trip to North Dakota. To Elgin. So different," Trudie whispered.

"Times may change. But goodness and honesty and the laws of God remain. We were too lenient with Irene, *Tay-Air-Oo-Day-Ee-Ay*. How does this look?"

Georg got up from the table to deposit his cup in the kitchen sink.

He stood at the kitchen window and looked into the back alley. Raindrops now pattered the house in intermittent bursts instead of slamming headlong, kamikaze-style, into it. The leaves of the big elm that hung over the house dripped on the roof. The rumble of thunder originated from the east, softer now, and a cool breeze freshened the air in the house. The quick Dakota storm was nearly spent. A couple of adventurous neighborhood children already played in the puddles.

"I need to think." Georg found his gardening hat on the hook by the back door, plunked it on his head and opened the porch door.

Trudie came to him. "Remember Luther's apple tree," she advised. She tried a smile. Her lips straightened, but she couldn't force them any further. She closed her eyes.

Georg turned away. The line that normally relaxed between his brows now formed a deep furrow on his forehead. He checked the sky. He slipped into his jacket and stepped onto the back porch.

Elinor moved to the window. She watched her father slow when he walked past his garden. He checked the seedlings and then disappeared down the alley.

Trudie, dishtowel in hand, circulated from open window to open window to see whether any rain had splattered into the house. Then she gathered the cups from the dining room table.

"Well, I know the right thing for me to do now," Elinor muttered. "I'm packing."

She dashed into the den and began taking Beat's favorite dresses off hangers. She folded them and arranged them into her valise. She added her new white suit, too, along with those pink pajamas he admired. She closed the door between the den and the kitchen when Trudie began washing dishes. She took out the enameled vial of Christmas Night perfume from Egypt and checked the stopper. She packed it into her purse with an extra lipstick. She remembered her hairbrush and ran upstairs to the bathroom to gather it in. Toothbrush . . .

Elinor was packed and ready for the trip when her father turned the handle of the front porch door and stepped inside.

He removed his damp hat and set it to dry on the shelf by his desk. "Come," he invited Elinor. "Let's sit and have a chat."

He led the way into the living room, removing his suit coat and shaking the raindrops off of it as he walked. Elinor tarried just a moment. She closed her suitcase and snapped the latches. Her father couldn't miss the metallic click. Then she followed.

They sat as they usually did when reading the Sunday *Forum*. Trudie joined them, on the sofa beside Elinor. No one spoke. The cuckoo clock ticked a couple of minutes away.

"The clocks are ticking in Long Beach, too," Elinor thought.

Georg reached for his pipe. The keys in his pocket jingled as he stretched his arm toward the corner table. He didn't look at her. He clicked the lid of the tobacco can open and began to fill the bowl of his pipe. A few flakes dropped into his lap. He stared at them, then brushed his pant leg. He tamped down the tobacco and added a pinch more, then closed the tobacco can with a snap.

He concentrated on lighting a sturdy wooden match, which he had removed from the box of matches on the table beside his chair.

Elinor tried to control her impatient breathing. She rearranged herself on the sofa. The old horsehair cushions sighed as she settled. Her father still hadn't looked at her.

Georg flicked a match across the matchbox. Nothing. He swiped it again and the match snapped. He tossed the pieces into his copper ashtray on top of the pile of ashes, damp and rank in the afternoon humidity. He retrieved another match from the box.

The hands on the cuckoo clock moved with a slight click. The bird, freed for a few moments on the hour, would hop out overhead any second.

Georg looked at Elinor then for an instant. His eyes wore red rims. They seemed to sag. His usual twinkle had evaporated. She thought her father had aged. He seemed tired and worn-out.

He struck the match across the box and watched the spark ignite. The acrid smell tickled Elinor's nose. He moved the flame over the bowl of his pipe and drew on the stem.

A car drove by outside, splattering the curb. Children laughed.

"Bunny," her father struggled to find the words, in English or in German. "*Ach!* It's hard to get used to." He settled back in his armchair and puffed on the pipe to encourage the flame to kindle.

Finally he looked into her eyes. "So," he said, "you're leaving."

Elinor nodded.

Georg set his pipe into its copper ashtray on the table beside his chair. He leaned toward his daughter. He paused and looked into her eyes. Tendrils of smoke rose from the ashtray behind him.

"You've been raised in the church. You know the ideals we've set before you. And we trust you. If this is truly what you want . . ." His voice was tender. Elinor sensed a tear back in there somewhere.

"It is, Papa."

Her mother dabbed her eyes with her handkerchief. "*Meine liebe*," she whispered. "My love."

"Then we'll help you, of course," he sighed. "Do you need money?"

Elinor shook her head. Beat would wire enough for the train ticket.

"A ride to the depot then."

Elinor nodded. "Thank you. I'd like that." Her parents would need to see her off. They'd fret until her return. But her need to see Beat drove her. Long Beach. She had to hurry.

More Trouble

July 14, 1944

ELINOR WOKE IN THE Mayflower Hotel in Seattle. She rubbed her eyes, then sat up slowly. She didn't know where she was. The room, dark and unfamiliar, came into focus. Beat lay beside her. Garbled words from somewhere mixed with his breathing. She turned her head to gather in the scene. A crack of light slid under the door but dissolved as it entered the gloom. Faint sounds floated into the room.

As her head cleared, Elinor remembered that sleep had come slowly to her last night. All that scheming, fretting. Had she ever arrived at the perfect solution? She tried to remember, to organize, her options.

She rubbed her temples, but she couldn't escape her early morning dream. Frightening visions still drifted in the back of her mind. Bloody medical equipment. Screams. Her father's disappointment.

Beat rolled over and splayed himself crosswise on the bed. Elinor moved to the edge to accommodate him. He snored and rolled closer. Awake now, Elinor slipped out of their bed and tiptoed into the bathroom. She turned on the light and found her watch by the sink. 5:34 A.M.

One look in the mirror told her that she needed to freshen up. Maybe it was all this worry. If only "those people" would come. She washed her face, brushed her teeth, and applied her usual make-up, adding a bit more color to her cheeks. She swiped her boar's bristle brush through her hair.

She exited the bathroom and sat at the desk. For a long time, she stared at Beat from across the room. He lay sprawled across the bed now, despite the practice of these past weeks. He had tried to hone his senses to avoid rolling over her or pushing her out of their bed as he slept.

Light began to edge around the hems of the drapes on the hotel windows. Elinor checked her watch. More than an hour had slid past. Beat's right arm moved slowly across her side of the bed as he felt for her.

He sat up, bleary. He pulled the sheet over his lap, then reached for his glasses on the bedside table. He put them on and took in the room. His eyes widened as they focused on her.

Elinor laughed. "Good morning, Beat," she called.

"It's so early, Bunny. What were you staring at?" he asked. "You were so still there, so dreamy eyed."

"It's already late," she said. She walked to the window and raised the shade enough to let more early daylight into the room.

Beat stood and stretched. He snapped on the room lights. "Now I can see you," he said. The open closet door revealed Beat's uniform and his khakis along with Elinor's outfits. On the desk lay her purse, a Mayflower pen, a sheet of stationery with doodles across the top, and the black desk phone. The chair in the corner of the room held Beat's half-packed duffel bag.

"G' morning," Beat whispered as he walked to her. He kissed her ear, then touched the hickey underneath it with his nose. His lips feathered down her neck.

Electricity shot through her. She moved closer to him, and he tasted her. "Mmmm," he nuzzled into her neck.

She spanked his naked rear and giggled.

"I guess I need to get going, huh?" he asked.

She laughed and reached for him. "Oh, Beat," she murmured. "Let's make this day memorable." She stood and he put his arms around her. They held each other for a moment, then parted, smiling at each other.

"I'm glad you're up. We're off to an early start," she said. "I'll run down and get us a newspaper and something to eat."

Beat laughed. "Always my hungry Bunny," he said as he opened his wallet and sorted out the money that was left. He gave her a couple of bucks.

She stepped to the closet. For this last day she chose her white suit, now a bit wrinkled, but one of Beat's favorites. She ducked into the bathroom to slip into her clothes. She dabbed a bit of the Christmas Night perfume he'd brought her from Egypt behind her ears before combing her hair.

Dressed and ready, she kissed Beat as he arranged himself, hands behind his head, in a comfy heap on the bed. "I'll be back in a jiffy, " she said. "The Coffee Shop opened at six."

Elinor checked the hall as she exited the room. She wanted to avoid a certain hotel guest, an old pal of Beat's from Fargo, who had showed up at their door last night.

The guy had held a bottle of Hamm's in each hand. "Thought we could talk over old times," he laughed, holding a bottle toward Beat. "And war stories, too." When he noticed Elinor there in the room, he quickly apologized. "I didn't know you were married," he said.

And Beat replied, "I'm not," before he thought about Elinor's situation.

If he really loved her, he could've said they were engaged. At least. The whole situation had made her feel funny. Dirty. But it was all water under the bridge this morning. They'd talked it through last night, and Beat was genuinely sorry for the whole mess.

When she returned to the room with breakfast, Beat was drowsy again, but the sight of an up-to-date newspaper piqued his curiosity. Those were rare where he was going. And where he had been. He sat up on their bed, dressed now in a sleeveless undershirt and his undershorts.

Drinking his coffee, Beat devoured the news while Elinor sat at the desk and nibbled a maple sweet roll she had found in the restaurant below.

A door slammed. A group of men called to each other down the hotel hallway.

"Have you heard? There's a war on," one yelled. That was followed by laughter. Then momentary quiet.

"Yeah, see you back here when it's all over?" someone replied in a softer voice.

Elinor opened the curtains completely and let sunshine flood the room. She stood at the window and looked over the city. The past five weeks had been so busy that she could hardly remember the June train ride, when she had dashed from Fargo to Long Beach. This time Beat had been there to meet her. She smiled as she remembered falling into his arms at the depot.

For nearly two weeks, during the morning hours, he had waited aboard ship for the black gang to get the engines of the *San Carlos* in order. He checked and rechecked his equipment but mostly twiddled his thumbs.

During those weeks, Elinor spent the mornings searching for work. She read the want ads in the papers even before she tried the daily crossword puzzles. The jobs available for women insulted her: hatcheck girls, cigarette girls, or camera girls in nightclubs. No modeling at all. Nothing for a woman with a college degree, *summa cum laude*. Nothing for a girl with real talent.

Despite the war, Hollywood still cranked out movies, but the roles were reserved for already popular stars—Bette Davis or Hedy Lamar or lucky Lana Turner. There were lines of girls applying for even the most minor roles, and the possibilities for acting or singing in nightclubs were nil. How did Judy Garland and the Andrews Sisters, both acts from Minnesota, make it big?

A few mornings while Beat was on the ship, Elinor window-shopped and dreamed of owning store-bought clothing. She studied the styles and copied them the best she could in the homemade outfits she'd brought with her. Beat thought she looked fantastic. But when she looked into the mirror, she saw only a Bishop's daughter dressed *a la* Fargo style, not a fashionable *femme fatale* ready for the stage.

In the afternoons and evenings Beat returned to the hotel to spend time with her. They traveled from Long Beach to Hollywood three times. The two of them tried to get into Ciro's in West Hollywood, a place where the stars were known to hang out, but they were turned away at the door, despite Beat's best efforts.

Becoming Something Big? She began to think that The Fates had Something Else in mind for her.

Elinor raised the open window to allow in the last of the cool early morning air. The day would warm up soon enough. She noted the first stirs of activity in the city below, then turned to Beat.

"Here it is, Bunny," he said as he handed her the crossword puzzle.

She settled at the desk again and began automatically. "One across. 'Before the deadline.' Five letters."

She watched Beat read. He hadn't heard her. She stared out the window. She couldn't concentrate on the puzzle.

"Bunny, the Normandy beaches! We're moving in toward St. Lo," he laughed. "Hitler's had it now." Beat turned the page of the newspaper, delving into another section. Was he oblivious to how quickly the minutes were flying? Their last hours together?

Elinor stood and returned to the window.

After ten days of waiting for repairs to the engine, Beat had given up on the *San Carlos*. These new-fangled tankers had technical problems. And just when the war was really heating up, they were docked for overhauls. He had two weeks to find a new ship in San Francisco. So the two of them had taken a crowded train up the coast together.

The first few days in San Francisco had been a dream. Beat treated her like a movie star. Good food in famous nightclubs. Surprises as they shopped together. Doormen, even. And fresh sheets every morning. They had visited San Francisco's famed Chinatown. Beat bought her two friendship rings just because she had admired them in a trinket shop there. Over drinks and dinner at the Top of the Mark, they could see the enormity of the ocean Beat loved. They strolled the Embarcadero and the beaches. Beat introduced her to the good life, the easy life, the bigger world. He certainly knew his way around! And he thought she was Something Big.

Elinor walked back to the desk, picked up the pencil, and tried the crossword again. "Five across. Pacific Ocean sighter. Six letters," she thought. The answer could be E-L-I-N-O-R. She had seen the Pacific, all right. She doodled hearts in the margins.

One day Beat had run into their hotel room. "Bunny!" he laughed. "I've got a tanker for the next trip, another new ship. I signed on this morning at the WSA."

"Another tanker? Beat, those are sunk first." How could this make him so happy? Everyone knew that German and Japanese fighter planes looked for tankers for target practice.

He took her hand then and said, "Bunny, it's what I want. If I'm going to be cruising on the ocean, I want to go as fast as a ship can go. The *Buena Ventura* can escape those planes."

Elinor turned away from him.

"Bunny, I'm a good swimmer, and I'll survive, even if the Japs catch up with us." He walked behind her and put his arms around her waist. He kissed her neck. "No one can catch me."

She turned toward him, then. "Beat, I wish you didn't have to go." Missing D-Day had been a big disappointment to him. She realized, seeing Beat's excitement about getting back into the war, that their time together was nearly exhausted, their vacation over.

From then on, Beat had to report to the ship in the mornings to ready the equipment for the trip. He had new equipment to learn, and he had two assistants to train. The crew assembled, and some of the machinery of war came aboard in San Francisco. The aviation fuel would be laded last in Seattle. Then he'd be off into the battle.

Elinor and Beat had raced each other up the coast from San Francisco to Seattle. She caught trains, one connection after another, while Beat sailed north on the *Buena Ventura*. She wondered whether they'd ever see each other again, and then there he was, waiting for her in Seattle as her train pulled in.

Elinor threw her arms around him when Beat took her to the elegant room he had reserved for the two of them at the Mayflower Hotel! It was perfect.

For the past week and a half, while his ship was lading in Puget Sound, Beat escaped whenever he could to be with her. Those early July days were now a whirlwind of memories of happy times together.

They had had no trouble at all in the Romance Department. Elinor knew Beat was dangerous. She couldn't resist him. She had become one of those girls her father preached about, a girl who lost control of her passions, no longer able to calm the raging ardor—the sexual delirium—of her man.

Oh, she had been confident, nearly smug. After all, she had been assured that she didn't have to worry like other girls did. The headaches and the endometriosis were blessings, after all. She could get around just like the stars. She welcomed this new romantic life of hers, and she had taken advantage of the past five weeks to flirt boldly.

But "even good things have to come to an end," as her father often reminded the family. She heard his voice now.

And today it would end—their time together. Beat's new ship would sail after midnight. Toward some flaming islands in the Pacific. Into the war.

Elinor used her handkerchief to blot her nose and eyes. She stuffed it into her pocket, straightened her shoulders, and stood. She smoothed the wrinkles in her skirt as she walked toward Beat. She sat on the bed beside him and studied his face.

She would have to tell him.

He set down the newspaper and put one arm around her shoulders. "I love you," he declared.

She drew back a bit and looked into his eyes.

Noticing her face, then, he asked, "Bunny, is something wrong? Have you been crying?"

"Beat, 'those people' haven't come. I think I'm in trouble." She looked down at her lap.

He stared at her, his eyebrows lowered. He straightened his glasses. "What are you saying, Bunny?"

"I could be pregnant, I guess." She tried to smile. Her lips wobbled. When she pulled the hanky from her pocket, she frowned at the soggy mess.

"But, the doctors . . ." Beat reached toward her and wiped a tear from her cheek. "Bunny . . ."

"They said it wasn't likely. But I'm afraid . . ." Elinor brushed her hair back behind her ears. "Oh, Beat, I don't know for certain. Sometimes 'those people' are late. And the doctors have told me . . ."

Beat walked to his duffel bag, retrieved his white linen handkerchief, and handed it to her. He kissed her ear.

She blotted her nose and eyes.

"But I leave tomorrow. Well, tonight after midnight," Beat reminded her as he sat back down beside her. "The next trip into the Pacific will be a long one, Bunny."

Elinor straightened and faced him. "I just thought you'd want to know. Before you leave, I mean."

Beat sat quietly. He looked into his lap.

"I am so sorry if I've made you worry just before a trip, Beat. But I thought I should tell you before . . ."

He sneaked a peak at her lap. "What can you do?" he asked. "I mean this is such a surprise, Bunny."

"I could try to get rid . . . if I am pregnant, that is." She started to rise off the bed.

He took her hand and she sat again, an inch or two further from him.

"Well, you don't even know if you are expecting, Bunny. Let's not rush into anything." He tried to look at her, but averted his gaze. Instead, he looked toward the window in the hotel room.

Elinor caressed the sheet beside her on the bed, straightening it. "If I turn out to be pregnant and without a husband . . ." She stared straight ahead. "There's a Dr. Haugen in the Cities. The girls at college used to whisper about him. I could try to find him."

Beat stood up and walked to the open window. He stared outside at nothing in particular. "If anything happens to you . . ."

Elinor stood, too. She stuffed Beat's hanky in her pocket. "I'd have to try. My reputation . . ." She joined Beat at the window. "My father . . ." She sighed.

The noise from the traffic below interrupted their conversation. They stared together, for a moment, at the real world infiltrating their space.

Beat turned to her and put his arm around her waist. "This would be my child, then?" he asked. He pulled her close and smiled. He tickled her side.

She jabbed him with her elbow and giggled, then quickly sobered. "Beat, be serious."

He saw his opportunity and asked, "Will you marry me, then?"

Elinor turned away from the window. "Today?"

He nodded. "You look like a bride to me." He raised his eyebrows and grinned. "Let's do it."

She giggled. It sounded funny to her. Maybe she was hysterical. Getting married. He sounded like he really wanted to.

Beat drew her into a hug. He opened the top hook of her suit jacket. Then he kissed her neck and finished the unbuttoning. She stepped out of her clothing. They both tumbled back onto the bed. He crawled on top of her, and she reached for him.

"Remember the night we wrestled the bed to the floor? What hotel was that?" he teased.

Elinor sighed and relaxed under Beat. "Our last day together," he reminded her. "We have to make every moment count, Bunny. Who knows . . . how long . . . until . . ."

And then, speechless, he entered her. Elinor couldn't breathe. She caressed his chest as he powered into her, then lay still until his climax. When he was spent, she snuggled into his armpit as he lay beside her.

It all seemed easy to him. To her it all boiled down to two options. Disgrace or marriage. Unless "those people" would magically arrive. Today.

And so they spent their last hours together—to their mutual surprise—making wedding plans.

They dressed and then left the hotel to locate the courthouse. Because Beat was in the service, they were able to forego the normal waiting period for a marriage license. With signed papers in hand, they lined up with other military couples at the offices of the Justice of the Peace.

Beat checked his watch. The queue moved slowly, and he had an appointment with inspectors in his radio room after lunch.

Elinor looked at her watch, too. "Beat," she whispered in his ear. "It could be tomorrow before we'll get to the front of this line."

"Bunny, I . . ." Beat started.

"We could try to find a pastor to marry us. Someone who can make this official?"

"We have the license. Sounds perfect," Beat laughed as he took Elinor's hand.

He walked her to their hotel room and, while he ran to the pier to catch a launch to the *Buena Ventura*, Elinor searched the Yellow Pages for the nearest American Lutheran church.

"If it's a church ceremony, maybe Dad . . ." she thought as she dialed. The phone rang on the other end.

"Reverend Rasmussen?" Elinor could scarcely breathe. "Would you by any chance be free to do a little marriage ceremony this evening?"

Her hand gripped the black phone.

"Around seven, then? Thank you." Elinor set the handset into the cradle and put her head down on the desk.

"Oh, God," she moaned. "I should tell someone."

She debated calling her parents, but they'd be out in some congregation, away from home and the phone. Anyway, what could she say? And if "those people" arrived after all? They might never have to know.

She should call Mickey. But it was Wednesday, and Mick would be at work. Mickey would tell her to drop Darrow. And fast. Was that even possible at this point? Party boy or not, she and Beat had been playing with fire, and Elinor had played along. Willingly. How could she possibly explain her situation in a three-minute phone call?

Anyway, a long distance call would cost—money she didn't have.

Elinor located her valise. She began to fold her things, organizing them into neat stacks in her small satchel.

That evening Beat returned to the hotel in his dress uniform, with as much gold as he could muster on his cap and jacket. He knocked on the door of their room. When she opened it, he whistled.

"Oh, honey," Elinor laughed. "Just look at *you*! I'm all wrinkled."

Beat took her hand. "You look beautiful to me, Bunny," he said. He put his arms around his girl and she relaxed into him.

"I thought you'd be here earlier," she murmured.

"I had to run all of those tests and then the inspectors showed up. I did my best. After all it's our wedding night." Beat smiled down at her. He raised her chin and they looked in each others' eyes. "I'm starved. Let's get a bite first."

They took the elevator to the main level and entered the hotel dining room. The tables there had been set with white linen tablecloths and napkins. Tiny candles winked from the centers. Beat pulled out a chair for her. Elinor kissed his cheek as she sat.

A waiter arrived to take their orders. The bride-to-be sat on the edge of her chair. Beat leaned back in his. They looked at each other and smiled, at a loss for words.

When the food arrived, Elinor watched her groom eat. She had no taste for the chicken on her plate.

Beat cut into his steak. "Beautiful," he commented as he chewed.

Elinor sipped her drink. She tried to think of something to say.

Beat polished off every bite of his steak and all the side dishes, too. As he emptied his plate, Elinor said, "Darling, let's forget about getting married tonight. 'Those people' are bound to come. The doctors at Mayo . . ."

Beat interrupted. "But you called a pastor?"

"We arranged a seven o'clock ceremony, but you were still on the ship then. It's so late now. We missed our chance."

"Damn, Bunny, I . . . What can we do?" He reached for her hand. "We have the license. We should be able to find someone, even at this hour."

"We're not in Las Vegas, Beat. Don't worry. I'll be fine. It's not likely that . . ." Elinor folded her napkin and set it on the table." Anyway, I have plans for my life. I'll be okay."

They moved into the bar and sat there in the Mayflower Hotel with nothing more to say. The hands on Elinor's watch moved to 11:00, and Beat ordered another round. He reached into his pocket and felt for his lucky gold coin.

"I wish you didn't have to go, Beat. To war." Her voice sounded muddled. Had she said that right? How many drinks had she had?

Close to midnight, Elinor excused herself. "I'd better run into the restroom to freshen up. For our last good-bye." She stood up carefully, then remembered to smile.

Beat nodded, wiping his mouth with the back of his hand. He snapped his fingers to call the waiter over for the check.

Elinor made her way toward the ladies' room across the lobby. She entered the too bright space, avoiding the mirror as she rushed toward a stall. She locked the door and crumpled against it.

"Please God," she prayed. "I promise I'll be so good from now on." She set her purse on the floor by the toilet. "No matter how he tempts me." She proceeded to check her underwear.

"Damn," she whispered as she pulled her panties back up. Although she never swore out loud, in case her parents might hear, in this private space, under these conditions, she needed to exhale a real curse.

She slammed the door of the stall as she exited.

Alone in the restroom, she stood before the mirror. As she washed her hands, she studied her face—so pale under the bright lights. She pinched her cheeks. "I have to buck up," she murmured. She dabbed a dot of lipstick on each cheek and spread it into her skin. "There! Some color."

She stretched her lips to put on fresh red lipstick, then dabbed some of it back off with a toilet paper square. She combed her hair, then straightened her back and threw her purse strap over her left shoulder.

When Elinor exited the restroom, she spied Beat across the lobby at the front desk.

"Anything for Darrow Beaton?" he asked. He paced, his right hand in his pocket, while the clerk checked. "Oh, thanks!" Beat left the guy a tip. Civilians these days were eager to help a serviceman.

Elinor laughed then, seeing Beat there unwrapping the florist's paper from around a nosegay of roses. "You're so sweet," she whispered as she walked to him and kissed him on the cheek.

He grinned and handed her the bouquet. "For my bride," he laughed.

"But, Beat," she put her hand on his.

"I've called your Reverend Rasmussen. Think I woke him. But he's waiting for us. For our wedding."

"Tonight? Now? This late?"

"Bunny, I want to get married, and he's still willing to help us out."

"Oh, Beat." Elinor dipped her nose into the flowers. "It'll seem almost like the real thing with these."

They caught a cab outside their hotel. Since they would be driving away from the piers, there would be no additional sailors going their way. They were alone. Darrow put his arm over the back of the seat and around her shoulders. Elinor sat stiffly. Their eyes met. She saw tension in his, but love, too—probably a mirror of her own eyes. He grinned at her. "It's gonna be fun," he coaxed. He patted her shoulder.

She snuggled into his chest, then reached up to kiss him, a soft promise.

Reverend Rasmussen and his wife met them at the doors of the church. The building was empty, cool, and dark.

"We're so sorry to interrupt your sleep." Elinor tried to apologize.

"For a serviceman," the good reverend replied with a tired smile, as he fumbled for the light switches in the gloom. When he found them, he invited Elinor and Darrow into the nave. They walked to the front with him and stood before the altar.

The vows that took forever at Yupps' wedding weren't really all that interminable. There were no sermons this time. No ceremonial marches up and down the aisle either. No family or friends to celebrate with them. No formal music, the usual backdrop of the pledges. A long life ahead began with just a couple of minutes of promises.

As she pledged to love and obey her husband Elinor thought, "What an odd tradition for the modern age!" She pushed her hair back behind her ears, turned toward Beat and winked.

Beat laughed out loud. Then he slipped a friendship ring, one that he'd bought her in Chinatown, on Elinor's finger. It would have to do.

At one o'clock A.M. on July 14, Reverend Rasmussen signed the marriage certificate and gave it to the bride.

Elinor wondered, after all the rituals she had attended, whether a person could take such a scanty ceremony seriously? Was this really legal?

The four of them exited the church, locked the doors and walked next door to the parsonage for coffee. Mrs. Rasmussen offered an after midnight snack for the occasion.

Elinor protested, "We really have to run."

She thought of her parents and the many times they had entertained in the parsonages of their lives. They had wanted her to marry into the clergy. And then she would've had such a role—a pastor's wife, the baker of cakes, the hostess for guests to the parsonage, the mostly invisible support for her husband. But what role would Beat's wife play? Well, the same as any wife, she supposed. A good wife supported her husband in myriad ways.

"What are your plans?" Reverend Rasmussen asked.

Beat and Bunny turned toward each other, shrugged in unison, and laughed.

"I guess we haven't exactly made plans," Elinor confessed. "That's hard to do these days." She pushed her hair behind her ears and smiled. She hoped that The Fates were in control, but these days it seemed that they had abandoned the world.

"There's a war on, you know," Beat added. "And I'll be back in it in a couple of hours."

Mr. and Mrs. Beaton excused themselves and taxied back downtown to the Mayflower, where they took the elevator to their room.

"Beat," Elinor murmured when her new husband picked her up and carried her over the threshold. It was like a scene from a movie. She laughed and then reached to kiss him for thinking of that.

They sat together on the bed.

Beat fidgeted. He checked his seaman's wallet. Everything was in order. He settled it into his back pocket and sat again. "Have you got your ticket home?" he asked.

Elinor found her purse on the floor by the bed where she had dropped it. She patted the front pocket.

"It's okay, Beat," she assured him. She smiled at him. "Can you believe we did it?" she asked. "We're married, and it's our secret." She rejoined him on the bed.

Beat put his arm around her. "Bunny, this is going to be a long trip. Will you write to me? I want to know how things are going with 'those people.' And with your parents." He stroked her hair.

"Oh, Beat, there's never much to say. Nothing happens in Fargo, but I'll write. As soon as I know anything."

"You'll see the doctor right away, then?"

The serious look on his face made her smile. She probably wasn't pregnant, after all. This quick marriage was just in case. "Don't worry, Beat."

He leaned over her to kiss her cheek. "My little wife," he whispered. "My own wife." He checked his watch. "This is it, honey," he reminded his bride. "1:40."

Elinor leaned toward him and offered a tight smile. "Well, now you have a wife, Beat. No more 'girl in every port', huh?" She rested her head on his shoulder for a moment.

Beat shrugged his shoulder. "Sure bet, Elinor. I'm a one-girl man." He turned toward her. "And you'll be on the train tomorrow. Back to Fargo. You'll need to let your 'old friends' know right away." He stood and picked up his duffle bag. "We clear the decks, Bunny. We're married now. No more girlfriends for me. Or 'old friends' for you."

Elinor looked away. She stared into the distance. "It was a short honeymoon, Beat." Her voice sounded far away. "One day, I hope we can afford a proper wedding ring. A diamond. Big as Ginny's?" She stood and wrapped her arms around Beat's neck.

Beat nodded. "Sure. Whatever you want, honey." He leaned toward her. "After the war."

"For now, though, let's keep our arrangement a secret," Elinor continued. "Then we can have a big wedding when you come back. Lots of girls are doing that these days. If I'm not . . ."

"It's a secret until you tell your parents." Beat brushed his lips across her cheek. "Damn, Elinor. You have to tell your parents."

"That'll be a problem," Elinor said as she pressed the fingers of both hands into her temples and rubbed circles. "If I am pregnant . . . That's another story." She closed her eyes. "Well, I just can't be."

"It's gonna be great," Beat reassured her. He patted her shoulder with one hand and pulled out his wallet with the other. "You can handle it, sweetie." He checked his papers and looked at his watch. He kissed his wife gently on the forehead. "I hate to run, but I'm already late, honey."

She murmured, "I love you, Beat. Bon voyage."

Beat opened the door just as Elinor remembered his shaving equipment.

"Your razor!" She ran into the bathroom to get it. She handed the razor to Beat.

He stuffed it into his duffel bag and turned quickly away from her. He threw his shoulders back and strutted down the hall.

She stood in the doorway and watched him leave. At the elevator he turned to wave to her, and she blew him a kiss. She stood tall, too. She had to be brave, to see her man off to war. She couldn't let him know how much she worried about what they'd done.

Then she slipped back into their room and closed the door with the merest click. She threw herself onto their bed, squeezing his pillow in her arms, alone now.

An Explosive Cargo

July 14, 1944 in the early morning hours

IN THE CAB ON the way to the wharf, Beat checked his seaman's papers again. He ran through his list of preparations before leaving port. He was ready. Everything for the trip was set.

But the home front wasn't settled. He couldn't be much help, riding from port to port, hoping to get mail, and sending advice in his letters to her. Would she have misgivings about this rushed ceremony?

Marriage to Elinor. His dream come true. He sighed.

He caught a launch to the tanker, now moored further out, away from the city, loaded with its cargo of aviation fuel for delivery in the South Pacific.

As he climbed up the gangplank, Beat put his hand over his nose, bothered by the strong fumes emanating from the fuel tanks. He'd have to get used to it. This would be a long voyage. Perhaps the ocean breezes would alleviate some of the odor of the many gas tanks aboard.

He made the last jump to the deck of the *Buena Ventura* and turned to look back toward Seattle. His wife was faced with so many decisions just as he was exiting the scene. "God in Heaven," he prayed as he looked upward at the dark night sky. His nerves jangled, he resorted to a god he didn't even believe in.

He took a last look at the stars overhead. He had to remind himself that the troops just over the horizon, on the other side of the earth, needed this cargo. And they were desperate. He had to leave. A cold sweat crept over him.

He turned toward the ship. His eyes took in the antennas above him as he began to automatically check his equipment. In his dash toward the radio room, he nearly ran smackdab into the Master.

"Nearly time, Beaton," the Captain warned.

Beat ducked into his quarters. He snapped the desk light on. He removed his jacket and cap and threw them on the spare chair. He flipped on the emergency receiver speaker and breathed in the static of 500 kHz. He twisted the dials to test the transmitter. He couldn't do that after they moved into enemy territory, and he needed assurance that the radio could send out a message if necessary. Amber lights glowed on the controls. Beat finished recording in the logbook, then stood.

He slapped his back pants pocket. His fingers found his lucky World's Fair coin. A smile curled at his lips. "Thanks," he muttered as he gave it one last rub with his thumb.

Then he reached for his jacket and found his cigarettes in the inside pocket. He slid one out of the pack, tamped it on his desk, and lit it with the cigarette lighter he'd bought on the last trip. His fingers shook and the flame danced. He returned to his chair, took a drag and tried to calm his breathing. A thin thread of smoke curled into the gloomy air in the room.

"This is no way to begin a marriage," he muttered. "Goddamnit!"

The deckhands stood ready to push off at high tide. He heard their shouts to each other as they double-checked the lashings holding the PT boats on the deck, then the neoprene gaskets on the fuel tanks. Everything was battened down, all right. He heard their laughs, their bravado, as the ship began to pull away, moving further into the Pacific.

This time Beat didn't dash out onto the deck to watch as they moved away from the States. He couldn't bear to think of the girl he had left behind. His wife, for godssake.

He sighed. He set his cigarette into the ashtray where it waited, glowing red. He leaned over his mill, inserted a piece of onionskin, wrapped it around the platen, and began a letter to his wife, the first of this journey.

He wondered what he'd hear from her at the next port. Or the one after that. Would she be happy?

Or pregnant?

Courage

July 14, 1944

July 14, 1944
Bremerton
0230

My Darling Wife,

It seems somehow improper to type this letter
to you, my darling. It should be handwritten,
I'm sure. There are so many things going through
my mind, Bunny.

This is a day we shall long remember, Bun,
and it seems to be a bit mixed up for us both.
There are so many things that have to be
settled. As soon as things are straightened
out, this day will assume the importance for us
that it should have. I know you still have the
"big job" ahead of you, darling, and I wish,
too, that I could be of some help to you when
you get home and talk this thing over with the
folks. Try some way or another to convey the
confidence we have in our marriage to them.

At last I'm sure of what I want for life.
As I sit here this morning, I feel a lot older

and ever so more important to the world and civilization. I want to deserve you and all of the good things you are, Elinor.

I'm ever so lonesome for you now. It's an old familiar feeling. This time it is even harder, as we've just been married seven hours now. I'm listening to Frisco overseas radio, and the music reminds me of the times I shall be sitting in some place a long way from you reading your letters. And it reminds me over and over again of the very wonderful times we have had in the last month and that it will be some time before we are together again.

Never shall I forget how you have come through in the toughest times with flying colors and proved to me beyond any doubt that you possess the necessary courage to go through life happily. I'm mighty proud of that, Bunny, as I like to have you have a lot of backbone. We both must have our share of it to have been married this way.

You'll be wandering out soon, and I imagine calling Alfred. It's darn nice to have someone to help you get your train and all. Your ride home won't be too bad on the *North Coast Limited*, as it isn't as crowded as the other railroads you have been traveling. You'll be home Sunday afternoon and see the family and start resting up. As soon as we get in, I shall call you and see how things are with you there. Be good to hear your voice again, Bun.

"I'll Be Seeing You" is now playing, and it echoes my sentiments quite perfectly, darling. It's been so long that I've wanted to marry ya and all, and all along things were happening to make me wonder if we ever would be married. And now we are married and all my dreams have come true. This time as I leave you, I don't have to reprimand myself for not having married you.

I'm more or less excited yet. Even though I didn't get much sleep, I'm darn sharp right now and starting to wake up a bit. And I find myself so happy, Bunny—so darn perfectly happy. I've got all kinds of wonderful plans, and I'm going to make all of them come true for us soon.

We're just embarked on a long life with each other, so let's have fun all the while. We have some time now to prepare for our life together, and I plan to make it count as much as possible. We'll go on having the same kind of fun as before, darling, with a bit more purpose added. We're finally started on the life we have so often dreamed about.

Your loving husband,
Beat

Toward Home

July 15, 1944

ELINOR CHECKED. THE TICKET was still in her purse. She dressed in a rush, jumped into her yellow sundress and ran a comb through her hair. Then she finished packing for the train ride back to Dakota. She scoured the hotel room for anything she might've missed.

And while she reorganized her life, she prayed. "'Those people' would be welcome visitors any time," she begged, "even with a headache."

Before checking out, she tidied the room and closed the window, pulling the drapes shut, too.

She walked the two flights downstairs to the Coffee Shop in the Mayflower. She set her valise, her book, and her purse beside her on a chair. The bellboy had brought her larger suitcase to the desk. Then she ordered her usual, a maple sweet roll and coffee. As she nibbled, she wondered what Beat was doing, exactly where his ship would be going.

What about her parents? She gulped her coffee. Hot! She coughed.

She breathed a short prayer for her husband's safety, then a longer plea for her period. And when she looked up, she saw Alfred coming from the lobby through the door of the restaurant.

He took off his Army uniform jacket and draped it gently over Elinor's shoulders. "You look cold," he whispered. He kissed her on the cheek.

"Thanks," she managed. She was. "I'm shivering. I don't know why."

She paid for her breakfast and they walked slowly out of the hotel, Alfred carrying her big satchel and her valise, she with her purse and her book for the trip. The sun winked as a few high clouds passed over its face. The day would be, predictably, hot. A few clouds lingered way out over the water, and she imagined she could smell the ocean breezes, the same ones she and Beat had enjoyed while they relaxed on their way up the coast.

She could almost hear the waves slapping away at Beat's ship, even though she knew the tanker had moved away from the city to take on aviation fuel. She studied Seattle as they walked. These would be her last views of the city, and she wanted to remember everything.

She and Alfred walked on together, to King Street, to the train station.

Alfred handed her suitcase to a Red Cap, then turned the valise over to her. "Well, it's been nice seeing you again, Elinor. I'm sure glad you looked me up again when you got to town."

"I always check in on my 'old friends,'" she replied with a quick hug.

The locomotive wheezed and panted but remained in its spot waiting for the signal.

Elinor shivered as she removed Alfred's jacket. "Thank you, Alfred . . ." She returned the jacket to her old friend and kissed him on the cheek. "If you hadn't come along, I'm not sure I could have found this place."

"You know, Elinor," he stammered, "not long ago, this was us, saying good-bye. When I signed up."

Elinor nodded.

"I remember how you thought there would be no American involvement in this thing, this war," he went on. "I sometimes wonder how things might've been different." He caught the frog in his throat before continuing, "For us, I mean."

Elinor nodded and smiled tenderly at her old friend. She remembered their fun times. "Mmmm," she murmured. "You never know what The Fates have in mind." Elinor patted his hand. "Now you've met Helene and your life has changed."

Alfred stepped forward and gave her a quick hug, then turned to go. Elinor waved at him until he disappeared around the corner of the station.

Then she opened her purse and checked. Her ticket was still there. She had the marriage certificate. Everything was in order. She snapped her purse shut and pulled the strap over her shoulder. She slid her book under her arm, picked up her valise, and stepped resolutely toward the train.

The porter set down a stepstool for her. She hastened up the trembling iron steps of the *North Coast Limited* and entered the passenger car.

This train wasn't as crowded as the one coming to Seattle. Then the train had been filled with servicemen. Guys who had joined the Navy or the Army were jamb-packed into the cars, destined for their training camps somewhere on the coast. It was a party then, as they traveled together, alcohol and laughter. The time in the train had simply flown by.

She found a window seat. A sailor helped her lift her small valise up to the shelf overhead. She thanked him and then, arranging her skirt, she settled herself lightly, her purse by her side. She placed the book on her lap. *Thirty Seconds Over Tokyo*, Lawson's report on Jimmy Doolittle's raid on Japan.

She looked out the window. Soldiers and sailors scurried around on the platform, rushing to trains that would take them into or further out of the war. A porter, pushing a cart of luggage toward the depot, dashed past. In his mother's arms, a small child waved at a serviceman who rushed to board another train.

Elinor wished she hadn't packed her sweater. Now it was somewhere in the bowels of this big train, in the luggage car, along with the matchbook covers she and Beat had saved on their travels and the souvenirs Beat had brought her from the exotic ports he'd seen. She twisted the friendship ring on her left hand.

The two seats facing her were taken up with boys from the Navy on leave before shipping out. Recent high school grads, she guessed—like some of the students she had taught in Pelican Rapids. Was that really only a year ago? They were already busy swapping stories and wouldn't disturb her much.

A Catholic nun arrived to take the seat next to her. Destiny. That's what it was. God must be reminding her. Sex before marriage was a sin. She nodded to her seatmate, then turned away.

She needed to think through this last turn of events. For Pete's sake! She was a married woman now. If only her seat were a phone booth, something she could close off and steam up with her thinking!

Elinor had only two days until this train would pull into the Fargo station. Two days to plan a cover story that her father would find feasible. She would be held accountable. She was an unchaperoned woman, and her parents had trusted her.

"All aboard."

The whistle. The jerk of the procession of passenger cars as they awoke in turn and, startled, began the parade away from the station. The train threaded past another train crawling into the station.

"Probably loaded with servicemen," Elinor thought. Everyone seemed to be coming and going. Mostly saying good-bye, it seemed, in this war.

The train, a torpid snake, left the depot behind and lumbered through the town.

Elinor stared out her window. She remembered last night—the roses, their wedding. Beat carrying her into the room.

The nun, sitting stiffly in her habit beside her, asked in a soft voice, "So, where are you heading, my dear?"

"Fargo." Elinor turned back to her window and her thoughts.

The *North Coast Limited* began picking up speed. Downtown buildings behind them now, they passed houses, rows of cozy homes with children playing in the yards. The train pounded across a trestle over a serene river. The water, of course, ran to the Pacific, and that brought Elinor's thoughts back to Beat. Her husband, for Pete's sake.

The train accelerated, a runaway stallion. It moved too fast to focus on any single place more than a few seconds. Every once in a while the engineer sounded the whistle as they flew through the countryside, past railroad crossings and through small towns.

Elinor opened up her book. Jimmy Doolittle. He'd already gone down in history! Even though she wasn't in the mood for reading, she felt even less like talking with her seatmate, a stranger. And a Catholic, to boot. Lutherans and Catholics weren't supposed to mix. But then, neither were Germans and Irish.

The conductor arrived to check tickets. Elinor put her book down and dug into her purse to find hers. She pulled out the folder for it, found the ticket inside and presented it to the conductor for punching. She returned it to her purse and leaned back in her seat. She opened the book, tried to read, and found herself staring at the pages, thinking about her parents, planning the next step.

The train pounded down the track, nearer to Dakota by the minute.

"Main Street of the Northwest"

THE AIR-CONDITIONED

NORTH COAST LIMITED

Ticket to Fargo

I Have You Forever

July 1944

LETTER 2
July 14, 1944
AT SEA

My darling wife,

Told the guys I was married this morning, and we had a big celebration here. Of course I took a lot of kidding and a lot of advice from the old-timers. Somehow I didn't feel much like laughing and kidding about it. It's something quite serious and important to me, darling, and too much of such banter kinda gets me. When a guy misses his wife so darn much as I miss you, Bunny, there just can't be any feeling but sadness. There are so many situations and complications to be thought out as best a guy can, and that has occupied my mind for the most part today.

You'll be trying to sleep tonight on the train in one of the hard and uncomfortable coach seats, and you'll no doubt do much in the way of thinking, too, my darling. The saddest feeling comes over me when I think of you all cuddled up there getting farther and farther from me all the time. I've got a cigar in my mouth to give me a bit of false courage now.

I'll call you the first night. By that time some of the difficulties should have been aired. Please, whatever you do, darling, don't let me go on worrying about how your parents feel and all. I want to know right away, as it will get all of this worry off my mind whatever the outcome is.

I know that we have been fortunate to have had all of this time together, but I'd have liked to have spent a few days with you after we were married to grow used to the idea with you near me. It would be fun to call you "wife" and other pet names for a few days so that I could know how it feels. When I think of you as my wife, my heart could almost break into pieces. Our letters will help us to learn what married life is like, more or less. But it would have been good to have had a few days in which to map things out.

As long as we live, I'll always feel indebted to you for things you have done for me, darling, and always a bit surprised, too, that I actually have you forever. I love you so terribly much, darling.

Your loving Husband,
Beat

※ ※

July 15, 1944

It's getting dark now, with the air full of clouds and a touch of fog and cold. It's a dreary sort of a night. You're on your train now, going toward home and the folks. It's after eight thirty now, and I suppose you are in an animated conversation with some old lady or some sailor or soldier who won't believe you are married.

Since marrying you, Bun, I've done a lot of thinking and finally decided what I'll work toward for making a living. There are so many subjects which will help a man in any number of jobs, all of which I would enjoy and work hard at. I'm re-reading my salesmanship book and reviewing all the important points in it. There are a few good books on politics here which I shall read. My book on business law hasn't been cracked for some time, and I'll study through that, too.

※ ※

LETTER 4
Sunday
Off Frisco

Dearest Wife,

This is the big day for you, and I know that as you sit on the train drawing within minutes of Fargo there are many thoughts going through your mind. It's just about three o'clock in that part of the country, so the train is not too far from Fargo.

You'll be wondering how to tell the folks we are married, first. Maybe you'll try to put it off for a day or two. You'll be wondering what the doctor will tell you tomorrow morning when you visit him. There are so many problems for you to attempt to straighten out all at once. I know you are getting those nervous chills and getting more or less afraid of the outcome again. But if I can help you from way out here, I'll be trying hard to think things out for you until I call tomorrow. Maybe some bit of mental telepathy will give you some added courage and make you sure that we have done the wise thing.

If "those people" come, it will automatically loosen the pressure a lot on us right now, Bunny. I know things will come around our way, darling, and I just hope you feel the very same way.

Well, you should have met the folks by now, darling. It's three thirty there, and the train is supposed to come in about that time or close to it. There'll be many sighs of relief from them at seeing you back home safe again, I know, and I think they will know right away that you have something to tell them. If only I knew for sure that you were going to tell them before tomorrow night, I could call for the first time for Mrs. Beaton.

I don't relish the idea of hiding this greatest event in my life from people who should mean so much to me. They'll think I'm trying to be sly or something, when I really want to run outside and let the whole world know I'm married to you, darling.

Life will be so much more enjoyable when we once get settled and find ourselves together with everyone accepting the fact that we love each other and that we plan to make a success of our life together. I wish so much that we had been able to do this thing in the right manner. Oh, Bunny, it is going to be wonderful if the home front comes around!!

If things are all right, darling, we shall be able to work things out perfectly. We may be able to have a wedding as you have always wanted. I'm using all my brain power trying to contact you in Fargo with my thoughts here!

Your faithful husband,
Beat

So Much for Plans

6:25 A.M.

ELINOR STOOD AND STRETCHED. She set down the last letters and walked to the front of the house to open the door. Ching rubbed against her leg. She bent over to scratch him behind his ears and felt the rumbling before she heard it. Thunder? She opened the porch door.

A runaway breeze blew through the porch and into the hallway, swirling through 1135. Elinor's pile of onionskin letters on her father's desk trembled in the fresh gust. She dashed back into the study and settled the copper ashtray and the round typewriter eraser on her papers. Then she stepped back to the front door.

A cool fall rain now splashed on the front sidewalk. The last reluctant leaves that still dangled in the trees began to loosen their grip as gusts of wind played tag in the branches. Oak and elm and cottonwood leaves twirled as they neared the ground and, at last, congregated under the streetlight on the corner, where they settled, wet and clean.

Elinor breathed in the fresh night air. She shivered. How she loved these prairie rains! In a month—maybe next week—this would be snow.

When the cloudburst calmed, Elinor closed the door again and returned to her work. She put away the weights she had arranged to hold her papers in place.

She sighed. Well, she'd cooked her own goose. It had been a mistake to keep this whole affair a secret. A mistake to hope that life would go on a different track. She had trusted The Fates—fought against them, too—and now she had to accept their decision.

So much for Something Big.

It was time to face her life.

Little White Lies

July 1944

T HE *NORTH COAST LIMITED* passed the scattered streetlights of Fargo and rumbled through intersections. With the bell clanging and a screeching protest from the brakes, it lurched into the station and came to a stop. A cloud of steam hissed upward as the engineer vented the boiler.

The sailor Elinor had been talking with for much of the tiresome journey leapt up to see her to the door of the car. He grabbed her valise off the overhead shelf, handed it to her and put his hand on her arm. She thanked him and turned toward the door of the passenger car.

"Here I go," she called to him. "Good luck on your leave at home."

"Will I see you again?" he asked.

Elinor laughed. She remembered slipping her friendship ring off and stashing it in her purse. As she turned away, she supposed she should have mentioned that she was newly married.

Over the loudspeaker, the stationmaster announced, "Now arriving. The *North Coast Limited* from Bismarck, Dickinson, Bozeman . . . Seattle."

Reverend Landgrebe greeted his daughter. "*Sei gegrüsst!*" he shouted, the usual opening to his German sermons. "Be greeted." He laughed as he reached for her. "Good to have you home again," her father whispered.

Elinor hugged him. She looked around at the tired looking city. She missed the tense energy of a busy port during wartime.

Elinor located her old brown suitcase on the baggage cart, grabbed it, and handed it to her father.

"I'm so glad you're in town," she thanked her father. "I feel so tired right now. I don't think I could walk a single block with my luggage, Dad." She handed her valise to her father, too. "That train ride was exhausting. I can't sleep very well in those seats. How do you do it?"

Georg laughed. He was often so tired on his trips around the synod that sleep was no problem, no matter the seating.

They hiked to the car, and Georg deposited the bags into the trunk. The two of them settled themselves into the black Pontiac.

"It's so hot and humid," Elinor said, as she rolled the windows down to vent the car. "And gray," she added in a whisper.

"How was the trip, then?" her father asked.

"Okay, I guess." Elinor stared out of her window of the car. The sky threatened rain. Good for the garden, but she missed California's sunshine. "There aren't jobs on the coast. Not for me, anyway." She felt the motion of the wheels underfoot again, the norm of the past days.

"Well, then, we'll have you at home a while yet?"

Elinor nodded. "Maybe, Dad. If that's okay. At least on the weekends. If I teach again this fall."

Georg laughed, "Of course, Bunny." He reached toward her to pat the hand she had put out on the seat between them.

"I wonder if I'll be able to walk," she laughed. "I've been cooped up so long on that train."

The big car swooped down the alley and then into the driveway at 1135, and the family rushed out of the house to greet them. Elinor stepped out of the car. She felt woozy as she stood and leaned just a moment on the Pontiac. She noticed her mother's eyes following her movement, so Elinor pulled her purse strap over her shoulder and straightened her shoulders.

Trudie hugged her fiercely. "I'm glad you're back," she whispered. "Are you feeling well? You look a little pale. Are you tired?"

Elinor hugged her mother. "I am. Long train ride, Mother. I missed you," she said. She sighed. Home.

Then Irene and Mickey surrounded their sister. "C'mon, Bunny. We want to hear all about it," Mickey laughed. They walked, arm in arm, three sisters with Elinor in the middle, into the house.

There they gathered around the dining room table, ice water in their glasses, while Elinor spun a few stories about her adventures trying to find a job. "I tried in several cities. I went from Long Beach to Seattle. Still no good jobs in Long Beach, Mickey, and it's a lot more crowded than last year. It's hard to even find a place to stay." She sipped her drink. Then she scratched her head and pushed her hair behind her ears.

"What did you do then? Where did you stay?" Her mother seemed unusually curious.

"I found some old friends, Mother, and stayed with them. In sleeping rooms. Then I tried San Francisco." Well, it wasn't exactly a lie. Just a small white one.

"You saw some of your 'old friends?'" Trudie asked. "Who? How are they?"

"Some of the gals Mickey and I knew in Long Beach. And I found Alfred in Seattle, Mom. He's doing well. He won't actually be going over. He's stationed in Seattle for the duration. He saw me to my train as I was leaving." Elinor looked into her lap, then into her mother's eyes. "I know how you love him, Mother."

"And . . . ?" Irene, the tease.

Elinor looked away from the family. She focused on her piano. "Johnny's gone now. I don't know where. You know how it is in this war. Secrets. Dale's shipped now, too. I couldn't find either of them this time." Elinor wiped her damp hands on the napkin in her lap.

Irene grinned. "But what about Darrow?" She had a familiar glint in her eyes.

Elinor looked directly at her sister. "Well, I did look him up. Beat's fine. He joined the crew of a different ship, and they're heading into the Pacific now." She snapped out the words she'd practiced on the train.

Her mother, head tilted a bit, eyebrows thinking, squinted at her.

"So you saw Darrow then?" Her father's voice rumbled. "He's finally heading into the war? Out of this country?"

Elinor nodded. She swallowed the last gulp of her water. She couldn't look at her father.

"You must be so tired," her mother declared. She stood then. Irene had already ducked into the kitchen to deposit a few glasses in the sink. Trudie joined her and hugged Irene.

Georg put on his gardening hat and exited into the back yard. The screen door slammed as he left.

Elinor sat at the piano. She started with "I'll Walk Alone" and "There Are Such Things."

Mickey stood behind her sister. She closed her eyes as she listened to the tunes Elinor had selected. "Good to have you home again," she whispered in her big sister's ear. "Everything okay?"

Elinor nodded as she played. She surely hoped everything would turn out okay. At least for the moment she had escaped the hard questions that were sure to come. If only "those people" would knock on her door!

Later that afternoon, Elinor unpacked her suitcases. Mickey sat on the daybed. The girls chatted about the West Coast as Elinor hung her things back in the family coat closet. She showed Mickey some of the trinkets she'd brought home from San Francisco. The girls both tried on the friendship rings and then Elinor settled them into her pink jewelry box. She hadn't mentioned Beat's name.

Mickey reached into her pocket and located a package of Lucky Strikes. She popped one out of the cellophane and settled it between her lips. She jumped up and located the box of matches on her father's desk. She sat back on the daybed.

"Okay, Bunny," she said with the cigarette between her teeth. She lit the cigarette and inhaled. Then, removing the cigarette from between her lips, she continued. "Let's have the real story, kid. Beat?"

Elinor grabbed her white suit from the suitcase and turned to the closet to find a hanger. The excuses she'd planned on the train melted away. She couldn't think. She turned to face her little sister. "I probably saw too much of him, Mickey. We had a lot of fun before he sailed." She pursed her lips and glared at her sister.

"Bunny, I warned you. He's no good. You've got to drop the guy," Mickey hissed. "And Irene . . ."

"I know." Elinor had nothing more to say. She kept unpacking.

At supper Elinor presented her father with film for his camera. Georg clapped his hands and stowed the rolls in a dark drawer of his desk. Film was hard to come by stateside, and Beat had purchased the correct size this time. Three rolls of 620, another diversion. She couldn't find the words to tell her father that Beat was the donor, that her husband had found the film.

All the rest of the evening, Elinor hung around in the den. She tried reading her book about Jimmy Doolittle's adventures, but she was distracted by thoughts of her Seattle wedding. She couldn't decide how to tell her family. What to tell her family. Whether to tell her family.

She drank coffee and paced. She felt nauseous. It was probably all the rich food on the coast. This might be an overdue migraine planning its arrival. Or, miracle! Could 'those people' be making an appearance?

Eventually she was drawn back to the piano bench. She played their favorites: "Sweet Eloise," "There Are Such Things," "Don't Get Around Much Any More," and "You'll Never Know."

Her thoughts shifted to the coast. She wondered where Beat was, how the weather was there, what he had been doing. She wondered whether he missed her.

She tried to put together a cogent sentence that would explain things to her parents, but she couldn't find words that fit together. "Married." The word sounded profane now.

At ten, she settled in the den at the Scott radio and listened to the news with her father. War news, the war her husband would sail into again. This time, she knew, his ship floated with a belly full of aviation fuel, and the deck held armaments of all kinds. She wished Beat would stop smoking, just for this run.

Maybe, she thought ruefully, she should ask her father to stop smoking, too. She worried that the Landgrebe house might explode when she announced her secret.

Much later, with everyone else abed upstairs, the phone rang. Elinor hadn't slept, hadn't even settled a sheet over herself, while waiting—hoping—for his call. She jumped off her daybed and grabbed the black receiver in the middle of the first ring.

"Are you okay, Beat? Where are you? How's the new ship working out?" Elinor spoke in a whisper, using her hand to cover the mouthpiece. She scrunched herself up on the floor away from the stairway to the upstairs bedrooms. She tried to pull the phone under her father's big oak desk, but the cord refused to follow her all the way.

"It's hot here, too. Humid and gloomy."

She watched the clock. Beat rattled on about his ship. She had no news.

When their time was nearly up, when he finally asked the question, she told him, "Mmmm. No. Not yet. But I'll tell them soon."

※　　※

On Monday morning, first thing, Elinor appeared in Dr. Hunter's office. As she opened the door of the clinic, the smell of the disinfectant nearly overcame her. She registered with the nurse at the desk, then sat quickly in a chair. Nausea overwhelmed her. She just needed a breath of fresh air, she supposed. She looked at her lap and sat still as a statue in order to settle her nerves.

In a while, a nurse led her to a white room which held mostly an examination table covered with a paper cloth. Elinor sat small in a chair in the corner. Dr. Hunter arrived.

"So, well, Elinor," he began. "A missing period?"

Elinor nodded. "But I don't think I could be pregnant. Do you?"

"We can do the test. It's easy. A little urine sample and then the lab will inject that into a rabbit. If the rabbit's ovaries have changed, we'll have an answer."

Elinor sighed.

"Have you married since I last saw you?" the doctor continued.

Elinor flinched. "I most certainly have," she answered. She sat up straight and looked him in the eye. She wondered what the doctor would've done had she said, "No."

She sat impatiently while Doctor Hunter checked her medical records. "I see the hospitalizations you've had, Elinor. From your cracked skull when you were in college?"

Elinor nodded. Her nerves today were tightropes and microscopic insects tap-danced on them. Probably the long train ride home, she thought. Or too much coffee yesterday.

"You were in a darkened room here for many weeks. Hmmm. And the debilitating migraines. I see." He took his glasses off to look at her. Then he put them back on to continue reading. "The Mayo report isn't complete in the Fargo files. However I see you have some pelvic inflammation issues. Now no periods. Are you still having headaches?"

Elinor offered, "I haven't had one since I left for the West Coast."

"That's another change. We'll do the rabbit test and then I think you should see a specialist." Dr. Hunter removed his glasses again. He nodded and then smiled, a quick grin to give his patient confidence, just enough of a grin to make her suspicious.

"A specialist?"

"Dr. Klein can keep an eye on you, Elinor. Reading these reports from last spring, it looks like there's little chance of a pregnancy. Pelvic inflammation can be serious. But I'd like an expert to re-examine you to see what's going on with this new turn of events."

Elinor stopped at the desk on her way out and scheduled a meeting with Dr. Klein. Her head throbbed. A sharp pain crackled across her brow and smacked its way into her brain. The lights in the room glittered. She ducked out of the cloud of disinfectant and hiked directly home where she threw up.

Three Days Married

July 1944

Sunday evening

My darling Bunny,

In a few hours we will have been married three days, darling. I know you have had time to think many of the complications out, too. One thing I want you to be sure of, though, and never doubt, is that I shall always take care of you and well. When the big landslide back to civilian life comes, I shall be more than prepared to step in with it and take advantage of the opportunities which will come my way. There are so many possibilities for a man that I know I shall find one of them and soon go ahead.

    I have your picture here on the bulkhead, smiling and wide-awake as ever, so why should I be a bit tired! Every night I kiss you good night and whisper to myself, "My wife!" It's got a sound to it that makes me go to sleep with a smile and wake up with a bigger one.

Your man, forever,

Beat

LETTER 5
July 17, 1944
Long Beach

My darling wife,

When the ships are launched at Sausalito, they paint some sort of picture on the bow. As our ship came out about Memorial Day, we had Flanders Field and poppies painted on our bow.

   We picked up the pilot outside the sub nets, and the first thing he did was run the ship full speed right into the center of the mine fields that you saw from the Hilton Skyroom. In other words, he missed the net opening and ran us over one mine field and into the center of another. There was still another one, and we don't know why he didn't take us over it, too!!!

   I was sitting in here right after dropping you a note, and suddenly past the ports here a bunch of guys ran like heck back aft. Of course, I was a bit interested as I was off watch and getting ready to go through some tests. Ran outside and then I went back there, too!! We still don't know why we didn't set one of them off, and the Coast Guard will no doubt have to investigate the effectiveness of their mine fields all over the world because of it.

   It took about three hours to get off the fields through the nets. Got on the air for about five minutes and talked with the Coast Guard station over here, and they sent about a hundred small patrol boats out here with officers. They were just visiting, it turned out, as they wouldn't come close to us.

We're anchored out now, but at this time (11 P.M.) they are supposed to be readying the ship for a move into Long Beach somewhere. By the time we get in there, I'll have to rush to catch you in bed very early in the morning sometime!! Hope to get the call through as soon as possible, darling.

Your faithful husband,
Beat

July 18, 1944
?? ??

Dearest wife,

The sound of your voice did things to me. I
came up to the phone with many fears and I was
so relieved to hear you there, darling, that
I felt kinda light and happy all over. I would
rather have had things settled in some way or
another now than have to wait until I'm overseas
to hear about it. The suspense is going to be
murder, darling!

Last night when I called you, I meant to
mention the big blast they had at Martinez. Port
Chicago. Three hundred some dead. It's quite a
horrible thing, isn't it? You see how dangerous
it is to be loading these things on ships bound
for the Pacific!

Your husband, with love,
Beat

July 18, 1944
Long Beach, Calif.

My darling wife,

This bit of writing could very well be titled "My Day" except for the infringement on copyright rights of Eleanor Roosevelt's column. I'll call it "My Day and Night."

We went downtown with a purpose today, and I accomplished what I went after. We found a good stationery store, and I have replenished my supply. The paper is lighter than this, so I will be able to get more in an envelope, darlin'. Then we picked up some transparent tape. I found a good large map to put up in my room, and tonight I taped it to the bulkhead over my settee. Before this trip is over, there will have been many heated discussions over the map. We picked up cigarettes by the pack— five packs each. We headed for the post office and found long lines to wait in, but when I got to the window I made it pay off. I have 100 airmail stamps, 50 three cent stamps, ten special delivery and 20 one cent. The rest of our shopping was confined to stuff for the radio room. So it was a good and busy day. I have three good bookstores lined up for my tour tomorrow.

We have a special detail of Coast Guardsmen on here because we have explosives aboard, or didn't you know? Neither did I! Seems there are about thirty or forty live torpedoes stowed up forward that came down with the PT boats, and the Coast Guard is here to see that they are protected. The ensign in charge says they are going to watch ships more closely now that the Martinez explosion happened at Port Chicago. The reports have it that some Merchant seamen were killed in the blast there, darling, so they must have been Merchant ships loading.

With all my love, darling
Your husband,
Beat

July 19, 1944
Long Beach

Darling wife,

I went in to mail my letters to you and the folks, wandered around for a while, and then on the way to a theater, I met an old classmate of mine from Fargo High! Now I can say I met a guy from home out here. And, before I forget it, darling, that same guy I met in the Hilton came up while we were talking. That made three Fargo boys there. He's the guy who came to the door that night, and, very embarrassed, walked away again. He asked me quite soberly tonight if I were married yet, and I assured him I had been married for some time.

Darling, I wish you would make arrangements some way to have a joint bank account set up for us. Then I could send the money to the bank without making any trouble for you at home. It's got me worried, and when I call tomorrow night, I'd like very much to get this ironed out. Hope you can be of help to me, my darling.

I've forwarded $100.00 a month to you at my parents' house'

Now, if and when things are straightened out, darling, you are to write Deconhill Shipping Company, 305 Avalon Blvd., Wilmington, Calif. They will gladly change your address so that you can get the money wherever you are. It's the best we can do under the circumstances, hmmm, Bun?

Add these to your code list:
Joe for Persian Gulf
Jerry for Aruba, Venezuela

Now I'm really not too far from you and I could still come to you in an emergency, but as soon as we get outside the breakwater here, I'll get all soft inside and I'll begin to want to get back again more than anything in the world. I'll call you tonight, Bun, and we'll have a few moments away from the world together.

Your husband,
Beat

SEAMAN'S ALLOTMENT NOTE*				WHEN WRITING ALWAYS REFER TO THIS NUMBER
UNITED STATES COAST GUARD				
NAVCG - 722				73994

NAME OF SHIP	NOW BOUND ON VOYAGE TO			DATE
S/S MISSION BUENAVENTURA	WESTWARD OF LOS ANGELES			7-19-44
NAME OF ALLOTTER	MONTHLY	SEMI-MONTHLY	BI-MONTHLY	ALLOTMENT AMOUNT	NO. OF MONTHS
Darrow R. Beaton		x		$100.00	Voyage

PAYABLE BY (NAME AND ADDRESS OF STEAMSHIP COMPANY)
Deconhil Shipping Co., 311 California St., San Francisco, Cal.

SIGNATURE OF ALLOTTER   SIGNATURE OF MASTER   APPROVED (SHIPPING COMMISSIONER)

NOTICE TO ALLOTTEE

1. The amount shown in this allotment note will be paid to you fifteen days, one month, or two months, as the case may be, after the date of this note.

2. Should payment not be made according to the terms of this note, please notify, in writing, the steamship company at the address shown on the note.

Name
Street No.   Mrs. Elinor E. Beaton,
City   1728 Fifth Avenue South,
State   Fargo, North Dakota

*It shall be lawful for any seaman to stipulate in his shipping agreement for an allotment of any portion of the wages he may earn to his grandparents, parents, wife, sister, or children, or for deposits to be made in an account opened by him and maintained in his name either at a savings bank or a United States postal savings depository subject to the governing regulations thereof.
(Act of June 26, 1884, Section 10, as amended—U.S.C., title 46, sec. 599)

2 - ALLOTTEE'S COPY (ALLOTTEE SHOULD RETAIN THIS COPY)

Seaman's Allotment Note
Part of Beat's salary went to Elinor each month.

Darling wife,

There are so many reasons why I thought you wouldn't wish to marry me during the war, at least. But having you actually agree to such an arrangement, darling, has had me in a dream for days now. I'm finally beginning to realize what has happened, and I can only say that I'm getting more pleased with Fate and this life each and every day, thinking of my life ahead.

I'm still bothered by the fact that your dad doesn't know about things yet. I'm still worried about financial matters. I'm wondering about whether or not we are to be parents. And, even more so, I'm worrying about your general condition to take such a thing, darling. When you write me about any of these matters, please be very frank and outspoken, darling. I want facts and more facts.

Your devoted husband—
Beat

Skipping, Just a Bit

Late July 1944

THE FOLLOWING WEDNESDAY AT 10:00, Elinor sat in the waiting room chair, perspiring in her yellow sundress. The pungent odor of disinfectant permeated the entire clinic, and the air was already—or maybe still—warm and stuffy, despite the fan spinning on the wall. Elinor's clothes stuck to the wooden seat. She hated the Dakota humidity and planned a powder bath as soon as she got home.

A woman strode to the check-in desk. "It's going to be a hot one today!" she declared before settling in the waiting room for her appointment.

Elinor knew she was staring, but her eyes focused on the woman's belly. "Thank goodness I've not got that to look forward to," she thought. She smiled, remembering the period she had just experienced. "I'm not really sure why I'm here at all."

She glanced around the room at the women in various stages of pregnancy. A woman, stuffed into a loose garment with the requisite bow at the collar, smiled at her. Elinor nodded and then looked away. To distract herself, she opened her purse and dug through things she already knew were there.

No need to focus on babies. That wasn't why she was here. Not now. But perhaps Dr. Klein had a solution to her persistent headache problem.

"Elinor?" the nurse called.

Elinor stood and straightened her damp sundress, her hand resting on her flat stomach just a moment before she followed the nurse's starched white hat. They marched single-file through the narrow hallway, the nurse leading the way in her white soft-soled shoes. "Here you are," the nurse said as she directed Elinor to an examination room.

Elinor wasn't sure what to do when the nurse left her. She set her purse on the floor. She walked to the window to look out at the traffic. People living their lives, driving along down Broadway, attending to business. Did they know there was a war on?

She wouldn't have to take her clothes off this time, would she? She sighed.

The door opened and Doctor Klein entered, smiling. "Elinor? Nice to meet you."

She turned from the window toward the doctor.

He continued, "Dr. Hunter wants me to have a look at you. But first . . ." He shook her hand. "Good news!" He held her file in his left hand.

"Nice to meet you," Elinor's eyebrows rose. She had good news, too.

"Have a seat," the doctor offered, and Elinor settled on the stiff wooden chair in the corner.

Dr. Klein sat at a narrow desk and spread out her medical file. "Headaches and endometriosis. Hmmm. But the good news . . ." He turned to smile at her again.

"I'm sorry I disturbed you with this. I just got my period. Two days ago. What a surprise!" She knew she was rattling on. "I'm surely glad . . . But the headaches . . ."

Dr. Klein referred back to the file on the desktop. He paged through the notes there.

Elinor leaned over to reach her purse. She pulled the purse strap over her shoulder. The corners of her lips edged upward. She couldn't help it.

"If you've gotten your period, it looks as though you have lost your baby." The doctor jotted something into his notes. Then he turned to look directly at Elinor. "The test results were positive. I'm sorry.

A miscarriage . . . But you're young yet and there's always another chance."

"Thank you, doctor," was all Elinor could manage. She leaned back into her chair and looked into her lap. She hadn't realized she'd folded her hands.

Dr. Klein nodded. "I'm going to give you a prescription for something to relax you. If the bleeding doesn't stop by Friday, I should probably take another look at you. With endometriosis, it's always good to be careful. Just call the office for an appointment."

Elinor smoothed the skirt of her sundress. "The bleeding is mostly over. And the cramps."

"You're married now?"

"But my parents don't know." She looked into her lap.

"Nevertheless, we should put your married name on these files. You can stop at the front desk and arrange for that. We'd need your husband's permission for any procedure, you know." The doctor smiled. "Congratulations. On your marriage."

Elinor nodded again.

"Your husband. In the service?"

"Yes. Merchant Marine." She knew this turn of events would relieve Beat. "He's just ready to sail, Dr. Klein. Of course, I don't know exactly where. His ship will make the rounds of some Pacific islands." She bit her lower lip.

The doctor twisted the cap onto his fountain pen and closed Elinor's file. He stood.

"He won't be home for a long time," Elinor almost whispered.

Dr. Klein opened the door of the examining room. His back to her, he looked over his shoulder. "Lots of action over there. We seem to be slugging it out." Then he was on to the next appointment.

Elinor remained in her chair a moment. So there had been a child? Should she even tell Beat?

Then she stood, pulled up her purse strap, straightened her hat, and sped through the waiting room and out of the clinic. She inhaled deeply as she exited the building.

Some kind of celebration was in order! She crossed the street and entered the drugstore. There, she dug into her purse and found a nickel and two pennies. She purchased a 6-ounce bottle of Coca-Cola. The soda jerk wrenched the cap off before handing her the cold green bottle.

"Thank you," Elinor smiled at him. Then, sipping, she exited the store, grateful for the chance to walk alone for a while.

Now, miraculously, her options had opened up. She strolled down Third Street in the heat of the day. The sunburned prairie breeze and the icy Coke kept her from evaporating entirely.

Nobody would have to know about this marriage. She could wait and marry Beat when he came home again. They'd have a church wedding and make everything official. Why, she could start planning the celebration right away. She'd need to pick out the silver pattern. And her china.

Her parents, of course, wouldn't be thrilled with her choice of husband. They admired Mickey's boyfriend—a rich man's son, polite, not a drinker, hard-working. All the things her father hoped she'd find, too, one day.

Elinor sipped her Coke as she walked.

Well, she could have the whole thing annulled and go on with her life as before. After all, she'd tried to break it off so many times.

But Beat was so . . . well, so exciting.

She turned the corner.

She could head to the coast again and get some job out there. A gal there never knew. A big shot Hollywood producer could discover her, like Lana Turner at Schwab's Drug. Could Miss Turner play piano? Or even read music?

She neared Grondahl's Market so she stopped in with her empty Coke bottle to get her two-cent deposit back.

She'd had her try at Hollywood. It wasn't for her.

She could teach again in some provincial town, but she hated all the extracurricular work involved—the baseball team, glee club, plays and the state declamation contest. Most of all, though, it was those study halls. It was hard to quiet kids who didn't think they had anything at all to study, boys who would be heading into the war in just a few months. Boys who didn't know whether they'd be alive in five years.

School districts were desperate for teachers these days. Not pregnant ones. Or wives with children. She'd qualify again now.

Maybe it was good after all that she and Beat hadn't sealed the contract with a ring. A good wife never took hers off. A ring just announced that you were taken, that you were out of circulation. Out of life.

Elinor walked faster as she neared home.

Beat was going along with the way she wanted to handle their elopement. The allotment check would be sent to his parents' home. He promised to write to her with her maiden name on the envelopes. Thank goodness!

The Fates had given her options. Now it was up to her to make a plan. She could decide the shape of her future. Perhaps she was in charge of her life after all. She threw her shoulders back and walked with a bounce in her step.

She passed Horace Mann School, a block from home. Elinor couldn't help skipping just a bit. She should celebrate. She was not pregnant!

She danced down the sidewalk, past the cheesemonger's house. Past the big garden at the Olsen's. She watched for the frost heave in the sidewalk, the one that always tripped up her mother.

Then, looking up, she saw her father in the front yard, pushing the old lawn mower. He had on his gardening hat. Walking up and down across the lawn, he often pieced together a sermon or solved some synod business, lost in his own thoughts. But today his eyes were following her as she skipped down the sidewalk toward him. He stopped mowing and waved. Then, laughing, he tipped his sweaty hat to her.

She streaked down the block, her yellow sundress reflecting the brilliance of the summer sun, as she ran to give him a hug.

We Wouldn't Have
to Advertise

Late July 1944

DAKOTA WEATHER EMBRACES DISASTER. It's in the wild winds. Blizzards in winter. Tornadoes in the summer as the temperature rises in the humid summer air. When the wind begins twisting on the prairie, anything might happen.

Elinor lay on the front porch, torpid, in her new sunsuit. Trudie insisted on keeping the windows and drapes of the house closed until the evening breezes kicked up, so the interior of the house had become a regular oven. The porch gave no relief. The heat compelled immobility. Beside Elinor on the table stood a glass of tepid water. The half-frozen ice cubes she had taken too early from the aluminum ice cube tray had melted almost instantly.

The sun slanted in through the porch windows. Elinor tried to avoid the sunbeam that aimed for her eyes. "I can't wait for those new venetian blinds Mother wants to put up," she thought, squinting, as she stood and moved into one of the chairs. She was deep into the book Darrow had sent to her, after reading it himself and declaring it no good for morale. It had some parts that were definitely interesting!

Was that Irene calling her to the phone? She popped her head out of Ilka Chase's steamy plot. "I didn't hear it ring." She roused herself and landed back in 1944. Fargo. When she heard her name called again, Elinor bolted for the phone.

"Oh, there you are. One of your 'old friends,' I suppose," her sister teased. Irene hid the phone behind her back.

Elinor grabbed the handset. She glared at Irene, squinting and nodding her head in the direction of the living room. Irene scooted away.

"Hello?" Elinor answered the call.

"Darling! Just got in. Seattle. The ride was fierce this time. The *Buena Ventura* came through some swift currents on the Sound!"

Did he ever breathe?

"A storm. Some of the new men got sick. Fun! She's now loading the final top deck cargo. PT boats. Planes. Trucks. So how are ya, my little wife?"

"Fine. Okay, I think." Elinor removed the phone from her ear for a second so she could listen and locate the other family members. Her parents were talking in the kitchen. She pulled the cord to the phone as far into the den as it would reach. She crouched close to her father's desk.

"Have you seen the doctor?"

"Last Monday. Not Haugen. Don't worry." Although Elinor whispered, her voice felt too loud.

"Well . . ." he hinted.

"Nothing to worry about," she whispered.

"'Those people'?" he asked. "Can you speak up?"

"They've come, Beat." She spoke directly into the phone, her right hand covering the mouthpiece for privacy. "Come and gone."

"So no . . . ?"

"I guess not." She pulled on the telephone cord. It refused to stretch any more, and she worried that she might pull the darned thing completely out of the wall.

"Have you told your folks yet? That we're married?"

Was he shouting? "Um, no. Not yet." Elinor fiddled with the phone cord.

"Are you planning to do that soon?"

Elinor thought she heard a stealthy footstep in the front hallway.

"Well, maybe. But we wouldn't have to advertise."

"I don't understand, Bunny."

"We could solidify things next summer. You know? A second time around in the church?" Irene would have trouble making sense of Elinor's cryptic message.

"Another ceremony? Your decision, sweetheart, but I think it's always wise to be upfront and honest. Especially with people who love us."

"Well, how are YOU? I was worried when you wrote about the mine field. Weren't you scared?" Now she spoke with energy.

"Sure. Everyone was. But we're fine. Nothing to worry about," he laughed.

Elinor sighed. "Good. It sounded so dangerous."

"They say we're leaving tomorrow, honey. South Pacific. We could be out a while."

Elinor was beginning to know those islands pretty well. And now that she had taken the job teaching geography and history, she'd be sure to track the war movements more closely. "I'll miss you, Beat."

"Me, too. But I'll write. Say! How shall I address the letters to you, Elinor?"

"Same address as always, silly. We haven't moved."

She couldn't see the disappointment on her groom's face, but she heard it in his voice. He had promised to write her maiden name on the envelopes until she told her parents about their elopement.

"Your three minutes are up."

"Good-bye, Bunny," he yelled.

"Beat . . ." The phone clicked.

Elinor stood. She coiled the cord around the phone to keep it out of Ching's reach, then replaced it on the shelf. That was that. They would have to handle the rest via their correspondence.

Elinor ducked into her closet and retrieved her pink jewelry box. She found the friendship rings Beat had bought her in San Francisco. She slipped her favorite onto the ring finger of her left hand. She spread out her fingers and stared at it. Not a diamond for sure. She returned the ring to the jewelry box and tucked the entire collection of her most precious jewels back into the family closet.

Then she sat at the piano and picked out the melody of "He's My Guy."

My Darling Wife

July 1944

July 21, 1944
Long Beach, Calif.

My darling wife,

I picked up two shoe stamps. I'm putting one in here for you, Bun, as I need only one. You may be able to use it there in Fargo if you are short of stamps, and I seem to remember your complaint on that subject. I'll save one in case I find something I like around here.

I have been trying to get to Long Beach to go through one of the bookstores over there. One has a wonderful collection of second-hand books on all subjects in the universe. I spent two hours there wandering from one subject to another and picking out the books I wished to read. There are two darn good books on seeds and grain which I shall be delving in soon now. Bought two books on philosophy—one with the history of philosophy from Greek times to ours, so it will be some job to get through it. There's a book on mental attitude in creating a personality and as in selling speech, etc. It gives many ideas on psychological problems which lead a person to fear things, etc. It may be interesting, and I know it will add something to my meager knowledge of such subjects.

They have been having some extra work to do in the engine room, but we are to get away from here tonight with a full load of cargo to move over to Wilmington for a load of planes.

Here is the general idea of what the trip holds for us, darling, and don't quote me or razz me if I'm wrong. We are supposed to go to Hawaii from here and discharge this cargo. Then we'll head for Panama to Aruba, Venezuela, for another load. From there we go back through Panama again, over to Australia or one of the islands down that way. After we discharge there, we are due to head for the Persian Gulf oil fields. If the rumors are right. If things hold true, we will be running around over there with our base at Abadan or Bahrain and running to India, Burma, and East Africa for a while. So don't be surprised if you get some mail with perspiration all over it, darling.

"Those people" could have complicated an already difficult situation, darling, and I'm certainly happy they have shown up around the Landgrebe home!

> Your devoted husband,
> Beat

July 22, 1944
Wilmington, Calif.

My dearest,

Last night when I went down to the gate and
told them the name of the ship, they laughed
at me, and I know they must have thought I was
a spy. They just didn't have any records of a
ship of this name coming in. That is the usual
thing around the world. And it does delay us
a bit here and there. I know ships that guys
have told me about which have come into ports
and the Navy gave them hell for being there,
sent them to some other port, and they were
shuttled around like that until they just tied
up and waited for orders from the States. It
happened like that on the *Oliver* a couple of
times with the Army and Navy fighting over who
was to get the cargo and then fighting over who
was to unload it.

I put in two shoe stamps, as I won't be able
to use them anyway now. Use them and get some
good shoes for yourself.

Captain Manuel in the show of the *Bridge of
San Luis Rey* was sailing on the *Buena Ventura*.
We saw the movie last night. It gave me a start
to hear him name the ship that way, and I had to
smile. We would have enjoyed the show together,
I know, as there were many speeches which would
have applied to this sailor and his wife. He
told the gal he knew of sailors who went away
only to come back and find their gals gone. She
promised to be true, but she wasn't, Bun. We've
no reason for mistrusting each other, and from

now on I shall forget it for the most part and talk of more pleasant and practical things, hmmm.

I'd like to get under way tomorrow night some time, darling. It's always better to leave the States in the night when it isn't so easy to see all of the beautiful buildings and people walking around enjoying themselves. The last view of the States always stays with a fellow until the sight of the Golden Gate Bridge. The first sight of the States after this trip will be doubly memorable to me as I know I shall be coming soon to you, darling Bunny.

Have a calendar here with a pretty picture on it, a desk pad with calendars on it, an ink stand with a good pen, a roll of Scotch tape (!), and many other things the usual radio room doesn't possess. I told you I had obtained a large map of the world again. Well, already it has been of use to us in tracing out possible routes here and there in the world. Yep, this is a class AAAAA1 room now, and it will be more than comfortable to work in for the trip.

I've a confession to make, darling. Hope you understand and approve of my dates every once in awhile out here, cuz I really do have them. The third mate and I usually meet back in the salon each night about twelve. And since we have been in here, we have found a good program each night from twelve to one. I just came back from my hour back there with him and our critic. The critic is a sailor, an able-bodied seaman (an ABS), who is an expert on classical music. We sit around and drink coffee and listen to music and talk over the good points of each composer. We heard Bach, Debussy, Ravel, Wagner tonight, and it was perfect. There was a selection from Wagner's "Lohengrin" which we worked over and talked about. Ravel's contribution was light and easy to listen to and understand as the fellow told us the story. When we get together, we close all the doors to the salon, get a cup of coffee and our cigarettes out and sit back and listen. We'll have some of these records some day to enjoy together as we sit around our home quietly contented with life.

The A.C. current was just shut off down below, and the D.C. may go off any moment. They're really hitting their troubles down there, and I'm surely glad I have such a nice soft job, Bun.

I'll start numbering the letters from now on so that you will know if you are getting all of them.

Your devoted husband,
Beat

❧   ❧

July 30, 1944
Port—Pacific

Darn Mrs. Bruns!! Bob told her about our wedding. She may say something and the word may get to your parents, Bunny. You say that the folks are ready for the announcement from you, darling, so you have probably already settled things satisfactorily—I hope!

LETTER 19
July 31, 1944

Darling,

Before I forget it, darling, here's the money I
promised to send once in a while. It's $500.00.
To be truthful, Bun, I haven't earned enough
to make it worthwhile to send any along as yet.
But there will be some soon.

So you suspect that the folks suspect strongly.
Have you told them by now? I'm sure they will
accept the marriage and do their best to make
us feel that we were right about everything,
Bun. It would hurt me terribly if I thought they
didn't feel a bit happy about it, sweets. From
now, though, they will have to worry about your
future—and mine! They will be a bit intermingled
from now on, hmmm?

Give my regards to Itch, Lanny and Jerry
[code] when you get the chance. Never forget how
happy we are when we are together, and nothing
in the world could change your mind or let you
forget the future we will share, too.

Your faithful husband,
Beat

LETTER 22
August 3, 1944
Pacific

My darling,

That book you mentioned—interesting! *How to Make and Keep Your Husband Happy* must contain quite a few pages!

Your review of *In Bed We Cry* was quite exacting, Bun. As you said, Bun, the one requirement of a best seller these days is some rubbish mixed with broken homes and emotions which are warped. I guess that takes care of the ultra-sophisticate Ilka.

I believe that much of the world's problems started when women were given equal rights. Don't misunderstand me, darling. I think it is perfectly all right. But, as with men, there are women who took advantage of this new-found power to play havoc with their lives and with others, too. It has led to a mutual distrust between the sexes which didn't exist over thirty years ago. It isn't considered too wrong for a woman to step out on her husband now. It doesn't even stir comment in some quarters—or some laugh at what a fool the man is. We'll live and let live, darling, and our happiness will be the kind that makes a nation strong and decent.

I picked up my favorite mags over here on my trip ashore, but I find I'm done with them already, with nothing but botany and stuff like that to read for the rest of this trip! Pity me. Time to go off watch soon, darling, and I'll kiss your picture good night and dream of you some more.

> With all my love, forever,
> Your husband,
> Beat

LETTER 24
August 6, 1944
Pacific

My darling Bunny,

We changed our clocks last night, but before we did, we had the blackest night I've ever seen at eight o'clock in the evening. The purser and I were back having coffee, and on our way back up here to our work, we were surprised by the very thickness of it. The wind was howling as per Hollywood, and we enjoyed struggling up here by sense of feel only. Both of us wondered just how we would get off the ship if we suddenly were called upon to do so, and my idea was just to stand still and let her go down until I was in the water! They say all this business of suction from a sinking ship is the bunk, so if I get a chance I'll find out. From about five miles, if I have my way, darlin'.

This afternoon I slept for want of something better to do. I guess it isn't that we have so much free time but that we don't know what to do with it most of the time. Back in the States people have no more work than we do, but there are always things to do at home or out in the evening.

Your guy,
Beat

August 7, 1944
Pacific

Jeepers, darling, this ship moves along! Two weeks at sea in this ship are really kinda enjoyable. As the guy off the other tanker back there said, "My god, cushioned chairs, even!" Such things as that make the ship much easier to live on, and the time goes that much more quickly. If I should list all the additional comforts we have on here, I'd be going at it for some time. It's not only the living comforts, but there are other ones, too. It's easier to charge batteries with the set-up on here. The engine room is perfect. Just about all they have to do when the ship is in good order is press buttons as you would to start the toaster in the morning. Everything which makes living and working conditions better seems to be put on here. It's quite typical of America.

We gathered back aft tonight after dinner. The seas were running away from us, as we sat there quietly watching and listening. There were old and young, dark and light, just every kind of person in the world represented there. Old "Pumps" Simpson with no known relatives in the world and a passion for poker and corny jokes even though he is over sixty. He's been a seaman all his life and his job is tending to the cargo pumps which a tanker depends so much on. Near him were fellows making their first trips to sea—guys of sixteen and seventeen. They were trying to appear tough and hard but they were acting a bit silly. The third engineer was there sitting on a kingpost, all 300 pounds of him. He's growing a beard and it's getting a bit long now. The bos'n was there with his "Ernie Wheeler" face. His young gang looks up to him with wide eyes, hoping some day to be as salty as he is. There were guys from all parts of the country and from every kind of home. There were fellows with college education and some without even the grades behind them. Some were dressed properly, but most were lounging around on the deck in remnants of "shore" clothes. There were torn shirts and trousers hanging on young and old, and they were quite acceptable out here. All of us were lounging on the various lines and anchor chains stretched out on the deck there. The big gun tub rested only a scant six or eight inches above our heads when we stood.

The sun was just setting aft of us, when we discovered we had talent in our midst. The third mate brought his accordion back and played a few numbers for us. Then one of the toughest guys I have ever seen, a fireman, offered to "try." He "used to play" the thing and thought he could "remember a few ditties." He did, and, darling, he was really good. He played music of all kinds, from the classical to the Beer Barrel Polka. It was a funny feeling, Bun, to be in the bunch tonight. We all seemed to be carried along with the good fellowship. Officers and men were all together having laughs at the same things and having fun. We sang song after song as the sun went down. The two cooks had raided the rag bag today and found themselves two women's aprons which they were wearing. One of them is the preacher, and he gave us a bit from the Bible. He said, "I expect to go broke gambling soon, so I'll have to go back to preaching to make some money again."

The evening was quite perfect, darling. As I've thought from the beginning, we have one grand crew. It is fun to sail with them.

Good night, darling—
Beat

⟫   ⟪

August 8, 1944

The purser has spread around the ship the new title for you, Bun. He calls you the "Woman I Would Most Like to See Widowed." It all started when he saw your picture on my desk and commented, "What a beautiful widow she would make."

⟫   ⟪

LETTER 27
August 9, 1944
Pacific

My darling wife,

Most of us are wearing shorts now, but the engine gang doesn't. They don't dare on their job, of course, due to the danger of escaping steam down there. But they get a bang out of razzing all of us up here who can take advantage of such clothing. The third mate walked in tonight and said, "Hello, girls." And we go merrily on our way with our shorts, making them a bit jealous—we think.

Wonder what you are doing now, Bunny. You know what I'm doing most of these nights, darling. But it's always something new and different for you back there. Wonder how the folks took the news and all, Bunny. You see, I still don't know the answer to that one. Then we can settle down to a normal married life, huh? Yeah, normal!

All yours, always,
Beat

❯❯   ❮❮

LETTER 28
August 11, 1944

My darling wife,

You're a fairly happy civilian in the Land of Plenty, so I don't know whether or not I should write you the following bit of news, Bunny. But, honesty being the prime requisite of a good husband, I'll tell you, darling. We had the biggest and juiciest tenderloin steaks you ever saw for dinner tonight. With a great big steak, we had French fried potatoes, creamed corn, asparagus and the other necessary things which go with a meal any place. We had big pitchers of pineapple juice to drink. It was iced and the pure juice, too. It's a funny thing, but we have grapefruit, grape, tomato and other fruit juices out here in pitchers. We drink as many glassfuls as we wish—just like water. I can just see you counting the ration points to get a glass of any of it, Bunny!

The meal tonight was in honor of Hank [enemy action]. I've written to you about Hank, along with Jerry and Itch and the others from other ships, Bunny. There seems to be a Hank on all the ships I've been on, Bunny. Makes life interesting in a way, though!

We spent more than the usual time out on deck today, when we weren't busy somewhere around the ship. There seemed lots to do, but we still found plenty of time to stay around the decks. There were fish of all kinds around us. We saw more flying fish in one day than we thought there were in the world. There were sharks and big turtles and other things, too. What a day for nature!

Right now I'm on watch, and I'm a bit more than a tiny bit busy. The trip has suddenly become one of interest and we all find that we are buddies and good friends of a sudden. Where before there were petty jealousies and bits of crabbing, there is good fellowship and cooperation. Wonder how long it will last.

> My love always, darling—
> Your guy,
> Beat

LETTER 29
August 14, 1944
Pacific

My darling wife,

This will always be one of our days, darling, won't it? One month of marriage and about four hours with my wife. That's not exactly the usual thing, my darling. But it is one of those months gone already, and soon they will pile up until I can have the time ashore with you when I get back to you.

We hit port this morning, as we had expected to do. There are some military men in the radio room now, as we run along, taking over the watch standing for us. They're giving us a rest, Bunny, and I'm quite thankful.

We expect to be back at sea in the dark hours tonight and back into another port in a couple of days. We're all anxious to get letters from home, but none more than I!

We had the doctor aboard this morning to look over some of the sick men. A couple of them the purser has been treating for various aches and pains were expecting to get off here, but they were found "fit for sea duty with proper care."

If I get ashore tonight, Bun, I'll buy you a wedding anniversary present. How about a dozen orchids? They're about fifteen cents each here! Often in such localities as this I have wished that I could buy a huge bunch of them and surprise you one day with them. For a while, though, roses will have to do, Bunny.

Your loving husband,
Beat

LETTER 30
August 14, 1944
Pacific

My darling wife,

We were supposed to be at sea, but right now we are tied up to a berth down here. They found some trouble with our big gun, so we have to stay here until it is fixed, darn Hank!!

I have mailed only two or three letters to you, Bunny, as I expected to be able to address them to you as my wife when I received the mail. It's a good thing I didn't address them that way on a hunch, isn't it? I really don't understand such things, but I wish your folks could be informed. It seems kinda screwy, Bunny, but I'll ride along with you and do as you say. As I've told you before, you're the one who decides things for both of us back there. You no doubt have your reasons, darling, so I'll accept them such as they are and hope that soon you will be able to inform them.

I was rather surprised to hear of your visits to doctors there, Bunny. I remember calling from Wilmington and asking you about things. You said at that time that everything was O.K., and I forgot that phase of our problems quite completely until now. I don't know just what to think, darling. Whatever you do, my darling, please go to good doctors and do things right. All of the headaches and things make me wish so darn hard that we could be together.

One of these days I hope to receive mail telling me that all is well. Your folks know.

You're in good health again. I've got a hunch that it may work out that way very soon. I'm surely hoping for such news, Bunny.

How do you like this new ribbon? Just put it in before I started typing. Thought you must be getting a bit tired of the old one. Your eyes, you know.

Your loving husband,
Beat

Fargo Café

Summer's End 1944

"I've always had so much 'female trouble.'" Elinor sighed.

Elinor and Mickey had grabbed their purses and summer sweaters. They planned to have a bite to eat—Elinor's treat—at the Fargo Café before Mick's 1:00 starting time at work.

There was no privacy in the busy home of the Bishop, but the girls could talk—and no one could hear them—in the noise of the café. Elinor knew her topic would surprise Mickey. She also knew that Mickey would control her response in a public place. That was, after all, part of their upbringing as clergy children.

The girls hiked down city sidewalks toward downtown Fargo. The sun hid behind the gray layer of clouds, and the morning remained cool. Mickey stopped to open her purse. She found her cigarettes and a matchbook.

"What are you getting at?" Mickey lit up a Lucky Strike. "Darn! I'm running out of cigarettes, kid. I hope Betty will loan me a few more until payday." Cigarettes were hard to come by during wartime, unless you were a serviceman in certain ports.

"Well," Elinor mumbled.

"I'm confused. What are we talking about?" Mickey turned to look at her sister.

Elinor looked at the sidewalk. "Well, Mick, 'those people' haven't been around to visit. For about six weeks now."

"Lucky! I just got done with mine. Why would you worry if you don't have to go through all this nonsense?"

Mickey flicked a few ashes off her cigarette and then inhaled again. She looked forward every year to this early fall weather—the cool air, the sky a steely gray. And she looked forward to her birthday, too, even if she had to share the day with Yupps. She pulled her sweater closer around her, then checked her penultimate cigarette to see how much was left to enjoy.

The sisters walked on.

Mickey worked at Kresge's every afternoon in the dry goods department, among bolts of fabric and cards of ribbons and buttons. Surrounded by thread, snaps, pins and needles, she wasn't as busy as most of the other clerks. She enjoyed her job when she could kibitz with her friend Betty in cosmetics or some familiar customer who dropped by to look at the Butterick or Simplicity patterns for the latest styles.

Elinor sighed. "Promise me you won't say a word to anyone!"

"Sure."

"Not Irene or Mom or Dad. Not a soul?"

"Okay."

Elinor bargained, "Not even Betty, Mickey."

"What on earth is up?"

Elinor stopped walking again and looked around to see if anyone were listening, but the business traffic in the late morning had settled, and they were virtually alone on the sidewalk at the north end of Broadway.

Elinor turned to her sister. "I could be pregnant."

"How? What's going . . ."

"Mickey, I need to decide what to do. Let's talk over lunch."

Mickey dropped her cigarette on the sidewalk and stepped on it, smashing it with her shoe. They walked on without speaking.

Elinor noticed the mess of cigarettes scattered on the sidewalk in front of Gene's as they passed, probably from people waiting to get into the bar last night. She remembered the bars of San Francisco and her evenings there with Darrow. Unconsciously, she straightened her back and stepped quickly past the place.

The girls walked faster as they neared Fargo's downtown. More people strolled the street. Several shoppers, strangers from one congregation or another, greeted the sisters. They smiled and waved back, automatic movements.

All those years of being The Preacher's Kids in Elgin had taught them a few things. They could seem nonchalant when talking about something serious. They could keep secrets better than most. They had code words for things—boyfriends were "old friends" and periods were "those people" and certain words triggered memories of past parishioners or pastors. They would be sedate on the outside no matter what. They had been schooled about what the neighbors might think of them. Demeanor. Composure. Prerequisites for being the Bishop's children.

When they reached the Fargo Café, they grabbed their purses tighter, smiled and nodded at each other, then disappeared inside. The noon crowd was gathering. The noise of conversations and the jukebox would cover up their conversation. Elinor saw a booth open in the back of the restaurant. She and Mickey bustled down the aisle to grab it.

A waitress brought them menus and glasses of water. "We'll need a few minutes," Elinor explained, "to look the menu over." The waitress stepped to another table to take an order.

"So, I think I have a few choices to make right away, and I'd like your advice, Mick." Elinor set her menu aside without a glance.

Mickey leaned over the table toward her sister.

The waitress reappeared with her order pad in hand. The girls sat up. Mickey ordered a Coke and a sandwich special. Elinor followed suit.

When their server had left again, Mickey leaned toward Elinor and mouthed, "Walt?"

Elinor grimaced. "No. Darrow."

"Bunny! How could you let this happen? Are you sure?"

"We were together most of my trip west. The whole month, Mick." Elinor ran her index finger around the rim of her water glass.

"But you know how Papa feels about Beat! What were you thinking?"

"I wanted to have some fun. An adventure. I didn't think it would matter in the long run." Elinor took a sip of water before looking at

Mickey again. "Why can't anyone in this family forgive a guy for something he didn't even do?" Elinor hadn't realized that the volume of her voice had risen until she saw people at the table next to them looking toward her. She sat back in the booth.

"Darn it, Elinor! I can't go through this family anguish again!" Mickey picked up her purse and began to move out of the booth.

"Mick, don't. Don't go. I need you. I need someone to talk to."

Mickey sat and set her purse back down on the bench. She turned, scowling, toward her sister.

"It's all so strange. When I got home I had a brief period right away. It was a relief," Elinor sighed. "But it's been six more weeks and nothing more."

"Kid, I don't know what to say."

Elinor leaned toward her sister over the table. "Well, I haven't been with anyone else. I had a period. How could I now be pregnant?" She shook her head.

"But the doctors told you . . .

"Have you heard of Dr. Haugen? He helps girls. Maybe I just need a cleansing or something." Elinor fiddled with the corners of the folded napkin in front of her.

Mickey leaned across the small table. She moaned, "Oh, Bunny . . . Do you remember what Mother told us about Aunt Minnie?"

Elinor closed her eyes for a moment. She remembered those warnings, the story of the coat hanger her aunt had used, so desperate she was to end the pregnancy. And the net result was the loss of two lives.

"But there are a couple of other options, too. I could go to Chicago. Mother and Dad wouldn't have to know."

"Remember how I had to room with Betty there just to stretch our salaries? We didn't last too long either. Who would you go with?"

"Actually, I haven't thought about that," Elinor admitted. She could see that Mickey wasn't anxious to try Chicago again. Even then, one person couldn't support another in that city. And a pregnant girl wouldn't be hired for any job.

Elinor spread a paper napkin on her lap. Then she folded up the corners again, one at a time. She straightened the corners and then folded them again.

Their sandwiches and Cokes arrived, slapped down quickly on the table in the noon rush.

Mickey scanned the restaurant. All the booths were full, and the air was busy with noon-time talking. Someone put a nickel into the jukebox and the "The Sweetheart of Sigma Chi" filled the room. Elinor remembered how Beat loved that song. She was his sweetheart, and he had spent his first earnings on that Sigma Chi pin. A smile curled at the edges of her lips.

Mickey leaned across the table again. Speaking softly, she advised her big sister. "An abortion. Hiding in Chicago and then giving the child up. Bad news no matter what. Look, there aren't a lot of options for a single girl in 1944, Elinor."

"Oh! We're married, Mickey. We were married in Seattle, just hours before Darrow had to get to his ship." Elinor picked at her sandwich. She lifted up the top piece of bread to peek inside, then made a face.

Mickey sat up in her seat. "*Married*? And you haven't told anyone?" She leaned toward her sister. "You didn't tell *me*?! Why?" She sat back in the booth and stared at this stranger.

Elinor looked into her lap. She straightened her napkin. "Oh, Mickey," she moaned.

"If you're married and pregnant, well, that's another story." Mickey rearranged her purse on the seat beside her. She removed the cigarette pack and began to play with it. "I'm not seeing the issue, kid," she whispered. "Why didn't you tell me you'd married?" She caressed the cellophane of the Lucky Strike pack. "But Darrow? What are you going to tell Papa?"

Elinor remembered Beat's letters. The joke about sending her $500 when he was really allotting her just $100. Beat was drinking again, after promising to keep a record of the drinks he had, promising to not drink until they were together again. So much for promises. She wondered what else he might be doing in those ports for entertainment. What kind of marriage was this, anyway?

"I got married in a hurry. I was worried." Elinor took a sip of her

Coke. "We were just having fun." Elinor remembered the laughter, the elegance, the way each day flew by when she and Beat were together. She leaned across the table. "You know, Mickey."

"Yeah, kid," Mickey agreed. "But Beat? Why did you have to play around with him?"

"I can't find a fellow who can compare to your Bob. At least in Papa's eyes." Elinor sat back in the booth. "Beat's interesting. Smart. Handsome in his own way. We just have great fun together." She leaned toward her sister again and spoke in a whisper. "And I admit it. The fact that he's on Papa's list makes him, somehow, more alluring."

Mickey sat speechless.

Elinor continued, "I didn't get a period the entire time we were together, and I was afraid to come home without a signed marriage license, just in case."

"You've had plenty of options. What not choose Walter or Johnny?" Mickey took a bite of her sandwich. She set it back on the plate.

Elinor stabbed the dull knife into her sandwich and sliced it in half again. She stared at her plate and shook her head.

The restaurant bustled with noontime energy, but the Landgrebe girls sat speechless.

At last Elinor looked up. "I didn't tell you we were married in case I could have this thing annulled. Or file for divorce. No one would have to know."

"Lots of gals are divorcing or dropping their guys these days." Mickey tapped her last cigarette out of the package she had been fondling. "Think about that, kid. It might be your best option."

"I wonder how they can do that. I think there are rules. A gal can't end a marriage without the groom's signature or something, and Beat's headed to the South Pacific, impossible to reach now."

"Bunny, you have to try," Mickey said.

"Anyway, it's demoralizing to the troops," Elinor mused. "To break up when they're off to war. That's what Emily Post says."

Mickey parked her cigarette between her lips. She crushed the empty cigarette pack and left it on her plate. She snapped her purse shut.

Talking with the cigarette still in her mouth, Mickey hissed, "Emily Post was never in this situation, Bunny."

"How can a girl have fun—get around—without these problems cropping up?" Elinor snapped open her purse, found two Anacin pills, and swallowed them with a taste of her Coke.

Mickey struck a match from the Fargo Café matchbook that lay beside the ashtray on the table. She lit that last cigarette and took a deep drag. Then another. She held the cigarette between the first fingers of her right hand and exhaled smoke slowly from the side of her mouth. She looked directly at her sister. "Bunny, a girl can't. That's all." She stared across the table. "It's simple. Girls can't take chances."

The waitress returned to remove their plates and to leave the bill. Elinor took out her wallet to pay the check. $1.05 for the two of them! She was glad she'd signed the contract to teach this coming year. She would need an income.

"Bunny, first you have to know if you are . . . You know. You've always had difficulty with that part of the month. Migraines, bloating, pains. You know what Mayo said. Kid, the chances are . . ." Mickey flicked the ashes from her Lucky Strike into the ashtray on the table. "Chances are you're imagining this." Mickey tried a smile.

"Okay. I'll see the doctor this week. But I need to make a plan. If I'm pregnant . . ."

"You have to decide if you want to be married. And how you'll tell Papa."

"I suppose I'll have to be. Married, I mean. I don't see how anything else is possible if there's a child in the picture." Elinor sat up straighter. "Darn it, Mickey. It's our fate, the expectation, isn't it? " She fiddled with her napkin.

"Well, we know a few women who never married. Their lives aren't that exciting either."

"But if I'm not pregnant . . ."

"You still have to decide about that marriage." Mickey exhaled again.

"Dad always hoped I'd be a pastor's wife."

"Yeah. Now that would be a boring life, kid."

Elinor checked her watch, the one Beat had given her for Christmas not even two years ago. A broken watch, the very watch he'd demanded back. The watch she had tried to return to him on her trip to San Diego just a year ago. And, just her luck. Now the watch kept ticking, as her time was running out. "It's nearly one already," she exclaimed.

Mickey grabbed her purse and stood. She was due at Kresge's to supervise those notions. "Gotta run."

Elinor stood, too, arranged her purse and, smiling now, thanked the waitress. She slipped a thin dime under her saucer. The girls exited the café.

They hugged outside the door. "We'll talk more tonight, kid," Mickey whispered. She turned south down Broadway, inhaling her last cigarette.

Elinor aimed herself north toward the Fargo Clinic. She tightened the purse strap over her shoulder. Then she brushed her hair behind her ears with her fingers. She organized her face. Composure. She would make an appointment to see Dr. Klein again.

One of These Days

End of August 1944

LETTER 36
August 22, 1944

My darling wife,

You suggested in one of your letters that it might be a good idea to let things go until we could have a real church wedding at home. Being honest, Bun, I've often thought of that possibility with pleasure, too. It would be the thing for both of us, if it could be arranged. It's all up to you back there, Bun, but I do want to know from time to time what you are planning for us!!

I'm glad that Mick is getting married to Bob when he arrives in the States. He's one guy who deserves all the breaks in the world. Think of the time he has put in on Guadalcanal, New Caledonia, Bougainville and others down there. The guy has been through a lot, and I'm sure that Mick will make him darn happy.

As this will be the last letter to you for some time, I guess I'd better quit worrying about what's to become of you back home, darling. It is up to you to do as you please. It will be fun to think of my wife back there teaching something this year.

It would be fun to be back there with you and the gang again, darling. Leo [Carolines], Norma [Mariannas], Gary [New Guinea] and Vic [Philippines] and the old bunch. Can't figure out which I would like the best to see, darling. Guess I'll see them all before too long, and I surely hope so. And don't forget Hank [enemy action] and Gordy [invasion]. They make trips go so much more quickly.

How I miss you, darling, and all the things you mean to me. But I am rather contented with this life, too. If I must be away from you, darling, this is the sort of thing I want to do.

Your loving husband,
Beat

LETTER 37
August 24, 1944
North Pacific

My darling wife,

I'm still one of the numerous uninformed men of
the world today, I believe, darling. You see,
Bunny, I still don't know whether I'm a married
man or not! Here we are married and we are
still going around with that cloak of intrigue
enfolding us ever closer and closer. Some time
it will all spill, darling, and things won't
look so very good for us.

In a case of this kind, I can't help but
think that truth will do (or would have done)
more for us now and in the years to come than
anything else. I don't mind throwing a bit of
a story to a guy I meet at a bar or some place
like that, but I know better than to try to kid
the guys I have to live with for a good long
time. You see, darling, they always catch up
with a person who tells bits of untruth.

I wish we had been a bit more frank and
outspoken with everybody concerned so that
everything would be all right and settled now.
I'm sure that they would have been as well
approached at the earliest possible moment as
they will now. I feel that the time that has
elapsed will only lead them to think that we
have a bit of guilty feeling about what we have
done. It's going to be hard for all of us to get
together, maybe, and really feel as one family
some day.

One of these days you had better inform the

folks that they have only two single daughters. I don't think they will be as surprised as we might think, Bunny. When we get all of those things out of the way, we'll be much happier, darling.

Oh, yes, I've spent a lot of time working on this, darling! It's been haunting me in and out of port when I have some free time. It would make me much happier to be getting letters from my wife with her name on the return address. It would more or less consolidate all of the things this partnership means to me, darling. When the mail comes, I immediately look for the return address to see if you have written me as my wife. It's always been a disappointment. It must be a strain on you, Bunny, to have to live with this secret inside you.

With all my love, always,
Beat

❧   ❧

August 25, 1944

There are the usual number of rumors flying around the ship. All we have to do is hit a few ports, and the stories of other ships come flying our way. One guy talks to a messman on such and such a ship, and he says that all of these ships, etc., etc. There are rumors that we will be here until around Christmastime, and others say we are due to stay out until the war is over. Silly, isn't it? I've more or less hardened myself to all of the bunkum and I just take what they give me. It saves a lot of worrying, and I won't get home any later than the others! But I surely do think about that day often, darling. And the good rumors make a much better impression on me than the bad ones. But, we'll just have to wait until this ship touches the good ol' USA before either of us starts making too definite plans.

≫   ≪

August 27, 1944

A couple of the guys were up here, and we were going all through the postwar problems of guys coming back home for jobs. I seemed to be the only one who felt sure that everything is going to be all right when we get back again! I've still got a bit of ambition, even after all these months out here, and I think a guy who gets a few breaks here and there will do all right if and when the opportunity to do so comes.

≫   ≪

LETTER 41
August 28, 1944
Pacific

My darling wife,

What a perfect day, darling. I helped check all of the lifeboats. We went over the lists of things which were supposed to be in them and saw that each boat had its quota.

The ship is rolling pretty much in this quartering sea, so today you may have a few more than the usual mistakes to read over, sweets. Every once in a while this typewriter seems to be sitting on one of its sides instead of being level like a civilized mill should be. When we get to the bottom of a swell, we can look straight out at other waves which seem ready to fall right on us. We always seem to rise soon enough to avoid that, though, so I'm still with you, darling.

I'd like to be back there now with the football season just around the corner, with the crisp cool days ahead. But not much further ahead are the days of real cold—and I'd just as soon be down here sweating it out!

Jeepers, Bunny, this war is going to be over before very long. The Germans will never last out the year, of course, and it won't take too darn long to clean the Japs up once the forces are marshaled out here. Then, darling, we'll be with each other all of the time. It will take us some time to get organized, Bunny, but when we are, it will be something really out of a dream!

We heard some good music from the States tonight, and it brought memories to all of us as we sat quietly listening to it. And they seem to make one know that those times will come again and be just as wonderful as before. "I'll Be Seeing You" seems to be the theme. We all know that we shall be back some day, but this music makes us feel more sure of it and makes the time go much more quickly and easily.

Last night I woke up again in the middle of

one of my rolls. Thought you were with me again, and I didn't want to roll over on you, darling. I'm quite set on that double bed life now. But this is a heck of a time to be thinking about it!

Your loving husband,
Beat

❯❯   ❮❮

LETTER 43
August 30, 1944
South Pacific

My darling wife,

Tonight as I sit here, the guys are outside playing the accordion and singing songs. We have what is known as a "happy ship." For days now the guys have been organizing and working on the initiation of the pollywogs when we crossed the equator. After lunch today, the "Jolly Roger" was suddenly raised over the ship. Somebody with genius had made a darn perfect flag with black cross and skull. Without warning, the cops struck and rounded up all of the pollywogs. The cops were armed with large clubs and a holster without the gun. They had uniforms, too—nothing but the holster! They quickly rounded up the boys and corralled them in the crew's mess.

I was part of the court, so we anxiously awaited the first initiate. There were many ideas for the court and the punishments to be dealt out. We had a king and queen, darling, and they were dressed for the part. The king wore a sheet, a mop for a beard and had a crown made of sheet metal. The queen had shorts, large breasts held in by some pink cloth and a mop for a beard.

The first very scared guy walked up, blindfolded, and court was in session. He was accused of many crimes, among which was failing to take the eggs from the crow's nest when coming off watch last night. Being defended by a shellback, he didn't have much of a chance! He was quickly put in the pillory and locked there. He was given a shot of "all cure" to swallow. It consisted of everything one can think of with a bad taste. He was duly painted and stripped of all clothing. Released from the pillory, he had to crawl through a wind sail, a canvas chute, of about seventy feet. There were two fire hoses shooting water at him from either end, and it took him some time to make it. He was paddled the entire length of the chute, so he had no choice but to get out quickly. After this, he went through the formal court and was declared a shellback. The others duly followed, and were accused, convicted and punished and then sworn in. It was a good day all around for such an initiation, and we all entered into the spirit of the thing.

This morning Doug, on his watch, started another one. He has a new ordinary seaman who hasn't been to sea before. He's been found very vulnerable, and this morning they heaped more sorrow on his back. He was instructed to get into the crow's nest and watch for the equator. The mate had to know when we passed it, so that we could change the compass cards, etc. etc. Doug would yell up once in a while to see if he had yet seen anything, and he would make another serious study of the skyline from his perch and yell down that he didn't see it yet. He questioned the old-timers on deck about the equator, wanting to know what it would look like. They gladly told him it would resemble a white line such as in seen on the highways back home. He thanked them and scanned the water for miles around. Of course, he never did see it, and he's feeling pretty badly about it tonight. He has been told that the compasses will be off now, and we may miss our destination because of his missing the line! He is quite gullible, as you can see.

Later: I'm back on watch now. Frisco radio is bringing all of the news direct to us from all over the world now, so we don't have our usual nightly arguments. We sit quietly and listen to the news over the radio. The war is being won, and we all hope that the end comes soon in Europe. There was a rather pessimistic guy on the air tonight with some news of the new fortifications which have to be breached before we can get at Germany proper. Let's hope everything comes out all right over there. Think of the work those Americans over there have ahead of them, darling!

I'm right up to date on the news and stuff on most subjects. Movies, sports, medicine, literature, war or what have you, I feel well prepared to say a few words on the latest. We have better facilities now for getting news. And much better company to argue in, Bun. We've got a college crew on here.

With about two weeks to go, darlin', I'm already thinking about getting mail from you. I'd kinda like to know just what your plans for the coming months are! Right now from your other letters, I don't know whether you're in Fargo, San Diego or Chicago—or in between! Don't you think your husband should know?

Your guy, forever,
Beat

⇒   ⇐

September 1, 1944

Read an article in *Esquire* today entitled "From Babe to Battle-axe." As you guessed, it's a poor guy, very seriously trying to find out why women change so after they are married. He asks, "Why does the shy, gentle, affectionate girl turn into the loud, bossy, frigid woman? The shrinking violet, domestic girl into the egomaniacal careerist? The girl of high marks in school with an apparently lively, alert mind into a mentally indolent, unprogressive woman, the prey of astrologers, cultists and other mental mountebanks? The girl of the Sunday School virtues into the woman of dubious character, addicted to one too many drinks?" Etc., etc. He writes in all seriousness, Bun, and it's quite a laugh some of the time. And other times I shudder to think you might do some of the nutty things some women do when they grow older! He sums up and makes the "ideal wife" the gal who can "cook a meal without making her husband

feel it was a sacrifice or chore to do it; if
she can entertain his friends without spilling
highballs down their necks; be a good lover and
good friend, and both at the right times." He's
quite a choosy sort of guy, darling, but I am,
too. And I know I've a gal who measures up to
even this idealistic sort of woman!

⇢ ⇤

LETTER 47
September 4, 1944
South Pacific

My darling wife,

We found out today that there is, after all,
some other life out here. And it was a real
pleasure to pass some other ships. We sneaked up
on them, I think, and it must have surprised one
particular crew. You see, there were two ships.
One had managed to pass the other by having
a bare advantage in speed. They were probably
feeling pretty good when we rushed past both of
them without any trouble at all. I know how they
must have felt, cuz I've been on those slower
ships and watched some other ship go flying by.
And I promised myself then that I would get
on one of these babies—well, needless to say,
here I am! And it's just as good a feeling as
I thought it would be, Bunny.

Your loving husband,
Beat

September 8, 1944

We had a beautiful sunset tonight, darling. It's really true what you see in those travel talks back home. The horizon was as clear cut as one could ever see. The clouds were like silhouettes set against a background of colors ranging from bright red to the deepest purple. The water down here is smooth as silk, too, and it took on all of the reflected colors of the sky. I couldn't really describe it, as you can see, but it's something one has to see to believe.

I'll always appreciate such things much more when I sit with you in some darkened theater in the middle of the winter back home, sweets. They really are true—"And as we leave this tropical paradise, we -----." We spent some time out on deck just admiring the sky. We're going to have something to tell our grandchildren about. But this war had better be done with in a hurry or there won't be any little ones around to tell all these stories to.

LETTER 51

September 9, 1944
So. Pacific

My darling wife,

We had gunnery practice today. The boys are really good, and our Merchant gunners did pretty darn well, considering everything—in fact, we broke more balloons at longer range than the Navy boys did. Our Deacon, the first time on a gun of this sort, hit two balloons without any trouble. He is from Arkansas, and he says his dad used to send him out in the morning with two rocks, and if he didn't come home with two squirrels, he'd beat him. He surprised all of us, and we are now calling him "Deadeye" instead of Deacon.

When I write here on watch, I always wonder the next morning how a guy could write such a letter!

Your guy, for always, Bunny,
Beat

LETTER 52
September 10, 1944
SW Pacific

My darling Bunny,

We've spent a lot of time reading maps and talking about things in history down this way. Our Chief, of course, knows all about the various naval actions, and we get the inside dope from him. We pool other things we have heard, and it makes the map come alive. We've become map conscious down here. I imagine that in my job I get a better idea of where we are each day, and most of the places stick in my mind. I'm always reaching for a map when I run across a strange place!

Often in the middle of these mysterious nights, surrounded by submarines and Jap warships, attacked by Jap planes and living through all the other "horrors" of war, I find myself addressing envelopes to "Mrs. Beaton." Somehow it makes me forget my other troubles. They're as nothing compared with my domestic ones.

With all my love, forever,
Your husband,
Beat

Hours to Recover

October 1944

"Bunny, are you okay?" Elinor heard her mother. Then she saw her, peeking through a narrow slit of daylight, as she held the door from the kitchen slightly ajar.

Elinor raised her head from the daybed in the den. "*Mütterchen?*" She opened her eyes, just a slit.

Trudie entered the study with a current of air that released the mixture of aromas of breakfast into the darkened room. Fried eggs. Dark toast. Coffee. She carried a few ice cubes wrapped in a washrag.

Elinor held the ice pack to her head for a couple of minutes before vomiting again into the wastebasket beside her bed. She lay back down with a moan.

It was day two of this migraine. She'd been through the aura, the premonition that she was about to get slammed. Now she was down for the count.

Her father had rolled his Royal typewriter on its cart to the porch to work on the Sunday's sermon. Periodically he peeked into his study to find something he needed, a concordance or a sheet of carbon paper. It was dark in there and stuffy, too, even with the windows open. Breezes couldn't make it through the drawn Venetian blinds and the layer of curtaining that kept any light out of the space.

Georg checked Elinor on each foray he made into his study. He leaned in toward her, hoping that he'd find her stirring and ready to begin the revival process.

But Elinor lay inert.

These headaches weren't as bad as the one that had hospitalized her. But, because there were so many of them, her life had crashed. Her weight had plummeted. Her thinking grew fuzzy. She wondered if this were her punishment for breaking the fourth commandment. She hadn't honored her mother and her father and now her days were bound to be short in the land that the Lord God had given her.

Migraines were mysterious. A doctor's best effort involved a hypo, a shot given during a house call. But by the time a doctor was finished at the clinic, the headache was already raging, and the hypo had little effect.

Elinor had made another appointment to see Dr. Klein. He was a specialist in women's issues. Menstruation was women's business. Weren't headaches women's issues, too? All the women in the family got these migraines and none of the men suffered.

As she lay on her bed, her head throbbing, Elinor prayed to be well enough to see him. Her appointment was scheduled for Monday. Just 48 hours to recover, to be well enough to bear the sunlight again.

Another Anniversary

September 1944

LETTER 55
September 13, 1944
S.W. Pacific

My darling wife,

Rain is coming down slowly but steadily and heavily. I'm here in the radio room at eleven o'clock in the morning and I have on most of the powerful lights—reminds me of the days of the "dust blitz." I've completed all of my checks, and everything is in A-1 condition as we near port.

I started things wrong this morning. We're starting on our atrabine (for malaria) course now and it'll continue until we leave these parts again. These pills taste like hell, as I found this morning. I put one in my mouth as I left here and walked back aft to get a drink of water before breakfast to wash it down. By the time I got there, I was in a good dead run. The guys in the salon when I arrived let out a yell and wanted to know what was the matter. I told them, after I had a drink of water, and it got a good laugh from them—the rats!

I've been trying to get letters ready to mail this morning, and I've really got a pile of them. There is still one large book to go through and get in envelopes—it's the book I have written you since I started this leg of the trip. Some day we may be able to read over those and get a lot of good stories started. I have no doubts but what they will someday rank with the other great letters of the literary world.

Tomorrow is our anniversary, Bun. Remember? Two months of married life and four hours awake with each other! As long as I live, I'll never forget your face when the judge asked you, "And is it your wish, Miss Landgrebe, that I sign this waiver?" Surprised—we couldn't have been more so—at the ease with which we were allowed to waive the three-day waiting period there in Seattle. The next thing we knew, we were walking down the street with a license!

Beat

LETTER 56
September 13, 1944
S.W. Pacific

My dearest,

Surprise! Yeah, I'm out again, and all I had time for was mailing a few letters to you by way of a guy in a bitty boat, darling, and I hope that he takes good care of them. We didn't get any mail, Bun, but we are still hoping to get some soon. I wrote the other letters to you as "Miss" so there will be need for no worry. But I'm getting a bit tired of it. Hope I get good news in our next mail, Elinor.

It's a good night, and we are still smiling to ourselves tonight due to some of the events today, Bunny. And, sorry to say, it is impossible to list them here. With all the excitement of things this day, I'm having a hard time settling into the dull routine business tonight, honey.

(Letter continues on same page)

September 14, 1944
Guess where

My darling,

I didn't finish last night—just wasn't in the mood, so I picked some letters from Hank (enemy action) up and got interested. The evening went before I knew it, and when I saw the above scrap of a letter, I had to laugh, Bun.

We're in rather interesting country, darling.

The skipper has clamped down on security on here, and the engineers don't know where we are going. They ask the mates and me in many roundabout ways, but we just can't give it out. When the Captain tells them, they'll know. On our last leg of the trip, very few fellows knew where we were going. I found that out as we stood on deck looking at the land. The guys were asking me where we were! But one has to know in order to have charts and things ready for broadcasts out here. Don't you like to have secrets?

Right now we're on a kinda "rest" basis, but we aren't through with this part of the world for some time, according to the rumors.

Hope we get mail soon. I need something to boost my morale. I just need to have you tell me you love me now and then to make me completely happy out here.

All my love always,
Beat

LETTER 58
September 19, 1944
Central Pacific

My darling,

And if you could only feel the emotions which
are going through me as I sit here, you would
be cognizant of the trembling in me as I write
"My darling." Suffice it to say that I'm more or
less of a wreck right now, and I really don't
know how I am able to type to you. The mail
arrived today, and, as always, it has made
me blue, nervous, worried, anxious for more
news and just plain homesick. Six letters from
you arrived today, dating from August 14th to
September 6th. There were letters from most of
the guys, too.

I'm worried almost sick about the clinic
reports, darling, and I wish you would be a bit
more specific about those things. Right now I
let my fertile imagination run away with common
sense at times, and it is definitely not fun. The
various troubles, which you describe in such a
roundabout way, seem to me to be quite serious.
I know that everything will come out all right
and that you will do things right, but I still
feel so out of this that there's a feeling of
uselessness I can't shake. This is hell, Bun.

With Johnny's arrival, your troubles will be
a bit tougher, Bunny, but I haven't anything
to do with those problems! Thank the Lord for
that! You've let him know for some time that
you weren't in love with him, so he should
understand. It's up to you to work that out—and

right away without any hedging and stuff, huh? If we work out all the problems we have, life ahead will certainly be easy for us, my sweets. I've worked out all of my problems, and now we have some community problems and a few of yours to settle. Then we're on our way to the easier days.

Your loving husband, always,
Beat

There are so very many things which have to be gone into, Elinor, and I've just about given up hope at times that they will ever be overcome. The folks, Johnny Holsen, Walt, etc. You don't seem to discard troubles, but rather to add to them. Somehow, darling, it isn't the way I imagined things would be for us. Only now when I really do want you for my very own have I ever objected to the things which seem to have you entangled so that you can't belong to me in name or entirely in your own mind. I'm what you so aptly describe as aggravated. I can see all of the ramifications of a sudden announcement and all, Bun. But, too, I can see all the possibilities for future unhappiness, darling, if things aren't soon worked out back home.

I guess I'd better resort to the weather again for a subject. It was a heck of a pretty night—starry and clear and warm. Blacked out ships and the smell of cargo oil and a rather static-y program from Tokyo.

LETTER 59
September 19, 1944
Central Pacific

Dearest Elinor,

I went to work this afternoon to get my mind
occupied for a while, and Doug and I set up
a lifeboat for the lifeboat transmitter. It
works darn well, but we just wanted to know! We
worked for some time on the rigging, as it is
a different kind of boat from any we have seen
on the ships. Just had supper now, and I wasn't
too hungry—just kind of nibbled. We all did more
or less. One of the guys lost a younger brother
on Guam, so the mail wasn't such good news for
him. I can only imagine how I would feel if I
were in his place. Getting news of that kind out
here is harder to take than back in the States.
It seems to be so much closer.

   We had some fun for a few days, but it's over
for a while now. We're just sitting here, and
we may be here for some time. I'll probably
get another letter from Hank, even, before I
leave these parts. Bruns saw some two or three
thousand Japs out here, so they are getting rid
of them gradually. The guys organize hunting
parties for the strays, and some of us are
talking about getting into one. Don't know if
it's rumor or not, but I think it's true.

   We're in a nice little bay—not so little
either. It's hard to realize that many good

Americans lost their lives for this place. A strange world, darling, and I wish somebody had the power to straighten things out once and for all

>   My love, forever,
>   Your husband,
>   Beat

❯❯   ❮❮

September 20, 1944

Over on the islands the vapor is rising from the jungle and it makes a rather pretty sight from here. I imagine the fellows over there are rather uncomfortable, though, with the very damp, warm air there. It looks a bit weird from out here, Bunny, especially right now at sunset.

I'm quite anxious to get to our next port and get some more info on the doings back home. There's really no use in worrying when there is really so little that I can do. But I will be happy and philosophical about things for the most part. I know that you will do the best you can under the conditions, and any advice I can give you from out here is out-dated by the time it arrives. So, my darling, 'tis in your hands for the most part, and I'm trusting you to work things out for the benefit of both of us.

September 21, 1944

Just heard another of the blasts around here. They've been blasting for some time, but we have more or less become used to it now. I used to run out and see if I could see anything flying in the air, but I got tired of seeing water, coconut trees, and mud flying, and I let them oversee their own work now. Suppose there are Seabees over there on land doing the work, building bases. From things I have seen, they do a darn good job on places out here, Bunny. Oh, those bell bottoms, hmmm!

"The closer the enemy comes to our homeland, the more advantageous our position," says Tokyo Radio. They have a long way to go now to dictate the peace in the White House! But let them dream for a few more months. And I hope they all commit hari-kari when the time comes. Bet the Emperor and other big shots don't have the nerve to do what they ask their subordinates to do!

⇒   ⇐

LETTER 63
September 22, 1944
Pacific

My darling wife,

Now the Philippines have declared war on us! What a mixed up sort of thing this war has become in the past few years. And how much more mixed up it will be when the peace draws nearer and nearer. I can just see the boys fighting over the peace now. It's going to be good newspaper stuff for many a month, darling. Or many a year.

Doggone, I just went outside to see what all the excitement was, and it was another of these storms. They come up suddenly, out of a clear sky, and they hit like a ton of bricks. This came across an island about three miles away, and it still carried most of the island's sand with it. It piled up all over the ship out here, and I got pretty dirty in just a minute outside. The wind is now whistling around the ship, the rain is driving down, and it is cooling off even more. It's dark and it reminds me some of one of those old dust storms—the ones we experienced a few years back in North Dakota. I'll take a good clean blizzard, tucked in bed at home with a good book and a nice warm fire going.

Just watched us tie up alongside another ship, Bun, and we did a good job of it. With the rain coming down so hard, we had to make two runs at it before we got in the right position for coming in close. Then we only nicked them a bit! Rain is dripping off this ship now like rain off a duck. There are many ingeniously designed drain pipes from one deck to another with much of the system left to the imagination and it is sometimes quite uncomfortable to stand in the "protected" areas of the ship. Ships are meant to be wet and uncomfortable outside, I guess, and they are. That's why it requires so many paint jobs during a trip—to try to combat the rust as it comes.

Oh, yeah, Bunny, I am taking two correspondence

courses from the State College of Washington. I sent from here for the books and stuff. Both business administration courses—marketing and a course in plain ol' administration. I'm darn interested in both courses. The only worry is the mail service and how it will affect the amount of work I shall be able to do. I have asked for a waiver of the rule allowing only two lessons to be sent out at once. Heck, I can finish that much in no time, and the rest of one of these long trips would be empty.

⇉ ⇇

8:00 AM—September 24

I had two beautiful eggs this morning, and as I reached for the salt and pepper, I thought of how you liked both. I got really lonesome for you, Bun. And at breakfast, too!

I thought of you during the church hours this morning, thinking back to the times I've seen you play for the congregation. Maybe you thought of me, too. I hope, sweets. Good night, my love.

Your loving husband,
Darrow

At the Organ
Sunday, October 22, 1944

THE MODEST WHITE CLAPBOARD church stood at the corner of Tenth Street and Twelfth Avenue, on the flat prairie outskirts of Fargo. A row of cars and a lone truck waited in the graveled parking lot outside the crowded sanctuary. A mostly leafless tree stood in the front lawn. Piles of yellow and orange leaves had settled around it.

The doors of the narthex stood wide open, to encourage any wayward breezes inside. The windows, planned for eventually holding stained glass, couldn't be opened. The sanctuary air was jungle-like, still and humid, on this rapidly warming October Sunday morning.

The hymn finished, Elinor played the last chords on the organ. Ah-men. She folded her hands in her lap and waited, partially hidden from the congregation by the console and left alone to her thoughts.

She spotted Mrs. Wolseth in the congregation. Her son was in the Pacific on one of those islands. Still alive, as far as anyone in Fargo knew. Children in the back rows began to squirm, and a baby cried. Its mother stood and carried the tiny one outside for a walk. Elinor pressed her fingers into her forehead.

The pastor, Reverend Keller, stepped down after introducing Reverend Landgrebe. Elinor's father, honored guest speaker for this service, walked to the lectern and spread open his big Bible. He stood straight and dignified in his black robes while the congregation rustled, arranging themselves into more comfortable positions as they settled their sweaty bodies in the pews.

Rev. Landgrebe began reading. "The Gospel according to Luke. Please turn to Luke 7, verse 36. The story of Jesus being anointed by a sinful woman."

Elinor knew what would be next. His wartime theme song.

He'd talk about the sins of modern society, the sheer extravagance contrasting this time of suffering and war. Movie stars gone wild. The drinking, partying, the immorality across the continent, the breakdown of marriage.

She wondered whether her father would mention the Ilka Chase book which Beat had sent her (and she'd actually enjoyed as she immersed herself in the love scenes). Had he even been aware that his daughter was reading such trash?

Elinor shifted uncomfortably on her bench. Her Sunday dress was getting tight, even though she vomited almost daily. Her head felt fuzzy. Her eyes automatically avoided the sunshine streaming through the church windows. These new headaches were such a curse. She looked into her lap.

"Brethren," her father spoke softly to start. "Forasmuch as each man is part of this human race . . ."

Elinor let her mind wander. Back to Seattle. Doing things her father would never believe . . .

"Marriage is honorable, insomuch as Christ Himself . . ." He began to gesticulate, robe quivering around his upraised arm. "Truly . . ."

Truly, she had difficulty keeping her thoughts focused these days. For she had let these Wretched Times and her inflated thoughts of love carry her away. Was she feverish? She felt her head. Probably this oven of a church . . .

"For what Christian man in these times . . ."

What Christian woman lies to her parents about what she's doing on the West Coast? What Christian woman parties with a fellow while he waits for his new ship? Even if the fellow is heading for long shuttle runs among war-torn islands in the South Pacific? Was that an excuse for such actions?

"For truly we must consider what this means to society today," her father was raising his voice now. Was he looking directly at her? She slid back a bit on the bench. People squirmed in their seats. Were they guilty of some of this immorality? More likely, in Fargo, they were trying to keep awake.

Elinor's thoughts returned to June. As the train neared the California coast, she had been filled with the sense of adventure—something she rarely felt in Dakota. When she flew into Darrow's arms at the station in Long Beach, she felt sure that leaving Johnny's engagement ring back home had been a good thing to do.

Reverend Landgrebe summarized his sermon. God was the protector of the Allies. God hadn't abandoned the world into chaos and hellfire. But the nation had to respond to the Almighty with prayer, family stability and support for our troops.

Elinor's thoughts snapped back to the present when Reverend Keller took back the pulpit. He thanked her father.

She began playing again as the ushers came forward for the blessing before they collected whatever spare change the congregants possessed.

As she played, pictures of the days with Darrow flitted through the hymn. Romantic evenings. Dinners out with drinks and orchestras playing songs from the Hit Parade. Traveling around Long Beach again, then the sights of San Francisco. Why, she'd taken a train north, following him to the final lading of his new tanker in Seattle.

She stopped playing on cue.

Reverend Keller invoked a blessing over the collection plates and then led the congregation in the singing of the doxology. "Praise God from whom all blessings flow. Praise Him all creatures here below. Praise Him above, ye Heavenly host. Praise Father, Son and Holy Ghost." The congregation, hot and eager to exit, was restive.

Elinor sat at the organ, coming back from far away. She prayed for help, for a plan for telling her parents—her sweet and kind parents, the ones who had expected more from her. She had broken the code, Post's code of behavior, the modern idea of trusting unchaperoned girls.

The announcements droned on. Ladies aid meeting on Tuesday, Luther League this afternoon . . .

Finally. "Turn to Hymn No. 149, 'The Church's One Foundation.'"

Hymnals were drawn out of their racks, pages turned quickly. Elinor played a few measures so any interested singers could find the key.

Anticipating the end of the service, the congregation sang with more energy, though no one would claim "gusto" in the voices of any Lutheran gathering. Her father sang loudest of all, trying to raise the volume in the chancel: "The church's one foundation is . . ."

Reverend Keller intoned the benediction, "The Lord bless you and keep you. The Lord be gracious unto you. The Lord lift his countenance upon you and grant you His peace."

Elinor played the recessional as the parishioners filed out of the sanctuary. At last she folded her music. She ducked out the side door of the familiar church, glided across the dewy lawn and evaded the other congregants who chatted outdoors.

As she began her hike home, she kicked at the fallen leaves on the sidewalk in front of her. It was time to face the music.

Life on the Benny

October 1944

LETTER 67
October 2, 1944
South Pacific

My darling wife,

We are short of water due to some trouble in the engine room, so we have to use a bucket of water for our showers now. It's not as much fun to shower, but it feels just as good, honey. I ordered a shower for myself, and it felt wonderful. One fills a pail with water, soaps down and then rinses off. Then a cold bucket of water is thrown over and drying is in order. It's quite a job to learn to do it properly, but, once learned, everything goes smoothly.

With all my love,
Beat

October 7, 1944

I was deep in a dream. I had walked out your front door with you. We talked about things so naturally that it's hard to believe it was a dream. I'm usually falling off a cliff, killing 4000 Japs with my bare hands, etc. So this was a wonderful change, honey.

→⇥   ⇤←

LETTER 73
October 10
Pacific
[handwritten]

My darling wife,

The Series is over, and we're once again caught with the quiet, unexcited sort of life which is the usual thing aboard ship.

We have a new game, darling. The first mate and I take turns at asking this sort of question: Where is X and how many miles from XX and how many days steaming for us? He knows the Atlantic better than I do, especially the Gulf, but I have the Pacific, Indian and Mediterranean with me. We've eliminated most of the well-known ports now, so we're beginning to learn together. By the time we're through with a port, we have exchanged all the news, stories, etc. about it—our own experiences and those of others. The world is full of things to talk about. Where is the Sea of Okhotsk and is it open all year 'round? That'll keep you busy while I dash back for coffee and a Frisco news report, honey.

Bunny, we're rolling closer to that third anniversary of ours each day. After this long away, the months seem somehow to be immeasurable. There isn't any medium for us to use in determining time. We remember rather vaguely hitting ports here and there. They seem far away, too, and rather dulled in interest. We're in one of the periods of stagnation. I'm sure we'll all emerge from this fantastic "Dreamland" a couple of days out of port. Word will get out, pools for arrival time will be organized, washing will be done, and everybody will begin making plans for some time ashore.

⇨   ⇦

October 11

Last night I was taken away from you suddenly, and this is the first chance I've had to get back. It's 24 hours exactly, so one might say I've had a busy day.

I had the most wonderful dream. We pulled into this port we're going to, and they informed us we were going to the States—with passengers. The Captain came in and told me that due to the number of passengers, all officers would share their quarters. I readied some room for my guest's clothes and things. Then came the big surprise. In walked my guest, and it was you, darling! Don't try to figure out how you got there. I didn't! Dreams sometimes show a person's frustration, and this one really did. I wanted to kiss you and hold you in my arms, but the usually very aggravating things (happened) in this dream—guys came in to paint the decks, inspectors arrived for the radio, Doug poked his head in a port to talk, customs came in to check your luggage and get passports cleared, the Captain came in to see if I had worked things out to your satisfaction. You might imagine that it took me quite some time to wake, but I did finally give up, darling, when they came in to tell me it was chow time! You looked so real, darling, that it is hard for me now to believe it really was only a dream.

Your husband—
Beat

Letter 76
October 16, 1944
Pacific

My darling,

Got rather hungry for a candy bar today—'twas a horrible yearning, too. After a day of recurrent attacks of dizziness when thinking of it, I thought of a solution. So, as I sit here now after supper, I have chocolate. I stole it from my abandon ship kit!

Everybody is happy again with port near us. All kinds of plans. Hey, Bun, I had another dream last night. I've had it before, too. Dreamed a letter from you had "Mrs. D. R. Beaton" in that upper left hand corner. Maybe I'll be lucky enough to see that this time, Bunny. Hope so.

Never forget my love, Elinor—
Beat

October 18, 1944
Port
[handwritten]

Darling,

The mail came and I've run through your six
perfect letters. You're having a time there with
so many things coming up, and you still find
time to write me a happy letter. I admire your
courage—just plain "guts," as we would say here.
I'll never again try to tell you what to do from
a safe, comfortable back seat—especially about
things you yourself must decide. Your attitude,
"Everything will come out all right," is flavored
with just enough serious planning so that I know
you're doing your very best, my darling.

Tomorrow I'm going to try to find a lawyer or
someone who knows about these things so that I
can send you my blanket approval for anything.
It might take months for us to be sending things
back and forth when something that should have
been done is put off until too late. Your
judgment is good enough for me, my darling,
and I want you to be able to do things when
they should be done, Bunny. What matters to me
is that I'm able to have you, Bunny. The other
things are quite secondary to that, honey. You
understand, don't you?

Doggone, Bun, 'tis good to hear that you're
teaching again. But what subjects for my darling!!
Some day you and I will have to have geography
classes together, huh? What makes it seem so
good is that you have a rather steady routine.
Your letters reflect your early season happiness

in the job, and, from what you say, you're going to be happy there right along. You can be home every weekend, too, which is pretty grand.

Your devoted husband,
Beat

A Bit Dizzy

the same Sunday, October 22

"LUNCHTIME!" TRUDIE CALLED THE family to gather at the dining room table, which had been set with her best dishes (the slightly cracked plate at Trudie's place), their wedding flatware and a white linen tablecloth that announced the Family Best.

They gathered quickly, the preachers from the den, Elinor and Mickey from the kitchen where they had been gathering last minute dishes to set the table, and Irene from the upstairs bedroom. It was Sunday afternoon about one. Sunday morning church services were finished. The next services were scheduled toward evening.

It was surprising how her mother could devise such meals, carefully meting out the ration coupons that each of the sisters contributed. The china bowl of leftover gravy and a few chunks of beef steamed in the center of the dining room table. The *kartoffelkloesse*, those delicious German potato dumplings her father fashioned from leftover mashed potatoes, lay steaming on the green glass plate. Somewhere down the table there were a few carrots from their Victory garden, pared and cooked.

In the days before the war, butter melted on the carrots, and a table wasn't set properly without bread and butter at every meal. Elinor remembered the taste of real butter, remembered playing with the fancy yellow pats in the San Francisco restaurants just weeks ago when she and Darrow had vacationed together.

This meager Sunday feast would have to make it around the table set for the five family members currently in residence and Rev. Hoeger, guest speaker at the late afternoon missions meeting.

The good reverend said a quick blessing. Georg passed him the meat and he helped himself. Elinor's father took several spoonfuls from the dish before starting it around the table. Mickey and Irene took small portions, noting the decrease in the dish as it was passed.

As the bowl neared Elinor, she smelled the gravy first. Her stomach turned. She couldn't look at the tiny chunks of meat left swimming in the bowl she held. Woozy, she set the dish down on the tablecloth.

"I'm feeling a bit dizzy today."

"Oh, Bunny," her mother sympathized, leaning in toward her across the table. "Another migraine? Or is it the same one?"

Elinor excused herself. "I think I'll lie down a while. Perhaps it's this heat."

She heard her mother excusing her absence as she left the room. "Bunny has had a miserable series of migraines lately. It was fortunate that she could play for church this morning."

"We're ready to try Mayo again," her father explained.

Her daybed tucked away, Elinor rushed up the front hall stairs, past the bedrooms, to the single bathroom in the house. She closed the door behind her. There she paced the small room, from toilet to bathtub and back again, four steps each way.

"Those people" refused to come. She remembered her brief period shortly after she returned from Seattle, a relief to her and to Beat.

She sat on the edge of the bathtub, willing her body to cooperate, praying for a reprieve. "I've been a good girl since Seattle," she thought. What could be the matter?"

In the study below, her father and his guest, now finished with supper, settled in to listen to the news from London on the Scott short wave radio. Elinor could hear the reports from all the war fronts as the reporters' voices reverberated through the house.

She plugged her ears. "Damned war!!" Her mind raced. She stood and paced again. Bathtub to toilet. Toilet to bathtub.

Elinor stopped in front of the mirror, grabbing the small sink for support. Her reflection alarmed her. Was she anemic again? Maybe it was that pelvic inflammation acting up. What a fix!

She heard a tap on the bathroom door. She quickly washed her face and dried it with a threadbare hand towel. She pinched her cheeks, an emergency rouge job, then opened the door to find her sister standing there.

"You okay?" Mickey asked.

"I guess so," Elinor answered.

"You don't look so good, kid."

"I've got to play for the service this afternoon. Just pulling myself together." Elinor attempted a grin. She flushed the toilet for good measure.

"C'mon, let's get some fresh air. Those pastors are smoking up the place," Mickey suggested. The girls walked downstairs.

"Be careful, Bunny," their mother called to them as they passed through the kitchen.

On their way out the front door, they paused a moment in the porch where the men had settled.

The pastors were just starting their after-dinner routine. They took out their pipes and filled the bowls with tobacco. Georg passed his new silver lighter to his friend. They leaned back into the wicker porch chairs. The conversation, after general talk about the evening's mission meeting, focused on the war in Europe and heated them up. Even the small rotating electric fan, aimed directly at them, couldn't find enough cool air to fling around the room.

"Hitler," Rev. Hoeger's tone judged the man. "How could the good Germans be following this tyrant?"

Her father nodded as he drew on the stem of his pipe. Smoke curled around the pastors' heads and hung there a while before dissipating into the late afternoon sunshine. The men were drowsy, the conversation languid, allowing for reflection between tidbits of talk. Eventually, as usual, they would turn to relatives in the fatherland. No way to communicate with them now.

Mickey and Elinor ducked out of the door. They returned just in time for the short walk to the late afternoon service at church.

Later, after Rev. Hoeger's missions meeting and his subsequent departure, the family settled into the living room.

"This must have been the warmest October day on record," her mother declared, opening up the curtains and then the windows to let in any available evening breezes.

"We have to appreciate these days, though. We know what's coming," Mickey chimed in.

A fall chill with the setting of the sun reminded them all, as the cool air slipped into the house, clearing out the stale, smoky air.

Elinor played a few tunes on the piano, but her thoughts of the upcoming appointment with Dr. Klein distracted her. She left the piano bench and went into the kitchen where she began to put away a few dishes that had been drying in the draining rack.

Georg put his papers down on the table beside him and picked up his pipe.

Instead of the usual bedtime coffee, Trudie passed around glasses of icy water. She had used all the ice cubes from the two aluminum trays, some of them only half-frozen after the afternoon lemonade. It would take all night for their busy refrigerator to freeze some solid cubes again.

When they were done with the news and the drinks, Trudie set all the glasses in the sink and turned out the lights in the kitchen. Georg turned off the short wave radio and locked both doors of the house. He yawned. Then, with Trudie in the lead, the Landgrebes drifted upstairs to bed. Mickey and Irene had dashed ahead of them, vying for the single bathroom.

Alone in the den, Elinor spread her nightie out on her daybed. She fluffed the pillow and found the sheets and the chenille bedspread in the closet. In a few minutes her bed was ready. She sat on its edge.

Tomorrow, Dr. Klein. Maybe he'd have an answer.

Business

October 1944

Letter 79
October 19, 1944
1:30 A.M.
[handwritten]

My darling wife,

You'll be proud of me before too long, Bunny.
Washington State sent me the correspondence
courses, texts and all—all the lessons at once,
too!! So, I've got another interest in life out
here. As soon as I get things cleared up with
the college, I'm going to get more such courses
and come darn close to a degree before leaving
the sea. Wouldn't it be wonderful if I could
graduate while on a trip to the South Pacific!
Boy, I'm happy about this thing.
   My war ballot arrived, too, but I won't tell
you how I vote, darling, not for a few years.
You may be sure I'll exercise my citizenship
rights by voting for the best man. We may have
different ideas on these things, but I don't

wish to carry on a fifty-year feud with my sweet
wife about the election of '44!

I'll dream of you, I know, and they'll be
wonderful dreams. You're sleeping soundly now.
I'll soon be sound asleep in . . .

Your husband,
Beat

October 19
10:30 A.M.

My Bunny,

I changed my insurance over to you in full—in case (and I say "in case" with a smile on my baby face) anything happens. Be sure to insist on $5,000.00!! Maybe I'm not worth it, but this is another generous gesture of our government and I want you to take advantage of it "in case." Guess I'll send the policy to you under another cover, as they have some information stamped on it and the censors will no doubt hold it up for a while. It's just a bit of routine business so don't dream anything up to worry yourself, Bun darling.

My mail is really good. Harry writes about life on his tanker—the only one afloat that blows smoke rings. Ships these days have devices to prevent smoking. Smoke can be seen for miles and gives a ship away to subs or planes. They lost part of their stack out in the Pacific in a "hot one" so they blow rings—and fire at night.

Think of me often, my sweet. I think of you day and night, no matter what comes up. Such as, "Elinor makes better coffee than this." And putting cream in my coffee, I remember you don't use sugar. All kinds of little happy thoughts pass by as I live through a day here.

Your guy, forever—
Beat

Letter 80
October 19, 1944
[handwritten]

Dearest wife,

Guys have been stopping in during the evening to share my Planter's peanuts, so the time has gone only too quickly. I told Mom I was going to write Jim [code] tonight, but you see how it all ended up. Tomorrow I'll write him and Vic. It's been a long while since I wrote them!

You're taking up every moment I have these days in port. I either write you or write about you to others. If you could see some of those recommendations! Full blown as some of the adjectives are, they can't come close to describing my wife.

My love, always, Bun,
Beat

❯❯   ❮❮

October 20, 1944 P.S.

I was just about asleep last night when my door was opened and some guy hollered for me. It was a radioman off a badly pummeled ship looking for a place to sleep. Of course I gave him a place on my couch, and we began talking. I should say, rather, that he began talking! And so on into the wee, small hours. He's on a [censor cut out with a razor] like this with a big hole in the bottom and she should be in near us today. He'd gone looking for her before I got up.

⋙   ⋘

Letter 81
October 21, 1944

My darling Bunny,

Have you ever seen tugs go to work on a huge ship? Two are working us around now, and it's a real sight to see them shoot around the ship to the right place, give a grunt and shove like mad, then run to the other side to stop us and start us another way. They really can maneuver a ship in these cramped places. A ship would be the proverbial "bull in the china closet" if it weren't for them. And they have the screwiest whistle and bells, too. Bet those guys who are slinging lines and things around down there on the tug aren't enjoying the beauty of the tug's performance!

And, darling, I'm mailing Doctor Hunter a letter giving you every right to do as you please. I don't know just what is going on, but I shall ask Doctor Hunter for the details when I write him. I'll send you a carbon copy of the letter so that you will know what is going on, Bunny. Sometimes I get all worried about the whole thing, and I can't shake the feeling that even now you may be going through something so darn tough. You told me in one letter that you didn't want to tell me because I had seemed worried in a letter in answer to some of the details you had written to me. I want to share this with you as a husband should, sweets. So, please send me all the news no matter what it is. And you needn't worry about the censors touching your mail cuz they still haven't opened any of the letters I've received this trip. Sit down soon and tell me all about it, Bunny, cuz your guy is more worried now than if he knew exactly what the situation is.

Your devoted husband,
Beat

Sunrise

The following Saturday, October 28

Elinor heard the train whistle. The *North Coast Limited* would be pulling into the depot just five blocks away. Her heart skipped a beat. She was nearly out of time.

She felt the sunrise, even before she saw its light. The night shadows began to vanish into the faint blush that announced the prelude to daylight. Elinor looked up. She brushed her hair back out of her eyes.

The light from the desk lamp lit the letter she still held in her hand. A stack of envelopes from her stash rested atop her father's papers on the desk. She had scanned these last letters, letters she knew nearly by heart from multiple re-readings of them.

Elinor glanced at the clock. She pushed the red button on the desk lamp and the fluorescent bulb dimmed over the mess on the desk. The family would be coming down for breakfast any minute.

She dashed into the kitchen and set her empty coffee cup, the one left over from last night's reading, into the kitchen sink. She poured water and ladled coffee grounds into the Coffeemaster, just as the milkman appeared on the back porch with their quart of milk. The glass bottles in his delivery basket clinked together, a gentle chiming of the dairy bells. Although the new war rules required daylight deliveries of milk, the family wasn't usually awake and in the kitchen this early. Elinor opened the door to greet him as he leaned over on the back porch to collect the cleaned glass bottle from the previous week.

"You're up early," he laughed as he handed her the glass quart bottle of Cass Clay milk.

She laughed, too. "I guess I've worked through the night. And I'm still not finished." She thanked him, closed the door, and stowed the fresh milk in the refrigerator. "I actually haven't even started," she thought, as she plugged in the coffee pot.

With a sigh, she hustled to her father's commodious desk.

Ching roused himself and, padding quietly, disappeared into the awakening house.

Elinor stretched the large rubber band around the thick packet of letters she had been reading. She stuffed those last envelopes back into their box, where they joined the ones she'd read overnight. Then she plunked the lid on and stashed her collection behind the daybed again. Concealing her letters was a practiced art, a war secret of her own.

She dug into the closet, feeling around in the near dark. She located her stationery box, exited the closet, straightened her back and then her hair. She set the box on her father's desk and removed two pieces of lavender paper and a matching envelope. Spreading the first sheet on the auxiliary pull-out shelf over the top left-hand drawer of her father's desk, she smoothed it.

"Arrive safely," she whispered. "Somewhere in that Big Ocean. Through the stifling heat and between typhoons. Through the torpedoes, mines, bombs. Past those damned Japanese planes. Directly to him."

Then she placed the paper on the desk blotter, a space she had cleared when she packed the letters away. She found her father's Parker fountain pen in the top desk drawer. She unstopped the ink bottle he kept by the desk lamp.

Now! No more lollygagging. It was time to let him know. "Those people" were not coming. No chance of a visit at all.

She gripped the pen in her right hand and faced the empty sheet. How to begin?

Beat prowled the Pacific on his tanker now, delivered aviation fuel, ammo, tanks. Waited for mail, surely wondered what was happening back home. The men on the *Buena Ventura*, like the other mariners on the seas, counted the days until the ship pulled into port, hoping any letters from home had landed safely on the island ahead of them.

Elinor tried to picture the port where Beat would receive this news. But, other than photos in her father's *National Geographic* collection, she had no idea what a South Pacific isle looked like. Not a war torn isle, a bombed out beachfront.

Instead, she imagined the ship. That was easy, since she had been on it in Seattle in July. A lifetime ago.

She scratched her head and then pushed her hair back from her forehead. So many memories! She pictured her husband in his uniform, standing there at the hotel desk, a bouquet of wedding flowers in his hand. He could be so thoughtful. He was smart, too. He read books and learned all those codes, and now he took care of all of that important machinery on the massive ships he sailed. Second in command, respected where he worked. She pursed her lips. He was by far the most romantic guy she'd dated. Which was, she thought, exactly how she got into this mess.

She pressed the white button on the fluorescent desk lamp. The bulb blinked three times before waking completely. The tip of her tongue rested on her bottom lip, as Elinor filled the fountain pen.

"Dear Beat," she began.

And then her parents arrived in the kitchen. She screwed the cap back over the nib and set the pen down. "Good morning!" she called, as she rose from the chair and walked the few steps to the kitchen from the den.

Her parents responded with good morning hugs.

"Did you sleep well?" her mother inquired as she organized breakfast—a bit of bread of bread, some cheese, and a couple of fried eggs. Elinor poured coffee for everyone.

Mickey and Irene were, thankfully, sleeping in. This was her chance. When her parents sat down in the breakfast nook for a bite to eat, Elinor slid onto the bench beside her mother.

Trudie gave her daughter a piece of toast from her own plate. Elinor fiddled with it. She couldn't look at those eggs on her father's plate.

Georg gulped his hot coffee with obvious relish, then dug into his breakfast.

Elinor sipped her coffee. She nibbled the crust of her toast. Her stomach was unsettled. Nerves.

"Bunny, what is it?" her mother asked. "Another headache?"

Elinor looked down at the table. "No, Mother. But I have had some news. Monday I took the day off school. I saw Dr. Klein."

"The headaches," her mother sighed. "What does he say?"

Her father looked up, his cup in his hand.

She met her mother's eyes. "*Mütterchen*, it's not the migraines. I'm pregnant."

"But how . . .," her father interrupted. He smacked his cup down on the table. Startling, even to himself. The single swallow of black coffee still in the bottom splashed over the lip of the cup and onto the tablecloth. Georg stared at his mess, his commentary on the situation. "Who . . . ?"

Elinor looked at him in surprise. She rose out of her seat to face her parents. "I went to the West Coast to see Beat and I stayed with him until he shipped out. I didn't really try to find a job there."

"Bunny?" her mother's voice shook. "I don't understand."

Her parents stared at her, not at all comprehending what she had just announced, plain as day.

"How . . . Who?" her father stuttered.

Elinor looked directly at him. "Darrow. Beat and I were together on the coast."

The electric clock on the kitchen wall hummed softly as the minute hand touched the XII. The Black Forest cuckoo in the living room popped out of its wooden nest to announce the hour. Eight chirps and then a bit of a song. The three Landgrebes, as they always did, stopped to count the chirps.

"We wondered why, Elinor . . . when you were in such a hurry to go to . . . to the coast," her mother tried to fill the silence.

Her father rose from the breakfast nook. He walked past her to the coffee pot where he poured a second cup for himself.

"We thought you might come home married. To Johnny. Maybe even Dale. But you had no ring," her mother explained.

"Darrow?" Her father seemed able to utter just one word at a time.

"Well," Elinor tried to clarify. She pushed her hair back from her forehead and held her hand on the top of her head while she thought of an answer. "He's smart and funny and we have such good times whenever we're together."

"So it's Darrow, then?" her father managed. He set the cup on the table of the breakfast nook.

Elinor turned to her father. "Dad." She brushed a couple of tears from her cheeks. "I got carried away, Papa. He treats me like a movie star."

"So does Walter," her mother piped in.

"But Beat . . ." Elinor started. She stood straighter.

"Your plans?" her father asked. "We can't send another of our daughters to Illinois." He eased himself onto the bench on his side of the nook, then turned to Elinor.

She wiped her face with her linen hanky. She blew her nose. "I thought I'd stay here with you, if that's okay. I'll keep teaching until . . ."

Her parents stared at her.

"Oh! Dad, Mother. Beat and I got married. When I first got to Seattle."

Georg's eyes met Trudie's for just a moment. They both turned to their daughter then.

"So you're pregnant," her mother asked, "but you're married?"

Elinor nodded. Trudie's hands fluttered to her chest.

"Darrow?" her father repeated.

"We found a Reverend Rasmussen, a Lutheran. And he married us. In Jul . . . June." She looked at her folks. "We didn't have time to get a ring. But we're married."

"So then it's all legal?" her mother asked. "You signed papers?"

Elinor nodded.

"A marriage certificate?" Trudie closed her eyes, bowed her head and raised her folded hands to her chin, one of her silent prayers. She looked up then and asked, "But why didn't you call us when you married?"

"You were out of town, and I didn't know where to find you. And I wanted to tell you in person."

"But, Bunny, we've been around these past months, and you said nothing until now?" Her father's voice rumbled. She had never seen his lips quiver before.

"I couldn't. I didn't want to disappoint you and Mother. I wanted to have a big wedding. Like you wanted for me. I thought Beat and I could go through the ceremony again one day." Elinor looked at her feet. "But I'm somehow pregnant."

"Georg, a grandchild! And Elinor has married." Trudie got out of her seat, too, and stood by her husband. "In Seattle. They found a Lutheran minister there. It was legal." She looked into his eyes, then patted him on the shoulder.

"But Darrow?" he repeated. He shook his head and swallowed a gulp of coffee.

"Come, Georg," Trudie directed. "Let's talk in the living room." She escorted her husband to his chair. Georg set his coffee cup on the corner table. He reached for his pipe.

Soon smoke curled into the cool morning air around the corners of the living room, then seeped into the kitchen and mixed there with the breakfast smells. Elinor's nostrils twitched as the aroma of tobacco tickled her nose. She listened for sounds from the living room.

"Georg," Trudie started. Then she stopped. Elinor heard the sigh from the cushion of Trudie's soft chair.

The cuckoo ticked some minutes away.

Georg settled his pipe in the copper ashtray with a clunk.

A whispered conversation in the living room murmured around the corners of the kitchen. Elinor tried to eavesdrop, but it was useless.

In a while, as she began the breakfast dishes, her father arrived in the kitchen. He put on his old gardening hat.

"*Tay-Air-Oo-Day-Ee-Ay*, I must walk and have a chat with my God," he called to his wife as he opened the back door.

Trudie met him on the back stoop, put her hands on either side of his face, and smiled up at him.

"Now would be a good time to plant that apple tree," she whispered. Her husband had often used that analogy, a quotation from Martin Luther himself. "Even if I knew that tomorrow the world would go to pieces, I would still plant my apple tree," Luther had written.

Georg tried to smile but his lips weren't in his control. He strode down the back steps, past his gardens without checking a single plant, and into the alley.

Trudie reentered the kitchen and hugged her daughter. "Don't worry. We'll work this out. Darrow is such a surprise. You know . . ."

Elinor hugged her mother. "I'm a little surprised, too."

"Your father will pray about it, and so should we. But I'd better get dressed first," Trudie whispered. "This, too, shall pass." She hugged her daughter once more, and then hustled upstairs to her bedroom.

Elinor exhaled. She dropped her toast into the garbage and put her breakfast plate into the sink. She'd finish those dishes later. First things first.

She opened the back door of the house to let the brisk morning air through the screen. Luckily her father hadn't put the storm windows on the house yet.

The apple tree in the back yard had lost the last of its leaves in the rainstorm during the night. A couple of apples had escaped her father and were hanging, withered, off the top branches. There would be new apple blossoms in the spring, and a fresh supply of apples next fall. And there would be a new life in the house then, too.

She walked to the front door and opened it, too. Crisp air circulated through the main floor of 1135. Elinor stood in the doorway. She breathed in the invigorating air and scanned the brightening sky. The night had been long, and she was weary. She really needed to sleep.

But first. They knew, and it wasn't the end of the world as she had predicted. Now she just had to tell Beat. She returned to the den, curled into the wooden desk chair, swiveling it toward the desk, and flipped the light on again. She glanced at her stationery. Well, she had a salutation anyway.

"Dear Beat."

How difficult could this be?

"It's warm here already today. But October can be like that in Dakota. Do you remember? We're having a long and lovely Indian summer. I suppose you're plenty warm wherever you are among those islands, too."

What an inane start! And for an English teacher. She paced the couple of feet to the phone, where she had waited for his calls so many times. She forced herself back to the desk.

"Well, I talked it all over with my folks this morning, Beat. You were right. I should have told them right away. They are always gracious about mistakes, and I guess you could call this a mistake. I mean, that we married secretly.

"I told them we were married in June. I think that will have to be our story or people will gossip. Can we make our anniversay date June 14 instead of July 14?

"And since they know now, I think I'd better tell you, too. I saw Dr. Klein again yesterday. He says I am pregnant. For sure. Those doctors who said I might never bear a child would be surprised, I guess. We are having a little one.

"I had a period with all that short burst of bleeding. Remember when we talked on the phone? 'Those people' had come?

"But it is something Dr. Klein called the vanishing twin syndrome. One of our babies left me, but we still have one trying to grow.

"I took a job teaching English, Beat, before I knew about this. But I'll quit soon, probably after Thanksgiving. They don't like it when teachers 'show' and my belts are getting tight. It's a good job, though, with a fine faculty. It'll be hard to give up, I think. I like it much better than the other places I've been. I feel like I finally know what I'm doing. Even in those study halls.

"My parents believe that God is good. That He sits in Heaven and watches us make decisions for good or not. I guess I believe that, too, but I also have a feeling that those old Greeks were on to something with The Fates. Sometimes we are fated to meet someone, to fall in love, to change the paths of our lives. And I think The Fates put us together, Beat."

Elinor set the pen on the desk and walked into the kitchen to refill her cup. Enjoying the aroma of the coffee, she meandered to the front three-season porch. She pulled the cord on the venetian blinds, raising them. She slid a window open. She loved the smell of the air and the damp earth after a late night storm. She settled into one of the wicker chairs. How many summer and weekend days had she sat there, waiting for any mail to arrive!

She thought about the next part of her letter. Honesty. No dissembling. No little white lies.

Her mother joined her on the porch. She had Post's *Etiquette* in her hands.

"Bunny, is it okay? I just thought I'd sit out here with you on such a nice day. To read."

"Of course, Mother. I just need to think."

Trudie leaned over her daughter to give her another hug. "I'll be very quiet," she breathed. She settled on the wicker sofa beside her daughter and began to page through Elinor's copy of "The Blue Book of Social Usage."

The two women sat side-by-side, quiet in the early morning sunshine, the fresh beginning of the day, getting used to the reality.

Trudie located the wedding section. "Parties for the Engaged. The Engaged Couple and the Chaperon." Too late for all that now. "The Ring."

"No ring, Bunny?" she asked.

Elinor shook her head.

But "The Announcement of the Engagement"! No, "The Announcement of the Marriage." Even too late for that now.

Elinor contemplated her resolute mother. Elinor had disappointed her. And all the ladies of the church, too. But she would make it up to them all one day. For now the two women sat side by side, quietly absorbing this turn of events.

Elinor glanced up and down the street. Her eyes caught the gold star in the window of the Hinschberger home. The war.

She wondered where Beat was now. What was happening in that big ocean today? The war made everything so unpredictable. What would her future hold now that she had stumbled onto this new path? Only The Fates knew.

She thought of her past plans, her dream of becoming Something Big. A popped bubble. Water under the bridge.

Her father opened the back door. Done with his walk, he was humming.

Elinor kissed her mother. "I have to finish that letter," she explained. Then she ducked into the dark interior of their home and returned to her father's desk.

She picked up the pen again, refreshed the ink supply, and continued.

"I will love being a mother to your child, and when you return, I will be the best wife you can imagine. I'll help you in any way I can. We'll get along all right. We'll have a sweet home of our own one day, and our friends and families will come to visit. And we can 'get around' together.

"It's okay now to address the envelopes to Mrs. Darrow R. Beaton when you write. I'll be looking forward to your mail.

"I promise I'll tell Walter and Johnny and the rest of the 'old friends' as soon as I can. And maybe one day we can get real rings for each other? After the war, I mean.

"I love you, Beat.

"Love,

"Elinor

"P.S. We never did have that long talk."

Elinor folded the paper, slid it into an envelope, and weighed the letter on the postal scale her father kept on the top of his desk, left-hand corner. He stored airmail stamps in the top drawer of his desk—pink six-cent stamps and green eight cent ones, along with penny stamps to cover most any postage cost. Elinor found the current postal rate sheet there, too. She weighed the letter and then carefully released one green stamp, tearing it exactly at its perforations. She found the mucilage bottle in the top drawer and cracked the shiny frosting of dried glue off the top of the rubber cap.

Eight cents. This rectangle of paper allowed her letter to ride on an airplane headed for the Pacific. Right into the middle of the war.

She tipped the bottle, applied a dab of glue to the back of the stamp and pressed it hard onto the corner of the envelope. Then she sealed the envelope and kissed it for good luck.

"Done!" she called to her father. "Papa, will you walk to the mailbox with me?"

Georg donned his going-to-town hat. Elinor put on a sweater and the two of them set off to mail the letter at the green metal mailbox on the corner of Broadway and Twelfth Avenue, a three block stroll.

The sky, often gray at this season, was lit with bright sunshine. They walked down the six porch steps, then the stone path that led to the sidewalk. The two of them passed under the boulevard elms, now a mass of twigs and branches and abandoned birds' nests over the sidewalk and street. A few last raindrops dripped from the trees.

Elinor trotted to keep up with her long-legged father. He hummed intermittently, as was his habit when walking along. Hymns. His faith in the goodness of mankind. She smiled. That used to embarrass her, but it didn't any longer.

He turned toward her. "Will you be staying with us all along, then?" he asked.

"I'm going to teach, Dad, as long as they'll let me. Darrow and I need some funding for this adventure of ours."

"You'll be home on the weekends then?"

They stopped at the cross street, and he took her arm, another habit that used to embarrass her. Her fingers relaxed in his warm hand,

and they walked together through the still damp piles of leaves at the curb.

"Sure, Papa. If that's okay. And when it's time to come home to stay, I'll squeeze in somewhere."

Georg nodded and turned toward his daughter.

"Good. Your mother knows just how to take care of a little one." He chuckled, remembering. "We'll make a good home for both of you."

Elinor hugged her father. "After the war, though, I'll need to find my own home, Papa," she cautioned.

Georg cleared his throat. "Of course." He helped Elinor up the curb on the other side of the street. "Darrow? What's happening with him?"

"Well, he'll be in and out. The Pacific, you know. Mostly. He'll call when he gets into a port. We'll try to see each other."

Elinor stopped on the sidewalk. She pulled her purse strap over her shoulder and faced her father. "Dad, you can't blame him. For Irene."

"Bunny, your mother reminds me of that, too." They walked on again, a few steps. "Forgiveness is central to the Lord's teachings," he added. "But Darrow . . ."

Elinor looked at her father. "Papa, I know what you're thinking. But I can change him."

"That's a most difficult prospect, Bunny. Men like Darrow aren't easy to change." Her father put his hand on her shoulder.

"But Beat listens to me. I can help him become a better man. He's an officer. I'll help him get places, Dad. Together we can be Something Big."

"Bunny," Georg looked at his daughter. Then he dropped his eyes and sighed.

"And that's really a gal's job, isn't it? To give a guy confidence and love?" Elinor continued.

Georg removed his hand from his daughter's shoulder. He straightened his hat. They strolled the last block in silence. At the mailbox, Georg stood, his back to the road, a bulwark safeguarding his daughter from any traffic that might move past on Broadway.

Elinor checked the envelope. The stamp? She pressed it again. She checked the seal on the envelope flap. This letter had such a long, long way to go.

"Done," she said, turning to smile at her father.

"The Fates have spoken," she whispered under her breath as she opened the mail slot and deposited the letter.

The Best Letter

November 1944

November 22, 1944

My darling Elinor,

You're positively the best wife in the whole world, my darling. The skipper and I just got back from shore side with all the dope and stuff, and there were four letters from you with them—and, best of all, two of them had "Mrs. D. R. Beaton" in that upper left hand corner. To tell you how very pleased and happy and glad I am at this time is just impossible.

And about our little one, darling, I think you'd better quit teaching soon and rest and take it easy. We'll be the happiest and proudest parents in the whole world. And I know right now I have expanded at least twenty inches around the chest.

I mailed Doctor Hunter a letter as you asked, and I imagine that you can use either copy—the one I sent you or his copy—to give Dr. Klein all the information and authority he wishes. Please, darling, take care of yourself.

What more could people want out of life? We'll settle down soon, when the war is over, darling. We'll have something to work for and make plans for and keep us company on a cold winter night in our big double bed. Everything is so settled and final and wonderful that I really am just too happy for you and for me. Whatever happens, I know that both of us will do the very best we can for the other. And if anybody ever tells you again that I'm not the guy to settle down to a happy married life, you have my permission to whack them!

Your folks won't be sorry. I promise them that I'll be the very best husband in the world, darling. I'll write your Mom and Dad a letter from our next port, huh? Don't you worry about those "too small" belts. I understand that it's the natural thing in these things, darling! Maybe I'll pass cigars now, hmmm?

> My love for always, darling,
> Your devoted husband,
> Beat

Acknowledgements

I'M GRATEFUL TO MY mother, Elinor Landgrebe Beaton, who so carefully saved these wartime letters from my father's voyages in the Pacific. She moved them eight times, from one home to another, and not one of us children knew they existed. I wonder whether she ever opened them and reread the story that changed her plans for her life.

My father, Darrow Beaton, was a fine writer, even when he was young, and I'm thankful he put so many of his honest feelings on paper. I wonder whether he knew Mom had saved his letters.

I honor all the men and women who lived through the war years: the participants in the battles all over the world, those who supported them with materiel, the families who grieved after receiving telegrams, and the women on the home front who lived such uncertain lives. Thank you, all.

I want to thank the experts who pitched in to help with the history: Don Wagner of the Soldier's Museum (www.soldiersmuseum.com); John Hallberg, historian at NDSU; Chief Radio Operator (WWII) Lawrence Owens, whom I know through email and phone calls and who was always ready to answer any question about ships or procedures; Audrey McComb, historian at the Mayflower Hotel in Seattle; and the Sigma Chi fraternity for the photo of the pin from the Forties.

To the readers who helped me improve the flow of the story: P.J. Heine, D.Ed.; Yvette Louis, Ph.D.; Allyson Perling; Neil Ross; and Chris Gordon, Ph.D. To our Wednesday writing group—Joan Mikitis,

M.D.; Charyn Fly; Walter Strach; as well as part-timers Jack and Boots Bjork.

Thanks to Mary Carroll Moore who teaches fabulous writing classes on-line as well as at the Loft in Minneapolis and to the editors at iUniverse who helped the book take shape.

And, most especially, to my husband, Jerry, who cajoled, read, commented with honesty, and believed.

Songs listed in these letters:

Don't Get Around Much Any More

GI Jive

Have I Been Away Too Long?

He's My Guy

I Don't Want to Walk Without You

I Had The Craziest Dream

I'll Be Seeing You

I'll Walk Alone

It Had To Be You

Jingle, Jangle, Jingle

Long Ago and Far Away

Moonlight Cocktail

On the Sunny Side of the Street

Pistol Packing Mama

Sleepy Lagoon

Spring Will Be a Little Late This Year

Stardust

Sunrise Serenade

Sweet Eloise

Sweetheart of Sigma Chi

There Are Such Things

When the Lights Go On Again

White Christmas

Why Don't You Do Right?

You'll Never Know

All references to Emily Post are from *Etiquette, "The Blue Book of Social Usage,"* Funk and Wagnalls, 1942. Original edition copyright, 1922; revised in 1927, 1931, 1934, 1937, and 1940.

CPSIA information can be obtained at www.ICGtesting.com
Printed in the USA
LVOW13*1524301113

363318LV00003B/247/P